SET THE CONTROLS FOR THE HEART of SHARON TATE

FOR THE HEART:

RON TATE

vel by Gary Lippman

RARE BIRD BOOKS

LOS ANGELES, CALIF.

THIS IS A GENUINE RARE BIRD BOOK

Rare Bird Books
453 South Spring Street, Suite 302
Los Angeles, CA 90013
rarebirdbooks.com

For more information, address:
Rare Bird Books Subsidiary Rights Department
453 South Spring Street, Suite 302
Los Angeles, CA 90013

Set in Dante
Printed in the United States

10 9 8 7 6 5 4 3 2 1

Library of Congress Cataloging-in-Publication Data

Names: Lippman, Gary, 1963– author.
Title: Set the controls for the heart of Sharon Tate: A Novel /
by Gary Lippman.
Description: Los Angeles, CA : A Rare Bird Book | Rare Bird Books, 2019.|
Includes bibliographical references and index.
Identifiers: LCCN 2019019670 | ISBN 9781644280263 (pbk. : alk. paper)
Subjects: LCSH: Authors—Fiction. | Threats of violence—Fiction. | Tate,
Sharon, 1943–196—Fiction. | Manson, Charles, 1934–2017—Fiction. |
Cults—Fiction. | Hollywood (Los Angeles, Calif.)—Fiction. |
Psychological fiction. | GSAFD: Mystery fiction.
Classification: LCC PS3612.I6456 S48 2019 | DDC 813/.6—dc23
LC record available at https://lccn.loc.gov/2019019670

For Verka,
for Ettie Pearl,
and for my three guys—Billy, Buddy, and Gabou

I can't help it, you're so good it hurts.
It's like magic, or some kind of curse.
I want to be wherever you are.
'Cause I'm a big fan of you...

Who's in a most peculiar dream,
Spreading happiness for free?
It's you, it's you, it's you.

—The Wannadies, "Big Fan"

Among the road maps, cards, old addresses—the lost world never put in order—
there is, I know, a photograph: the brilliant, almost demonic director on a couch
with a tall, graceful girl. It was taken one night when we had dinner. I envied
him his wife. It is difficult now to imagine the woman she would have become.
She remains as she was, as if among all the herd there had been this exceptional
creature, slightly awkward perhaps, but without blemish and carrying in her
person the essential traits...

—James Salter, *Burning the Days*

Let me go, let me go, people!...
I am criminal, I won't eat people anymore.
The country has changed.
Criminal says
I won't eat people anymore.

—Voodoo Chant

CONTENTS

1

SHARONOPHILIA

(Saturday)

RED was the color of his true love's Ferrari—but he couldn't afford to rent one, so Lunt Moreland settled for a Mustang that was not quite the same hue. Pretending it was *her* car while driving north from LAX, he'd made two stops before the cemetery: a fast-food drive-through and a flower stand whose owner secretly grew poppies for an opium den downtown. It was a scorching, sticky day, the hottest so far during this summer of 2003.

"Is this your first time with us, sir?"

After munching on a chicken burger in the flower stand's small parking lot, Lunt had tossed the trash in his back seat. (Nearly two weeks later, a pair of officers from the West Hollywood Police Department would find the trash there.) Because he was about to turn forty, Lunt wondered if senility was the reason he'd missed the familiar left onto Slauson. Was his memory crumbling already? What would be next, hair sprouting from his ears? With a muttered oath, Lunt had turned his car around on La Cienega to take the proper route to Holy Cross Cemetery. And after paying his respects to his beloved and placing a bouquet of roses beside the glossy black marble plaque that read *Beloved Wife of Roman, Sharon Tate Polanski, 1943–1969*, he'd come directly to the hotel.

"Mr. Moreland?"

This time the voice broke into Lunt's reverie.

"Sorry?"

"I asked if this is your first time with us."

Lunt had been gazing blankly at the Hotel Ofotert's sunken lobby, its mismatched sofas, antique lamps, and candelabras, all bathed in amber early evening light while black-vested servers darted past a Steinway Baby Grand. Thanks to the gray stone walls and timbered ceiling, the hotel's visual vibe was of a spinster's sitting room transported to some feudal sanctuary. Since 1938, when the Art Nouveau–influenced building rose above Sunset Boulevard, this upstart rival to the Chateau Marmont and Garden of Allah quickly surpassed those show business hangouts as the place to see and be seen. At the Ofotert, Clark Gable had canoodled with Carole Lombard, Paul Newman rendezvoused with Joanne Woodward, and everyone from Boris Karloff to Marilyn Monroe leapt headlong into exclusive Hollywood orgies.

"No," said Lunt. "I mean, yes—my first time *staying* here. But I've visited a lot over the past, like, twenty years. Just, you know, poking around."

Facing Lunt from across the polished mahogany registration desk stood the hotel's general manager, a stooped, ruddy-complexioned, middle-aged man in a brown sports coat. His name tag read "RANDY TRUEAX." On the wall behind Trueax, a curved mirror competed for space with a wooden matrix of pigeonhole mail slots. In the mirror Lunt tried to catch sight of his own slightly weak-chinned, rather fleshy face, but a view of the manager's bald spot was all he could see. Trueax gave a lopsided grin when he heard the term "poking around." The lopsidedness derived from his having just smoked a self-rolled cigarette, his second so far today. Although no one but his unemployed boyfriend knew it, Trueax liked to mix the drug WHF (street name "Plonk") with his tobacco. Not much Plonk, just a smidgen—the minimum required to calmly handle each day's rigors.

"In any case," he told his new guest, "we're glad to have you here until"—glancing at the guest's registration form—"the thirtieth."

"Yes, I'm here for the Tate-World Conference next weekend." Lunt gestured to his T-shirt, where a luminous young blonde woman's face was accompanied by the words "I'VE GOT THE FREAK HOTS FOR THE GIRL!" "I'm a 'Sharonophile,' which is what us Sharon Tate enthusiasts call ourselves. 'S-phile' for short."

"Ah," said Trueax, "the murdered actress, yes. Charles Manson is still locked up for that awful crime, I hope."

"Along with the other killers," Lunt said.

"Well, I'm glad that you and your friends remember Ms. Tate." The manager fiddled with a button on his coat sleeve. "You certainly have plenty of days to spare until your gathering."

"Which is just how I've planned it," Lunt said. "I'm trying to finish a literary project, and I had some vacation time, so I decided to do my work here."

"You're not our *first* early bird, you know."

"I'm not?"

"Another member of your group checked in last night."

Uh-oh, Lunt thought, tensing. "A man?"

"I believe so, yes."

"His name's not 'Glen Mandrake,' is it?"

With pursed lips, Trueax considered the name. "I don't believe that's it, no."

"You're sure? Because if Mandrake is here..." Lunt meant to continue with, "It would spoil my whole trip," but he decided to clam up and simply wait, fingering the brass bell on the desktop, its edges gone green, until Trueax had given his computer keyboard a few strokes and squinted at its monitor and finally said, "Randang."

"Ran-what?"

"The other early bird is in Suite Twenty-Nine. A Mr. Melek Randang. Does that sound familiar?"

"No," said Lunt, "it doesn't." He had believed he was acquainted with all his fellow Sharonophiles, but Melek Randang? Was this another sign of impending senility? "Melek" sounded Arabic. Some new Sharonophile from Dubai?

"Would you like me to contact this fellow Randang?"

Lunt declined, saying he'd "look for the guy tomorrow," and Trueax felt a throb of Plonk-borne pleasure surge through him, further lopsiding his grin. "What kind of project are you working on, Mr. Moreland, if you don't mind my asking?"

Lunt said that he was curating a book about Sharon Tate. "Ordinarily I write essays for this specialist journal, *Sharing Sharon*, but they're scholarly stuff, like my latest piece, which is about how Sharon's menstrual cycle affected her work on the film *Valley Of The Dolls*. With this full-length book of mine, though, I want to break out of the specialist ghetto—reach a wider audience. Get the world interested in Sharon more than it's ever been before."

"Fascinating!" said Trueax. "I'm sure you'll be successful."

Lunt knocked lightly on the reception desk for good luck. "Let's hope so. I'm not quitting my day job just yet…"

"And what's that, may I ask?"

"Real estate." Lunt worked as a residential broker in his hometown of Sulphurdale, New Jersey, but decided not to elaborate. Better to let Trueax believe he *owned* a bunch of buildings. After all, he was finally staying at the elegant, fabled Hotel Ofotert!

"Will there be a lot of photos in your book?" asked Trueax. "Glamor pictures will probably help sales."

"We'll have an *extensive* photo section," Lunt said, his voice rising with excitement. He loved talking about Sharon, and about his work in honor of Sharon, whenever someone he met seemed truly interested. "Plus a filmology, celebrity testimonials, a fashion section—maybe even a psychoanalyst to write about Sharon's psyche. It's still in the planning stages, but I've got a top literary agent repping me—Vishwa Mukherjee, in case you've heard of her—and

I'm already nearly finished writing the book's centerpiece, which is a memoir."

"Your own memoir?"

"No, that's the cool part—it's *Sharon's*. A memoir in her voice. Sharon's own 'from-beyond-the-grave Sharon Tate story.'"

Trueax looked impressed. "Are the other fans coming to the Sharon Tate conference here also writers?"

"No, but everyone's more or less as rabid about her as I am. We talk about Sharon nonstop, what she was like, and we collect what we call 'Sharonabilia,' which are objects connected to her. You know, posters, photographs, clothes that Sharon wore, her correspondence. She had this beautiful regal handwriting..." He paused to cough, making sure to cover his mouth. "We go on pilgrimages, too, visiting places where she spent time. Places like Big Sur, and Joshua Tree, and the Chelsea Registry in London, where she got married to Roman Polanski."

"The film director."

Lunt made a sour face. "Or 'that perverted dwarf bastard,' as we usually refer to him. He wasn't faithful to Sharon, he didn't deserve her. But did you know that after their wedding Polanski and Sharon lived right here?"

"Here at the Ofotert?" Trueax felt his left eye twitch, a typical sympton of the Plonk. "I hadn't realized..."

"Yeah, back in the sixties they stayed in Suite Fifty-Six, which is why we're having our Tate-World wingding here this year."

They'd finally arrived at the subject Lunt needed to broach with this hotel manager, so he placed both hands on the reception desk, whose gleaming surface felt as smooth and as cool as Sharon's glossy black marble gravestone had felt earlier, and he got right to it, saying, "In the late sixties Sharon and Polanski lived in Suite Fifty-Six for a few weeks before moving into the Chateau Marmont and then into their rented house in Bel Air. That house is where she ultimately lost her life. Meaning if she hadn't left *here*, most likely she'd still be alive."

"Oh, *now* I understand why all you Sharon Tate people have been asking for Suite Fifty-Six!" said Trueax, cutting into Lunt's spiel. "I can't say I'm surprised. We've had so many creative types at the Ofotert. As a matter of fact, in the junior suite where you'll be staying, the author Dorothy Parker spent a stretch of time. If you'll forgive the ghoulishness"—Trueax leaned forward to lower his voice conspiratorially—"the story goes that she tried to, well, *take her life* in your bathtub." He waited for Lunt's expression of awe, then capped it with, "Fortunately, Ms. Parker's suicide attempt was not successful."

"That's a relief," Lunt said. "Because I like to take baths. And I appreciate the history of the room, thanks, but"—finally getting to his point—"are you *sure* Suite Fifty-Six isn't available for me? I called ahead three or four times about it."

"Sadly," said Trueax, shifting into the apologetic tone he needed to use so often with pushy people, "as my staff and I have been telling everyone from your fan group, Suite Fifty-Six is occupied by a certain long-term hotel guest."

"So I've heard. Is he or she a Sharonophile?"

"Sharonoph..." The manager's left eye twitched again. "Oh. No, I don't believe so."

"Anyone famous?"

"Absolutely not. But he's someone who values privacy."

"And this guest won't be leaving any time soon?"

"Not until the autumn, I'm sorry to say. Autumn at the earliest."

Just my luck, Lunt groused to himself. *Suite 56 is one of the few patches of universe Sharon ever occupied, actually slept in, and this fop Trueax is denying it to me!*

Lunt loved to visit places where Sharon had spent time. The only "Sharonized" locale in the world that he categorically refused to visit was 10050 Cielo Drive in Bel Air, where La Tate was murdered. The mere thought of being near that ghastly place creeped him out. Once, while visiting LA in the late 1980s—before the new owners tore the structure down—he'd *nearly* visited the place. Deciding to "Sharon up" (his own version of the expression "man up," because Sharon had faced her violent death at age twenty-six with such courage), Lunt drove toward the death-house in another rented red Mustang. A few blocks away, however, he'd started to tremble. Fear went xylophoning up and down his spine, and in the end he fled, vowing never to go again. This left the Hotel Ofotert's Suite 56.

Not giving up yet, Lunt said, "I don't suppose the occupant goes away on weekends? Because if I could spend even *one night* there, I'd be grateful."

"Alas," said Trueax, "it's impossible. When a room is occupied, it's our policy that—"

"Even if the resident goes out for, like, one *hour*? I mean, even if it's fifteen minutes, I'd love to get inside that room."

Trueax's grin straighted out, then commenced to fade from his florid face. Before he could deny the request again, someone walking behind Lunt caught the manager's attention.

"Hello, Mrs. Kruikshank," Trueax said.

Lunt turned to face the newcomer, an elderly woman who smiled politely at Trueax as she went by. Stout and Asian-featured, with a dried fig of a face, she was clad in a gray polyester uniform with her sleeves buttoned tightly around her wrists. Something about this woman—Lunt couldn't tell what, exactly—reminded him of his mother. His mother, in fact, during her last years, the years before the car crash that eventually ended her life and left Lunt's father paralyzed.

As Mrs. Kruikshank disappeared around a corner, Lunt turned back to Trueax, who was saying, "I think you'll like the junior suite we've assigned you, sir," and Lunt sighed, accepting failure for the moment. So close 56 was, yet so far! Even locked out of her suite, he knew that, with the proper attunement, he would still be able to feel Sharon's vibrations humming through the rest of the hotel. This reception desk, for instance—how many times had she stood right here, resting her adorable hands or elbows on its shining surface?

By all accounts, Sharon had loved the Hotel Ofotert during the weeks she spent here. She loved its blend of charming design and louche decadence, not to mention the musicians, painters, and actors who were its main clientele. Creative types had continued flocking to the hotel in the era after Sharon, and they'd multiplied: every time over the past two decades that Lunt came to "poke around," the lobby and garden were crowded with artists, many famous. Clearly they loved the place for the same reasons Sharon did—and loved it for the Ofotert's long-time ban on the paparazzi.

Today the celebrity quotient was as high as ever. Stealing a glance at the lobby while Trueax fiddled with his computer, Lunt was able to recognize half a dozen minor film stars. A few seemed to be on a romantic meeting while others chatted with what looked like agents or managers.

The most notable of the lobby denizens was Benny Pompa, bass player and lead vocalist for the well-known music combo Memento Morey Amsterdam. This week the group's latest album, *I Wanna Die in My Sleep Like My Dad Did (Not Screaming in Terror Like All His Passengers Were)*, teetered on the cusp of platinum status. To Lunt, Pompa was important not for his music, which was tuneless dreck, but for his birthday, January 24. Lunt knew the pop star shared his birthday with three great movie thespians: John Belushi (whose 1983 fatal overdose took place in the neighboring Chateau

Marmont), Nastassja Kinski (with whom Roman Polanski wooed and worked in the 1970s), and Sharon Tate herself.

Pale and clean-shaven, his Afroed hair a natural copper hue, Pompa sat sprawled across a burgundy-colored couch, cupping a knee with interlaced fingers. Flanking him were two middle-aged brunettes—hardly the jailbait you'd expect to find consorting with the notoriously hedonistic (and, like Lunt, closing-in-on-forty) Pompa. Neither pouting woman resembled Sharon, yet Lunt still found them comely. Their attire made them a curious contrast to the pop star's. While he wore torn blue jeans and a red football jersey that read across its front "I'LL DO ANYTHING BUT BREAKDANCE FOR YA, DARLIN'," the women were decked out in luxuriant animal-skin clothes: one outfit made from leopard (probably faux) and the other from rattlesnake (possibly authentic).

What Lunt didn't realize was that, in nearly two weeks' time, he would become as famous—or rather, *infamous*—as anyone there. And, brief as Lunt's lobby survey was, he failed to notice a tall, bald, rather sunburned man seated alone two sofas over from Pompa. Just one glance at the tall man's crisp white suit would have alerted Lunt to his identity. So would the man's jug ears, pronounced Adam's apple, spade-shaped beard, and protuberant eyes, which all combined to make him look a bit grotesque. Yet this man had *not* missed Lunt. In fact, as soon as he had spotted the Sharonophile, the man in the white suit ducked his head and concealed himself behind an orange, orchid-shaped lampshade, then plucked his Japanese smartphone from his lap, pressed two buttons on it, put it to one of those jug ears, and said, "He just arrived, the poor lamb. He's got *no clue* about the *scheiss*-storm we've already sent his way."

"Mr. Moreland?"

Lunt's attention snapped back to the hotel manager, who was sliding a red-tasseled key across the reception desk toward him.

"For your junior suite, Forty-Seven. Would you like the local paper delivered to your door each morning? Or we can do *The New York Times.*"

"Neither," said Lunt. "I don't read newspapers. Who needs daily reminders that psychopaths like Manson are making chopped meat out of this world?"

As Trueax's left eye twitched once more, Lunt fished his wallet out from the front pocket of his khakis, removed a twenty-dollar bill, and pushed it across the desktop.

"My gift to you," he said. "And if Suite Fifty-Six *does* become available, even for just five minutes, I hope you'll remember *me* instead of any other Sharonophile."

WITH its modestly sized bed and small kitchenette, Lunt's junior suite turned out to be less suite-like than he'd expected. Still, the closet space was ample, the air-conditioning worked well, the wall-to-wall carpet was colored a pleasant butterscotch, and waiting on the writing table was a complimentary bottle of Dom Perignon Champagne. (Not that Lunt drank much alcohol—his hangovers tended to be atrocious.) The writing desk he'd requested was actually just a simple scratched-up wooden table, a far cry from the splendor of the reception desk downstairs, but it had a worn-in literary quality that Lunt liked. Best of all, this *sanctum sanctorum* was as silent as the grave: not a sound got past its thick walls and heavy wooden outer door.

Lunt couldn't stop smiling. Finally he was staying in the Ofotert, just as Sharon once had! He decided to drop the word "junior" from his conception of the suite. And when he considered the reasonable rate that Randy Trueax had agreed to extend to Lunt from the conference weekend to his entire more-than-two-week stay, how could this Sharonophile complain?

After unpacking his clothes and hanging the black, circular "DO NOT DISTURB" sign on his front doorknob, Lunt tugged open the nightstand drawer. Someone, obviously aware of the celebrated previous occupant, had placed a book of Dorothy Parker's stories and poems in it. Lunt took out the hardbacked volume and set down in its place a package of ribbed latex Instigator condoms. Here in libertine Hollywood, he had high hopes for those condoms; and the Dom Perignon, come to think of it, would assist him with potential Sharonesque seductees.

For a few minutes Lunt sat on his suite's gray swayback sofa and examined the Parker book, flipping through it with an eye peeled for any reference to suicide or bathtubs or the Ofotert. He found none and went on to wonder if Sharon had ever read Parker's work. A subject for future research.

Tiring of the book, Lunt dropped it onto the nightstand and began to Sharonize his room by sprinkling Sharonabilia around and Scotch-taping pictures of his true love to the walls. Before he got far, the black and shiny old-fashioned room telephone rang, its cry piercing the low murmur of his television set, which Lunt liked to leave switched on. By the phone's second overly loud answer-me-right-now ring, Lunt jumped across his bed toward it, delighted, figuring that the caller must be Trueax bearing good news, the hotel manager saying, "I've decided to let you stay in Ms. Tate's former suite, Fifty-Six. Shall I send a bellhop up to move your luggage?"

But the caller wasn't Trueax. Nor, to judge by the solemn male voice, was it anyone else Lunt knew.

"Whosoever treats his fellows without honor or humanity," the caller announced, "he, and his issue, shall be treated with commensurate inhumanity and dishonor."

"Uh...*what*?" said Lunt. "I didn't quite catch that."

The caller repeated the message verbatim and then went quiet, though he remained on the line: Lunt could hear the man's faint, patient breathing.

"Buddy, if this is some kind of telemarketing thing, it's not grabbing me, okay?" said Lunt right before he coughed, not bothering to cover his mouth. "Where'd you get that quote, the Book of Revelation?"

For the third time, the caller delivered his strange message.

"Yeah, yeah," Lunt said, "I heard you. But I just checked into this room, so if you're trying to reach the *previous* guest, I'm the wrong party, okay?"

As his response to this, the caller launched into his message yet again. He only got about halfway through before Lunt hung up. Then, for several moments, the Sharonophile stared at the phone. That loopy call had given him a brain wave. So he picked up the receiver and dialed, room-to-room, Sharon's former suite. Who needed Trueax when he could appeal directly to the current big-wheel occupant?

A woman, sounding bored, answered after three rings by saying, "Speak."

"Hello there," said Lunt, trying to sound sophisticated. "This is Mr. Moreland. I'm staying downstairs from you, and I was just wondering if—"

"Do we *know* you?" the woman interrupted him.

"Er..." Who was this woman, the rich guy's wife? Mistress? Aerobics instructor? Business manager? Dominatrix? "Not yet, but—"

"Have we *heard* of you?"

Disconcerted by the question, and by her brusque tone, Lunt said, "Well, probably not, no, but I was wondering if—"

"If we don't know you, piss off. Don't call again or we'll fucking *burn you down*."

BEFORE Lunt had ever heard of Sharon Tate, his life was already linked with hers. More specifically, with her death. This was because, unbeknownst to either of them at the time, Lunt's sixth birthday, the eighth of August in 1969, was the same day the Manson Family slaughtered Sharon. (In fact, they did this an hour past midnight, thus technically August ninth, but Lunt always ignored this inconvenient detail, savoring as he did any link to his beloved.)

—

2:00 P.M. (NEW JERSEY TIME)/11:00 A.M. (CALIFORNIA TIME): As guests began arriving at the boy's Sulphurdale home for the Friday afternoon birthday party, his mother insisted that he drink a glass of milk before indulging in the 7Up he loved. Sharon, unlike Lunt, was a milk enthusiast, and at her brick-and-redwood house on Cielo Drive in Bel Air—a rustic place with a swimming pool, three bedrooms, and an enormous two-story living room—Sharon had just finished gulping down a frosty glass of skim.

For the pregnant woman, it was just another day in the "fairytale world" in which she once told an interviewer she lived. Patchouli-fragranced incense were burning, Janis Joplin and Leonard Cohen and The Doors were on the stereo, the front door stood open (slightly claustrophobic, Sharon hated closing her doors, even in hotels), and she was lounging in a blue-and-yellow floral-print bra with matching underpants when her phone rang. Polanski was calling from London. He'd been laboring on a screenplay about dolphins trained to assassinate a US president, and asked Sharon how she was feeling. Her due date was less than two weeks away. Chewing on a fingernail, she told him she felt boiling hot since LA was sweating through a heat wave. But she loved being pregnant. She had been exercising to get ready for the baby and reading books on childcare. The director promised that he'd be home soon. And though Sharon was never very self-assertive (in an interview, she once said, "I'm so afraid of hurting other people's feelings, I don't speak out when I should—I get into big messes that way"), she hadn't been too happy about Roman's recent absence. In fact, she insisted that day that he return in time for the start of a night-school course she'd enrolled him in. It was a course for expecting fathers.

Before they rang off, Sharon also gently complained about Polanski's friends, Voytek Frykowski and Abigail Folger, who'd been staying at the house with her. She wanted alone time with her husband when he got back. "But let's not hurt their feelings," she added, glancing at herself in a bathroom mirror and nibbling on her lower lip. She tended to feel embarrassed by how beautiful she was.

Sharon's next phone call of the day was to a neighbor whose kitten was missing. Always an animal lover, Sharon assured the neighbor that, yes, she'd found the tiny creature. She'd been feeding it with an eyedropper and would return the kitten whenever her neighbor wanted. Just then the doorbell rang. A delivery man stood outside with two steamer trunks sent by Roman. Each was filled with mementos Sharon had amassed when she'd last been in London. She couldn't bear to get rid of anything, believing that to do so would be, as she phrased it, "giving up who I am."

—

4:00 P.M. / 1:00 P.M.: Lunt was playing on the lawn behind his house with various cousins, kindergarten classmates, and friends from the neighborhood when his mother called out, "Come inside for cake, kids!"

Meanwhile, two of Sharon's own friends, Joanna Pettet and Barbara Lewis, had arrived at Cielo Drive for lunch. Before sitting down in the kitchen, Sharon showed the two women the baby's room, and let them feel the baby kicking in her belly. She also praised a vibrator she'd bought recently, saying, "It's great for stiff necks, too."

Once Pettet and Lewis had departed, Sharon was on the phone again, speaking this time with her ex-beau Jay Sebring, the ultra-innovative barber, a self-described "hair architect," who'd remained a close friend. Most of their mutual acquaintances believed that Sebring still carried a torch for Sharon and was waiting for her to tire of the constantly philandering Polanski. On the phone, Sebring and Sharon discussed their dinner plans for the night. After ringing off, the pregnant woman took one of her customary brief naps, clad in just bra and panties.

—

8:00 P.M./5:00 P.M.: With all the party guests now departed, Lunt played with a G. I. Joe, one of his birthday gifts, while his father watched TV and his mother washed dishes. She had just announced "Bedtime!" to Lunt when Sharon woke up to munch on some nuts and take a call from her sister Debbie. The teenager asked if she could bring some school friends over to Sharon's home, but Sharon declined. "I'm too tired," she said, "but come visit another night, okay, Pumpkin?" employing her usual nickname for Debbie.

Given the grisly events to come, Sharon's declining to have Pumpkin over to visit probably saved the teenager's life. And the fact that Winifred Chapman, the starlet's housekeeper, turned down Sharon's invitation to sleep at her home that night ("It's so hot outside, Winifred!") likewise might have saved Chapman's life. Nevertheless, it was the housekeeper who would find the four mutilated victims the next morning, and the supremely gruesome sight would set her sprinting wildly from the house, screaming, "Help! Murder! Blood! *Dead bodies!*"

—

9:30 P.M. / 6:30 P.M.: Exhausted from his hectic day, the newly minted six-year-old Lunt Moreland, now wearing blue pajamas, kissed his parents goodnight, climbed into his bed, and fell asleep before a minute had passed.

Across the country—and a few dozen miles from Bel Air—a man in baggy cotton pants and shirt brought together four members of his cult, The Family. "I want you to do something witchy," Charles Manson said in a low voice. "Drive straight to that house on Cielo Drive, pull out the people's eyes there, and hang them on the mirrors. And if they ask you who you are, tell them you're the devil come to do the devil's work."

Always a snappy dresser, Jay Sebring arrived at Sharon Tate's home wearing black boots, a Cartier wristwatch, a deep-blue shirt, and white trousers with vertical black stripes. Accompanied by long-time houseguests Frykowski and Folger, Sharon and Sebring went to dine at El Coyote, a popular Mexican restaurant on Beverly Boulevard, then returned home.

(The adult Lunt would go on a pilgrimage to El Coyote during his first visit to Hollywood, but he could hardly feel Sharon's presence there. What's more, the food upset his stomach.)

Around midnight in Bel Air, a dusty yellow '59 Ford pulled up to the gate outside 10500 Cielo Drive. Manson's four acolytes climbed out. In the guesthouse on the property, a caretaker played loud music (drowning out the sound of subsequent events) while in the main house, Sharon and her three friends relaxed, digesting their Mexican dinner. In time Abigail Folger wandered off to her bedroom to read, and Voytek Frykowski drifted to sleep on the American flag–draped living room couch, close to the TV set. On this TV three weeks earlier, he and Abigail, Sebring, Sharon, and the Tate family had watched the historic moon landing.

Cozy once more in bra and panties, with a negligee draped over her shoulders, Sharon lay on the bed in the master bedroom, her long, glossy blonde hair draped on the headboard while Sebring sat facing her.

(*What were they kibbitzing about? the adult Lunt would often wonder. Their last carefree words, their last carefree thoughts...Sebring probably wanted to kiss her, especially with Polanski thousands of miles away. How did he restrain himself? Once you've been La Tate's lover, how can you settle for anything less? But maybe that's true love,* Lunt pursued the thought, *love where you're content to simply orbit your soul mate without expecting anything in return, just grooving on the pleasure of being near them.*)

The door to Sharon's bedroom stood ajar. Ajar—until a stranger's hand touched the doorknob.

"Gee," one of the killers later said, "were they *surprised!*"

The devil had come to do the devil's work.

But the birthday boy, on this nation's opposite coast, kept sleeping.

ON the wall above his bed in Suite 47, Lunt Scotch-taped a certain well-worn poster. In it, a woman who wore a brocaded velvet dress and sunset-colored wig was gazing skyward, as if attempting to glimpse an angel. A curl of glowing wig hair dangled to her shoulder, which was bare and milk white. No inscription revealed the name of the woman, yet emblazoned beside her head was a word in Gothic letters: "WHY?"

Lunt was gazing at the poster while he spoke on his BlackBerry with Bronson, his favorite fellow Sharonophile and dearest friend. "It's pretty astounding," he said, "that after all these years and all my travels with it, the 'WHY?' poster's still in good condition."

"I'd be flabbergasted if it *wasn't* shipshape," said Bronson. "It's not like you've mistreated it, right? Plus, it's an image of Sharon, so there's magic in that."

"Pity I can't hang it in *her* old suite in this hotel."

Which made Bronson chortle. It had a distinctive sound, her chortle, and this sound annoyed Lunt as often as it amused him, although he'd never mentioned his annoyance to Bronson.

She said, "Maybe you could try bribing your way in there?"

"No dice. Whatever heavyweight moneybags is holed up in Fifty-Six seems to have a vise-grip on the place."

"According to whom?"

"According to the goofball, eye-blinking hotel manager. God, imagine sleeping in the *same bed* Sharon slept in. Of course, it's probably a different mattress."

"Not to worry," said Bronson. "I have a feeling, one of my intuitions, that you'll make it into that room of hers sometime soon."

"You think so?" Lunt had come to trust his friend's intuitions. "How soon?"

"Even if you need to bribe a housekeeper," Bronson said. "Or sleep with the housekeeper. Just don't jerk off in Shar's bed, okay?"

Both of them laughed at this—Lunt uncomfortably, because he'd already toyed with the idea of doing so.

He would have loved for Bronson to join him at the upcoming Tate-World Conference, yet she had demurred, saying she couldn't manage to get away from her work as an executive with Amway. This did not surprise Lunt, for in spite of their closeness, the two friends had never met face-to-face. He knew what Bronson looked like—auburn hair, sleepy eyes, lantern jaw—because she'd sent him some photos of herself. But their only contact had been by way of telephone; Bronson was for some reason as opposed to text messages and email as she was to personal meetings.

Their first contact occurred as a result of one of the earliest Tate-World Conferences, a Philadelphia gathering of Sharonophiles from Europe, Japan, New Zealand, Brazil, South Africa, Kenya, Israel, and Brunei. One of the S-philes present, a six-foot-tall woman with red hair cut low on the sides and a wealthy husband at home, took a friendly shine to Lunt—she'd read his articles in the extravagant fanzine *Sharing Sharon*.

"You ought to meet my friend Bronson," Loretta told him. "Not for romance, mind you. She's a lesbian. But she's got the same sense of humor you've got. I'm the one who got her interested in Sharon, back in high school. Trust me, I just *know* you're going to get along."

Lunt, nodding his head, said, "Sure." He knew it wasn't uncommon for lesbians to be Sharonophiles. There were many gay male S-philes, too—including Thornton Pisher, the publisher of *Sharing Sharon*. But the majority of S-philes were straight men.

"The only problem is, you won't get to *meet* her." Loretta licked her plump lips. "In person, I mean. She's physically disabled—multiple sclerosis—and *majorly* self-conscious about it. I hardly ever see her myself."

"Bronson's her first name?"

"No, her last. But that's what she goes by."

Always glad to make a new Sharonophile's acquaintance, Lunt phoned Bronson a few nights after he drove home from Philly. She was avuncular and hilarious, everything Loretta said she would be. Within minutes, they were kibbitzing like old comrades.

"Ever wonder how different Sharon's life would've been if she'd never met Roman, or never hooked up with him?" Bronson had asked Lunt that first night.

"All the time" was his response. "Or if she never got murdered?"

"If she'd lived, I guarantee you they would've split up. All the catting around that Roman did? Sharon would've gotten fed up."

"No doubt," said Lunt. "She told him she was liberated, but his cheating began to bother her. Most S-philes have this dreamy thing about her and him, where they cling to this kitschy happily ever after."

Such a lovely woman, Lunt thought. How awful that she was disabled, and too ashamed of her condition to meet new friends in person. He said, "One thing's for certain: Being a mom would've deepened Sharon, matured her. And if she'd lived on and eventually dumped Roman, she probably would've married again and had more kids."

"Agreed. An actor?"

"For a hubby? No, more like a writer." He was thinking of someone like himself, yet didn't know Bronson well enough yet to say it. What he did know, as they spoke on the phone for ninety minutes that night as well as two hours the next, was that a friendship—albeit an exclusively long-distance, non-face-to-face friendship—had been born.

"Have you seen the schedule for this year's conference?" Lunt asked Bronson tonight. "Even better than last year's. There's a slideshow about Sharon's early teen beauty pageants and a panel about her TV work."

"So far I'm not hearing anything to make my mouth water," Bronson said.

"Trust me, the Sharonabilia for sale alone is worth the trip."

Bronson chortled again. "I know what Luntie wants *most*—it's those Sharon lookalikes they hire to lounge around. Are the rumors true? That those girls do private Sharon fashion shows?"

"I wouldn't know. I couldn't afford them, anyway." Peering into the mirror above his writing table, Lunt checked out his brown hair, which he combed to resemble the hairstyle of Jay Sebring. Not only had Sebring been the king of Hollywood hairdressers, thereby knowing a thing or two about looking good, but he'd perished right beside La Tate, heroically striving to protect her, loving her until the end. Lunt brushed a lock of hair onto his forehead, getting it more Sebringesque, and changed the subject back to Suite 56, Sharon's former home at the Hotel Ofotert, saying, "Well, if I can't stay there, at least Mandrake can't, either."

"Mandrake." Bronson made a growling sound. She'd never met the man, who was Lunt's only enemy in the Sharonophile community, yet Mandrake's poisonous reputation had inclined her against him even before she knew Lunt. She asked, "Is he bringing Pandora to the conference?"

"According to the Tate-World listserve he is. But don't fret, Bron—by this point, I'm fine with it. No more flipping out about Pan, I promise."

Both suspected that this was untrue, but Bronson let it pass.

Turning from the mirror to the wide picture window above his sofa, Lunt walked over and pulled on the cord that opened the wooden Venetian blinds. A hill sloped up from Seething Lane with red-roofed houses, scrub oak, creeping figs, New Zealand ferns, and pepper trees. No lights shone from any of those houses (odd—didn't people dine at home anymore?), though a yellow half-moon cast some radiance on the view. The look of the moon made Lunt think of something he'd read once. According to Gurdjieff, one of Sharon's favorite spiritual authors, the moon nourishes itself on human souls, devouring our dead spirits as avidly as we ourselves eat breakfast.

"When're the other S-philes arriving?"

Bronson's question slammed Lunt back to the now. "A week from Friday," he said. "Though I'm told there's already one Sharonophile here now."

"Juliette?"

"No," said Lunt, "it's a guy. Not Mandrake, thank God."

"Crosby, maybe? He's such an eager beaver."

"It's 'Melek' something. 'Melek Randang.'"

"Randang...hmm."

"I haven't heard of him either." Lunt yawned, loud enough for Bronson to hear it. "Oops."

"Is Luntie getting bored with me?"

"Nope, just jet-lagged."

"You're still on Jersey time. I'll sign off, my soon-to-be-birthday boy. Forty years old, wowee. I already know what I'm gifting you for the big day."

Lunt said, "And you still won't tell me *your* age."

Bronson chortled again. "Can you keep a secret?"

"Yes!"

"Are you sure?"

"Absolutely!"

"Well, so can I, Luntie, so can I."

"Bitch!"

"Sweet dreams. And if your dreams can't be sweet…"

"I know, I know—*enjoy my nightmares*."

The problem was, Lunt never dreamed. Or never recalled his dreams or nightmares once he woke.

2

TRIPS: EGO, STAR, GUILT, BUMMER, AND DEATH

(Sunday)

LUNT'S first full day in West Hollywood began well. He'd slept deeply, and woke at eleven feeling invigorated. The only problem was a persistent cough that seemed to originate deep in his chest. Had he caught a bug on the flight over from New Jersey? Was the cough caused by the A/C in his suite? *Or maybe*, he thought with a smile as he climbed out of bed, *my lungs haven't yet grown accustomed to the Ofotert's debauched atmosphere.*

The first thing Lunt did after freshening up was to cue the suite's stereo system to one of his iPod's "Sharon Playlists." The music included "Star" by Stealers Wheel, a 1970s-era Scottish pop group, and a dozen other numbers that evoked Lunt's true love. Opening the Venetian blinds revealed a world drenched in sunlight. He sang along with Stealers Wheel as he cranked a metal latch to open the window. The heat outside was down, no longer as oven-like as yesterday. In fact, it would remain mild, sunny yet mild, for the rest of Lunt's spectacularly ill-fated time on the West Coast.

While heading to his kitchenette to brew coffee, he noticed something odd resting on the carpet at the suite's entrance. Someone had pushed an unmarked manila envelope beneath his door. Lunt assumed that the envelope contained some banal hotel business. Wrong. Once he'd cut open the package with his silver, scimitar-shaped letter opener (a gift from his mother for his eighteenth birthday), he found an adorable eight-by-ten photograph of Sharon Tate dressed as Santa Claus. There was this photo and nothing else, no note or explanation, except for two added elements. Using a red Magic Marker, someone had childishly decorated the image, drawing a halo of hearts around Sharon's winsome Santa-hatted head. The other added element was more bizarre. On the reverse side of the envelope was a pre-printed white sticker that read, "NO SENSE MAKES SENSE."

Despite the mystery of the package's provenance, Lunt's delight was immense since he'd long heard on the Sharonophile grapevine about this fabled "Santa Shot." It was the result of a Yuletide photo session for which Sharon once posed. *Did this come from Bronson?* Lunt wondered while placing the photo and its envelope on his writing table. *The birthday gift she mentioned? But why no identifying message besides the cryptic "No Sense Makes Sense" jive? And how'd she get it delivered here without postage?*

Enjoying the rising scent of the coffee, Lunt powered up his laptop and renewed work on his Sharon book's centerpiece, which he called *Excerpts from the Memoirs She Didn't Live Long Enough to Write: The Life of Sharon Tate as Told from Beyond the Grave to One of Her Biggest Admirers, Lunt Moreland.*

He'd started writing scholarly articles about La Tate during his college years, publishing them in crummy Xeroxed fanzines and eventually in *Sharing Sharon*, that slick-papered Bible of Tate-World studies. He thoroughly enjoyed writing about Sharon. It felt devotional, a true labor of love. So it was a no-brainer for Bronson to suggest that Lunt put together a full-length book on Sharon, one which would "break her out" into mainstream culture; and it was Bronson again who'd soon thereafter gave him the concept for the book's centerpiece, the "from beyond the grave" Sharon memoir which Lunt himself would pen. He wasn't sure he had the chops for it, but Bronson had pumped him full of self-belief. Not only was she his great comforter, she was his writing's champion, often reminding him, "Life's too short to doubt yourself. Look at Sharon—that's one grand lesson her young death can teach us."

After five months of painstaking, though necessarily part-time, labor (damn his "civilian" job for wasting so many vital hours!), Lunt was about three-fifths finished with the memoir work. Employing the dead actress's "own" voice, the text's main conceit, had made him feel awkward at first because his Sharonophilia had always been predicated on admiring Sharon from the *outside*—knowing her, that is, as another person would, not as she knew, or might have known, herself. Fortunately, Lunt had over the years acquired such a wealth of knowledge about Sharon's life and times—her tastes, aversions, and opinions—that he found he was quite able to access her psyche, to project his mind into hers, and thus to "speak" in "her" voice.

Eighty minutes into today's writing session, Lunt took a break. With a last slurp of coffee, he jumped online to his email account. Waiting for him was a missive from his boss at the realty office inquiring about a minor business matter. There was also an invitation to a benefit for a victim's rights organization (a charity that Lunt supported to honor Sharon's memory), and a message from Vishwa Mukherjee, his literary agent. Vishwa wanted him to contact her "ASAP—it's not urgent, but *important*."

Lunt frowned at the italicized word. Was this good "important" or bad "important"? Was "Vajillion Dollar Vishwa," as publishing industry wags enviously dubbed the agent, on the brink of her latest nervous breakdown? If so, how would Lunt ever replace her? It had already taken him so long, and cost him so much energy, to land Vishwa; no other literary agent had been interested in his Sharon opus. The rejections he'd received had been legion: "No one cares about Sharon Tate anymore," and "Why not write about Manson or Polanski instead?," and "Only Tate's relatives or lovers have any commercial appeal as authors," and "Publish some other subject's biography and then come back to us." Each dismissive agent's words hurt. So when Vishwa said yes, Lunt felt jubilant for months, and set to work with renewed purpose.

Not that Vishwa came free of complications. Despite her exquisite taste in cinema-oriented literature, her senior position at New York's prestigious agency The Gutenberg Gang, and her top track record with books devoted to film figures, Lunt's agent was, to say the least, emotionally fragile. Vishwa, during the past few years, had suffered two major bouts of nervous exhaustion. While the first of these had a banal cause (a dashing Farrar, Strauss, and Giroux editor had broken her heart), the second episode, in 2001, was caused by a case of uniquely bad timing. Only a day after her release from a psychiatric hospital in the Berkshires, Vishwa was seated in a taxi in New York's Financial District, late for a morning meeting, when a human body fell from the sky and crashed through the taxi's windshield. The date was the eleventh of September, and back to that hospital in the Berkshires Vishwa was sent.

As Lunt showered this morning, the deep, dry cough he'd woken up with returned, and it continued while he pulled on pressed khakis, black pebble-grained sneakers, and today's Sharon-themed V-necked T-shirt, one in which her eyes, colored International Klein Blue, were superimposed over the words, "SHARON TATE IS THE LIGHT OF THIS WORLD." Lunt's coughing only subsided when he called the hotel switchboard to ask about the Santa Shot he'd received.

The operator was a cheery young woman who volunteered her name as Nancy. ("Rhymes with 'fancy'—and 'chancy,'" she told him). Nancy promised to look into the matter. While thanking her, Lunt reminded himself to stop by Suite 29 to say hello to his fellow "early bird" S-phile, this guy Melek Randang. He would need to call his agent Vishwa, too. But his stomach had commenced burbling. Time to eat. The minibar in 47 was stocked with delicious snack items, but their nutritional value was as low as their prices were high.

Time for a late breakfast.

Elevator, going down!

The trees in the Ofotert's courtyard restaurant were strung with Christmas lights. Candle pots rested on each wrought-iron table, and sunshine sparkled everywhere. A plane sliced through the cloud-flecked blue dome overhead, skywriting an advertisement for Triple O Toothpaste. One table in the sparsely populated courtyard was occupied by a pair of chattering executive types. At another table sat the actor Keith Carradine, at another sat Dustin Hoffman, and at the table next to Lunt's reclined the ginger-Afroed pop star Benny Pompa. He was stroking his chin with the filter of an unlit Codex cigarette, smiling beatifically, and the two foxy, middle-aged brunettes from yesterday sat with him. Both women chainsmoked, the cloud of their mingled Codex fumes hovering above their heads before it dispersed. The trio wore the outfits Lunt had previously seen them in, as if—this being likely—they'd slept in them, or hadn't slept at all.

While Lunt eavesdropped, Pompa spoke in a raspy voice seasoned by his own consumption of cigarettes. He was talking to a black-vested waiter who stood rigidly beside the table. The waiter, a bespectacled young man with a long mulish face, fire-red horn-rimmed glasses, and a crew cut, appeared to hang on Pompa's every word.

"After our last gig in San Sebastian, I drank some moonshine absinthe. It was in a vat in someone's basement. The promoter's cousin, someone like that. You had to dip your face in the vat to drink that shit. No cups or goblets allowed, right? And it fucked me up for nine days straight. *Nine bloody days!* I felt like I got hit by lightning all over again!"

How predictable, Lunt thought, shifting his weight on the cushion tied to his metal chair. What was predictable was not Pompa's cryptic lightning reference (whatever that meant), but the "fucked up" bit. As even many non-fans of Pompa's were aware, this pop star was all too typical in his fondness for unlawful intoxicants. ("Noticed a shortage of fun drugs for sale in your town lately?" went one gossip piece in *Popfart Magazine*. "This shortage means Benny Pompa and his group Memento Morey Amsterdam are on a concert tour again!") Pompa's drug abuse stood in contrast to his reputation as one of show business's most philanthropic figures. His "Pompa Pride Foundation" gave millions of dollars each year to orphanages. Free tickets to his concerts were set aside for parentless children, and they were regularly brought backstage afterward for a meet and greet with the band. The result of all this? No one begrudged the man his illicit substance issues. "Let the mensch have his fun," was the public's reasoning. "Benny does so much good—who are we to judge his victimless pleasures?"

What a buffoon, Lunt thought. All the same, he wanted to talk with Pompa—to introduce himself and ask if Pompa knew that he shared his birthday with Sharon Tate. Then Lunt would see if the pop star would be amenable to contribute a few pages' worth of homage to Sharon for Lunt's book. Given how charitable Pompa was, and how friendly he acted now with the Ofotert waiter, it seemed worth a try. And yet, and yet...something about the pop star—about his female companions, actually—struck Lunt as not right. Lunt couldn't put his finger on it; he lacked his friend Bronson's fine-honed intuition. Yet finally he got it: it was the way the two women regarded Pompa, gazing at him so hungrily, savoring each word he uttered. This was how Lunt imagined Charles Manson's followers behaved.

"You couldn't meet a nicer group of people," one of the Manson Family had described that "Hippie Kill Cult" of dropouts and runaways. The notion of "nicer," in this case, included mescaline-fueled sado-orgies, prostitution, armed theft, dope-dealing, and crazed lectures by the small-statured, bearded messiah they called "The Wizard," "The Soul," "The God of Fuck," or simply "Charlie." His lectures to them concerned a coming genocidal race war that he referred to, after a Beatles song he loved, as "Helter Skelter." In Helter Skelter's aftermath, Charlie and company would escape to a purported massive hole under Death Valley where a sea of gold, a river of milk and honey, and a tree boasting twelve kinds of fruit would supposedly sustain them. This subterranean refuge, cribbed by Charlie from Hopi legend, was the goal of endless questing by the "tuned-in" Family.

The way Lunt saw it, Manson's scene was a hippie idyll with a brutal prison consciousness superimposed over it. Locked up in reform schools and penitentiaries for more than half his life, an armed robber by the age of thirteen, Manson had learned a lot. In prison, an old con who'd been a member of the Ma Barker Gang taught Manson to play guitar, someone else taught him to play croquet (picture Manson playing croquet!), and there were also lessons in hypnotism, Scientology, Silva Mind Control, and Masonic hand signals, all of which Charlie would later try to utilize against his enemies. (Manson called his put-on crazy behavior "the insane game.") Perhaps most useful to the young convict were pimping lessons: how to control women, especially the most psychologically vulnerable, and how to "turn them out" on the street. A Dale Carnegie book he got a hold of helped with this program as well. (Picture Manson reading Dale Carnegie!)

As soon as he left prison in 1967, Charlie started attracting followers in the Bay Area with the preferred ratio being four females to each male. He called them his "slippies," as opposed to "hippies," because they'd "slipped through the cracks of society." Said one of his disciples, "We were little kittycats who were mentally gone." Hence they were ripe for the picking, believing Manson when he claimed he could pet rattlesnakes and revive dead birds by breathing on them.

Before long the ex-con decided to bring his "slippies" south; they traveled in a school bus painted black with a goat head nailed to its front. (A rumor that the bus had been found in a lake with children's corpses inside it only boosted its appeal to The Family.) Down in Death Valley, they squatted in caves, raced around in stolen, fur-lined dune buggies with machine guns mounted on them, and settled at last on an abandoned movie set called Spahn Ranch.

"Bow like sheep," Charlie would command his women. "Die for me." Because pleasing him meant everything to them, they obeyed. They also ingested every drug he offered and were forbidden to ask "Why?" about anything. They wore their hair long for the "witchy" look Charlie favored, and believed his promise that they would soon sprout wings, and went everywhere naked except for undies, with Bowie knives attached to their belts.

"Creepy crawling," a demented game The Family liked to play, involved their quietly breaking into the homes of middle-class "pigs." At first they didn't hurt the residents, just watched them sleep and mischievously rearranged the furniture. In time, though, the "creepy crawls" became outright burglaries, and then the murders got underway. Said one member of the Family, "Charlie would think no more of killing one of us than he would of stepping on a flower. In fact, he'd rather kill people than step on a flower." According to another Family member, "I've finally reached the point where I can kill my parents."

Why had Manson singled out for slaughter Sharon Tate and Jay Sebring and their two friends? Some believed that Manson meant to spark Helter Skelter by having African-Americans blamed for the murders of rich, young, attractive white people. Others believed that he was seeking to punish the record producer Terry Melcher for failing to advance Manson's career as a singer-songwriter. (Melcher had lived at the future death house before Sharon and her husband moved in.)

Lunt's own belief about the motive for Sharon's murder was that Manson, reportedly in a foul mood that fateful August night in '69, knew that Sharon lived at the house and wanted her dead because she represented to him all the privilege and beauty and goodness that his warped life so obviously lacked.

Before Lunt's reverie at the Ofotert could go any further, it was interrupted by a new arrival to the courtyard, a presence which Lunt now sensed looming above him. It was a tall, sun-burned bald man in a white suit who'd sauntered over to Lunt's table without Lunt noticing.

"Well, well," the new arrival said. "Another early bird."

At first Lunt wasn't able to recognize the man who'd managed to position himself so that the sun shone directly in Lunt's eyes. All Lunt could make out, squinting up into the light with the seven-storied cream- and gray-colored castle behind him, were vegetable-like protrusions coming from both sides of a dark globe. Soon enough, though, these protrustions resolved themselves into ears and the dark globe into a head. A head with a very familiar face.

"Oh, *fuck*," Lunt said.

LUNT'S literary opus-in-progress, *Excerpts from the Memoirs She Didn't Live Long Enough to Write: The Life of Sharon Tate as Told from Beyond the Grave to One of Her Biggest Admirers, Lunt Moreland,* began as follows:

The last word I ever spoke—the word I gasped as blood seeped from my knife wounds—this word was "Mother." But so much of my life was about my other parent.

People who knew Paul Tate in his hometown of Houston, Texas, found him to be a serious, hard-working, self-assured man. When he enlisted in the US Army at the start of World War Two, those solid qualities helped him rocket to the rank of colonel in the field of Military Intelligence. Ironically, my father's solid qualities were the very things that alienated him from me. Whereas my mother was warm and available during my childhood, teaching me how to sew, giving me dolls to play with, and encouraging me to help her in the kitchen, Colonel Tate—"PJ" to Mom and their friends—seemed remote to me even when he was home with us, which wasn't very often. He just smoked his cigars and glowered at us a lot. I wanted him to love me the way my mom did, and my father simply couldn't.

Another thing I resented Dad for (though only subconsciously, I suppose) was my being a military brat. By the time I was sixteen, we'd lived in Houston, Dallas, El Paso, San Francisco, Richland, and Washington State. Making me even less of a Daddy's Girl were the subsequent appearances of my sisters: Debra, when I was ten; and four years later, the baby of the family, Patricia.

Don't get me wrong, I treasured my sisters, and when Patti, "Patti Cakes," was born, I knew for the first time that someday I wanted to be a mother myself. Unfortunately, heading an expanded family just drove my father deeper into himself. No matter how hard I tried to win him over, to make him demonstrate his love for me in the open way that Mom did, it felt like a losing battle. When he hugged me after I won a baking contest, I felt like I'd gone to heaven, and I considered becoming a chef when I grew up. This was mainly to please him, although I did love to bake. If I hadn't discovered my passion to act, to become a film actress, maybe I would have enrolled in some culinary academy! I also dreamed about becoming a psychiatrist or a ballerina.

In the end, my acting success did please my father, and now I'm thankful for my strict upbringing—it helped me learn discipline, and that's very important in show business. Still, I only realized the degree to which Dad loved me, and how proud of me he was, after I was gone.

Here's what I mean: Dad believed that the police were dragging their feet in investigating my murder, and this frustrated him so much that he decided to search for the murderers himself, using his training in Military Intelligence to go undercover. That is, he grew a beard, let his hair get long, and started hanging out in Hollywood's hippest scenes, everywhere from the posh Daisy to the raunchy Whisky A Go-Go.

From my vantage point here in heaven, I thought Dad looked pretty silly as a hippie, especially when I heard him use phrases like "freak out," and "what a bummer," and "wow, man, you're blowing my mind." How could any hippie think of him as one of their own? But I also thought, Oh, Daddy, now I see how much you love me.

Like the rest of my family, Dad really broke down in tears at my funeral at Holy Cross Cemetery. To the strains of Pachabel's Canon, I was buried in my favorite flower-print dress, and Father O'Reilly's eulogy for me touched even the most image-conscious show business friends of mine, people like Kirk Douglas, Warren Beatty, Peter Sellers, Peggy Lipton, James Coburn, Yul Brynner, and Lee Marvin. One of my closest pals, Steve McQueen, wasn't at Holy Cross that day, but I forgave him since I knew that Steve feared he'd be the killers' next target, whoever those killers were. Steve had a reason to be worried, too: it turned out that his name was on a "Celebrity Kill List" that the Manson Family drew up and planned to follow. (Others on the list included Elizabeth Taylor, Richard Burton, and Frank Sinatra.)

Needless to say, it was painful for me to witness how upset everybody got after my murder. My intimates became suspicious of each other. Crazed with grief, my husband threatened people with knives, demanding that they confess to my murder. My hope was that the pain people felt in losing me would weaken as years went by; I believed the adage about time healing all wounds. Sadly, it didn't work this way. My death, and its grisly circumstances, went on haunting everyone who loved me. If I'd perished in an accident or from an illness, bad enough—but homicide? It's like a black hole from which no light escapes.

TIME juddered and jumped track as Lunt looked up at the tall man in the white suit.

"Oh, *fuck*. You?"

"Who's this '*You*,' dear boy? Be precise. My name is Melek Randang."

Shaking his head in disgust, Lunt said, "An alias, I should've guessed. Where'd you steal it from, some high school classmate of Sharon's?"

The bald man smirked at Lunt's disgust, showing perfectly white teeth. "It's an anagram from my name. I register incognito at hotels; it's an old quirk of mine. Each time I use a different anagram, and Melek means 'angel,' I'm told, in some language I don't speak. But you probably don't speak it *either*, Monsieur New Jersey."

Lunt straightened in the seat, feeling the hard struts of it against his back, and sucked in his paunch in case Pandora was watching. From what vantage point? A window, he figured. He didn't glance around. He wouldn't give her that satisfaction. Still, there was no doubt that, *wherever* she was, she was enjoying how her current boyfriend Mandrake had ambushed her ex-boyfriend Lunt.

"What brings you here so much earlier than the Tate-World Conference?" asked Glen Mandrake in his lordly tone of voice.

"Is it necessary for you to know that?"

With a sneer—something he specialized in, along with scowls and that smirk of his—Mandrake said, "Allow me to quote the incomparable Lichtenberg: 'If people should ever begin to do only what is necessary, millions would die of hunger.'"

Mandrake's incessant spouting of aphorisms from the hunch-backed, eighteenth-century, German intellectual Georg Lichten-berg was an affectation of his, along with Mandrake's white suits, which were supposedly made for him by the same Manhattan-based Italian tailor that the author Tom Wolfe used.

"Nothing like a little Lichty to start your day," Mandrake went on, putting his fists on his hips. "God, the *brain* that man had! Did you know he was a scientist as well as a quip-meister? He built Germany's first lightning rod. Drafted a map of the moon. Examined people's dreams, a century before Freud, and still my 'humpy-backed homey,' as I call him, found the time to write *bon mots* in his famous *Waste Books*. Pearls like, 'The most entertaining surface on this planet is that of the human face.'"

"Fuck you and fuck Lichtenberg" was the best Lunt could do for a comeback.

Mandrake went into a fake body collapse, as if defeated by Lunt's wit. Then he tut-tutted, which was another of his annoying habits. "My, how *unlettered* of you. Turning the other cheek as any gentleman would, I hope you'll permit me to say that your recent article in *Sharing Sharon* wasn't bad. Credit where credit's due. Certain bits I even found perceptive."

Lunt rolled his eyes. The phony way Mandrake spoke cried out for a pince-nez to be slammed down on his nose.

"If your projected Sharon book turns out to be as esoteric as that article, dear boy, I wouldn't feel so inclined to campaign against it. May I sit down?"

"One step closer," said Lunt, grabbing hold of the bread knife from his table, "and I puncture your throat."

Assaulting Mandrake, he knew, would impress the probably-observing-from-somewhere, violence-loving Pandora. Not that Lunt had the will to stab a fellow human being, even such a despicable one. It was a matter of cowardice, too: Mandrake was bigger than Lunt, a few years younger, and reputedly a student of Jeet Kune Do, the martial arts system developed by the late kung fu legend (and FOS—"Friend of Sharon") Bruce Lee.

"Temper, dear boy, temper!" Mandrake tut-tutted again. "You need better nerves. What Lichtenberg called 'nerves of thick cable.' Don't you know that threats are the last resort of the powerless?"

Lunt glared up at the jug ears, toad eyes, hairless pate, Adam's apple, and spade-shaped beard. "'Last resort?' Is that another quote from Lichtenberg?"

"Jumping Jehosaphat, as *if!*" said Mandrake, his mouth tightening, seeming to take offense. "No, it's mine. I'm capable of my own pithy observations, you know. And I recognize the powerless when I see a prime example."

IT was mostly about Pandora.

Lunt had first encountered Mandrake four years earlier at a Tate-World auction held in Brooklyn's prestigious Luther Bix Gallery. Glorious lots of Sharonabilia had appeared on the auction block that day, and in spite of his relatively meager finances, Lunt could not resist bidding on one savory item. It was a toe ring said to have a strand of Sharon's hair woven into it. Lunt had desperately wanted the toe ring, of course, but he'd also placed his bid because he meant to show off for the young woman he'd brought along to the auction.

Lunt had been dating Pandora Dibble for two months by then. She was an alluring philosophy grad student at Columbia whose thesis-in-progress was entitled "Nietzsche's 'Will-to-Power' Concept As Exemplified By Middle-School Cyber-Bullying." Pandora's appeal to Lunt when he'd first encountered her at a restaurant in Soho had been instant: one glance at the woman seated near him and he could tell that she possessed the sacred qualities he sought in a lover. He called these qualities his "Five S's"—smart, sweet, sexy, Sharonesque, and sane. In Pandora's case, the Sharonesque part came not from her hair (brown) or physique (willowy) or face (angular) but from her eyes, which were the exact shape, size, and color of Sharon's.

In beholding Pandora's peepers, Lunt felt his heart begin to hammer against his ribs. Pressure filled his chest, sweat sprang to his skin, an erection stirred in the boxer briefs beneath his khakis, and he whispered to himself, "Oh, my stars!"

Lunt sparked a conversation with Pandora about her tofu stroganoff dish, then contacted her via email that night. He told her at their first rendezvous, over lunch in the East Village, about his Sharonophilia. On their second date he mentioned how identical Sharon's eyes were to Pandora's own. And Lunt made sure that they kept unbroken eye contact when they consummated their relationship on the third date.

During those early days, Pandora found Lunt's preoccupation with her eyes, and with Sharon Tate in general, rather odd. Nevertheless, he seemed so open and confident in his passion that she came to find it sexy. Moreover, she was no stranger to pop-culture obsession; in her teen years she'd been a high-ranking officer in "The International Tintin Fan Club."

As Lunt expected, he'd failed to snag the Sharon toe ring at that auction. At least Pandora felt impressed by his boldness in bidding. Unexpected, though, and most unwelcome, was the approach of the auction winner moments after the gavel fell.

"Your eyes are just *extraordinary*," Glen Mandrake told Pandora as he walked up to her, ignoring Lunt. "They're *Sharon's* eyes, precisely!"

"So I've heard," Pandora said.

"Congratulations on bagging the toe ring," Lunt put in civilly.

Once again, with his lips forming a smirk as his gaze stayed locked on Pandora, Mandrake pretended not to notice her boyfriend.

Long before that day, Lunt had heard of "The Bad Boy with Blue Blood," as *Sharing Sharon* had referred to Mandrake in a cover story. He was wealthy, the scion of a bicycle parts manufacturing empire, and socially prominent—his bloodline was reputedly Mayflower WASP. Despite his grotesque looks—"unconventional physical luster," as he himself phrased it—Mandrake succeeded prolifically with women.

Burnishing the weirdness of Mandrake's image were those white suits, that propensity for the aphorist Lichtenberg, his pretentious "Dear boy"-laden diction, and his decade-long public feud with his stepmother, who was a six-term state senator in New Jersey. Mandrake's denunciations of his stepmother in the *Sharing Sharon* feature bordered on the libelous. Yet Senator Mandrake's counterattack was impressive, demolishing as it did her stepson's Mayflower pedigree. In a letter to *Sharing Sharon*'s editor, the stepmother revealed that Glen's great-grandfather, a self-hating Jewish tailor, had changed the family name to "Mandrake" from "Manevitz."

"Maybe you didn't hear me, Mandrake," Lunt had said at the auction, giving his voice some edge as he set a proprietary hand on Pandora's shoulder. "I said 'Congratulations.'"

"Oh, *I'm* sorry," said Mandrake, finally addressing his fellow Sharonophile, although his gaze stayed trained on Pandora. "Thank you, dear boy. And apologies to you and your Sharon-eyed daughter here for my outbidding you."

"*Daughter?*" Lunt clenched his jaw, feeling his heart rate and blood pressure shoot up. "Listen—"

"She's not your daughter?" said Mandrake. "Then she's a much younger sister, I'm sure."

Tightening his grip on Pandora's shoulder, Lunt said, "Try *girlfriend*, you asshole."

"Oh, my." Mandrake went with a sneer. "As Lichtenberg says, 'Much can be inferred about a man from his mistress—in her you can see his weaknesses as well as his dreams.'"

Pandora wrinkled her nose at Mandrake. "What's that supposed to mean?"

"Oh, nothing *personal*, please believe me." He turned back to Lunt. "Same with the auction—nothing personal. I simply couldn't, could *not*, bear for any lock of Sharon's hair to end up in, urgh, New Jersey." Then he paused to season his next statement with some drama. "They call it 'The Garden State,' but there's nothing *Edenic* about it."

"What makes you think I'm from Jersey?" Lunt began to grind his teeth. "You don't know me!"

"*Of course* you're Jersey-stock, Lunt Moreland, because you and my accursed stepmother look alike. All you Jerseyans have that same look about you. And I do know you, because I make a point of knowing all the S-philes who publish in *Sharing Sharon*."

Lunt turned to Pandora and said, "Can you believe this clown?" assuming she felt just as offended by Mandrake's rudeness as he did. Unfortunately, Pandora was smiling at the rude one now, and he continued to stare into her Sharon-eyes, his nostrils quivering slightly with sexual ardor. Having accurately "read" the personality of Pandora—Pandora, the scholar of Nietzsche and cyber-bullying—Mandrake predicted that the more cruelly he treated his rival Sharonophile, the more he'd impress the rival's lover. This prediction proved correct. That very night, Pandora reached out to Mandrake with an email, and by the following weekend she lay naked in his bed, her Sharon-eyes blinking expectantly at him.

AFTERNOON shadows dappled the Ofotert courtyard, where most of the wrought-iron tables were now occupied. A breeze tickled Lunt's Sebring-styled hair. In spite of the temperate weather, he felt his insides boil as his rival, disobeying him, settled into the empty seat opposite Lunt.

"How's your junior suite?" Mandrake asked. "Forty-Seven, isn't it? Probably not as comfortable as mine, but not *rancid*, I'm supposing."

"There's nothing junior about my suite. And however nice *yours* is, *Maneshevitz*, it's not Sharon's old place."

"Fifty-Six, yes, that honor eludes us both. I did a bit of research. Seems that the resident is some obscure and privacy-minded investor. A Belgian named Ziggy Rosenwach. Surprisingly nothing about him on the web. Probably an intimate of my stepmother, *nouveau riche* cow that she is. I can't tell you how much damage that woman does to my digestion."

"Never heard of Rosenwach," Lunt said, not mentioning his telephone call last night to the suite once occupied by Sharon. Maybe the surly woman who'd answered the phone was the Belgian investor's secretary?

"*Whoever* this Rosenwach is," Mandrake said, consulting his watch and sighing as if late for an appointment, "he's not a Sharonophile. We would have heard of him if he was, yes? But my current inability to reside in the Sharon suite is no biggie because I've stayed in that paradise before. Half a dozen times or so. Haven't you?"

"Of course I have," Lunt lied.

"And," Mandrake added, "I'm sure I'll be setting up shop there again on my *next* visit to the Ofotert."

Enough of this, Lunt decided. He would end their useless conversation, now, by snarling at Mandrake, "Shove off or I'll call the management and have *them* do it." Yet before he got this threat out, both men were distracted by the trio at the neighboring table. Benny Pompa pushed his chair back, got to his feet, and stretched his arms toward the temporarily cloud-blocked sun, his fingers tickling air. Then, the stretch completed, the pop star loped into the hotel, trailed by his female companions.

"That churl's music is insufferable," Mandrake said. "But you *do* know his birthdate."

"Duh. John Belushi's, too."

"And Nastassja Kinski, Polanski's post-scandal jailbait. I actually met Nastassja once, and nearly got to sleep with her. Which would mean, you realize, that I'd be someone who slept with someone who slept with someone who slept with Sharon. A community of linked loins! At any rate, how lucky that Benny Pompa is. The same birthday as Sharon! How well-aligned can someone's zodiac *be*? Pity that Pompa's such a dolt. Drug abuse tends to do that. *Plus*, he got struck by lightning once. So his press bio claims. Lightning bolts can't be healthy for brain cells, can they? It must be why he gives away so much money with his foundation. Still, I do like how Pompa travels, always with not one but *two* pulchritudinous pals. Success has gone to his crotch, as they say."

"Buzz off," said Lunt. "Scram!"

In response, Mandrake threw back his head to laugh, exposing the cords in his throat. "Speaking of pulchritude, just imagine how awkward you'll feel when my girl Pandora arrives here next week. How fantastic *that'll* be—all conference long, you'll be hiding here, hiding there, ducking everywhere to avoid us. Burn, baby, burn!"

So Pandora hadn't arrived in LA yet? Lunt sat back, relieved, but tried to hide it, saying, "Sorry, Maneshevitz, but I've got better things to do than pay any notice to you out here in Hollywood. My work, for instance."

Mandrake put his bulging eyes on Lunt, full weight, and contempt dripped from his voice when he said, "Calling me Maneshevitz, mispronouncing my family's Semitic name, doesn't faze me in the slightest. I know who I am. Do *you*?"

"Sure. I'm an author, the one who'll introduce the world to Sharon. *Really* introduce her, and for keeps."

"You're delusional, dear boy."

"My powerful literary agent Vishwa Mukherjee doesn't think so. Vajillion Dollar Vishwa says I'm *Oprah Show*–bound."

Mandrake's opposition to Lunt's book about Sharon had started two months earlier, with an open letter he'd penned and gotten printed in *Sharing Sharon*.

"Popularizing Sharon for a new generation of the public may sell a few books," went Mandrake's elitist argument, "but only by vulgarizing our Ms. Tate. If he makes her a mainstream figure, Lunt Moreland will only malign her. So let's keep Sharon safe. Let's keep her for ourselves. Besides, do we really need more books in the world? As the great Lichtenberg tells us, 'Many people read just to prevent themselves from thinking.'"

Lunt's reply appeared in *Sharing Sharon*'s following issue.

"My goal," Lunt wrote, "is not to 'vulgarize' Sharon, as you phrase it, Mr. Mandrake, but quite the opposite—to ennoble her, to elevate her to the pantheon where she belongs, alongside legendary screen sirens such as Marilyn Monroe, Brigitte Bardot, Sophia Loren, and Jean Harlow. Obviously, I trust my fellow citizens more than you do. To 'protect' Sharon from them, you would imprison her in a golden cage. We true believers are not as selfish as you would have us be; we're not snobs who would deny our pleasures to anyone else. Sharon is not our exclusive property. She belongs to the ages. She deserves the recognition, and the applause, and the love of the whole world, not just our loving corner of it. We have the responsibility to share her, and my book will start this process."

To judge by the letters subsequently mailed to the journal, Sharonophiles were equally divided in their support of Mandrake's or Lunt's viewpoints, while Thornton Pisher, *Sharing Sharon's* publisher, carefully remained neutral about the matter.

"*Scram*," Lunt said, furious. "I *mean* it. And next time you approach me—either before the conference, or during—I'll call the cops and press charges for harrassment!"

"How touchy you are, dear boy. Mind your mind here. Don't go loony like your literary agent Vishwa tends to do. Southern California is not for the emotionally fragile." Then, flapping his right hand at the cream-and-gray edifice looming above them, he said, "But as the great Lichtenberg puts it, 'We cannot truly know whether, at this moment, we are sitting in a madhouse.'"

LUNT learned of Sharon Tate's existence when he was eleven years old. At the shopping mall in his hometown of Sulphurdale, a long, low, red-brick building where the only child and his parents spent weekend afternoons browsing, Lunt's favorite spot was a Brandisi Bookstore. He didn't have crushes on girls yet, but he loved to wander the stacks at Brandisi and peruse the paperbacks he was usually too young to read from cover to cover.

One rainy Saturday while Lunt's parents were buying lawn furniture—"We'll be back in forty-five minutes," his father had said—Lunt drifted into the true crime area of the bookstore. A thick hardback on display, recently published, bore the title *Helter Skelter*. Until he'd scanned the book's black and blood-red dust jacket, Lunt had not known about Charles Manson, his Family, their crimes, or their most illustrious victim. Yet as soon as the boy opened the book and started turning pages, he was riveted.

Most compelling at first was Manson's affinity for the Beatles, who were also Lunt's favorite musical group at the time. Songs like "Nowhere Man" and "Piggies" and "Blackbird" sounded so friendly, so welcoming, so human—how could a murderer appreciate the same music Lunt did? And how did Manson hear, or claim to hear, strange messages in the songs, secrets about an approaching, violent Doomsday?

Thumbing through the book, Lunt knew he had to own it. He would read the book carefully and learn how this "Nowhere Man," as Manson dubbed himself, would help black people, "Blackbirds," destroy Lunt's own people, the white "Piggies." This book— it was essential!

"Not a chance," said Mrs. Moreland when she and her husband returned to Brandisi.

"But, Mom—it's about the Beatles, my favorite group!"

"Sorry, Mister." She waddled over to him. With her free hand (the other was holding two plastic Sears bags), she snatched the copy of *Helter Skelter* from Lunt and placed it back on its display shelf. "I know about this Manson character, I heard all about him on the news. That's no person for you to emulate."

"But I'm not *emulating* him, Mom" (Lunt wasn't familiar with the word, but he could guess), "I'm just—"

At which point Lunt's father, who'd been brushing lint off the shoulder of his coffee-stained blazer, spoke up on the boy's behalf. "It can't be *that* bad, sweetheart. It's not like, I don't know, *Mein Kampf*—or some book about homosexuals."

This was a rare outing for Curtis Moreland's boldness; he didn't usually challenge his wife—or his child, for that matter— in anything. From the couple's first encounter at the college they both attended, she seduced him away from his foreign girlfriend. And since then, Shirley Moreland had called all the proverbial shots. Resistance, Curtis learned, was futile. Their son had learned the same lesson about his mother. So when she raised her voice to say, "Forget it, both of you! We're leaving," Lunt gave one final mournful look at *Helter Skelter* and his father shrugged his shoulders, looking away. Then the woman gave each of them, man and boy, a Sears bag to carry, and led them out of the bookstore.

WHEN Bronson's name appeared on the grimy BlackBerry screen, Lunt was on a hiatus from his afternoon writing session and humming some of Sharon's favorite songs while strolling west along the Sunset Strip. He encountered a few pedestrians, the occasional mosquitos, the smell of scorched metal, a broken, left-behind acetylene torch, busstop benches with ads for a twelve-step program, and billboards—endless billboards, including one near the Ofotert where a massive "Marlboro Man" figure had once stood. Back when Sharon had lived at the hotel, there'd been an odd drum-majorette statue here, an advertisement for a Las Vegas casino. Lunt had seen a photo of this statue on the cover of *Myra Breckinridge*, the Gore Vidal novel. What had Sharon thought of the statue? Had she ever read Vidal's book? Was it published before she died?

Lunt knew he ought to know this. Damn his failing, nearly forty-year-old memory!

Well, he thought, *another subject for future research.*

Bronson was her usual buoyant telephonic self today. After hearing about Lunt's confrontation with Mandrake, she said, "You're perfectly right to notify someone if Mandrake keeps bugging you. But start with the hotel management before you shout 'Cop,' huh?"

"Good idea, Bron. Hearing you, I feel calmer already. Where would I be in a Bronson-less world?"

Strangely, Lunt's mention of the photograph he'd received today, the valuable 8x10 glossy of La Tate dressed as Santa Claus, seemed to surprise his friend. Bronson said, "I didn't send that, no. Why would I give you a birthday present without a card? Not my style, hon. And weeks before the actual date? Bad luck. Besides, I wouldn't mess up a pristine Santa Shot by Magic-Markering hearts all over it. I wouldn't even know how to *find* a Santa Shot. Don't the PP have a lock on the whole batch? That's the tale I've heard—the PP bought the whole series of Santa Shots from some movie memorabilia shop in Georgia back in the eighties."

"Who's Pee-Pee?"

"*The* PP—'Polanski People.' Assholes."

"Ah. That weird fan club who wrote to me last year."

"Don't feel special. They've solicited all of us, Luntie."

"*Having learned of your interest in our Roman's late wife Sharon,*" began the letter that Lunt had received, "*we are hereby offering you a chance to join, at a special discount rate, our exclusive group—'The Polanski Devotee Organization That's so Much More Than Just a Fan Club.'*"

The letter went on to enumerate a series of "advantages" conferred to "PP Members." Despising Polanski as he did, Lunt stopped reading before the end and got busy crafting a response.

"*To the Slavish Adherents of a Confirmed Scoundrel,*" Lunt wrote. "*My interest in Sharon Tate does not concern rank strangers like yourselves. And it most certainly does not entail that I have, or want, anything to do with 'your' disgusting dwarf Roman. Not only did he shame Sharon with his unfaithfulness to her, but he has shamed her memory with his subsequent misbehavior, the outrageousness of which I hardly need to mention. Even his storytelling sense is corroded: as he put it himself in an interview, 'I generally like female characters who are victims.' Finally, although his film* The Tenant *does have its satisfyingly creepy moments— and a male victim, for a change—Polanski is a cinematic failure. He is, as someone once remarked, 'the original five-foot Pole you don't want to touch anything with.'*"

Bravo, Lunt had congratulated himself when he completed the letter. Even so, a faint disquiet lingered after he had mailed it to the

PP's "World Headquarters" in Des Moines. The truth, although he was reluctant to admit it to himself, was that his hatred for Polanski was intermixed with envy. Obviously, Lunt wished he could have been married to Sharon, and he also wished that he possessed the Polanski dwarf's fame, his artistic reputation, and his unbridled access to hedonism. The Pole seemed to be, *was*, his better. Except for ethical purity, Polanski trumped him in every way. Which only increased Lunt's hatred.

"Hey," said Bronson, "do you think someone from The Polanski People, some 'Polanski Person,' put that Santa Shot under your door?"

Lunt pondered the question before he said no. "Even if they're smarting from the letter I sent them, I doubt it."

"Was there anything written on the envelope?"

"Nope, just a sticker that said, 'No sense makes sense.'"

With her trademark chortle, Bronson said, "Which itself makes no sense!"

Whizzing cars, shiny storefronts, the glitter of sunlight everywhere. On the south side of Sunset, Lunt shuffled past a striptease club called Corpus Co-op.

Lunt wasn't much of a habitué of strip clubs. Although he did appreciate gazing at naked women in three-dimensional motion, he disliked the sleazy ambience of such places, along with the growly, tuxedoed bouncers, the diarrhea-mouthed disc jockeys, the *schlock* music those deejays played, the grating waitresses, the Visigothic clientele, the laughably phony stripper names ("Pumpkin Pie," "Fancy Free," "Delta of Venus"), and the strippers' greed for the patrons' lucre. This greed, though understandable, was just as naked as the rest of them.

"Hey," Bronson started onto a new subject, "did you use your Beige Milk yet today?"

As she'd explained to him when she mailed the expensive oint-ment to her friend as last year's Christmas present, Beige Milk Mois-turizer was made from marigold petals. "Apply it to your face twice a day," ran her advice, "and you'll look thirty instead of forty."

"The jar's back at the Ofotert," Lunt said today. "I'll use it later, I promise." Yet he couldn't shake the previous subject from his thoughts. "You don't think *Mandrake* gave me the Santa Shot, do you?"

"No, stupid!" She growled. "Why would he give you something valuable?"

"Fair point."

As Lunt went by the Corpus Co-op, he ogled some female silhouettes on the club's facade, wondering about the actual strippers employed there. Would any of them have legs, or other body parts, that resembled Sharon's? Next to one of the silhouettes was a strange graffito Lunt nearly missed. "THIS PLACE WORSHIPS DEATH," someone had written in black spray paint. Meaning that the strip club worshipped death? Or that all of Hollywood did?

"If Mandrake isn't your mystery-gifter," said Bronson, "then maybe you've got a female admirer. Some gal from the stable of that rock star Benny Pompa, maybe? Is he the only celeb you've seen so far?"

"Give me time, I just arrived. Anyway, I'm not here to star-trip."

"No, but in LA it's impossible not to go on a star-trip. Which, don't forget, is based on all the gawkers' *ego*-tripping. With the occasional guilt trip and death trip thrown in."

"Now you're putting me on me a *bummer* trip, Bron."

She chortled. "How I do love that sixties lingo, son. Sharon's lingo. It sounds like a law firm, doesn't it? 'Star, Death, Ego, Guilt, and Bummer—Attorneys-at-Law.'"

"I saw him again, by the way."

"Who?"

"Benny Pompa. You know he was born on Sharon's birthday, right?"

"Along with Nastassja K. Smoking hot, that Kinski cutie. I'll tell you, if I wasn't gaga for Sharon, I'd be a Nastassjaphile. Exotic, plus she does have one thing that I wish Sexy Sharon had: *she's alive.* Hasn't it ever bothered you—just, like, a little—that we love someone who can never love us back? Or even know how we feel about her?"

"Not at all, Bron. Love is blind."

"And in my case," Bronson said, chortling again, "love is physically disabled, too."

Lunt laughed politely. He never knew how to react when she made light of her disability, which she did fairly often. (She was fond of quoting Richard Pryor, another multiple sclerosis sufferer, when referring to her illness: "It's God's way of making me slow down.")

"I take Sharon as I find her," Lunt said. "Dead, alive—if you love someone, you don't stop just because they're no longer with us." He felt a cough coming on, swallowed it back, then said, "My guess about the Santa Shot—not that my intuition rivals yours—is that it's another Sharonophile. Someone else who came out early for the conference."

"Another Tate-Worlder, huh? How many S-philes are aware that you're at the Ofotert?"

"Pretty much all of them. I posted my plans on the listserv."

"So that explains it. Since the whole Sharonverse knows where you are, it could've been anyone who sent you the Santa Shot. By mail, with instructions to deliver it to your door."

Unable to withstand it, Lunt broke into a new coughing fit, one more extreme than the others. Stopping at the corner of King's Road (a fortunate name—Sharon loved to shop on a different King's Road, the ultra-chic one in the Chelsea neighborhood of London),

Lunt remained in place and hacked away for half a minute, back of hand pressed to mouth, the phlegm at the base of his throat tasting bitter.

"You okay?" Bronson said when the coughing finally subsided.

"Yeah. Just some germs I must've picked up on the plane."

"No other sign of cold or flu? Stuffy nose? Headache?"

"None. No fever, either."

"Guard your health, hon—you've gotta be in prime shape for that Sharonfest next week."

"Don't worry, I will be."

But just after he said this, he remembered a remark that Sharon once made to a journalist: "Something more powerful than we are decides our fates for us. I know one thing: I've never planned anything that ever happened to me."

DESPITE Lunt's mother denying him ownership of *Helter Skelter*, the boy always made sure to rush straight to Brandisi's true crime section—and that jewel of a book it contained—each time he went back there unsupervised. Meanwhile, adolescence loomed. At the age of eleven, he still had no romantic crushes. This changed the night when he first beheld Freya—"Freya Carlson," the pride of the Danish Tourist Bureau.

The movie being broadcast on Channel 11 that night was *The Wrecking Crew*, a bad, late 1960s James Bond knockoff. In the flick, an aging, turtleneck-clad Dean Martin starred as "Matt Helm," a hip fashion photographer who moonlighted as a Bond-like secret agent. Against the film's band of villains, what help did Matt Helm have? Only another American spy, one whose cover assignment was as a guide to tourists in Denmark.

Newly arrived in Copenhagen, Helm is checking in to his hotel when a prim woman in tight slacks with pillbox hat and goofy, square-framed spectacles comes dashing through the lobby— "*Mr. Helm!* Oh, *Mr. Helm!*"—and promptly does a pratfall, landing flat on her back on top of his luggage.

"I'm Freya," declares the woman from her prone position, clearly unflappable. "Freya Carlson!"

Lunt Moreland blinked at the TV set. Seated alone in his family's den, the boy felt his heart rate begin to accelerate inside his pajama top. Sweat began to moisten each pore. Wow! There was so much deliciousness here: Freya's red-toned hair (a wig, Lunt would soon learn), her honeyed voice, her kind eyes, wide mouth, lustrous skin, and razor cheekbones. Everything about her was delectable. Perfect. More than anything, though, Lunt loved Freya's klutziness. Being a klutz himself, he could identify with this woman. (And, by extension, whatever actress played her.) *We're the same*, he told himself. Lunt and this woman, they were birds of a feather, he knew this, simply knew it. And with her, only with her, his angel of mercy, it seemed okay to be a klutz.

To be uncool.

To be *himself.*

It was as though she'd reached through the glass TV screen and out into his home to grasp Lunt's hand and guide him to the portal of puberty. His bubbling hormones would require more time before he could actually pass through that portal. But while he waited, the actress playing Freya Carlson waited with him, and she did not release his hand. Lunt wouldn't let her. He held on tight.

Watching *The Wrecking Crew*, the boy was incapable of clear thought. He was under the actress's spell. This spell got shattered an hour later. As soon as the good guys, Helm and Freya, had kicked some serious villain ass, the words "The End" came flashing across the screen, the credits rolled, Dean Martin's name appeared beside "Matt Helm," then next to "Freya" appeared a name that horrified Lunt once he read it. This name—he recognized it from *Helter Skelter.*

"Oh, God!" he cried out, startling his parents in the kitchen two rooms away. "But she's the one, the pregnant actress who that psycho Manson—"

Yes.

AS soon as Lunt got off the line with Bronson, still ambling on foot along Sunset, he remembered that he needed to call Vishwa, his literary agent. Given the time difference, it was too late to reach her in her office, *Tomorrow*, he promised himself.

A few blocks past La Cienega, Lunt came upon a trendy-looking seafood restaurant named Gush. On the pavement outside, hot, hip-looking young women, all in miniskirts with cigarettes, stood chattering among themselves, probably waiting for tables to open up. *Seems like a prime place to investigate*, Lunt told himself. *The kind of spot Sharon probably would have adored.*

One street beyond the restaurant, Lunt decided to head back toward the hotel. Ordinarily during his visits to LA, he spent each afternoon driving around, checking in at known Sharon sites as well as Lunt's own haunts from his college days. He intended to see more of the city this time, too. But since he was finally settled in at the Sharon-sacred Hotel Ofotert, he liked the idea of not straying too far from it. To hang out at the Ofotert would keep him Sharon-pure, and also throw up less distractions that could tempt him away from writing.

Glancing down as he walked, Lunt noticed two spiders hurrying along the cracked, yellowish sidewalk. They moved in a kind of spider-lockstep as they approached a dirty portion of Bubble Wrap. It was the size of a CD case, all its bubbles popped. The spiders piqued Lunt's curiosity. Were they related to each other? Didn't spiders travel alone? Where was the nearest web? Lunt didn't care much about the answers, actually. He even considered stepping on the spiders, to make them experience death together, just as Dorothy Parker claimed that she liked to stomp on earthworms. "Aha, my little dear," she'd written in a poem Lunt had read last night in his suite's Parker book, "your clan will pay me back one day."

Another reason Lunt had for treading on the spiders was his having once read of Charles Manson's fondness for the creatures. When a friend of Charlie's had killed one, Manson scolded him by shouting, "Better to ice a human being than a spider!" Remembering the Manson quote, Lunt stared some more at the creepy-crawlies, his right foot poised to strike. In the end, he resisted his violent urge because Sharon, the eternal animal-lover, considered all life sacred, and he always tried to follow her lead.

When Lunt arrived at the Ofotert's narrow, white-walled driveway, he came upon two hotel employees. The first was the squat, sunken-chested garage attendant who'd parked Lunt's Mustang yesterday. *"Hola, señor,"* the attendant called to Lunt, waving a hammy hand. Lunt waved back. The second employee, a high-hipped Latino man in white Oxford shirt and plaid slacks, was less welcoming. He smelled of Brut cologne and had the lean, planed-down body of an athlete. With his right hand raised in a "Stay back" gesture, the man asked if he could "assist" Lunt "in any fashion."

"I'm a hotel guest," the hotel guest replied.

"What room, sir?"

As soon as Lunt told him, the man—whose name, if his name tag could be believed, was "BABY SON"—checked a clipboard he held in his left hand. Finally, after a moment of paper-flipping and rhythmic tapping of his right foot, Baby Son said, "Mr. Moreland?"

"That's me."

The man's mouth, which was encircled by a precisely shaved goatee, eased into a smile. Which made the goatee seem to wobble. "Sorry, sir. Welcome back." His English bore no Hispanic accent, Lunt noted, but his chin rose slightly with the last word of each sentence. "Our *casa* is your *casa*."

GARY LIPPMAN

Lunt returned the smile while giving Baby Son a once-over, studying the Latino man's face especially. It was the color of coffee-flavored ice cream and filled with out-of-place-looking freckles. "You the official greeter?"

"Something like that. Security. House detective."

"Ah, a pleasure. Now, about the name tag, which intrigues me. Mind if I ask what 'Baby Son' stands for? Is that a nickname?"

"It's my given name, sir. Courtesy of my parents."

"What were you, the baby of the family?"

"That's exactly right, sir. "

"Come on—seriously?"

"I'm always serious, sir."

Oops, Lunt thought, his face quickly flushing. "Well, uh—at least you escaped being a wretched only child like me."

A look of sadness seemed to enter Baby Son's eyes. "I'm the last of twelve children, sir."

"Twelve?" Lunt chuckled good-naturedly, hoping to win over the man. "Wow, your parents really went for it! But why didn't they go the extra mile and have thirteen? They superstitious?"

"They *did* have a thirteenth child," Baby Son said. "My little brother. But he died at age three."

Oh, shit, thought Lunt. "Jesus, I'm sorry."

Baby Son shifted his clipboard from one surprisingly small hand to the other. "Thank you, sir."

Seeking to defuse his embarrassment, Lunt changed the subject. "Listen, I'm glad I bumped into you, man. I need to ask you a few quick questions."

"I'm here to help, sir."

"I'm curious about Suite Fifty-Six. It has, like, historical meaning for me, so I'm wondering about the current occupant, how to approach him. Apparently he's this bigwig named Rosen-something, right?"

74

Baby Son exhaled. "That's correct, sir. Mr. Rosenwach."

"What's his story?"

"I'm not at liberty to say, sir."

"I understand. At least—is he into the actress Sharon Tate?"

"As I said, I'm not at liberty to say."

"Roger that. I'm only inquiring because, well, I want to visit the room when that Rosenwach goes out."

Baby Son slowly shook his head.

"As I said, it's of great importance to me, and—"

"I understand, sir. But you visiting there won't be possible."

"Then maybe…" Lunt tugged his wallet from his front pocket, drew out a twenty, and held it out it to the house detective, who accepted it with his free hand as if expecting it all along. "Maybe," said Lunt, "*this* will improve my chances?"

As Baby Son slid the bill under the silver clamp on the clipboard (Lunt feeling encouraged by the loud *pock* sound it made), the man's eyes took on new vigor, all sorrowfulness dispelled. "I'm sorry, sir," he said. "As I told you, it's impossible."

"Wait," Lunt sputtered, "*still?*"

"It's still impossible. Sorry, sir."

"But I—I just gave you money!"

"And I thank you for it. My *tio* Huberto used to say, 'Never turn down money when someone offers.' My children will benefit from your kindness, sir. But I cannot help you with Suite Fifty-Six."

Lunt began to grind his teeth. "I only gave you that twenty as a *bribe!* For access to Fifty-Six!"

"I understand, sir."

"So give it back!"

Baby Son smiled again, his goatee wobbling. "Do you really want me to return this, sir? After all, I'll be protecting you in the hotel while you're here."

Knowing he'd been beaten, Lunt said, "Okay, fine, just keep it."

"Thank you, sir."

"But there's another problem."

"Sir?"

"Someone left an envelope under my door sometime this morning. I was sleeping, and it just, like, materialized there. An envelope with a photograph in it."

"I don't know anything about that, sir. Have you spoken to your housekeeper? Or Mrs. Kruikshank?"

"Mrs. Kruikshank?"

"She's our night clerk."

"But this happened in *the morning!*"

"It might have happened in the *early* morning, sir. And no matter when it was, Mrs. Kruikshank will probably know who left it for you. She's very wise. Like a guru person, or the Yoda."

Lunt considered this for a moment. "Mrs. Kruikshank"— he recognized the name. Wasn't she the old woman who'd been greeted by Trueax, the Ofotert manager, last night when Lunt was checking in? The old woman who reminded Lunt of his mother for some reason?

"She's Asian, right?" Lunt said to Baby Son.

"I believe her parents were from the Philippines, sir. Filipino people know a lot."

"Maybe," said Lunt, still indignant about his failed bribe, "I ought to talk to your *tio* Huberto."

"That's not possible," Baby Son replied. "My *tio* died last year, sir."

In his suite upstairs, remembering Bronson's mention of Beige Milk, Lunt took the jar of moisturizer from his writing table, twisted off its top, and rubbed a few fingertips' worth of the gunk into his cheeks, chin, and forehead. The odor was musky, terribly so, and he made sure to wash his hands after the treatment. Then, plucking up his courage, Lunt left his suite (almost forgetting his red-tasselled key) and walked from his suite up the crimson-carpeted main staircase to the fifth floor.

His plan was to snoop around Sharon's former suite. Maybe he could learn something about the Belgian fat cat Rosenwach. Unfortunately, the door to the suite was shut and no sounds could be heard from within.

Lunt didn't linger—he recalled only too well the threat he'd gotten from that hostile woman when he'd phoned there. Before descending to 47, though, he noticed a balcony on the fifth floor, a little public patio from which he could watch the sunset. Perfect for writing, too! So he bounced back to his suite, brought his laptop upstairs, and got to work.

Scudding clouds drifted overhead. The scent of patchouli, Sharon's favorite fragrance, seemed to linger around Lunt for a moment. Or was he imagining it? It didn't matter. As the daylight melted to pastel orange, then to marbled blue, he felt like he was melting, too, in the best way: melting into a state of pure contentment.

For thirty minutes, Lunt worked efficiently on the balcony, his fingers plucking away at his laptop's keyboard. Sometimes he glanced down at the kidney-shaped Ofotert pool. He would have to stop by there tomorrow, check out the female flirting possibilities. Meanwhile, the sunset went on being delightful, and just before it ended with a final vivid flare, a hawk, or another raptor with a vast wingspan, began to circle slowly, lazily, high above him, threading its way through the now-purple clouds. Who'd have guessed that hawks could be glimpsed over West Hollywood? Lunt didn't think of this town as a natural setting for wildlife, but of course, with the haze-shrouded hills north of the Ofotert, it was. Squinting his eyes, he could just about discern the bird's brownish stripes, its rounded head and narrow, reddish tail. He'd learned about hawks from a book he'd read years ago, a volume on his informal "Sharon Reading List." It was *A Paradise of Peregrines* by Gabriel Egset, who'd been one of Sharon's favorite naturalist writers. Around and around the hawk cruised, lifted sometimes by gusts of thermal wind, dipping and swooping as if its flight was just for fun, no effort required.

In LA, even the hawks are laid-back, Lunt mused. *Even they go for joyrides.* He smiled at the winged one, feeling a kinship.

But then it dawned on him that the hawk was hunting, using its terrific vision to search for prey.

And he remembered what Sharon once told a journalist: "Everything that's realistic has some sort of ugliness in it. Even a flower is ugly when it wilts, a bird when it seeks its prey, the ocean when it becomes violent."

MOST likely it was because of my father that I always felt attracted to powerful men. These men didn't have to be emotionally remote like Dad was, or physically striking—they just had to be the sort who took control of life. Roman, for example: despite his short stature, he had such presence. I'd never met a man so self-assured in his manner (overly self-assured, many would say), so chic in his fashion sense (perhaps too much so, what with his "Beatle Boots," velvet bell-bottoms, and paisley ascots), and so unashamed of his promiscuity ("The Krakow Shagger," people called him). Roman dominated me, just as, in his own way, my father had.

Sometimes things were difficult for me with Roman, but it made life twice as interesting. Because of him, I started to see things for what they were worth. I used to take everything at face value; when I said something, I meant it, so I felt that everybody else meant what they said, too, but of course that wasn't so, and life, in fact, wasn't always so sweet and simple.

Was I too indulgent of the men in my life? Probably. Whenever Roman complimented one of my outfits, for example, I dashed right back to the shop and bought a few identical ones in different colors, or else figured out how to make them myself. Then there was my smoking cigarettes, which I found so relaxing. Roman didn't want me to do it, so I had to hide my ciggies from him. I was even afraid to tell him when I learned I was pregnant because I worried that he wouldn't let me keep our child.

As a little girl in Texas, I saw the handsome actor David Niven in a movie, and wowee zowee! I decided that when I grew up I would marry him. I really only became interested in boys at the age of fourteen, though, which was pretty soon after boys took to liking me. By that time, we'd moved to the Tri-Cities in Washington State, where my father was posted at Camp Hanford. I especially remember one Saturday morning at *a shopping center. My mom and I were there with my sisters, and I was pushing Patricia's stroller, which I loved to do, when these three young men in golf outfits passed us and looked me over from head to toe. At first I figured they were focused on my dress, but the expression they had in their eyes—their expression made me feel so uncomfortable. Uncomfortable in a way I'd never felt before. So I blushed and I glanced over at my mother, who'd witnessed what happened. She was also staring at me strangely.*

"Is something wrong, Mother?"

She just smiled and said, "It's starting."

Mother used to say that I was just as beautiful as a teenager as I was in my twenties. Whether that was true or not, she did encourage my being noticed for my looks. It was Mom, for example, who entered me in beauty pageants and then hollered with delight when she saw me on the stage in my swimsuit. "Miss Richland," "Queen of the Autorama"—winning these titles did make me feel proud, but not as proud as they made her. Soon we set our sights on the biggest local contest, "Miss Washington," although my father was growing more and more upset about my competing in pageants. He wasn't keen on my dating boys, either. Dad was typical for 1950s fathers, I guess. But "strict" in Paul Tate's case was really strict! Most of the boys I liked he turned away—this one didn't look wholesome enough, that one supported Adlai Stevenson in the last presidential election.

As for the few boys Dad did authorize to take me out (only on weekends; school nights were for homework), well, each boy got a big interrogation as soon as he arrived to pick me up. "What are your intentions with my daughter tonight?" It was humiliating for me, as you'd imagine. And don't even ask about the curfew he imposed!

In 1959, Dad got promoted to captain and was sent to the G2 Southern European Task Force at the Passelaequa Army Base near the Italian town of Verona. I hated the idea of moving to Italy, and tried everything I could to prevent it: starving myself, refusing to pack my clothes, and giving my parents the silent treatment. Nothing worked, of course. I let them think that I was resisting going to Italy because it would prevent me from participating in the Miss America competition, but the true reason was that leaving the States frightened me. Italy, Europe, a new home across the ocean? It all seemed so adult. And I wanted to go on being young, a teenager, a non-adult, forever.

"HI, Mrs. Kruikshank, I'm Lunt Moreland, in Suite Forty-Seven? Someone slid this package under my door earlier today, and I'm wondering if you have any idea whom it might be."

Behind the mahogany reception desk, the Hotel Ofotert's elderly night clerk smiled pleasantly, her name tag slightly askew on the front of her gray polyester, buttoned-tight-at-the-wrists uniform. So here was the "wise Yoda" mentioned by Baby Son. Well, she did look rather wise, and neat as a pin, as she leaned forward to peer at the envelope Lunt held out across the darkly glowing desk top. Lunt waited, giving her time to check out the package with the Santa Shot inside it, and he wondered, *How many years until I look as old as she does? And why does she remind me so much of my mother? My mother didn't have a drop of Asian blood!*

Mrs. Kruikshank looked up from the package, gazed into Lunt's eyes, and frowned. The facial movement redrew the map of many wrinkles on her Asian-featured face. But when she opened her mouth to speak, nothing emerged. Not, at least, for eight long seconds. Evidently she had suffered a stroke in the past, or was afflicted by some other neurological disorder, which meant that her responses to other people's words took time, and obvious strain, for her to get them out. Lunt felt pity for her.

"No," Mrs. Kruikshank said, the odor of mustard on her breath, "to tell you the God's honest truth, I don't recognize this envelope, Mr. Moreland. At what time was it left for you?"

"Sometime last night or this morning. While I was asleep."

During the long pause before Mrs. Kruikshank spoke once more, her eyes blinked while looking into his own eyes imploringly.

The night clerk's heavily lipsticked mouth quavered, too, and a fat vein on the right side of her throat kept pulsing. As she struggled to get the words out, Lunt looked at the curved mirror mounted on the wall behind her. He'd hoped to catch a glimpse of himself there but all he saw was the back of the night clerk's small, gracefully shaped, white-haired head. Next, he peeked at the hotel's sunken lobby, which teemed with glamorous cocktail-sippers. None of them, Lunt was glad to find, were Glen Mandrake.

Since returning from his afternoon stroll, Lunt had kept a wary watch for the white suit and misshapen features of his enemy. Where was the bastard? And when would Pandora arrive? From beyond the open, Gothic-spired wooden doors to Lunt's rear came more sounds of revelry. Was Mandrake out in the courtyard? Was the pop star Benny Pompa outside, too, showing off with more druggie anecdotes?

"I understand," said Mrs. Kruikshank, able to respond at last. "I do work at night, but I'm afraid I can't help you."

Lunt offered her a placid smile while fingering the green-edged brass bell on the desktop. All of a sudden the inside of his right ear tickled him, so he jammed a finger in it and moved it around, hoping he'd feel no hairs growing there. Ear hair, of course, was another sign of middle age. To Lunt's relief, his ear felt hair-free.

"Have you asked Mr. Trueax?" the desk clerk added. "He's the manager."

"Well, it seems that—" But Lunt could not finish his sentence, because—again!—he sputtered into a cough. From deep in his lungs it came, and the coughing spasm went on and on. Covering his mouth with one forearm so that he didn't spray phlegm all over the night clerk, Lunt thought, aghast, *I'm tearing up my stomach lining! What is this thing, tuberculosis? If it is, then why aren't I manifesting any other symptoms?*

"Would you like a glass of water?" Mrs. Kruikshank asked after four seconds.

Lunt shook his head, nearly doubled over now, trying to will the hacking to stop. But whenever a cough felt climactic, the grand finale, a new cough would follow.

"There's a water cooler around the corner there, free for guests to use."

Lunt shook his head again.

"Have you tried Mucaquell?"

"Mucawhat?" Lunt managed to get out.

"Mucaquell," said Mrs. Kruikshank following an eight-second pause. "It's a syrup, a cough suppressant. 'Muke' is how they refer to it in advertisements. Charming advertisements, I must say! '*Make your cough a fluke—come on, get on the Muke!*' There's that, and '*Bad cough treating you rough? Mucaquell, do yer stuff!*'"

Upstairs in the air-conditioned cool of his suite, the coughing jag trailed off and stopped. For now. While checking emails, the Sharonophile found a new "Need to talk" message from his literary agent Vishwa Mukherjee. Lunt promised himself he would call her as soon as he woke in the morning. Then he turned to beam up at the Sharon "WHY?" poster Scotch-taped to the wall above his bed.

"That guy Lichtenberg was wrong," Lunt whispered. "The most entertaining surface on earth isn't *any* human face, it's *yours*. How gorgeous you are, such a vision! I wish you could see me— I've made real progress writing my book, my Great Work, since I got here. You'd be proud."

Later, while soaking in the bath, his back muscles unknotting, Lunt thought of Dorothy Parker. Was it true that she'd tried to kill herself in this tub? Had she cut her wrists or used pills? Splashing up from his prone position, Lunt took hold of some Tate-World Conference brochures. While he leafed through them, he wondered how many Sharon lookalikes would be hired to lounge around this year's Sharonfest. As he'd assured Bronson, he couldn't afford to hire any of them for the "private Sharon fashion shows" they gave wealthy Sharonophiles. That was Mandrake's thing, not Lunt's.

Maybe, Lunt thought, leaning back in the warm water far enough that it wetted the hair at the nape of his neck, *one of those hired Sharon lookalikes will fall in love with me, anyway! I'm a Tate scholar, after all, and not as unattractive as most male S-philes. Plus, I'm currently standing at the cusp of a great career in Sharon publishing…*

Still in an aroused mood after climbing from his tub and drying off, the naked man turned off the TV, placed his laptop on the bed, and summoned up a film he kept on the hard drive. It was a long silent color video clip of Sharon in a bikini, just months short of the oldest she would ever be. With a commendably intent look, she was shampooing a dog, the actress Patty Duke's Russian wolfhound Shadrach, in the backyard of a house. Of all the moving images of Sharon that Lunt possessed, none turned him on as swiftly and surely as did "The Old Standby," as he called it.

Once the clip got going, he took one of the smooth pillows from his bed, stuck his penis inside the pillowcase (not so hygienic, but he would shower in the morning)—and then he did to that pillow what he longed to do to Sharon.

BY the time Lunt turned twelve, six years after Sharon's murder, the actress had seized control of his inner life, holding him fast in her web. In the decades to come, he would ask himself repeatedly (though never aloud to other Sharonophiles except for Bronson), *Why Sharon Tate?* What was it, aside from her obvious appeal, that caused him to fixate so intensely on this dead woman? Some alchemical process had ignited during that moment when he first beheld Sharon on TV and thought, *With her, only her, I can be myself.* Yet this alchemy's precise nature remained beyond his ken. It felt as elemental as any personal "given"—his liking girls, his hating mayonnaise, his feeling frustrated when his mother bossed him or bossed his father around.

Lunt just *knew*, knew at his core, that the woman for him was Sharon—and he grew comfortable over time not knowing why this had to be, why it was Sharon and no one else. He was a Sharonophile through and through—although in the early years "crypto-Sharonophile" would be a more accurate description. This was because his mother rejected his chaste Sharon-love, calling it "sick, sick, sick" whenever he spoke to his parents about it. In fact, Mrs. Moreland forbade her boy from mentioning or even thinking about "that poor dead blonde girl Sharon Fate."

"It's 'Tate,' Mom, not 'Fate.'"

"Whatever," said Mrs. Moreland. "She might've been a movie star, but you can bet your bottom dollar she wouldn't want someone worshipping her the way *you* do."

"You don't know that, Mom."

"Speaking of 'not knowing,' you don't even know a *thing* about who she really was, so why go around pretending you do?"

"Give me time!" Lunt fired back. "I'm still *learning* about Sharon. If you'll let me, I can learn enough to love her properly."

Lunt's mother wasn't listening. "And the awful way they *killed* her, that poor thing. Can't you just leave her in peace? Find a girl in school, someone you actually know, who's your own age, and still alive!"

"No living girl is as good as Sharon."

"Too bad. If a live one is good enough for your father, it should be good enough for you. Like the TV commercial goes, 'Like father, like son.'"

"My life's not a TV commercial, Mom."

"No, and it's not a freak show, either."

To support her thesis, Mrs. Moreland produced the latest *Reader's Digest* and read to Lunt a quotation she'd discovered there: *"He who treats another human being as divine thereby assigns himself the relative status of a child or an animal."* Then she added, "See? You're making yourself an animal!"

Mr. Moreland, sitting nearby, looked up from *Starsky and Hutch* on TV and took another rare crack at challenging his wife. "Look on the bright side," he said. "Isn't it better that our son loves a dead girl instead of loving homosexuals? This is probably just a stage Lunt's going through."

"It's not just a stage!" Lunt replied.

Mr. Moreland shrugged his shoulders at that. But there was no reasoning with Mrs. Moreland—no bright side to look on. To her, Lunt's Sharon-love was not just impractical, it was emotionally harmful and morally wrong.

Instead of yielding to his mother, Lunt went underground. His unsupervised visits to Brandisi Bookstore became treasure hunts for any tomes that made reference to Sharon, while solitary television watching meant hunting for Sharon's films. In that dark age before the Internet, videocassettes, and DVDs, to be a Sharonophile was a meager business, with the big finds, since they were so rare, seeming like nothing less than gifts from God. Like manna dropping into the boy's lap from heaven's highest ledge.

The more Lunt learned about his beloved, the more he used this information to model his adolescent suburban life after hers. Take the American flag, for example: because Sharon had draped the sofa in her last home with the Stars and Stripes, Lunt asked his parents to do the same. (Figuring he was going through a patriotic phase, they obliged him.) It was not that Lunt wanted to *be* Sharon—all he wanted was to revere her, and feel intimate with her, by living life as much as possible the way she'd lived it. So Sharon drove a red Ferrari? Fine, when Lunt could afford it, he'd drive one, too! Or at least rent one.

During his first year of Sharonophilia, Lunt also turned against the Beatles, purging their record albums from his collection and vowing never to listen to them again. Nothing Charles Manson valued would have any place in Lunt's own life. And the more he learned about Roman Polanski, the more he hated the man (and secretly envied him).

Sweetest of all the manna that the fledgling crypto-Sharonophile received was the repeat opportunity to see that bad Dean Martin movie, *The Wrecking Crew*. After his fateful first glimpse of Sharon as Freya Carlson, Lunt pored over the *TV Guide* each week, scrutinizing the rerun listings as if he were a Talmudic scholar. The day he finally hit the jackpot, he began to hyperventilate, and watching Sharon again nearly put him into cardiac arrest. Unfortunately, just before Sharon/Freya's final kung fu battle with the evil villainess Yu Rang (played by actress Nancy Kwan—another hottie, but no Sharon, of course), Lunt's mother came waddling into their TV room and caught him masturbating to La Tate's moving image.

This was only Lunt's third time "interfering with himself," as his mother called what he was doing, and her enraged shrieks did nothing to enhance the experience.

To punish him, Mrs. Moreland grounded Lunt for a month, forbidding him to see friends or go to Brandisi Bookstore after school. Unbeknownst to her, this merely served to strengthen the boy's resolve. His Sharon-love grew and grew. Then, at Lunt's twelfth birthday party, his father once more proved to be an ally. Out of his wife's view and earshot, Mr. Moreland gave his son a meaningful birthday gift. It was the "WHY?" poster which Lunt would go on to relish for many years to come.

"I know how it is to be in love," said Mr. Moreland. "I was in love once…"

"With Mom?"

"No, with the young woman before Mom."

Lunt was amazed. Before he could ask about this provocative statement, however, his father said, "You should know, son, that this poster gift comes with three conditions. First, you can't let Mom ever find it."

"Don't worry, I'll hide it good," Lunt promised.

"Second: if she *does* find it, for Christ's sake, don't squeal that I gave it to you! Got me?"

"Loud and clear, Dad."

"And third, the most important thing…"

"Yeah?"

"Don't you ever, *ever*, look at any posters of naked men."

LUNT took his time on the bed in number 47.

Again and again, he brought himself to the brink, then drew back. Stretching it out, making it delicious. He'd been doing this a long time; he had his special ways to "interfere with himself."

Oh, wonderful interference!

Unfortunately, at an especially fine juncture tonight, a shrill sound shattered the reverie. The overly loud black and shiny room phone was ringing. "Bullshit," Lunt muttered. He rolled away from his Sharon pillow, stretched his arm to the nightstand, grabbed the receiver from its cradle, and put it to his ear.

"Whosoever treats his fellows without honor or humanity," said the same solemn male voice from last night's wrong-number call, "he, and his issue, shall be treated with commensurate inhumanity and dishonor."

Outrageous, thought Lunt, who was livid. He'd gotten interrupted for *this*? In the most threatening tone he could muster, he said, "Look, Mr. Bible Studies *Bitch*, you've got the wrong party, okay?"

For his response, the mysterious caller repeated his cryptic message.

"This is a hotel, okay?" Lunt hissed, cradling the receiver between his chin and shoulder. "I'm *on vacation*. And if you fucking call again, I'll—uh, *crucify* you. Or throw you to lions. Whatever scares you Christ freaks the most!"

For the third time, the caller delivered his message. Or tried to. Before he got to finish, Lunt shouted, "Fuck you!" and slammed down the phone with gusto.

Enough gusto, he figured, to make the caller's eardrum crack.

3

GREENERY

(Monday)

THE cough again, but deeper, drier, more wrenching than last night. Sitting up in bed with a palm pressed to his mouth, the newly awakened Lunt coughed until his chest burned. He still had no clue what was causing this distress. Once the fit passed, he climbed out of bed, and while padding toward the bathroom to pee, he glimpsed a flat object on the butterscotch-colored carpet near his door. During his slumber, someone outside, in the hallway, had pushed a new manila envelope into his suite. Lunt detoured, opened the door, and looked back and forth, from the crimson-carpeted main stairwell in one direction to the glass "Emergency Exit" door in the other.

No one to be seen, not even a housekeeper. And silence but for a distant vacuum cleaner's whine.

Back inside, Lunt studied the new envelope. Again, the front of it bore no markings, and on the reverse side was a white sticker. "DEATH IS NO MORE IMPORTANT THAN EATING AN ICE-CREAM CONE," the sticker read. Lunt smiled. Whoever his benefactor was, he or she had a esoteric sense of humor. First, yesterday's "NO SENSE MAKES SENSE," and now this quip about death. Envelope in hand, Lunt hurried to his writing table, which was where he'd last seen his letter opener—the miniature silver scimitar his mother had given him for his eighteenth birthday. He used the blade to slice open the package. Inside was another Santa Shot, identical to the previous one, except for one thing: the red Magic Marker had been used this time to inscribe the numeral "6" in three places around Sharon's Santa hat.

For a few moments, Lunt peered at the photo, confounded and disturbed. Three sixes—was this "666," the number of Satan? That *couldn't* be what was meant. Or could it? Who would deface a rare

Santa Shot, *any* Sharon photo, so horribly? Not even Mandrake would disrespect Sharon this way. Yet if he *had*—and if Lunt could prove it—then Lunt's enemy would have hell to pay with the Sharonophile community. Lunt snapped into action, pulling on fresh clothes and running out of his suite, seeking someone to question about the package. None of the housekeepers or handymen he buttonholed said they knew anything about it. Down in the lobby, Randy Trueax had the day off, but Lunt got to question his replacement, a grim-looking woman with cropped hair and penciled eyebrows. Like the other employees Lunt found, Su Wing Schmidt (as per her name tag) couldn't help him.

Outside, the noon sun felt as forceful as ever, but the air temperature had dropped from the scorcher-level that greeted Lunt two days before. An ambulance was parked in the Ofotert driveway, its red lights flashing yet its siren stilled, and EMT workers slouched around, chuckling at a ribald joke one of them had just shared. The only thing missing, Lunt figured, was a body, either dead or still fighting to keep the light of life from flowing away.

"*Hola, señor!*"

Lunt waved back at the squat, sunken-chested garage attendant, but his attention was mostly aimed elsewhere—at a tall man who stood beside the ambulance. Today, in addition to his clipboard and odor of Brut cologne, the Ofotert's house detective brandished a walkie-talkie.

"You're just *itching* to tell me what's happened here, right?" Lunt said.

Baby Son cleared his throat. "Are you staying with us, sir?"

"You don't recognize me? We already went through this!"

"What room, sir?"

"I'm Lunt Moreland, in room—no, *Suite* Forty-Seven."

Baby Son frowned, which made his goatee wobble amidst the freckles on his cheeks. Today the thin lines of facial hair looked even more precisely delineated than yesterday. "Oh, yes. My apologies, sir."

"You can make it up to me by telling me why the ambulance is here."

"I'm sorry, sir, I can't do that." As Lunt remembered, Baby Son's chin lifted sharply with the last word of each sentence he spoke. "Confidential matter, sir."

"Got it, got it. And if you accept *another* twenty from me, it still won't loosen your lips at all?"

"Loose lips sink ships, sir. I'm sure you've heard that expression. But I never turn down gifts, sir. My *tio* Huberto—"

"Yeah, yeah," said Lunt, growing annoyed. "Well, I've got some more bad news. Another package." He held out the defaced Santa Shot to Baby Son. "*This!*"

Baby Son didn't understand. "Sir?"

"Someone just shoved this vile thing under my door, and I don't know who it is!"

"You mean you don't know who the woman in the photograph is?"

"No, that's Sharon Tate! I mean I don't know who *gave* this to me!"

"So you'd *like* to know?"

"Of course I would!"

"I'll look into the matter, sir," Baby Son said, and yesterday's sorrowful look reentered his eyes just as a voice, unintelligible due to static, crackled out from Baby Son's walkie-talkie.

"I see you're busy," Lunt said. "One more thing, though: if I were you, I'd keep an eye on one of your guests. He might be the one leaving me the stuff under my door. A troublemaker. His name is Glen Man—no, uh, 'Melek Randang.' Suite Twenty-Nine."

"Yes, sir."

"He's already hassled me, and when the Sharon Tate gathering gets underway here next weekend, he'll probably be bothering the other guests, too."

While Baby Son acknowledged this with a nod, smiling again, his goatee a wobble, Lunt thanked him and set off on Sunset Boulevard. Raising a hand to shade his eyes as he traipsed along, he left Bronson a voicemail about the new Santa Shot defaced with three sixes, then reminded himself to call his literary agent after lunch.

The air smelled clean, no trace of smog, as cars swept past him, slowing only slightly at a bend on the Strip. A speeding gray Volvo nearly clipped him as he ran across the street. On the sidewalk, regaining his breath, Lunt found himself again in front of Corpus Co-op, which looked melancholic. Someone had left a strange new graffito on the club's facade. Right next to the one from yesterday ("THIS PLACE WORSHIPS DEATH"), someone had written "GIRD YOUR LOINS, JIVE TURKEY!" in black letters.

Next to the graffito was a crude, spray-painted stencil, one depicting the Tarot-card image of Death, but Death was done up as a surfer here, with a long board serving as his scythe.

Chuckling at this, Lunt turned back to regard his hotel. Midday favored the appearance of the cream- and gray-colored turrets and towers. The Ofotert seemed to belong to a different galaxy than the striptease club and its graffiti. A better galaxy. Despite that larcenous house detective, the hotel was far from the "madhouse" that Mandrake, via Lichtenberg, had suggested.

After Lunt had walked for a few blocks, passing King's Road, his shoulder bag began to feel heavy, though it contained only a paper writing tablet and his hardcover copy of *Roman by Polanski*. Lunt had read the Polish director's autobiography many times, and felt scornful of its self-justifying horse crap, yet he needed it for research purposes. (He was due to write a passage about Polanski today in his Sharon memoir.) Forced to stop for a red light at the downward-sloping, ever-busy La Cienega Boulevard, Lunt glanced at his black pebble-grain sneakers. No spiders in the area today. No filthy popped-out sheet of Bubble Wrap, either. Nothing but empty, heat-cracked yellow pavement.

THE first psychotherapist Lunt was forced to see was named Greta Tanley. Prompting the consultation was his mother's shocked discovery of a certain flashlight hidden under a pile of her husband's *Sports Illustrated* magazines. The flashlight bore images of Sharon Tate and the message, "I'M REFLECTING ON HER MEMORY." Lunt had purchased the object by clandestine mail order, having seen an ad for it in an issue of *Movie Star Mementos Quarterly*. In the same mail delivery, he'd received two other items: photos of Sharon in her film *Twelve Plus One*.

"*Her* again!" Lunt's mother shrieked on discovering the flashlight. "That Sharon Fate!"

"Why can't I love who I want?" Lunt shot back. "And her name's not 'Fate,' it's—"

"I suppose you've been interfering with yourself, and with a *flashlight* this time! A goddamned *flashlight!*"

To upbraid the boy, she read to him a new quotation that she'd found in *Reader's Digest*: "*Anyone who idolizes you is going to hate you when he discovers that you are fallible. He never forgives. He has deceived himself, and he blames you for it.*"

"What's that supposed to mean, Mom?"

"It means you're *deceiving yourself*, Mister! Your blondie was only human, not the goddess you think she was. And someday you'll *hate* her for it!"

More harsh words were spoken. Mother confiscated son's specialty flashlight. Worst of all was the new bonus punishment: Lunt was grounded for two months. This damaged his social life since the boy had started to be invited to weekend parties. At these parties he tended to moon over three classmates of his. One girl had hair that was the same blonde tint as Sharon's; another's voice sounded a little Sharon-like; and a third had once lived in Houston, Sharon's hometown.

Several weeks after the ban on Lunt's going out ended, Mrs. Moreland discovered a further outrage: the stash of Sharon images he'd purchased at the same time as the flashlight. Lunt had hidden the photos in a chemistry notebook from his previous school year. This time his mother's response was to forbid Lunt from socializing for six months. And something else: she sent him to the South Orange office of Greta Tanley, MSW.

"Of the four shrinks I ultimately got sent to," Lunt would recall decades later to his friend Bronson, "Ms. Tanley was the only one I could stomach. She didn't judge me harshly, or judge me at all. If she hadn't alienated my mother by supporting my Sharonophilia, saying it had value for my development, I would've gladly seen her again."

Eyeballing the vintage rock concert posters that adorned Ms. Tanley's office, Lunt pegged the therapist as having been a hippie back in the 1960s. Thanks to the middle-aged woman's braided hair, her paisley-patterned peasant dress, and her white go-go boots, Lunt could tell she'd preserved a sense of the hippie ethos, too. Even her view of Lunt's Sharon-love was colored by that halcyon decade when Sharon and Polanski had galvanized Hollywood.

"It's touching," the therapist said to Lunt after he'd explained his feelings for Sharon. "I'd say you've got yourself a clear case of what I call 'sixties sadness.'"

Unsure what this meant, Lunt looked absently at the wolfsbane that grew from a miniature garden arranged on Dr. Tanley's desk.

"This condition," she said with a thoughtful nod of her head, "chiefly troubles people like you whose early childhoods occurred during the sixties. You perceive adolescence as painful, Lunt, overwhelming—so you yearn to regress, to be a child anew, and this you rationalize with a keen nostalgia for the flower-power era."

The office smelled of disinfectant. Dr. Tanley took a sip from her red coffee mug. Inside it was valerian tea that she'd fortified with distilled juniper berry.

"A writer I used to go to bed with, this guy named Thomas, he said that everyone feels a homesickness for the decade they were born in. But for someone sixties-born like *you*, Lunt, this must be more than just homesickness. Something about that decade was just *special*. And you feel so out of place here in the anticlimactic seventies that only a sixties-flavored existence can bring you bliss."

In the years that followed that single psychotherapy session, Lunt would often wonder how Greta Tanley was faring. He'd even had a wet dream about her once, which was odd, considering that she'd been his mother's age, or older, and she looked nothing like La Tate. Was it the go-go boots that turned him on? Sharon had adored wearing footwear like that.

THE restaurant Gush was jammed, and looked as sleek on the inside as its posh exterior suggested, with brushed silver surfaces and white leather banquettes. A canary yellow tapestry stretched across the ceiling, pots of flowers hung by chains from the ceiling, and the walls were adorned with painted fish, bubbles, and other aquatic shapes. Just as visually sumptuous was the Gush lunchtime crowd, which matched the Ofotert's best-looking guests and visitors. What a pageant of beauty there was in Gush!

Clearly, Lunt realized as a bossa nova version of "Seventy-Six Trombones" blared from the eatery's stereo system, *I've come to the right place to find a local girlfriend.*

"So," he whispered to himself, using an expression he'd once heard from Bronson, "set the controls for the hearts of Sharon-esque women!"

The restaurant's hostess, Lunt happily discovered—*Here we go!*—was a comely, buxom African-American woman who wore a fur vest and frosted lipstick. "Table for one?" she said, stone-faced. "Follow me."

As she led him to his table, Lunt went back to scoping out the female customers. Alas, so intent was this scoping of his that he slammed into a waiter with a shag hairstyle. Thanks to the waiter's dexterity, a silver tray of oysters didn't end up decorating the bald head of a young man in a nifty black suede jacket.

"Whoa, sorry!" said Lunt.

The waiter, he realized, was actually a waitress, though her face looked similar to Jim Morrison's, The Doors' late lead singer. The waitress and Morrison could have been siblings. Quite a hipster she was, too: peeking out from her black ruffled shirt, which went well with her white tuxedo pants, were tendrils of tattoos on her wrists and throat.

Having recovered from the collision, the hipster waitress showed her tongue to Lunt, sticking it out at him the way a petulant toddler would, and then she scurried off, the silver tray once more balanced on her raised hand. The not-exactly-friendly fur-vested hostess dropped a menu at Lunt's place, a small round table in the rear of the dining room. But Lunt hardly saw this— he was again busy admiring the lovely female customers. To his disappointment, none of the lookers he zeroed in on bore any resemblance to Sharon.

The celebrity quotient in Gush was also a letdown. Although a few faces appeared familiar to Lunt—character actors on TV, probably—there were no old-timers who'd personally known La Tate. Too bad: Lunt would have relished a chance to meet some of Sharon's people. Over the years, he'd sent interview requests to Warren Beatty, Mia Farrow, the producer Robert Evans, and other still-living friends and relatives of Sharon, and none ever responded—not even with a polite "no." Undaunted, Lunt still welcomed any face-to-face encounters, knowing that once a Sharon intimate met him, they would recognize how noble his Sharon-love was.

Making himself comfortable in his hard molded-plastic seat, Lunt pulled the Polanski book from his satchel, set it beside his menu, and glanced at the menu's front. Printed there was the restaurant's fanciful motto: "WE'RE FOREVER BLOWING BUBBLES." He hadn't realized how hungry he was until now. Did they serve lobster bisque? How about seafood gumbo? Those were two of Sharon's favorite soups. Before Lunt got his menu open, however, more human scenery distracted him. Out of the restroom just behind Lunt, a young woman materialized. She was the occupant, it turned out, of the small round table right next to his. And what an occupant!

As she seated herself, placing her already sauce-stained napkin in her lap, Lunt sucked in his paunch and studied the woman. Most likely no more than eighteen or nineteen, she was flat-chested, petite—and green. That is, her miniskirt was emerald-colored, her boots (Doc Marten knockoffs) were forest green, her top was Kelly green, the choker around her neck was lime green, as were her tinted contact lenses and eye shadow, and her long, straight, free-hanging hair had been dyed a seafoam green. Eyebrows, too. As for her jewelry—bracelets, a necklace, and rings through her nose and on her fingers—it was uniformly jade. And mint glitter dusted her cheeks and hands. By far the girl's most arresting feature, though, was her mouth. It bore acid-green lipstick, yet was shaped precisely like Sharon Tate's mouth. The similarity was even stronger than the one between Pandora's eyes and Sharon's.

Once he saw this new girl's kisser, Lunt whispered to himself, "Oh, my stars!" And his physical reaction was profound, the same as when he'd first beheld Pandora with her Sharon-eyes. Pressure filled his chest, his heart began to bam-bam-bam against his ribs, sweat sprang to his skin, and his penis stirred in the boxer briefs beneath his khakis. (His nostrils, it should be noted, did not quiver when he was aroused the way that Glen Mandrake's did.)

Noting the empty seat and table space across from her, Lunt deduced that his neighbor was alone. Next he stole a glance at the green woman's sauce-spattered plate, trying in his mind to fashion a suitable opener. Something about her meal? Yes. But she beat him to the punch. In a congenial yet surprisingly direct voice, she turned to him and said, "This your first time here, dude?"

Lunt, pretending he hadn't been aware of her till now: "You could tell, huh?"

"I come here, like, *daily*, and I don't recognize you." She moved her green eyes to the hardcover on Lunt's table-top. "What're you reading?"

The question rattled Lunt. Normally, until he felt at ease with a fetching non-S-phile female, he was reluctant to discuss his Sharonophilia. So he dodged the issue. "Just something about a Polish film director."

With a quizzical expression, the girl craned her neck to get a better glimpse of the book. "*Roman by Polanski*, huh? It's the guy who directed *The Tenant*! That's one of my favorite movies."

"Really?" said Lunt. He couldn't believe his luck. "Me, too! Well, sort of."

Here was serendipity of the most sublime sort. *The Tenant*, of all Polanski's films to 2003, was the only one Lunt liked. In this blackest of black comedies, a *schlemiel* played by the dwarf director himself gets driven insane by his neighbors in a Paris apartment house. *Or*—we're compelled by the film to wonder—is the schlemiel just imagining the abuse? That is, driving *himself* insane?

Lunt stole a peek at the woman's Sharon-mouth again. He didn't dare to focus on it because he knew from experience that too much lust might cause him to lose his conversational grip (and thereby put off the lust-object). Even so, he couldn't yank his eyes away from the mouth for long. Despite her youth and daffy greenness, he truly fancied her. Accordingly, he hoped that she'd had problems with her father. This was due to his having read somewhere that most father-troubled women were drawn to older men. Which was certainly the case with Sharon. In fact, Polanski himself had once said, "Thank God for my fame, my foreign accent, and my girlfriend's fucked-up daddy issues!"

As they spoke more about *The Tenant*, Lunt wondered about his neighbor's fetish for green. Was it some kind of political statement, a nod to Europe's left-wing Green Party, or else to the burgeoning Green ecology movement?

The young woman shifted excitedly in her seat. "Don't you love that scene in *The Tenant* where the hero finds a human tooth stuck in a wall? It's, like, so freaky!"

"That's an awesome moment," said Lunt. With both hands, which were now sweating, he brushed at his hair, trying to get it closer to the Jay Sebring style.

"Did you know that Polanski got busted for screwing a teenaged girl? They got him on the Mann Act. In the seventies."

Uh-oh, Lunt thought. *Step carefully here.* If he corrected her erroneous statement, he might seem smarty-farty, which could turn her off. Then again, being knowledgeable was part of an older man's charm, so he straightened his posture and pointed out that it wasn't the Mann Act but statutory rape. As he considered what to say next, he noticed something else about her lips that fascinated him, something apart from their Sharonness. It was how they moved when she spoke. Rather, how they *didn't* move. She voiced sounds, constructed words, in such a way that she never exposed her teeth or gums or tongue or anything else inside her mouth.

"You sure about that statutory thing, dude?"

"Trust me."

The green woman stuck out her lower lip and blew upward. Then, as if to test his intellectual credentials, she asked, "So do you know how Polanski's girlfriend died back in the sixties?"

Here we go, Lunt thought, and he pointed to the front of his V-necked T-shirt, which today bore an image of Sharon along with the word "SUPERCALIFRAGILISTICEXPI-*SHARON*-DOTIOUS." "Actually," he said, "she wasn't just 'his *girlfriend*,' but his wife, and I'm wearing a picture of her right here on my chest!"

Arching an eyebrow, the woman took in Lunt's shirt, and her green-painted eyes lit up.

"Hey, you're right, that's her! Sharon Tate!" And she favored Lunt now with the cutest smile he'd seen in a long time. It wasn't identical to Sharon's—La Tate opened her mouth when she smiled, showing off her gorgeous pearly whites. Still, watching the girl's Sharon-lips create a closed-mouth smile made Lunt's nearly forty-year-old heart thrash around inside him.

"You from around here?" he said. Lame as this question was, it was the best thing he could think of to prolong the conversation.

"Right down the street, on North Guidry. Know where that is, Jeepster?"

"Jeepster?"

"Yeah, it's what I call people. Check this shit—I live at 1313 North Guidry."

"Wow! That's, er, unlucky."

She tilted her chair back and balanced herself by bracing her knees against the table's edge. "Wrong. It's extra-lucky. And guess what my apartment number is?"

"Another thirteen?"

"Wrong. *Two* thirteens! So that makes four in total." She gave him a victorious look. "How cool is *that*? Nobody believes me."

"I do," said Lunt.

"Promise?"

"Promise."

"Fantastic! Anyway," she said, leaning over from her table to hold out a tiny hand out, "I'm Jopp."

"Joss?"

"*Jopp.*"

Bingo, Lunt thought, *we're connecting!* He told her his own name and extended his hand. How soon would he have her naked in his Ofotert bed? How soon would she be gulping down his suite's complimentary Dom Perignon while he rolled on one of his Instigator condoms? Soon, he hoped, very soon! He sucked air through his teeth, thoroughly excited. But at the moment their hands touched—and how bony, how fragile her hand felt—his horrid cough began again.

Amazed at this misfortune, Lunt turned away from Jopp, spewing phlegm onto a raised wrist. Something seemed trapped in the deep of his chest, and no matter how hard he coughed, he couldn't unearth it. Why *now*, of all the times to be cursed with this thing? Jopp waited patiently while Lunt hacked away, watching him with her serene green closed-mouth smile, and when he couldn't get his coughing under control, she advised him to order an omelette.

He glanced at her in mid-cough, a forearm now pressed to the lower half of his face.

"Eggs get rid of coughing," she explained.

Bending over beside his table, Lunt shook his head. He was too occupied by the latest paroxysm to reply. And too embarrassed, too, thinking, *She probably sees me as some modern male version of Typhoid Mary.*

As if this wasn't bad enough, other customers in their vicinity were staring at Lunt now, some perhaps having also arrived at the Typhoid Mary idea. He wished he could assure everyone, "It's not contagious," even though this might be wrong, but speaking was still impossible. So he decided to retreat. Jumping up, he made a "Just going to the men's room" gesture with his hands. Jopp nodded, she understood, but spoke up loudly so he could hear her as he tore off.

"Eggs, dude!" she said. "Should I order you an omelette?"

The restroom doors were marked "BOY-FISH," "GIRL-FISH" and "DIAPER-CHANGING FACILITY." Briefly speculating why

Gush had a special place for diaper-changing (it was hardly a family style restaurant), Lunt pushed through the boy-fish door and found the bathroom decorated, like everything else in the place, with aquatic imagery. He stood beside the sink until his coughing attack finally tailed off.

Now, what excuse should he make to Jopp when he got back to his table? What charming quip would put the sexy green one at ease? Coming up with something serviceable, he examined himself in the slightly smudged mirror. No spittle on his chin, good. A few passes of hand through hair got Lunt looking pretty Sebringesque. Not bad for a guy who'd just coughed his throat to ribbons! Sucking in his paunch again, Lunt advised himself to follow the advice of the graffito he'd seen earlier—that is, to "gird his loins." Then he started back to the dining room, ready for romance.

The bad news was that the sour-faced, fur-vested restaurant hostess was currently seating a young Yuppie couple at Jopp's empty table. Every trace of the green woman was gone. She'd flown away, his gorgeous Sharon-mouthed bird. But there was good news at Lunt's own table. This news took the form of a bright green sheet of notebook paper resting on Lunt's unopened menu. Written in dark-green ink on a diagonal across the paper was a West Hollywood cell phone number.

ITALY took some getting used to. At first I was somewhat withdrawn from my classmates at the Vicenza American High School. They were mostly the children of other Yanks living abroad. I spent a good deal of time being a loner. That probably had something to do with the way we lived—always on the move, never living in one town very long. It's hard to make lasting friendships that way. Eventually, though, I found some good friends, and I got popular, I suppose—there wasn't much of the envy and gossip and lust-fueled bitterness that I would later find in Hollywood. At Vicenza I was known as a practical joker, just a bit of one, yet I was kind to everyone, too, or at least I tried to be, since this was how I wanted to be treated. "Sweet-Natured Sharon," is what my mother called me. ("Pretty is as pretty does," she also liked to say.)

I garnered a lot of attention when I joined the cheering squad. I loved being a cheerleader because the other four girls were all sweeties and we got to travel to different Italian cities to show them our American team spirit. Another thing I was known for in high school were my clinging sweaters and my short skirts. The other kids, and even some teachers—the women as well as the men—would stare at me a lot, but I got used to it, and came to expect it. Contrary to what many thought, I didn't wear these clothes to show off how I looked; I already got enough attention for my face, my blondeness, and my figure. It was just that I loved fashion, all kinds of fashion, and wearing sexy clothes felt fun. Liberating, too.

(For the record, I was 5'6", wore a size 6 dress—now it would be a 2—and my shoe size was 6 1/2. I preferred tailored clothing, white suits, miniskirts, antique camisoles, wide belts, big hoop earrings, and love beads. I wasn't big on heavy necklaces or rings, though— I bit my nails a lot and didn't want to bring attention to my hands.)

As everybody knows, so much of life is determined by pure chance: what if you didn't glimpse that certain hardcover book in a store, or that certain movie rerun on TV? In my case, what if my family never went to Italy, for example? Or else how different would my life have been if I was a redhead, or homely, or overweight? Or a conniving diva instead of "Sweet-Natured Sharon?"

Or what if—I'm really stretching here—I was exactly who I was but I didn't get murdered and in time divorced Roman and then had some unfulfilling affairs while I became world famous and finally found true love many years later with a much younger man—a humble real estate agent from New Jersey, let's say, someone who finally adored me the way I deserved to be adored?

Putting aside most of those "what-ifs," I feel pretty sure that, no matter what, I would have become an actress. For as long as I can remember, people were telling me, "You ought to be an actress or a fashion model, something in show business," and that sort of sank in. I wasn't tall enough for modeling, so being an actress is what I settled on.

RIDING the clanging elevator to his suite, tapping on the old-fashioned metal grille wall with his red-tasselled key, Lunt remembered Vishwa Mukherjee. Again, it was too late to phone his literary agent in her office; he would call her first thing tomorrow. As for the here and now, he was itching to phone Jopp, to reach out to the green woman and dazzle her with his Sharon-erudition and other personality strengths.

This reaching out to her got delayed, however, by the object awaiting Lunt on the carpet inside his doorway.

At first he assumed it was the same package as earlier, transferred either by sorcery or a chambermaid from his writing table to its original location. But this new envelope was sealed, and the white printed sticker on it, its sole outward marking, was a new one. New, and slightly ominous: "MY MIND IS TUNED TO MORE TELEVISION CHANNELS THAN EXIST IN YOUR WORLD— AND IT SUFFERS NO CENSORSHIP."

There was another disturbing aspect to this latest "gift." The Santa Shot inside the envelope was not so much decorated as defaced. Instead of red hearts or sixes inked in around Sharon's head, this time a single thick black line had been Magic-Markered across her eyes. Which was supposed to mean *what*, precisely?

"Any brain waves about it?" Lunt said out loud to the poster of Sharon above his bed. If she had some, she didn't share them; she just kept gazing skyward. But someone else did have ideas, for just as Lunt was replacing his silver letter opener in its usual place on the writing table, Bronson rang him on his BlackBerry.

"Someone's toying with you," she told Lunt once he'd filled her in on the day's two successive gifts. "These sticker messages are goofiness, that's all. Some S-phile who's staying there, someone you don't know about. Whoever it is, don't let it distract you from your Sharon book."

"It's gotta be Mandrake behind the packages, it just has to be. And the stickers must be, like, updated quotes from Lichtenberg."

"Updated?"

"Yeah, there wasn't television in Lichtenberg's day."

"Oh. Hmm. Seen him lately?"

"Mandrake? Nope, which is *itself* kind of odd. Shouldn't he be pestering me more? Not his style to leave me in peace. Especially since Pandora supposedly hasn't arrived yet."

"Don't question it, pally. Just keep your eyes on the prize. Sharon up and get back to writing."

"First, though, I've gotta call my new love interest."

"Whoa! Slow down. Love interest?"

"I *thought* that would snag your interest." Lunt began undressing, his shoulder pressing his BlackBerry to his ear as he hopped around on one foot, trying to tug off a khaki trouser leg. "Picture this: Sharon's mouth—Sharon's mouth, like, *exactly*—the same-shaped lips, everything. The only difference is green lipstick."

"Green? For real?"

Lunt gave his friend a run-through of the meeting with Jopp at Gush, recounting details and answering Bronson's questions. While he did, he settled his naked-but-for-boxer-briefs self into his gray sofa and turned to regard Seething Lane. The green hills and houses that dotted them seemed to shimmer in the weakening daylight. "I only spoke with this Jopp for a minute," Lunt concluded his spiel, "but I can tell she's gonna be important for me."

"Is that a bona fide intuition, or just wishful thinking?"

GARY LIPPMAN

"The former, I think. Of course, my intuition pales next to *yours*, Bron, but…"

Bronson, bracing herself against a cabinet in her Carson City kitchen, moved the cell phone from her ear so she could stretch her powerful arms. The big muscles came from her refusal to use a wheelchair. ("Crutches are a true bitch," she'd explained to Lunt once, "but I use them because I like to meet my boss and colleagues at eye level, not from a subordinate position.")

"Well," she said to Lunt now, "*cherchez* your Sharon-lipped *femme*." She chortled. The sound made Lunt wince. "Just be sure you get me a picture of that mouth of hers. I'm still grooving on the snapshots you sent me…"

"Which ones?"

"Of Pandora's Sharon-eyes, remember?"

"Ack. Don't mention Pandora, please."

"Fine. But, hon? Check that this green chick's not, like, actual jailbait. Have her show you some ID. I can't afford you getting Polanski-ish on me!"

Lunt grew still for a moment. *Good point*, he thought. *What if Jopp isn't the age of consent yet? Just my luck—I meet a girl with Sharon's mouth, my sexual salvation here in LA, and she's not legal!*

After saying goodbye to his friend, Lunt stepped into his bathroom to urinate, then tried Jopp's number. It shot to voicemail without a ring. "Tell me something green," Jopp said to callers before the beep, her voice sounding more girlish than it did in person.

"Something green, huh?" Lunt was beaming as he stretched out on his bed and left her a message. "Well, green wasn't Sharon Tate's favorite color, but your green presence today sure captivated me. Actually, I'm calling to apologize for my coughing—that was some *hack-attack* I had at Gush, right? Don't worry, I'm free of tropical diseases, and every other disease, so no worries." He raised his eyes

112

to the Sharon poster. "And, uh, at the risk of sounding overeager, well, are you free for lunch tomorrow? I don't live in LA, I'm from New Jer—er, from New York, and I'm only here for, like, another ten days, but like, er, anyway...well, let me know!"

As he clicked off, Lunt rolled his eyes, thinking how stupid he must've sounded, though the New York lie was shrewd. He wouldn't need to tell Jopp the truth about where he lived until some distant day, if ever.

Lunt's father phoned eight minutes later, saying, "I'm not disturbing you, am I?" and Lunt told him no, he'd been hard at work on his Sharon memoir, which was false: he'd been lost in a fantasy of himself conducting a ménage à trois with Jopp and Sharon.

"Going to finish that book of yours soon?" Mr. Moreland asked from the elaborate hospital bed in his room in Sulphurdale, New Jersey. It was the house Lunt grew up in. "And publish it and make me proud of you before I croak?"

Lunt's gaze returned to the Sharon poster. Specifically, the word "WHY?" printed there. "Oh, absolutely, Dad."

"How's that fancy-pants hotel you're staying in? Can you get anything done with all that fancy-pantsiness?"

"Lots of work," said Lunt, wanting to hurry his father off the line so he could play out the rest of his sexual fantasy.

"Meet any nice West Coast girls yet?"

"As a matter of fact," said Lunt, pleased to be able to give the old man a positive reply that was also truthful, "I did meet someone today, at lunch."

"I hope she's not another freethinker like that bad-news Pandora."

"Far from it."

"Good. Because freethinkers will always lead you wrong. Into homosexuality, for one thing. This new gal got your five S's?"

"Er...I think so."

"What are they again?"

"Smart, sweet, sexy, Sharonesque, and sane."

"Sane, yes! I was just telling this new nurse here, Extina…"

"You've got a new nurse?"

"Nah, a substitute, just for one night. Jah Victor has a problem with his mother."

"Is he okay?"

"Oh, sure, fine. His mother, too, it turns out."

"And the replacement's name is 'Extina?'"

"No, *Christina*, but she's an atheist, she says, so she insists that I say her name with 'Ex' instead of 'Chris.' And I was telling her about your five S thing but I forgot the sane bit."

"Dad, never forget the sane bit."

"I know. Especially when it comes to you! You need a stable girl, son. Someone who'll keep all the fancy-boys away from you! Is this new prospect a blonde, brunette, or redhead?"

"Well…"

Lunt would have liked to say, "seafoam-green-haired," but he knew this would dismay his father, since a girl who dyed her hair a color not known to nature (for hair, anyway) would most likely fall under the category of "freethinker." And so, in honor of Sharon, "blonde" is what he went with.

IN secret defiance of his mother's anti-Sharonophilia campaign, the teenaged Lunt persisted in his devotion, searching for books at Brandisi that mentioned La Tate, studying *TV Guide* for relevant movie reruns, drawing up a list of Sharonabilia that he would buy someday, and listening to the haunting soundtrack for Sharon's flick *Valley Of The Dolls* as well as other Sharon-oriented music.

Owing to the *sub-rosa* nature of Lunt's Sharon worship, Lunt viewed himself in self-mythologizing terms. He imagined himself as a *converso* Jew still practicing his faith as an outlaw in Catholic Spain circa 1500, or else as a librarian of the thirty-first century, one who hid the fruits of global civilization on microchips lest marauding neo-Ostrogoths destroy those fruits out of ignorance or spite.

Like many during their teen years, Lunt masturbated whenever he got the chance. ("Spending time with Mother Fist and her five lovely daughters" was how a schoolfriend put it.) Lunt keyed each of his auto-erotic sessions to mental movies that featured Sharon or else high school classmates who somehow resembled Sharon, and the more he jerked off undiscovered, the more chances he took. Hence it was only a matter of time until Mrs. Moreland—as crafty as a spy for the Spanish Inquisition, and as brutish as a neo-Ostrogothic thirty-first century goon-squad leader—came home early from her job one afternoon (she worked at the same local realty company that would eventually employ Lunt as an agent), burst into the TV room without knocking, and caught her teenaged boy "interfering with himself" while watching a rerun of *The Fearless Vampire Killers*, the cinematic horror spoof on which Polanski and Sharon worked together for the first time.

"*Her* again!" Mrs. Moreland bellowed.

Back to a psychotherapist went Lunt.

"And *this* time," his mother announced, displeased as she'd been with the "over-tolerance" of Lunt's previous therapist, Greta Tanley, "we're getting ourselves a *male* headshrinker."

Lunt's other parent, as it happened, disagreed with this strategy. A male shrink, he pointed out to his wife, might convert their progeny into a "flagrant homosexual." As usual with their battles, the wife won.

Lamar Fractawill, a middle-aged and bushy-bearded though still cherubic-looking African-American man, welcomed Lunt into his spartanly appointed Livingston office. The place smelled of shoe polish, and beyond the single window, drops of rain that looked like blobs of mercury fell.

Once he'd heard about the boy's Sharonophilia, Fractawill plucked a hardbound volume from a crowded bookshelf behind him, placed the book on his unvarnished desk, blew (or pretended to blow) a coat of dust from its cover, opened the book to a certain page, and then read aloud:

"According to *The Book of Glory* by Rabbi Judah the Pious, '*The spirits of the dead roam the world, to harken to what has been decreed. Sometimes they invite the living to go along with them, but if a man accepts the invitation, he will die. "No," he must say to the spirits of the dead, "no, in the name of God, I do not wish to join you, or join any other dead." On the morrow then, he should go to the graveyard and remove his shoes and prostrate himself on their graves and say, "For the sake of God, who desires that man shall live, do not come after me anymore. It is God's will, and it is my will, that I refuse to join you, and refuse to join any dead. Do not stalk me or my loved ones, not you and not your agents. Because I want to live in this world, not in that world!"'*"

Now the therapist shut the book, a pudgy index finger still holding the relevant page, and he went quiet, beaming at Lunt.

"Wow," the boy said at last. "I'm not sure that..."

"What's not to be 'sure that,' young man?"

"Well, uh..." Lunt gazed at a goose-necked lamp on the shrink's desk. "For one thing, I'm not Jewish."

"Doesn't matter. I'm not a Jew, either. This ritual is nondenominational. Rabbi Judah's words apply to everyone. Your actress Susan Tate, her soul is troubled. The cruel way she left this world, I'm not surprised. Violence never leads to a good death. It's never a plus to die screaming in pain or fear. And her soul is so troubled that it's calling out to you. But you have to, you *must*, resist the call."

"First of all, it's *Sharon* Tate, not Susan. And I don't *want* to resist it. Resist *her*, I mean."

"No, not 'her.' Souls have no gender. Not anymore. Don't tell your father this, because he seems a bit uptight about male-on-male bonding, but your dead lady-love might even be a *he* now. It doesn't matter—this soul is hungry for you, and it *must not*, repeat, *must not*, have you." Fractawill opened his book again and reread the passage about how if a man accepts an invitation from the dead, he's bound to die. Fractawill paused for effect, then: "You don't want to *die*, do you, young man? Emotionally, or in any other way?"

"Of course not." Lunt took a deep breath. Was this guy some kind of joker?

"Therefore," the therapist went reading on, "you '*must say to the spirits of the dead, "In the name of God, I do not wish to join you, or any other dead."*'" The therapist closed the book, his finger once more strategically inserted in it. "Simple as that."

"You're not a psychotherapist," Lunt said, "you're more like a faith-healer!"

To which Fractawill said, actually said, "Pshaw." Then continued, "I'm just a psychotherapist who believes in the power of rituals. If something works, why disdain it because it's outside the box? I take wisdom wherever I find it—even from our friends the Jews. Not Rabbis only, but gangsters, too—like the Jewish gangster Dutch Schultz, for instance. No one remembers Dutch Schultz anymore, which is too bad. He too had wisdom to offer us. Do you know what Schultz said when he lay dying? His famous last words. He said, 'Mother is the best bet and don't let Satan draw you too fast.' Words to ponder, hmm?"

"But all this stuff you're saying isn't just 'outside the box,' it's—"

"Young man, your interest in a dead soul is dragging you to the pit. Straight down."

"Not at all!"

"Your mother certainly believes that."

"Who cares what my mother—"

"Son, what did I just say? Dutch Schultz! *Mother is the best bet!* You may not *think* you're being dragged down, but you are. It's plain to see. It's written on your face." Dipping back into the book: "*'If a man accepts the invitation, he will die.'*" He closed the book. "Clear as crystal."

This guy is barking mad, Lunt decided. Yet before the session was over, he'd taken heart, because he knew he would never have to endure Fractawill again. All he had to do was report to his parents the therapist's ideas and they would bar Lunt from seeing the madman again. Maybe they would even send him back to Greta Tanley! And so, amusing himself with Fractawill now, Lunt said, "And I resist Sharon's…soul…like, *how*, exactly?"

"Just as it says here." The therapist opened the book and read: "*'On the morrow he should go to the graveyard and remove his shoes and prostrate himself on their graves. And say, "For the sake of God, who desires that man shall live, do not come after me anymore."'*"

"You really mean it? You want me to go to her grave in California and *do* that?"

"Rituals," said Fractawill. "Never underestimate a good one."

"IT'S your new green friend here."

"I know," Lunt said, his pulse accelerating. No sooner had he glimpsed the name on his grimy BlackBerry screen than it got his pulse going. "When you call, even the ring sounds green."

Not reluctantly at all, he'd suspended the literary work he'd been doing, saving his Sharon-memoir file, shutting down his laptop, and leaning back in the chair at his writing desk so he could give Jopp his full attention.

"How's your cough, Jeepster?"

"My lungs have given me the all clear, I'm glad to report."

"Dude, listen, you've gotta put more eggs in your diet. It's basic science. Eggs take care of coughing. And no eating tomatoes. Tomatoes are the devil's testicles."

"Never heard that one before. But be my lunch companion tomorrow and you'll be stunned at how many eggs I chow down."

Seated on the toilet in her grandmother's apartment at 1313 North Guidry, with green sweatpants bunched around her ankles, Jopp threw back her head and laughed. "I told you, Jeepster, I eat at Gush, like, *daily*, so tomorrow's not a problem if you wanna join me. I'll save you a place at my table. They always give me the same one."

"The one you had today."

"Yup. It oughta have my name carved in it."

Trying to envision Jopp's delectable Sharon-mouth, Lunt said, "The menu should read, '*We're forever blowing bubbles—and forever serving Jopp.*' How'd you snag that sweet deal?"

"Simple," said the green woman. "Bribery 101. You know the hostess there?"

"The black woman with the fur vest?"

"Yeah, she always wears that stupid shit."

"She's not exactly Miss Conviviality."

"No, she's a bitch, you got that right. Latreena, her name is. Those ridiculous gigantic fake boobies aren't fooling anyone. But I pay her a fixed figure every month so I can eat at Gush when I want. I just can't stay there too long. That's the deal, I've gotta eat fast and leave."

"Eating fast is fine with me," said Lunt. He pushed his chair back, stood, and began pacing around his suite. "The reason I'm in town from Nueva Yorka is to finish this big writing project, so I'm busy enough as it is."

"Yeah, you mentioned NYC. 'Fun City,' my grandmother calls it. Never been myself. Then again, I've got time, I'm only nineteen. Am I missing much?"

On hearing that the green woman was nineteen, hence above the age of majority, Lunt felt elated. *All systems go!* he thought. *Set the controls for the heart of green gal Jopp!*

"You cool with hosting visitors, Jeepster?"

"*Green* visitors? In New York? Without a doubt."

"My man Benny says, 'New York is like a bowl of underpants.' Is that true?" As Lunt pondered this—*Dirty underpants or clean? Why a bowl?*—Jopp added, "He's in town, by the way. I'm so stoked!"

Uh-oh. Lunt stopped pacing. "Benny? Is that, uh, a boyfriend or something?"

"Shit, I *wish*. Benny Pomps? I'd do him in a heartbeat. In one of your New York minutes!"

"Benny Pomps. Wait—Benny *Pompa*?"

"The rock guy, yeah, from Memento Morey Amsterdam. Red Afro? Legendary talent, like no one else. And *philanthropic*! You heard about the stuff he does for orphans? He's even got his own foundation—Pompa Pride! Word is, Benny ate at Gush when he hit town last year. Twice! Not when I was there, but let a girl *hope*, right? I just know I'm gonna see him this visit!"

Lunt felt his breath catch. "I've got news for you," he said. "Benny Pompa's staying at my hotel."

"Dude, are you *serious*? Where?"

"The Hotel Ofotert."

"Hang on, Benny's staying at *the Ofotert*? Fuck! Usually he stays at the Marquis, so when I heard he was in town, I just assumed, you know, that he was back there. I was gonna stake him out..."

"I guess he switched. Where does he live ordinarily?"

"At a suite in the Gramercy in New York—when he's not at his ranch in Australia, or at his geodesic dome near Spokane."

"Wow," said Lunt, trying to sound interested. Yet the bummer of all this was beginning to sink in. How could he compete for Jopp with Benny Pompa? Not bloody likely. He could hold his own with other older men, maybe, but not with a wealthy celebrity. At a loss for what to say now, he mentioned the birthday that Pompa and Sharon Tate shared.

"*Wrong*, dude, Benny's birthday is John Belushi's."

"Right, but it's also Sharon Tate's!"

"Polanski's girl? No way! What a day for world history! And you know what they say about history, right? Most of it gets made at night."

MY first movie, if you can call it that, was an American production, Adventures of A Young Man. It was based on a handful of Hemingway stories. Mom drove me and some girlfriends of mine to the Young Man set one hot, cloudy afternoon, and after we hung out there for awhile, we got invited to stand around in a big crowd scene. I didn't meet either of the two stars, Paul Newman or Susan Strasberg. Yet a handsome young actor, the second male lead, was eyeing me up and down, and after the director yelled "Cut!" for the actor's scene, he waved me over to him.

"Italiana?" the actor asked.

"No," I said, "I'm American, like you. From Texas."

Now that we were face to face, I recognized him—it was "Tony," from West Side Story, which was one of my favorite pictures!

"I don't believe it," said Richard Beymer, in a friendly voice. "The most beautiful girl in Italy, and she's a Texan!"

He invited me to join him for lunch with a few other actors, and before we finished eating, he asked to take me out to dinner.

"Sharon," said Richard during our first evening together, "have you considered an acting career? The camera will just devour you!"

I wasn't sure what "devour" meant (I had to ask my mother later), but I pretended to be delighted to hear this statement, and I mentioned how often I'd been told that I "ought to be an actress." Richard laughed—he had such a lovely laugh—and he handed me the business card of his talent agent back in the States, a man named Howard Gefsky. "Gefsky is one of the nicest people you'll ever meet in Hollywood," Richard promised.

When the Hemingway movie finished shooting and Richard flew home, I missed him. He was my first real lover, and a very thoughtful one. We kept in touch with letters, and in Venezia the next spring, on a trip with some school friends, we "invaded" another set, this time for TV. The singer Pat Boone was shooting a network variety program. I got to speak with Pat and his nice wife, and I even got an audition with his program's choreographer. Still, Pat threw a little cold water on my ambitions. He said, "Italy is a long way from California, Sharon, and it's a hard life in Hollywood, especially for young women."

Thanks to my talks with Richard, however, and thanks to the letters he kept sending me after he left Europe (I lived for those letters), nothing could dampen my ambition to be a Hollywood actress. Yes, I was starry-eyed. But what teenage girl doesn't yearn for that glamour and fame? It's also true that I wanted to please my parents. If they could "see Sharon's name in lights," as my mother kept saying, maybe my father would show me more tenderness. And I didn't want to let Mom down—the older I grew, the more excited she got about my becoming a star. It was like those early-teen beauty contests again. But for me, it was more important to be an actress than to be a starlet. Didn't actors and actresses do their jobs by being other people? In all the roles I'd play, I would get to be someone else—that is, I wouldn't be the military brat anymore; I wouldn't be the "pretty is as pretty does" Sweet-Natured Sharon, or even the sex-bomb blonde whose name was going to "be in lights."

No, in each role I'd be another person, someone who looked like Sharon Tate, but wasn't really her at all.

AFTER ringing off with Jopp, Lunt remained in bed for half an hour, fantasizing about her. No Sharon this time, just the green woman getting carnal with Lunt all around his suite. *Even if she's not strong on the "sane" part of the Five S's, he reflected, Jopp certainly meets the "smart," "sweet," "sexy," and "Sharonesque" requirements—and that's enough for a two-week-long vacation here. She can be my West Coast honey in the future, too, whenever I come back. Oh, my stars! How Mandrake and Pandora will be pissed off when they see me squiring her around the Tate-World Conference! Jopp's Sharon-mouth will drive Mandrake wild!*

Later on, drained by pleasure, Lunt got dressed, went out, and ascended the crimson-carpeted stairwell to the fifth floor, where he stood outside Sharon's old suite for a minute, listening for any sounds inside Suite 56. Nothing. Mr. Moneybags Rosenwach and his unfriendly phone answerer weren't "in residence" much, were they? Yet they were bogarting the room, wasting all those Sharon vibes!

With a parting glance at the fifth floor's balcony, that public patio where yesterday he'd watched the hawk on the wing, Lunt descended the stairwell to the lobby. Mrs. Kruikshank stood on duty behind the gleaming mahogany front desk, the sleeves of her gray polyester hotel uniform again carefully buttoned around the wrists. Cordially she asked if Lunt had discovered who left him "the package."

"*Packages,*" he corrected her, albeit in a polite voice. "It's plural now. Three. And no, not yet, but I will."

The stout old Filipina night clerk with the neurological condition smiled warmly, and after four seconds of quivering lips as well as eyes that blinked a lot, she said, "I hope so. By the way, how is your cough?" Her breath, like last night, was redolent with the smell of mustard.

Well," said Lunt, launching into a joke he'd heard once, "even with my bad cough, there's still plenty of people in the local graveyard who would trade places with me." He waited for her to smile at this, and when she did at last, her mouth forming a cute quavery circle, he felt he'd achieved something.

After five seconds, Mrs. Kruikshank said, "Have you picked up the medicine I mentioned?"

"What's it called again?"

Three seconds, then, "Mucaquell. 'Get on the Muke,' the advertisements say. My brother, he has a chronic cough and he swears by it. He likes to say, 'If you can't drink Muke, just freeze it and eat it—or else open up a rib and pour it in!'"

"I'll look for it," said Lunt. "In the meantime, how are you tonight?"

During the five seconds before she answered, Lunt seized the opportunity to do a fast visual scan of the lobby, which was empty except for an underaged-looking group of bohemians sipping Brandy Alexanders; a mountain man–type of bearded behemoth pecking away at what appeared to be some sort of an electronic abacus; the actress Connie Stevens; a nimbus-haired woman sitting with Tarot cards spread out in her lap; and a table where the shaved-headed singer of the rock group REM sat alone. No Mandrake. A further glance through the nearest window revealed tiki torches blazing in the garden as well as the usual crowd of revelers.

"Oh, it's been quiet here," said Mrs. Kruikshank, "but I'm glad for it." With a manicured fingernail, she lightly touched a fleshy crease in her neck. "There was a whopper of a commotion earlier today."

"Commotion?" Lunt didn't know what she meant until he flashed back to the ambulance he'd seen in the hotel driveway around noon.

After a four-second pause: "Oh, yes, what a stir! To tell you the God's honest truth, I imagine we have a new ghost on our hands."

"A ghost? *Here?*"

"Yes," the woman said, continuing without much of a pause, "we've had many ghosts at the Hotel Ofotert, it's thoroughly haunted. But Mr. Trueax has asked us not to discuss this with our guests."

"Come on, Mrs. Kruikshank, you can trust me!"

Following three seconds of silence: "Will you keep this confidential?"

"Cross my heart," said Lunt, making the corresponding motion on his chest.

So she beckoned him close, where her mustard breath smelled stronger, and after two seconds she began: "Late last night, or I should say this morning, a Dutch photographer who's been staying in Suite Sixty-Seven called down to the desk here. He was upset, in great personal turmoil. It seems he'd been asleep, and he woke suddenly to find a woman dressed in black standing beside his bed. She wore a black, tight-fitting outfit. Now, what did our guest call it? Hmm. A *cat outfit*, was it?"

"You mean a *catsuit?*"

"Oh, yes, you're right, a *catsuit*! And the woman in this catsuit, she simply stood beside our guest's bed, peering at him, and when he asked her who she was—why she was there, what she was doing in his suite—she moved away and went to his bathroom without saying any words. This cat woman moved nonchalantly, the Dutch guest said—though I imagine *he* wasn't nonchalant. He followed her to the bathroom, ready to confront her. But she was gone."

"Gone?" Lunt spread his hands on the desk. "Like…"

"Yes, vanished into thin air. The window was open, but Suite Sixty-Seven—like your junior suite, Mr. Moreland—has no balcony or ledge to speak of."

Lunt wasn't much of a believer in ghosts, other than possibly Sharon's. The way he saw it, people invented the concept of ghostly visitations because they couldn't fully accept the blunt fact of their mortality, and ghosts were a way around this fact. (Reincarnation served as a flip side of the matter—a projection of immortality into the past instead of into the future). Also a factor was people's great wish to reunite with their dead loved ones, which led to reasoning along the lines of "if a headless knight can come back, then my sweetheart can, too." Finally, in Lunt's view, people believed in ghosts because they took pleasure in being scared out of their skulls.

"Was this the same ghost you had at the hotel before?" he asked Mrs. Kruikshank. "The one you mentioned?"

Following a six-second pause: "No, we've only had *male* ghosts in the past. This explains why I found last night's visitation so mystifying. When I first began working at the hotel, in 1967, there was talk of a wrinkly old male spirit who wore a pale yellow ascot and paced around the third floor. Over the years, I have heard four different guests, four *completely unrelated* women, complain about Suite Thirty-Two. Each one said that when they were in bed alone, they felt ghostly hands and a ghostly—well, a ghostly *other thing*— touching them in a tender spot. This was always in Suite Thirty-Two, mind you. And each woman leapt up from the bed, as you would expect, and put the lights on."

"No one there?"

Mrs. Kruikshank, after just a one-second pause, slowly shook her head.

"Wow." The inside of Lunt's right ear tickled him, so he jammed a finger inside it. To his relief, he felt no hairs. "Weird," he said. "I've never seen a ghost myself, but I know about a guy who used to live in a haunted house. A haunted house right here in LA."

"Does he still live in that place?" Mrs. Kruikshank asked after four-and-a-half seconds.

"No, he's been dead since 1969. His name was Jay Sebring. A famous hairstylist. People say I look like him a little. My hair does, at least."

Three seconds later, Mrs. Kruikshank said, "You know, since you mention the sixties, I even saw a ghost myself once. Although it might have been the seventies. Oh, it was a *heck* of a thing! It was a boy who was standing right where you are now." Her eyes narrowed, forming a deep furrow in her forehead. "He looked like my college paramour, who jilted me."

Amazing, Lunt thought. *Ghosts everywhere!* Was Sharon's spirit here, as well? Lunt had always assumed that if Sharon's ghost existed and haunted somewhere in particular, it was the death house on Cielo Drive. Did she hang out in the Ofotert instead, happily haunting it, this being somewhere that held pleasant memories for her? Was she, in fact, the catsuit-clad ghost from last night? Just to *think* of it, Sharon's spirit in a catsuit!

Returning his attention to the desk clerk, Lunt said, "That ghost with the Dutch photographer—did anyone catch sight of her again?"

Mrs. Kruikshank blinked at Lunt, a strained look on her face. It took her five seconds before she said, "Oh yes, the mysterious woman in black. Well, our security guard Baby Son searched for her, and he found no one, no one at all. Quite a mind-bender, I must say. Baby Son seemed frustrated. He's *very* diligent. The matter seemed to end there. One more Hotel Ofotert ghost story, hmm? But then this morning, just as I was about to telephone my brother and tell him about it, my phone rang. Mr. Trueax was calling. He said that the gardening staff had made a gruesome discovery." She fell silent for three seconds. "Are you sure you will keep this confidential, Mr. Moreland?"

"Again, cross my heart"—and this time, he made an even more emphatic heart-crossing gesture, which drew a pleasant smile from Mrs. Kruikshank.

"Well," she said, once her smile had collapsed into two or three mild twitches of her mouth, "the gardeners found a corpse in some shrubbery on Seething Lane. Behind the hotel, you see. The corpse was female, and wearing a black, tight-fitting outfit. She was a burglar, it seems, a 'cat burglar,' and when she climbed out of our Dutch guest's window, she made her escape along the hotel's rear facade by holding onto a drainpipe. But she fell. The drainpipe snapped. It couldn't support her weight, apparently, and—"

"And *splat*," said Lunt, thinking, *My God, it could've been my own room she broke into! It could've been me waking up to find her! And what if she'd been armed, and I tried to confront her? Or if I kept sleeping and she stole my laptop, all my Sharon materials? What then? Without my Sharon book, my Great Work, where will I be?*

LUNT'S high school years emboldened the teenager to be less covert about his Sharonophilia. Which meant that his mother once again sent Lunt to a psychotherapist—"Walter Hutchins, PhD," as the new shrink insisted on being called.

Hutchins was a stern man with huge tortoiseshell eyeglasses and, behind them, heavy-socketed eyes. Reclining in his quaintly decorated Scotch Plains office, the therapist puffed on a cigarillo and told Lunt, "There's an old Basque saying: 'We seek the teeth to match our wounds.' Why do I mention this? Well, it's apt for your dead actress problem. Not just philosophically—I mean it literally. Why? Because in my view your problem derives from your fear of what can be termed 'vagina dentata.' In other words, vaginas with teeth, sharp teeth, the kind that will chomp your phallus off if it swings too close to them."

Lunt, still a virgin, gaped at his new therapist. The office smelled of boiled cabbage. Beyond the window at Hutchins' back, night was coming on fast, a swollen moon already visible.

"Women frighten you," Hutchins explained. "Why? Because you find them threatening, so you prefer an unreal woman, a mythic woman like your actress, who lacks that all-too-dangerous tangibility. The tangibility strikes you as dangerous, you see. And since death fixed your actress forever at a young age, she remains pure potential. Why? Because you never knew her, and *cannot* know her, hence you feel free to burnish her with fine qualities minus the fear of your phallus being torn up. Shredded." Hutchins blew two jets of smoke from his nostrils and inspected one of his yellow fingernails. "She cannot bite you, bite your phallus, but in a sense *you* bite at *her*, and there's the rub. You victimize her memory."

"No, I do the opp—"

"But it's your needs that are paramount here, young man, isn't that true? Not her needs, but your *own*."

"How can she have needs if she's, like, gone?"

"That's immaterial. To you, it doesn't matter that this poor woman even existed. Why? Because her name and face and reputation are just material to you, raw material, building blocks you've employed to build a lover who'll keep you company in your frightened, loveless life."

Lunt had the sense that this man was trying to peel him like an onion. He knew he couldn't endure more of Walter Hutchins. But he'd figured out how to get the better of him. To both his parents later that day, he announced, "Hutchins never laid a hand on me, but he sure talked about my 'phallus' a lot. Matter of fact, he hardly mentioned anything else!"

"I knew it!" Lunt's father cried out. "That man's a homo!"

"Well," said Lunt, "*whatever* he is, if I keep on seeing him, his influence will probably tempt me to experiment with his lifestyle. He really makes it sound appealing!"

Not even Mrs. Moreland could combat her husband on *this* one. Exit Walter Hutchins, PhD.

THE Sharonophile hadn't heard his room phone from the hall-way—the stone walls and heavy wooden door prevented this—but its shrill ring reached his ears as soon as he entered Suite 47. Was it Mrs. Kruikshank calling to tell Lunt of another ghost, perhaps? Or that "Whosoever" swine making his latest prankish night call?

The latter.

"Whosoever treats his fellows without honor or humanity, he, and his issue, shall be treated with commensurate inhumanity and dishonor."

Lunt waited until the solemn male voice finished its sermon, then he said, "You know, pal, I agree with every word. Message received. And I'm on your side—I get it! So you can skip me tomorrow when you're speed-dialing every room here, or every number on your list, or whatever the fuck you—"

Interrupting Lunt, the caller jumped into the sermon once more, carefully enunciating each word. Which caused Lunt to finally snap, yelling, "Fuck *you*, you fucker," before he slammed down the receiver.

While preparing for bed, and remembering to smear some Beige Milk moisturizer on his face, Lunt tried to calm himself. Easier willed than accomplished. When he finally plugged his BlackBerry into its charger on the nightstand and put his head on the pillow, he couldn't sleep. Insomnia was to be expected before a big romantic rendezvous, but tonight Lunt fretted less about tomorrow's lunch with Jopp than about the mystery caller. He'd assumed that the "Whosoever" phrase was from the Bible, but a Google search on his BlackBerry (which he had to fumble for in the dark) turned up nothing about the phrase except for a reference to a Japanese sci-fi film entitled *Battle without Honor or Humanity*.

As to the provenance of the call itself, Lunt investigated it by phoning the Ofotert's switchboard operator Nancy (that overly cheerful young woman who'd told him that her name rhymed with "fancy—and chancey!") and asking her to track it down if possible. Impressively, less than three minutes later, she called Lunt back and informed him that the "Whosoever" call had originated in Amarillo, Texas.

"*Amarillo?*"

"From a payphone in Amarillo," Nancy clarified.

Lunt gave a laugh that had little mirth in it. "Not only do I not know anyone in Amarillo," he said—his only Texan Sharonophile contacts were in Dallas—"I don't even know anyone who uses payphones anymore!"

Nancy's "educated guess" was that the caller used a payphone to block his personal number from being traced.

She has a gift for the obvious, Lunt thought. And once he'd thanked Nancy and set his head back on his pillow, he tried again to sleep. The air-conditioning was perfect, the room was dark and silent, but no luck, he couldn't help but continue brooding. Was Mandrake behind these annoying nightly calls? Had he hired some confederate in Amarillo to torment Lunt by long-distance phone? And were the calls somehow connected to the packages that kept arriving under Lunt's door? Was it all a conspiracy? A Mandrake-piloted project to harass Lunt into…into what? Into leaving LA? Or just leaving the Ofotert? Did they want him out of here before the Sharonfest, the Tate-World Conference, got cooking?

"Enough of this," Lunt said aloud, and he fumbled in the dark for his BlackBerry.

Time to dial for help.

"You awake?" he said when Bronson answered.

"Just getting ready for bedtime, Luntie-love."

"Am I bothering you? It's so late, I know, but—"

"No worries. Lately, in spite of my early rise-and-shine for work, I've been sorta night-owlish. Guess what I was watching until, oh, five minutes ago?"

"Something Sharon-related."

"Naturally," said Bronson. "The home movies of that Sebring-and-Sharon housewarming party."

Lunt grinned. "La Tate's wearing Jay's sweater in that one, right? Yeah, his hair looked terrific in that film. Wish the footage had some sound, though."

"You still combing your hair like his? Someday I'll see you in person, I promise. I mean, not just in pictures."

"No pressure."

"I know," said Bronson. "It's just that I—I need to keep my distance. From people I care about. It's strange, I know, but—"

"Hey, I understand."

"No," she said, "I don't think you do. No one does, least of all me. But you and I *will* meet face-to-face one day. I'll pluck up my courage, I'll Sharon up, and—"

"Maybe next year's Sharonfest."

"Sure. You dig this year's and then we'll talk. Who knows if I'll even still be into Sharon then?"

"Bite your tongue!"

"Really, I've been feeling drawn to Raquel Welch lately."

Lunt groaned.

"Hey, don't knock my Raq!" Bronson said. "I'm not claiming she's better than Sharon, just that she's to brunettes what Shar is to blondes."

"I thought you were swinging over Nastassja Kinski's way."

"I think I need someone just a bit lusher. More decollage, you know, if that's the right word? So it's Welch, or maybe Claudia Cardinale. You ever catch Raquel in *Bedazzled*?"

Irked by Bronson's talk, Lunt informed her in a bratty tone that Welch was inferior to Sharon in every category he could think of. Bronson countered him just as brattily, and they went on bantering in this fashion until Lunt changed the subject. He'd never argued with Bronson and didn't want to start. So now he filled Bronson in about Mrs. Kruikshank, the Ofotert ghosts, his upcoming lunch date with Jopp, and, at last arriving at the main reason for his call, the mysterious calls he kept receiving from Amarillo. Once he finished describing those messages, Bronson asked, "When you hang up on this Whosoever guy, does he ring you right back?"

"He hasn't yet, no. It's almost like he's got a quota, one call per night, and then he's through. Until the next time. The next night."

Bronson's trademark chortle.

"Don't laugh, Bron! This is *serious*. The guy is spooky. Even spookier than all the Santa Shots. You'd be creeped out too."

"Maybe it's a ghost, one of those ghosts the hotel clerk told you about."

"How reassuring. What does your intuition say? Got any tingles about this?"

"None. None so far, at least. It's nebulous. But what if this cretin isn't calling you *personally*? Like, what if he's just calling your room?"

"My room? Forty-Seven?"

"Yeah, he calls that room night in and night out, saying his shit, delivering his munificent statement to whoever's staying there." Bronson thought for a moment. "Which reminds me of something, actually."

"What?"

"This apartment I used to live in a few years back. More than a few years."

"Where?"

"Right here, in Carson City. It was this eensy-weensy pad in a nice building, nice and quaint, and maybe two or three months into my time there, I got a postcard in the mail. On one side was a smiley face, but it was frowning, and the written part was wiggy. The person wrote, 'Please light a candle in your apartment, because someone once got hurt there badly.'"

In his dark, cool, quiet suite, Lunt yawned, hoping Bronson hadn't heard it. "Wiggy is *right*, Bron."

"And here's the best part, or the worst," Bronson continued. "Every few weeks after that, I got a postcard with the same pic, the frowning smiley, and all they wrote was, 'Did you light the candle yet?'"

"Well, did you?"

"No. I didn't want to, I felt defiant. I mean, who the hell are they to issue me orders? Why should I spark up a candle just because some invisible stranger demands it? But after ten or twelve cards, maybe, I started thinking that it couldn't hurt. Besides, I was curious—if I *did* finally light one, would the postcards stop arriving? Would the postcard-sender realize I'd done it?"

"What if he didn't *need* to sense it?" Lunt suggested. "What if the writer of those postcards was living right across the street, watching your window every night? Or staking you out, stalker-fashion, standing right outside your building, and gazing up, Bron, at your window?"

"Nice effort to bug me out, hon. Except those postcards I kept getting were all postmarked from far away."

"Where?"

"Amarillo."

"*No!*"

"See that, jackass? I paid you *back*."

"So it *wasn't* Amarillo?"

"No, they were postmarked from where you are now."

"The Hotel Ofotert?"

"LA. Honestly. And it wasn't a man who sent them because the handwriting was feminine."

"It was? How'd you know?"

"Tell me, do boys dot their i's with cutesy heart shapes?"

"Mmm. I see your point."

"But finally, months later, I did light a candle and say a prayer for whoever got hurt."

"Thoughtful of you. And did the postcards keep arriving?"

"I don't know," Bronson said. "I moved out the next day."

"ALL things must pass," a former member of Charles Manson's favorite pop group once sang, and so Lunt's senior year of high school ended and off to Four Winds Community College in Los Angeles he prepared to go. Given its geographical centrality to Sharon's adult life and career, LA was ground zero for Sharon Studies, so Lunt had chosen to apply to colleges there and nowhere else.

His parents were not keen on this move. Each preferred that Lunt remain at home and commute to a local school. Typically, Mrs. Moreland's fear involved Lunt's connection to La Tate. She said, "If you're living somewhere outside our parental supervision, God help us how deep into *her* you'll go."

Mr. Moreland's fear was that Lunt would change his sexual orientation while in Southern California. He said, "College campuses, and especially dormitories, and *especially* college dorms near Hollywood, are unchecked breeding grounds for homosexuality. You might as well get a degree in 'Boy Love' at the University of Sodom!"

Time for an ultimatum, Lunt decided. Time for his first-ever open stand against his parents.

"If I don't go to the college of my choice," he announced (having practiced this speech in his room nightly for a week, saying the words softly), "I won't go to college at all. Instead, I'll run away from home, become a prostitute, sleep with men as well as women, and use the earnings to support myself while writing a book about Sharon." Then, as a spontaneous grace note, he added, "And when I can finally afford it, I'll get a sex-change operation that'll make me look as much like her as possible."

"You wouldn't dare," said Lunt's thunderstruck mother.

Lunt, needless to say, was bluffing, though the book idea did of course return to his life two decades later thanks to Bronson's suggestion. The teenager knew that, for his parents to believe his lies, he had to offer some proof of earnestness, so he saved enough money from an after-school job as a local diner's short-order cook to decamp from his house late one night, catch a Community Transit bus to Manhattan, and hole up for a weekend in a flophouse-style Greenwich Village hotel room.

Alone in the urban jungle, the boy was scared witless. He only left his hotel to dine at a restaurant called O'Henry's, which had sawdust on the barroom floor. An O'Henry's waiter with a handlebar mustache acted friendly, and with an odd wink he kept asking the boy if he'd read authors such as Walt Whitman, Arthur Rimbaud, Marcel Proust, Oscar Wilde, Tennessee Williams, and Truman Capote. Lunt couldn't wait to go home. Once he arrived there, however, he pretended he'd had a ball.

"Worried, *weren't* you?" he snapped at his parents. "Still, that was just a taste, a little *sample*, of what I'm capable of."

To Lunt's delight, both parents gave in. Still, his mother said she had a single last requirement for him. To wit, that Lunt see a therapist one more time before he went to college.

The office of the elderly female psychiatrist Dr. Gluck was decorated not with rock concert posters *a la* Greta Tanley but with the tri-color flag of France and with kitschy framed images of the Eiffel Tower.

"Why does that metal structure look so familiar to me?" Lunt asked in deapan fashion.

The long-necked Dr. Gluck was unamused. "I'm a Francophile," she stated crisply.

"Cool," chirped Lunt, "'cause *I'm* a Sharonophile."

He could afford the levity since in two months' time, he would be winging his way across the friendly (he hoped) skies to California. Dr. Gluck directed a chilly look at Lunt, as if scrutinizing her new patient for visible cracks. "Tell me, please, what you mean by Sharonophile."

Gladly Lunt obliged, running it all down for her until Dr. Gluck lifted a tiny-fingered hand to cut him off.

"May I inform you about what is causing this mania?"

"Mania?" Lunt put on an tetchy face. "You make me sound crazy. But I guess to a hammer, everything looks like a nail. Sure, bombs away."

"To you, this actress Tate represents a kind of *anti-mother*. They are two sides of the same coin, your maternal parent and the actress, and you feel persecuted by your mother, because she rightly belittles your fondness for the actress. Thus you have come to think of the actress as 'Good Mother.'"

Lunt clucked his tongue and glanced at the double clock on the wall, which showed the hour in France as well as in Jersey. The office smelled of chalk dust. Outside her window, not a cloud marred the azure sky.

"Like everyone," the psychiatrist continued, linking her hands atop her desk, "you seek safety in your world, safety and sanity and love, and you feel you have no choice but to project warm, maternal qualities onto this actress. Her presence, with all its appealing familiarity, seems to you ideally suited to reflect consistency."

Lunt waited for more, but Dr. Gluck said nothing else, intending that the wisdom of her diagnosis would ring in the air as if someone had struck a nipple gong.

"That's it?" Lunt asked.

"Yes. In brief."

"You make my Sharon-love sound like a, well, *defense mechanism*. But didn't I tell you that I'm happy? Happy the way I am?"

"You only *believe* you're happy. I promise you that you're not."

"Okay, fine, let's assume you're on the money. You've never met me before, you've only known me for twenty minutes, but let's assume you've got me *all* figured out. What now?"

"What now?" Flinty Dr. Gluck smiled for the first time in the session, but awkwardly, as if meaning to stifle the smile. "Medication. What you need, what I'll prescribe, is an experimental drug. I believe I can obtain it for you. *If* we're fortunate."

"What's it called?"

"The market name for this medication is—or *will be*, if the FDA approves it—'Lustrate.' Until now it has only been used on a West Virginia prison population, but I believe it will be effective for you."

"Prison popu—like, *convicts?*"

"Not to worry, young man, it's quite safe. And it won't give you criminal thoughts, I promise. It's tasteless, odorless, a clear liquid you dissolve in milk. Skim milk is my recommendation. Do you drink skim milk?"

"Nope, but Sharon Tate loved milk, any kind, so I can force myself if I have to. But what does this drug *do?*"

"Lustrate is a libido-suppressant."

"A libido sup—you mean it'll kill my *sex drive?*"

"Isn't sexual mania, an excess of affection, your problem?"

"With all due respect," Lunt snarled at her as he stood, ready to leave psychotherapy behind him forever, "f you and the Eiffel Tower you rode in on!"

His parents grounded him for that foul-languaged parting shot. Only for one month this time, but to protest the grounding, the teenager again ran away from home, spending the Memorial Day holiday weekend holed up in the same Greenwich Village hotel from months earlier. The handlebar-mustachioed waiter at O'Henry's remembered Lunt and winked at the boy and mentioned more authors: Jean Cocteau, André Gide, Somerset Maugham, Noël Coward, John Rechy, Joe Orton. And even though Lunt knew that his future would soon get brighter, he still felt scared witless until the time came for him to catch his bus back home.

4

MUCAQUELL, DO YER STUFF!

(Tuesday)

BEFORE Lunt could come up with any answers about his mystery caller from Amarillo, he fell asleep. And slept well. Unfortunately, the morning proved less productive than he hoped. His nerves were to blame: too much anxiety about meeting Jopp for Lunt to be able to write emails, much less his Sharon memoir. So he procrastinated with the Dorothy Parker book, where the only satisfying line he found was, "The only -ism Hollywood believes in is plagiarism." Post-shower, he spent ten minutes at the mirror, making his hair Jopp-ready. He prayed to Sharon's poster on the wall for her blessing re: his lunch date. Then, with a vow to work harder than ever after lunch—"Win, lose, or draw with Jopp," he told the poster, "I'll put my shoulder to the wheel!"—he donned clothing (his latest V- necked Sharon T-shirt read, "LOVE! VALOR! SHARON TATE!") and left his suite.

When Lunt arrived at Gush, which was less jammed than yesterday, a bossa nova version of "The Shadow of Your Smile" blared from the restaurant's sound system. This song gave Lunt a shiver, for it had been one of Charles Manson's favorites, something he played on guitar at bohemian showbiz parties when he was hustling for recognition as a singer-songwriter. (Manson's taste in music beyond the Beatles ran to early rock'n'roll as well as to crooners like Sinatra and Frankie Laine.) Charlie's failure in the music biz obviously rankled him. As Polanski later said, "He was an artist spurned, and it can be a very, very dangerous thing to spurn a certain kind of artist. Think of Hitler."

Shoulder to shoulder in the noisy Gush entryway with a bunch of hungry hipsters, Lunt craned his neck in order to survey the dining room. No Jopp yet: she wasn't at her table, which was unoccupied. Was she in the girl-fish restroom, perhaps? Or just fashionably late?

Lunt did spot two familiar faces: the busty, unfriendly, fur-vested hostess Latreena and the Jim Morrison look-alike waitress, whose tendrils of tattoos still peeked out from her black uniform onto her wrists and throat. From the foyer, Lunt also recognized a celebrity in the house. It was the exhausted-looking film actor Garth Chthonic, who sat splayed in the center of a white leather banquette with an enema bag nestled beside him. Chthonic had been on a bourbon jag since two nights ago, and the four tough-looking women who sat with him, all of them wearing pricey-looking pink leathers, were members of a local motorcycle club called "The Menstrual Cycles."

The sight of bikers, any kind of bikers, tended to unnerve Lunt. This was due to how chummy Manson had been with such ruffians. Intent on making the "Straight Satans" and "Jokers out of Hell" and other biker gangs he knew into his personal bodyguards, Manson would invite them to party with his women, who stole the bikers' wristwatches as they went down on them, saying, "What's does *time* mean anyway? You don't need time."

"Can I help you?" Latreena failed, or pretended to fail, to recognize Lunt's face from yesterday. "For one person, it'll be an hour's wait. At least."

"Actually," Lunt said, "I'm here to meet Jopp."

"Jott?"

"*Jopp*, the girl with green hair."

"Oh. She's not here yet."

"I know, I'm early for our rendezvous, but I want, uh—" What he wanted was to be at the table when she arrived, as if announcing to Jopp on her arrival, "Look, dear, I'm present and accounted for already, it's *our* table now and here we shall lunch together for many joyous afternoons." He grinned sheepishly at Latreena and said, "I wanted to get started eating so we can get out of here sooner and leave you the free table."

The hostess gave him a stony look as she mulled this over. Lunt, to add extra weight to his request, fished his wallet from his front pocket, peeled out a twenty, and held it out to Latreena. "Besides," he said, appealing to any compassion gene in her, "I'm really *famished*."

Still the hostess hesitated, which prompted Lunt to worry that, like Baby Son, she would accept the bribe and then refuse to help him anyway. Did she have her own "tío Huberto" in her life who promoted greed? Perhaps not, as it turned out: with a sigh to show her displeasure, the hostess accepted Lunt's bill, pulled a menu from the pile of them on her podium, and led Lunt to Jopp's table.

While crossing the space (and then from his seat), Lunt considered the dining room. There was as much female beauty in the house as yesterday, but no one Sharonesque at all, and zero people who'd been known to fraternize with La Tate. After he shared an amiable nod of the head with three button-nosed blonde housewives in yoga outfits at the table beside his, Lunt's gaze travelled to the front door. Except for occasional sidelong peeks at the soused actor Garth Chthonic, his female biker companions, and the yoga queens seated next door, Lunt's gaze remained at the entrance. Any time someone entered the restaurant wearing green, Lunt felt a jolt. Each jolt was a false alarm. But one great jolt came from his noticing a fellow Ofotert guest at a banquette on the other side of the dining room. How had Lunt missed seeing Benny Pompa until now?

Once again, the dissipated pop star was accompanied by his two brunette sirens of a certain age. The trio was eating heartily, decked out in what looked like the same attire from the last time Lunt had seen them. The only difference was that Pompa's football jersey today read across its front, "GUILTY AS FUCK." Other customers besides Lunt were also gawking at the copper-Afroed pop star.

From across the room, Lunt couldn't hear Pompa's husky-voiced mealtime conversation. He wondered what Pompa was talking about. The answer was that the pop star was recounting to his companions some lore about lightning. It was a tale the women had heard before, as Pompa well knew, but he still felt like telling it. To fulsome oh's and ah's from the women, the pop star took a bite of his meal, put down his fork, and nodded his head as he chewed, his eyes sweeping through Gush until they met Lunt's own eyes. Then Pompa grinned. It was a beatific grin, too, incandescent, and Lunt returned it. He even gave a coy wave of his hand, a wave that meant to say, "Hey, I've seen you at the Ofotert—we both stay there." To his surprise, Pompa made no acknowledgement of the wave; he just continued grinning at Lunt, his take-in-everything eyes not blinking. It was as if his face was paralyzed, or a mask. Which brought to Lunt's mind a quotation that he'd heard once: "Fame is a mask that eats into the wearer's face." Who'd said that? Dorothy Parker? Lichtenberg, maybe? Or was it one of Dutch Schultz's famous last words? And did Sharon's own fame make of her face a mask? If not, then would this have happened later, a transformation awaiting her?

Another question: If Lunt's book made its author famous, as he hoped, would the fame mask likewise ruin him? He couldn't say, of course. But he did know that the time was ripe for him to go speak with Benny Pompa. How impressed Jopp would be, walking into Gush to find Lunt chatting with her favorite rocker! Lunt knew how to make the approach: he would apologize for the interruption, mention their mutual good taste in hotels ("Stop by Suite Forty-Seven anytime for a chat, Benny!"), then cite the birthday that Pompa shared with La Tate and implore the pop star to write a birthday tribute to Sharon for Lunt's book.

The Sharonophile stared vacantly at the cover of his menu, not really seeing the words "WE'RE FOREVER BLOWING BUBBLES" printed there. *Gird your loins*, he told himself, self-respectfully leaving out the "jive turkey" part of the graffito he'd seen yesterday. With another sociable nod at the nearby yoga queens, Lunt pushed his chair back and got to his sneakered feet. Before he launched himself across the room, however, his peripheral vision caught a flash of green at the front of Gush.

Jopp?

No—*Glen Mandrake.*

The back of Lunt's neck went cold.

With a green scarf complementing his signature white suit, jug ears, Adam's apple, spade-shaped beard, and bulging eyes, Mandrake stepped confidently into the still-busy restaurant foyer. Sitting again, and fast, Lunt covered his face with a hand as if about to blow his nose into it. Concealed in this way, Lunt watched his rival go circling around a cluster of would-be lunchers and then say something to the hostess. He'd interrupted a conversation Latreena was having but she greeted him civilly enough, and even tittered when he pointed to her fur vest and made some remark. Was there no one whom Lunt's enemy couldn't charm?

Lunt wished Jopp would show up immediately, so he could do some charm-work himself. He needed to seduce the green woman as soon as possible. Even if she ended up not liking Lunt (or if she *did* like him but already had a boyfriend; or could only focus on her heartthrob Benny Pompa), Lunt needed at least to be *friends* with her, so that he wouldn't be alone at the upcoming Tate-World

Conference. And so that he could show off her Sharon-mouth. *Shit,* he thought, *I'll even pay Jopp to be my friend if I have to!*

The more Lunt mulled over the matter, the darker his imaginings grew. What if Mandrake glimpsed Jopp walk into Gush, beheld just how Sharon-like that mouth was, and then stole her from Lunt just as he'd stolen the Sharon-eyed Pandora? To avoid this scenario, Lunt considered leaving Gush right now, intercepting Jopp on the sidewalk, and diverting her to a different restaurant, far from Mandrake's view.

Before he could act on this, though, something freakish happened. *Good* freakish, actually. It was a series of mundane actions that led to one hell of a climax. As Glen Mandrake scanned the dining room crowd, no doubt to assess its most attractive female customers, his eyes landed on Benny Pompa. Mandrake had failed to notice Lunt, but he'd caught sight of the Sharon-birthday-sharing pop star, and Mandrake looked pleased at Pompa's presence. Then the expression on his face grew determined, and he breezed right past the hostess Latreena toward the banquette where Pompa sat.

Oh no, thought Lunt, panicking anew while he followed Mandrake's progress through the room. If Jopp showed up now to find her beloved Pompa chatting breezily with Mandrake instead of Lunt, she might be Mandrake's for the taking! For a moment, a horrible moment, Lunt pictured a sexual threeway— not Jopp entangled with himself and Sharon Tate, but Jopp fucking Mandrake and Pandora!

"*No,*" Lunt repeated out loud this time, yet he was paralyzed, unable to move a muscle, as Mandrake arrived, smirking, at Pompa's table. There, with the hue of his suit blending in with the banquette's white leather, Mandrake hovered above Pompa and made some friendly seeming statement that Lunt, across the dining room, couldn't hear.

By this point, Pompa had long ago stopped looking at Lunt, but when he glanced up at Mandrake now, his face still featured that mask-like grin. Pompa appeared to listen to every word that Lunt's foe uttered. The grin never wavered. But once Mandrake was finished, Pompa went into motion. With impressive speed, he lifted a tall, narrow glass from his table, a glass filled to the brim with some sky-blue-colored beverage, and he hurled this glass, not just the beverage but the glass, up at Mandrake. What's more, Pompa's aim was true: the glass struck Mandrake squarely in the face, bouncing off his nose. And along with the shattering of the glass on the glossy restaurant floor came the sound of the pop star's hoarse voice, which thundered at his victim, *"Don't you talk birthdays to me when me and my wives are feeding!"*

Silence enveloped the room, a shocked hush that felt as loud as noise.

Did I really see that? Lunt wondered.

Had he, indeed? Or was it just some wish-fulfilling hallucination?

Gaping at Mandrake and Pompa, his eyes zipping back and forth between the two men, Lunt entirely forgot about Jopp. How absurd Mandrake looked now! How humiliated he must be feeling! Lunt began to laugh, the sound of it cutting through the silence that still reigned in the restaurant. Soon other lunchers were also laughing, including the yoga queens near him—everyone laughing at how the pop star Pompa, famous yet nevertheless deserving his privacy, had dressed down what appeared to be an overzealous fan.

For Lunt, needless to say, what he'd just witnessed meant so much more. The gods, or maybe Sharon's spirit, had intervened in his life! *Favorably* intervened, because not only had Lunt been spared from the error of socially engaging Pompa, but someone else, his sworn enemy, had made the error instead. And had suffered the consequences.

While the laughter throughout Gush swelled, Mandrake remained too shocked to wipe the blue liquid from his face. Even once he finally did, mopping it away with the back of his hand and shouting foul language at Pompa, Mandrake's green scarf and white suit still bore the stains. As for Lunt, who was doubled over by now, laughing too hard to breathe properly, he hoped that Mandrake would turn to see him, to know that Lunt had witnessed his public shaming.

To his dismay, Lunt's laughter soon changed to coughing, more of that recent heavy coughing. He covered his mouth with both hands, a searing pain detonated in his lungs with each hack, and it kept growing worse, as though one gigantic cough lay buried *in potentia* within him, the ancestor of all coughs, and this whole crazy fit was the means by which to reach it, to excavate this *ur*-cough and soothe his chest and cough no more. But he could not release the *ur*-cough, so his coughing fit went on, growing severe enough that the onlookers moved their focus from the shamed man to the cougher. The yoga queens in particular looked disgusted with the Typhoid Lunt who was seated so near to them, and they watched with mounting horror as his germs infected their share of oxygen.

This is too much, Lunt told himself, *I need medicine,* panic setting in once more. He couldn't bear for Jopp to find him in this state. He thought of rushing to the men's room and holing up there till his cough passed. If someone was already in the boy-fish area, then he'd use the diaper-changing facility. But another huge cough changed his mind. *Medicine,* he thought. *As soon as fucking possible!* So he leaped up from his chair and rushed out of the restaurant.

DURING my senior year, our school newspaper featured a notice request-ing "actors to perform in the major motion picture Barabbas, a Biblical saga starring Anthony Quinn." As we soon learned, the phrase "actors to perform" really meant "extras to stand around in an arena wearing togas and watching fake gladiators pretend to fight," but my girlfriends and I didn't care. We loved wearing those costumes, and we found it great fun when the director instructed us to make a thumbs-down movement with our hands. By doing so, our characters condemned an unworthy gladiator to his death. A few years onward, I would think about this thumbs-down gesture whenever I stuck out my thumb on the California freeways to hitchhike. I would also remember the gesture later—a lifetime later, it seemed—when those mixed-up Manson people were stabbing me and my baby and they turned a deaf ear to my pleas for mercy.

On the Barabbas set, a particular actor caught my eye, and I guess I caught his eye, too. Jack Palance turned out to be terrific. Sure, he was mainly interested in me "that" way. But Jack also gave me lots of advice about coming to Hollywood, much more upbeat advice than Pat Boone and his wife provided. Jack even arranged a screen test for me in Rome. Of course, Dad didn't want me to do it, but Mom insisted that he give his daughter a chance to fulfill her dreams, so he finally allowed the two of us, my mother and me, to travel to Rome.

Unfortunately, the screen test did not pan out. I was too nervous, and too green, to act very well. At least Jack Palance didn't lose interest in me. One night while the Barrabas shoot was still happening, Jack invited me out to dinner, saying, "I've just set up a special record player in my sports car and you must experience it, Sharon." Nothing sexual occurred with Jack that night. I wouldn't let it, because I was still smitten with Richard

Beymer. *I even went to visit Richard in California after my graduation, and once I arrived, I really had stars in my eyes. Wow, the parties Richard took me to! All those palm trees and gorgeous homes, too—it was even groovier than I'd envisioned. The problem was, my parents kept writing me letters insisting that I return to Italy, and reluctantly I did. There was no way I could say no to my father. Even so, I told Richard before I left that I would be back soon, since Dad had recently gotten posted to Fort McArthur in San Francisco. And sure enough, it wasn't long before my folks, my two sisters, and I boarded the* USS Independence, *bound for the States.*

This ship has a fitting name, *I thought as we set sail.*

THE pharmacy nearest Gush was named Limsky's. It was a Mom-and-Pop establishment not far from the shopping mall built on the site of Schwab's Drugstore, that legendary soda fountain where aspiring starlets from decades past would congregate, hoping to be "discovered." (Not Sharon, who was too graceful to behave with such desperation, but legions of others.) Lunt had driven past Limsky's a few times, so he knew how to get there, and while hurrying along Sunset on foot, his coughing let off enough for him to leave Bronson a voicemail: "Wait till you hear about Mandrake's comeuppance!"

On reaching Limsky's, Lunt read a curious sign hung in the pharmacy's front window: "SORRY, WE DO NOT PERMIT CUSTOMERS TO ENTER WITH CONCEALED FIREARMS." Simple enough for Lunt to honor—he had never been into guns. Navigating to the area for "Cough Suppressants" proved simple, too, and there on a low shelf sat four chocolate-colored Mucaquell bottles. The drug's bluish label read, "NOW FORTIFIED WITH SPECIAL INGREDIENT 'SzV'" in addition to "EASING COUGHS SINCE 1968." The year of Sharon's marriage; one year before her death. Had she ever used this syrup? Why had Lunt never heard of it till now? Or did he hear about it and simply forget it, as he seemed to be forgetting so much with the approach of the dreaded age forty?

Outside once more, in the bright sunlight and mild air, Lunt drew his purchase out from its pearl-white, Limsky's-insigniaed bag. The bottle's safety seal, its instructions ("*One or two teaspoons once a day*"), and its warnings ("*Caution: narcotic—Drowsiness may occur—Do not operate heavy machinery*") seemed straightforward enough. Lunt hadn't planned to use the Mucaquell right off the bat, fearing that the drowsiness would inhibit his ability to operate the machinery (not heavy, admittedly) of his laptop. Hadn't he vowed to La Tate (that is, to her poster on his wall) that he would work hard on his Sharon memoir today? Yes, and he intended to keep the vow, to "put his shoulder to the wheel." Yet as he headed back to the Ofotert, the coughing acted up again. So Lunt reached back into the bag and screwed the top off. Then, muttering, "Mucaquell, do yer *stuff*," he put the bottle to his lips, tilted his head back, and drank down what he guessed to be the equivalent of two teaspoons.

The syrup tasted horrible, like a drunk chef's failed attempt at licorice flavoring. Lunt nearly vomited several times, which seemed to alarm two frail-looking Mexican girls who were skipping toward him on the sidewalk, hand in hand. Fortunately, the medicine seemed to work fast: by the time he was starting to dash across Sunset, Lunt was no longer racked with coughing.

His enjoyment of this relief, alas, was short-lived. First, a speeding gray Volvo nearly clipped him. Then, while he lingered on the sidewalk, catching his breath, his BlackBerry trilled. And the name that appeared on the grimy BlackBerry screen made him say "Shit!"

"Actually, before I even say hi, Vishwa, let me apologize for not calling you sooner. I *planned* to, but—"

"Sooner?" Lunt's literary agent sounded peeved. "You're not even calling me now—*I'm* calling *you*, yes?"

"That's true, right. But I've been busy with my book, so I haven't reached out to *anyone*. Not my father, not my friends… Plus, you wrote 'Not urgent.'"

"Lunt, I wrote, 'Important but not urgent,' yes? If I use the word 'urgent' every time something's *merely* important, people would stress out. They would feel stressy, yes? Does that make sense? And being a person who is so prone to stress myself, I prefer not to cause stressiness in others."

Remembering Vishwa Mukherjee's emotional delicacy, her history of nervous breakdowns, Lunt softened his voice in order to keep her calm. "Well, in the future, whether you indicate 'urgent' or not, I'll get back to you right away. Promise!"

"I'm glad that you're working on your project, Lunt," said the so-called Vajillion Dollar Vishwa. "Your work ethic is admirable, yes? Not every author cares about their subject as much as you do."

Lunt's heart quickened from the praise. He pictured Vishwa's burnt-gold face, her aquiline nose, and her forearms crowded with long, ink-black hairs. Plus the expensive clear retainer on her upper row of teeth. "Much obliged," he said.

"You should be proud of yourself, yes?"

"Er...I am." Still, something was different today with his literary agent, Lunt could tell.

"Is something *wrong*, Vishwa?"

"No, nothing is wrong. As I said, this is not urgent, yes?"

"Oh. Good."

"But regrettably I will no longer be able to represent your project."

"*What?*" The agent's words struck like an ax blow to the back of Lunt's now-sweaty neck. "Won't be *able?*"

"My deepest regrets, yes? I hope we can work together on a different project someday."

"*Someday?*"

"In the future, yes."

"A *different* project?" Lunt said. "Why not this one? Is it because I didn't call you back fast enough?"

Seated on the lavender-tinted chair at the ochre-tinted desk in her fushia-colored office at the Gutenberg Gang on East Forty-Ninth Street in Manhattan, Vishwa began to massage her forehead with her thumbs. "It's nothing to do with that, yes? I *do* expect when I use the term 'important' that my authors contact me with, well, *professional* haste. But I don't penalize anyone for faulty communication skills. Not unless it causes me stress, yes? Does that make sense?"

"Vishwa, *no!*" Lunt felt as though she'd blasted away the ground beneath him and he was falling. "You can't quit on me, we have a contract! You *signed* the thing. So did I! That's—"

"When you review this contract, you will find a clause that says that either party can dissolve our deal at a moment's notice. We discussed this, yes?"

"But why?" Absentmindedly, Lunt dropped the paper bag from Limsky's to the sidewalk and stuck the chocolate-colored bottle of Mucaquell in the left back pocket of his khaki trousers. "Did I do something wrong?"

"Again, you did nothing wrong, nothing at all. I simply choose not to go forward at this time. I…I have too much on my plate…"

Lunt felt like weeping. "Don't, Vishwa," he beseeched her, "don't quit on me!"

The dire sound of Lunt's voice disturbed the agent. Contrary to what she'd hoped, this was getting "stressy," threatening to smash her currently peaceful state. She needed to bring this matter to a swift close. "I'm sure you'll find another agent," she told him. "You have a worthy project, yes? I believe in it. So other agents will also believe."

"But I don't want *another* agent, I want you! You're—you're the best!"

The fact was, Lunt would have been content with *any* literary agent, but since Vishwa was the only one who hadn't turned him down, he clung to her the way a shipwrecked sailor would cling to the side of an overcrowded lifeboat. Her representing Lunt's book had validated it, validated *him*, gracing him with ego-salving approval. Without Vishwa, without an agent, what would he be? Just another barely published, nearly unknown, Sharon Tate–mad scribe lost in the literary tundra.

"You know, Lunt, I'm feeling some anxiety stirring. Anxiety not just for you, but for me, too, yes? This is *not* good. My doctors would want me to end this call. Does that make sense?"

Lunt's mouth, dry with anxiety, still bore the licorice taste of the Mucaquell. While Vishwa elaborated on her need to avoid stress, he looked down at the cracked sidewalk, where a lone spider was crawling around between his feet. Watching it made Lunt feel dizzy. Was it the cough syrup kicking in? Did cough syrup clobber someone *this* quickly? This *completely*? Or was it just the upsetting news from Vishwa? Either way, Lunt knew that as soon as he finished this call, he would need to put his head down somewhere.

"Please, Vishwa. When I'm back east, we can meet."

"I need to end this call, Lunt. I need to hang up."

"Don't hang up!"

"I find your eagerness *very* distressing. The anxiety you provoke is—it's poisonous for me. I don't believe you're stable. We can speak another time, yes, if you need closure? By email would be best. Does that make sense?"

"No, it doesn't! Why are you doing this?"

"Why?" She exhaled and fell silent, trying to control her breathing. *Better to end this now*, she thought, *than to let it drag on and on.* So Vishwa tried to end it. "Well," she started, "all I can say is that I received a communiqué from an associate of yours. He presented his case to me. And after careful reflection, I—"

"Wait—an *'associate,'* you said? What associate? I don't *have* any associates! I haven't hired any other contributors to my book yet—"

"In any case, your associate made a good case against my taking onboard your project. I wish you all luck in the future."

"*What* associate? Which associate did you talk to?"

"That really doesn't matter. The point is—"

"Yes, it *does* matter! I need to know!"

"One of your colleagues in the world of Sharon Tate fans, yes?"

"But which one? *Which?*"

Vishwa hesitated, her eyes darting to a certain orange bottle on her desk. The bottle, far larger than the one containing Lunt's Mucaquell, was half-filled with capsules of the antianxiety drug Onalull. Too bad that Vishwa had passed her daily maximum dosage already, because this phone call was really too difficult. She needed another dose. And she needed to disconnect the phone line. But she also needed to resolve this ordeal, and so, massaging her forehead with her thumbs very vigorously, she revealed to Lunt the name, which struck him like a second ax blow.

Lunt was too dumbstruck to speak at first, so she added, "He said he's only trying to protect the reputation of Sharon Tate."

"Vishwa, how can you be so naive?"

"Naive? You're calling me naive?"

"Mandrake hates my guts! He doesn't care about Sharon, he just wants to fuck me over! First he stole my girlfriend, and now—"

"You make insults now on top of shouting? I'm putting down the phone."

"*Last week* he called you? And you're not telling me till now?"

"I wrote you an email, yes?"

"Yeah, and *'not urgent,'* you said! This is the end of my *career,* Vishwa—how is it fucking *not urgent?*"

The agent's shoulders began to shake. *Not a good sign*, she knew. "I *did* write 'Important,' yes? And I prefer not to hang up telephones prematurely, but the stress you're causing—"

"*Fuck* important!" Lunt was grinding his teeth so much that they hurt. "Mandrake will say *anything* to ruin me! *Any* falsehood— and you believed him? You actually *believed* him?!"

While waiting for Vishwa's reply, Lunt glanced once more at the sidewalk, where another spider was crawling around between his black, pebble-grained sneakers. What was it with these little creatures? The Strip was infested! So Lunt lifted his left foot and then, remembering but choosing not to care about Sharon's creature-kindness, he stomped the spider flat.

As for Vishwa's reply, the one Lunt awaited, it never came. Or it didn't come in words. Energetically—but not so much so that it made a harsh noise or damaged her telephone—Vishwa pushed the button on the console that terminated her call with Lunt. Her hands were quavering even more than they had been during last week's blind date with the cookbook author's brother. Still, her hands weren't so far gone that she couldn't reach for the bottle of Onalull.

Who cared about "daily maximum dosage?" Surely she could hazard one more capsule...

LUNT'S four years of college were hardly hallmarks of scholarship. Instead of studying for his economics major, Lunt indulged his Sharon-love, bringing roses to her grave, poking around all the Sharon-charged locales in Los Angeles (including the Hotel Otofert's lobby), and buying Sharonabilia at a nostalgia shop on Hollywood Boulevard. Ultimately, he managed to graduate, but more important to him was the fact that, for the first time in his life, he'd experienced how it felt to worship Sharon openly, without the fear of hassles from his mother.

Throughout his college years, Lunt had intended to make LA his permanent home. "I'm here to stay," he vowed to his best non-Sharonophile friend. Ernest was a classmate who hailed from Altuna, Pennsylvania, and who worked at the same computer repair shop in Marina Del Rey where Lunt put in twenty hours a week.

It wasn't just LA's Sharon history that appealed to Lunt. The weather and the palm trees and the beaches, the luscious women everywhere (a few resembling Sharon in some facet or another), the Sunset Strip's charming seediness, and the casually hip vibe— these elements all played their parts. What's more, anywhere on the East Coast felt "too close to home," Lunt explained to Ernest. "I need the whole damn land mass between me and my parents in Jersey."

"But everybody here is so *phony*," Ernest retorted. "It's a cliché, but so true. You know the joke, right? How do you say '*Fuck you*' in Hollywood?"

"How?"

"'*Trust me.*'"

Lunt chuckled. Sure, there was truth to this—so many people he had met in LA were ultra-friendly right up to the moment when they'd stabbed him in the back. Or in the front. At least the citizens of New York—and New Jersey, for that matter—didn't go overboard in pretending they liked you. In fact, the insincerity of Southern California often reminded Lunt of a quip made by one of the Manson Family killers. When she sat on the witness stand at her trial and was asked, "How could it be right to kill somebody?" Her cheery response was, "How can it *not* be right when it is done with love?"

"I know Hollywood's not perfect," Lunt admitted to Ernest. "Far from it, man. But *where* is perfect? Nowhere. Which is what the word 'utopia' means, incidentally. For better or worse, I *belong* here, Ernie. This was Sharon's chosen town, and it's mine. I'm never leaving."

Twelve days before his college graduation, Lunt's parents were involved in a horrible car accident on the Garden State Parkway. According to the New Jersey highway patrolman who reached Lunt by phone, there was a pileup in a rainstorm, and the result rendered Mrs. Moreland comatose and left her husband permanently paralyzed from the neck down.

BLOOD boiling, stomach knotted with rage, Lunt stormed up the driveway to the Ofotert. He ignored Baby Son ("Afternoon, sir") and the squat, mustachioed garage attendant (*"Hola"*), who stood together inspecting something printed on the so-called house detective's clipboard. Noting Lunt's hostility, the two men exchanged a glance that seemed to say, *Another wealthy loco gringo, probably hopped up on some gringo drug.*

Despite his growing dizziness and rubbery legs (symptoms of the Mucaquell, he assumed), Lunt broke into a run halfway through the driveway, then attacked the crimson-carpeted stairwell to the lobby two steps at a time. He planned to confront Mandrake in his room, or if Mandrake was away, to wait outside the door until the son of a bitch got back. But while charging past the lobby, which glowed, just as it had when he'd checked into the hotel, with strong amber afternoon light, Lunt decided to take a fast peek there, and...

Jackpot!

A bald man in a white suit sat alone on a chardonnay-colored sofa (the lobby's largest) under an unlit electric candelabra. No stained scarf, and new unstained jacket and trousers. His feet were propped on the edge of a marble coffee table. Glancing up from the *LA Weekly* in his manicured hands, he watched a fuming Lunt come stampeding toward him, and Mandrake's protuberant eyes lit up for a moment, then seemed to flicker out. Instead of deploying a smirk, sneer, scowl, or something else from his gestural repertoire, the bald man merely nodded his head and said, "I'd offer you a seat, but I'm not in the mood for chat. You can put me 'under heavy manners' some other time."

"Up *yours*," Lunt shot back, chopping at the air in front of him with both hands, his voice piercing enough to alarm an elderly Armenian film-music arranger who sat nearby. "I'd rather stand and make you feel puny," Lunt added. "That's *your* style of social interaction, right? You and your power-pervert Pandora."

He'd assumed that his enemy would behave as usual and rise up to equalize their positions, yet Mandrake seemed too listless today to bother. And why had he flinched when Lunt mentioned Pan's name?

"*Touché*," Mandrake said, making a slow-motion-punch-to-his-own-jaw gesture. "Power-pervert. That's cute. I'll have to tell her you said that."

Lunt shifted his weight to handle the wave of dizziness that rushed through him. He'd never despised anyone, not even Charles Manson, as much as he now despised Mandrake. Where was a butter knife to stab him with? Lunt could run upstairs to seize his scimitar-shaped letter opener, hurry back down, and plunge it into the scumbag's chest—but then he'd be a killer, no better than Charlie M., and how would Sharon's ghost care for that? Not one bit. He was already guilty in her eyes for destroying that spider...

In search of a less homicidal weapon, Lunt's eyes jumped to a glass filled with pink liquid that rested on the coffee table near Mandrake's loafers. Could he hurl the glass at his foe—Benny Pompa style!—then make a break for it, run away before said foe could pursue him?

No, Lunt realized with a grimace, *Mandrake will catch up with me eventually, and with his supposed Jeet Kune Do skills, he'll beat me silly. Besides, if I hit him and run now, I won't even make it out of the lobby. With my head spinning the way it is, I'll probably trip and fall before I reach the elevator. Not a good visual for Pandora to learn about.*

"Did she arrive yet?" he asked.

"Who?"

"You know who."

Mandrake flinched again, then tried to cover it with one of his obnoxious tut-tuttings. "The power-pervert will be here soon enough, dear boy."

But why did he look so annoyed at the mention of Pandora? Had she been delayed in coming out west? Was this reason enough for Mandrake to look so bloodless now, so weakened? Or did that public shaming by Benny Pompa explain his distress?

"Guess you won't be going back to Gush," Lunt snapped, shifting tactics.

Bullseye! Mandrake's mouth tightened, as if he'd smelled something rancid. Trying to look unmoved, he said, "As Lichtenberg tells us, 'If all else fails, the character of a man can be recognized by nothing so surely as by a jest which he takes badly.'"

"What a *groove* it was," Lunt went on, driving the figurative blade in deeper. "What a buzz, watching your ego get gored in public. You'll *never* live it down."

"Jumping Jehosaphat," Mandrake finally exploded, complete with bared teeth and veins standing out on his neck. "Keep *still* about that animal," he roared. "I can't *believe* he and Sharon share a birthday. But *you*, you coughing, tubercular mess—let's discuss *you* for a change! You terrified that whole restaurant with those damaged Jersey lungs of yours. You've been inhaling too much industrialized swamp gas."

The old Armenian film-music arranger had heard enough of this clamorous, nonsensical talk. He got to his feet and trudged off to find somewhere else to sit.

And Lunt? He had the sense now (and now feared Mandrake also would notice) that he was swaying, actually *swaying*, on his feet. He felt as though he was encased in Jell-O, a block of unstable,

Mucaquell-infused Jell-O. This cough syrup was potent stuff. Lunt needed to lie down, to rest, to sleep. But his fury still burned bright, so he said, "My cough is history, but your shame will last forever. And your campaign against my Sharon book won't work. I'm forging ahead without Vishwa."

"Ah, yes," said Mandrake with a sneer, "my 'campaign.' So you've been speaking to your literary agent. The highly nervous Ms. Mukherjee. Vajillion Dollar Vishwa didn't have a good Nine Eleven, did she? Flying body parts *do* derail a head case's recovery, don't they?"

Lunt rubbed his glassy eyes. The lobby had started to tilt, making his body list to the left. He hoped to steady himself by leaning against a nearby orange recliner, making this move look as casual as he could, but his legs were going, too, buckling under his weight. He had to sit, there was no choice, so he plopped down into the recliner.

Not that Mandrake seemed to pay attention to any of this. He was still elaborating on how he'd "turned" Vishwa, saying, "I promised her big trouble. Simple as that! Picket lines. *Daily* picket lines with dozens of rabid Sharon supporters, plus dozens more well-paid faux-Sharonophiles who couldn't care less about Sharon. All of them would be marching in lockstep with me outside Vishwa's office. And outside her apartment building. Nasty, but effective."

"You wouldn't *dare*," Lunt managed to say.

"Oh, mere threats alone usually suffice with emotionally jangled targets. I told her to picture the signs we'd have, placards that mentioned her by name, linking Vishwa, to—*ta-da!*— Charles Manson. I informed her that she'd be 'killing Sharon' a second time. Just as *you* are, Moreland. You and your pathetically democratic need to coarsen Sharon by sharing her with the unwashed hoi polloi."

God, thought Lunt, blinking his eyes, struggling to stabilize his thoughts, *this chair feels comfortable.* Before he sank too deeply into it, though, he mumbled, "Publicity…even negative publicity…it just works in my favor…"

"True, the first law of publicity." As he spoke, Mandrake began to slide around and shimmer in Lunt's field of vision. So did the wall behind him and the candelabra attached to it. "Maybe your next agent, if you find one—and I hope you'll do a thorough search, since, as Lichtenberg says, 'He who wants to become Pope must think of nothing else'—maybe your next agent will be braver than Vishwa when I go on to threaten *her.* Or *him.*"

Lunt gnashed his teeth, his heart rate and blood pressure shooting higher, even as the lobby fractured into broad bands of color, everything flying off in different directions. "I'll *ruin* you," he gasped. "Somehow, *some* way…"

Mandrake cackled at this, showing lots of pink gum, and the sound of it was oppressive enough to incense the old Armenian film-music arranger, even at his new location across the lobby. "Another quotation serves here," Mandrake said. "'In the weak, a lack of strength to defend oneself passes over into complaining and threats, while the best always stay defiantly silent.'"

"Enough with the Lichtenberg!"

"That last quote wasn't Lichty, it was Artaud. As if you, or *any* Jerseyite, had ever heard of him."

With the lobby swimming around, settling for a moment, then swimming more, Lunt nevertheless managed to get a good grip on the arms of the chair and shut his eyes again. His hope was to stop the whole fucked globe from whirling, but colored smoke awaited him behind his eyelids.

Enough.

He couldn't do this, he was too befuddled to go on, and as good as this recliner felt, he knew he had to go, leave, claw his way up somehow, and get upstairs before he passed out, or dozed off, in front of Mandrake. Unfortunately, no matter how he struggled to push himself out of the recliner, he felt himself sinking farther into it.

Between grunts of effort as he tried to stand, Lunt said, "Is Pandora amused...amused by all those...those late-night calls to me that you commissioned?"

"Calls? Which calls?"

"Ha!...Amarillo...'Whosoever'...That...*that* ring a bell?"

"'Whosoever?'" Mandrake looked at Lunt quizzically. "What are you saying, dear boy? This is hogwash. Utter bilge."

Lunt tried to fix his eyes on his foe. "Or the Santa Shots...?"

"Santa Shots? *What* Santa Shots? You mean that Christmas shoot Sharon did? There's a Santa Shot for sale?" Lunt's foe brightened, speaking loudly again, though not from anger but excitement. "I didn't realize they're available! Doesn't the Polanski People group have them all? That's what I was told. I'd like to buy one!"

At which point, with a supremely irked "Harrumph," the old Armenian film-music arranger finally did what Lunt could not yet do: he tottered to his feet and left the lobby.

THE speaker slated for Lunt's college graduation ceremony was Chuck Barris, former host of TV's *Gong Show*, but Lunt never got to hear what Barris had to say. Twelve days before commencement, word reached him about his parents' car accident while he was lunching with his friend Ernest. With both Mr. and Mrs. Moreland hospitalized in critical condition, Lunt flew back to Sulphurdale and moved into his childhood home. *Just for now*, he told himself. *Just until things get sorted out.*

Lunt made daily visits to St. Matthias, the local hospital, and sat with his comatose mother, holding her soft, dry hands and wondering whether she would ever recover. She'd made his childhood so difficult with her efforts to stamp out his love for Sharon, but she deserved better than this affliction, and it gutted him now to watch her suffer. About a month after Lunt had returned to the nest, his quadriplegic father was discharged from St. Matthias. While at home, Mr. Moreland was cared for by a twenty-four-hour nursing staff funded by the family's insurance policies. The jovial head nurse, a rope-muscled, dreadlocked Jamaican man who called himself "Jah Victor," struck Lunt as being gay—flamboyantly so—yet Lunt's father seemed somehow oblivious to that fact. In fact, he often referred to the effeminate-acting Jamaican as "a real man's man."

By the time the nursing staff got functioning at full force, Lunt had converted his former bedroom into a Sharon shrine, openly displaying there much of his Sharonabilia and giving pride of place on the wall above his bed to the poster of Sharon with the word "WHY?"

"You've got a big love for this girl, yah?" Jah Victor said to Lunt when he first beheld the shrine. "So you go find her then, and you *marry* this girl."

"I can't," said Lunt.

"Why not?"

"She's dead."

Assuming that Lunt was joking, perhaps teasing him, Jah Victor went into a giggle. "Oh, don't let *that* stop yah, mon!"

Regardless of anyone's opinion, Lunt was proud of his Sharon shrine. Yet he was apprehensive, too: as he explained to his friend Ernest (in one of their last phone chats before their friendship faded away), "If my mother ever wakes up from her coma, comes home, and sees the shrine, she'll cut my head off!"

IN spite of his drugged state, Lunt eventually made it out of the recliner. Veering slightly yet steadily to the left, he lurched out of the Ofotert lobby, then rode the clanging elevator to the fourth floor, his back pressed to its grille rear wall, and at last collapsed on the bed in his suite, still fully dressed. *Just a short nap*, he promised himself as he reached, with his last reserve of strength, to take the chocolate-colored bottle of Mucaquell from his pocket and set it on his nightstand. The mattress felt as though it was composed of Sharon's breasts. Or so he mused to himself, yawning loudly. Sharon's breasts and—because of Jopp's own flat-chestedness—the green woman's buttocks. Yes, here were hundreds of breasts and ass cheeks, pillowy and smooth, into which Lunt eased gratefully, and before long the bed, with Lunt stretched across it, floated off. It went "Floaty P'Toaty," to use the term his father would playfully employ when teaching the five-year-old Lunt how to swim. Yes, Floaty P'Toaty went the bed and its occupant, and after many vague encounters, said occupant wound up walking barefoot along a dirt path.

Lightning forked through a cobalt sky but there was silence, not a single thunderclap. Cemetery vapors drifted past Lunt as if in a bad vampire movie. The path was worn smooth, like the surface of the Ofotert's mahogany front desk, the one Lunt had tapped on for good luck upon his arrival at the hotel, and the path led the wanderer to a vast hole in a desert, a corkscrewing kind of pit into which he carefully descended, placing each foot just so.

After a long time, Lunt found himself a tour guide, someone who took him by the hand. This tour guide was a woman in a catsuit, a sleek black Lycra catsuit, and her face was concealed by a Sharon Tate mask, one made of unpopped Bubble Wrap.

Lunt woke in darkness. To his amazement, it was night already. Past midnight, in fact! Another surprise came when he realized that he, who never dreamed, had just spent time in Dreamland. Still groggy, he checked his BlackBerry and found two voicemails. One was from Bronson, who apologized for not calling back sooner. She said, "The office this weekend has been like Dante's *Inferno*." (Dante's *Inferno*? This reminded him of his dream.) The other voicemail was from Jopp, who apologized for having missed their lunch date.

"I forgot I had to see my dentist" was how she began her explanation. "Really, truly! It was, like, *urgent*." (Lunt winced on hearing this Vishwa-associated word.) "But maybe you didn't show up, either? Anyhoo, let's meet tomorrow—same Gush time, same Gush table!"

Lunt planned to call Bronson back first thing tomorrow. He would also call his agent Vishwa, beg her to reconsider, to resume representing him. With Jopp, however, he couldn't wait. She answered her cell on the fourth ring, and Lunt told her that he'd indeed been at Gush, leaving out the news of his coughing fit.

The green woman apologized again for missing lunch. Unlike nearly every other LA-based female Lunt had met since his college years, she sounded as though she meant it. Then, abruptly changing the subject, she asked him if he'd seen "Benny the Pomp" around the Hotel Ofotert.

"Oh." *Him again.* "Actually—"

"Dude, I would *so* love it if you'd invite me over to the Ofotert. I wanna see your room. You're still checked in there, right?"

"Not only am I still here, and bumping into Benny Pompa almost *hourly*, but I saw him at Gush today."

"Wait. Benny was *at Gush*? Oh, *fuck!*" she shouted, hurting Lunt's ear a tad. "You mean I *missed* him?"

"Sorry. But serves you right, seeing your dentist instead of me."

"Dude, *really*? I knew he'd probably stop at Gush this week, but not the *one time* I'm away!" Lunt heard a smacking sound over the line and hypothesized that she'd slapped her forehead with a palm. "*Fuck* my dentist, dude! I'm never going to see that lame-o again! How'd he look?"

"Your dentist? Sorry—bad joke." He made a mental note to avoid such lame humor with Jopp in the future. "Well, *pissed off* is how Benny looked, and for good reason. This asshole I know from back east, he went up to Pompa and bothered him, interrupted his lunch, and Pompa threw some blue juice in the guy's face, glass and all."

"Wow, I can't believe I missed that! Sounds like Benny, though— he never suffers fools. Especially not while he's eating. '*Feeding*' is what he calls it. God, I would so suck Ben's dick. Or have him lick the place where my dick would be, if I had one, which I *don't*, in case you were wondering."

Breaking into laughter, a distinctly nervous laughter, Lunt felt his own penis pulsing. Sweat flowed through his pores, too, pressure filled his chest, and his heart boomed like a bass drum. He couldn't think of what to say next, but eventually came up with, "You ever meet him?"

"Ben? A few times, yeah. Little chats when I snuck backstage at his gigs, but I never *boinked* him. Not yet. Oh, I made out with Saffron once—does *that* count?"

"Who's Saffron?"

"One of his wives."

"One of them?"

"Hey, I thought you were a Benny fan!" Her voice turned snarky for a moment. "Don't you know *anything*? Yeah, Ben's a bigamist. It's no secret, he's open about it. *Too* open, according to his manager and legal team. But Benny's attitude is, 'Bust me or don't.' He's fearless."

Lunt asked if Pompa's wives typically wore leopard- and snakeskin outfits.

"Always," said Jopp. "That's them, Saffron and Trudi. So they're in town, huh? I thought he left them behind in Australia."

"And these wives never, like, get jealous of each other?"

"Nope, it's a polyamorous relationship. Saffron's the hotter one, but both are primaries. That means, like, equals in the poly world. Like I said, I made out with Saffron once, after a Memento Morey show at the LA Forum, and I'm not even bi! Not after what happened with that bull dyke in Vegas. But that's another story!"

Once they'd hung up, pledging to meet for lunch at Gush tomorrow, Lunt switched on the lights in his suite and started padding toward the bathroom, needing very much to urinate. On the way there, he found the night's next surprise. A new manila envelope had been pushed under his door. This package proved to be more ominous than usual. On the Santa Shot inside, someone had drawn with Magic Marker a black line through Sharon's throat. It looked like a noose. And the sticker on the envelope read, "THE COYOTE IS OUR MOST AWARE CREATURE, BECAUSE HE'S COMPLETELY PARANOID. FRIGHTENED OF EVERYTHING, HE MISSES NOTHING."

1962: By now, becoming an actress was an obsession for me. We lived in the Bay Area, but this seemed so close to Hollywood that I could almost feel the winds from that magical place blowing through my soul, calling to me. The day we arrived at our new house near the Army base, I took a business card from my purse and studied it, not for the first time.

According to Richard Beymer, his talent agent Harold Gefsky was "the nicest man in Hollywood." Mr. Gefsky certainly sounded nice when I spoke to him on the telephone. What a sweetie! We scheduled a meeting, and on the big day, I put on my sexiest outfit. Because Mom promised not to tell my father where I was going, I caught a bus to Palo Alto and then stood on the freeway with my thumb out. This was the first time I had ever done such a thing.

"You hitchhiked a ride here?" the talent agent said once I got settled across from him in his office, a cup of steaming-hot tea on his varnished desk. "I don't believe it!"

I told Mr. Gefsky that the truck drivers who'd given me rides were perfect gentlemen.

Gefsky grinned. He had a kind face, and looked sincere when he told me what many (most?) other show business men would not have been sincere about (because they were only after sex): "Honey," he said, "I can tell you got what it takes to be a star."

I worked hard from day one and did everything Mr. Gefsky asked me to do. Acting classes, photo shoots, auditions, wine promotions at restaurants, and TV commercials for Chevrolet and for Santa Fe cigarettes. (Not a regular smoker yet, I ended up fainting from the puffs on a cigarette I took on the soundstage while the cameras were rolling!)

Over my father's protests, I was able to move down to Hollywood, where my apartment was in a rooming house for young actresses. I had a rough first night at the Hollywood Studio Club—the roommate assigned to me kept insisting on giving me a "Swedish massage." But Mr. Gefsky sorted it out, and my replacement roommate turned out to be a lovely girl. Anyway, I spent a lot of nights at Richard Beymer's home. Richard was as dreamy and tender and supportive as ever. After a few weeks, Mr. Gefsky pitched me for a new television series, called Whistle Stop. (They later changed the title to Petticoat Junction). And this is how the blessing-and-curse of Martin Ransohoff entered my life.

"One of the shrewdest men in show business," "the most fearless and decisive man west of the Rockies," "the smoothest of all the world's smooth talkers"—Ransohoff's reputation as a film and TV producer was larger-than-life. At the time I met him, he was only thirty-two, though with his bald head and stocky build he looked ten years older. At least! According to Mr. Gefsky, the gum-chewing, chain-smoking Ransohoff was a "star maker"—he'd already built the careers of Ann-Margret and Tuesday Weld. (I liked both of those gals, by the way, although Tuesday later became my competition on one film, as you'll see.)

"I have this dream," Ransohoff told a journalist before I came along. "A dream where I'll discover a beautiful girl who's a nobody and turn her into a star everybody wants. But once she's successful, I'll lose interest. That's how my dream goes."

We did a screen test. The next day, with Mom by my side, we watched the test in the so-called "star making" producer's private screening room. As soon as it ended, he shouted to his assistant, "Get me a contract. Get my lawyer. I'll take this girl to the top."

He asked me to sign an exclusive, seven-year contract with his company Filmways, Inc. This contract made me a "ward of the state" until I turned twenty-one, which allowed me to work anywhere without parental permission. The monthly stipend of $750 struck us as an *astonishing amount—although my mother whispered to me, "Don't act so grateful or else he'll rewrite the whole thing and pay you less."*

Ransohoff and his people said they had a plan for me. I was *immediately put into training, like a racehorse. They told me, "Cream your face, Sharon. Put on more eyeliner, Sharon. Stick out your tits, Sharon." Ransohoff decided to publicize me as "The Texas Firecracker," despite the fact that my speech classes got rid of most of the "Texas twang" in my voice.*

My first audition while under the Filmways contract was for Whistle Stop, *but I got so anxious when the casting director yelled "Action!" that I blew some lines and lost the part.*

"Just do everything I say," Ransohoff told me, and I did. At least till I met a certain Frenchman who became the next love interest in my life.

DEAR MR. TRUEAX,

Since you greeted me at the Ofotert on my arrival, I have been having a pleasant stay here. However, there have been two major problems that you, as hotel manager, should be aware of.

First, every night I have been receiving a prank call on my room phone. According to Nancy at the hotel switchboard (she has been most helpful), the calls originate from a payphone in Amarillo, Texas. I do not know anyone who lives in Amarillo or anyone who would spend time there. Please ensure, perhaps with Nancy's aid, that I receive no more of these calls.

My second problem at the hotel is more serious. Already, in my less than one week here, multiple different envelopes with baffling sentiments written on them (in sticker form!) have been pushed by someone under the door to my suite, number 47. Inside each envelope are doctored photographs that I find upsetting. As with the phone calls, I have no way of knowing who is behind the packages, or if the packages and the phone calls are connected.

The only culprit I can think of is my fellow hotel guest (and fellow Sharon Tate enthusiast) Glen Mandrake, who is registered at the Ofotert under the name of Melek Randang. The fact that he is here under an alias should clue you in to his shady character and nefarious intent. Mr. Mandrake and I are on antagonistic terms, and this antagonism motivates his misbehavior toward me.

Needless to say, these are problems best resolved by hotel management. Your assistance will be most appreciated.

SINCERELY,

LUNT MORELAND

PS: As I have previously mentioned, I am highly interested in occupying Sharon Tate's former suite, number 56. Please let me know if the guest there, Mr. Rosenwach, has left the suite, thereby making it available for me. My moving over to Suite 56 will probably bring a halt to the mysterious giftings and prank calls. Without a doubt, it will help to ease the abuse I have suffered here.

Lunt underlined his name twice, then reread the letter he'd written on the distinctive cream-colored Hotel Ofotert stationary. A detailed drawing of the hotel was printed at the top of the sheet. He hoped he wouldn't alienate Trueax—he planned to stay at this hotel as much as possible in the future—but the packages and prank calls needed to stop.

"I'm so ashamed that this has been going on, sir," said Mrs. Kruikshank as Lunt set down the thin, black, Ofotert-monogrammed pen he'd been writing with. As usual, the sleeves of the stout, old, Filipina night clerk's gray polyester uniform were neatly buttoned around her wrists.

"Not to worry," Lunt said. He handed her the pen. "How are you tonight?"

What followed were five seconds' worth of quivering lips, pulsing throat vein, and eyes that blinked repeatedly in her small, gracefully shaped head. To pass the time until she answered, Lunt turned toward the candlelit sunken lobby. No sign of Mandrake, but the late-night crowd was as baroque as ever: business executives, some players from the Lakers, a hip-hop artist Lunt vaguely recognized, the hip-hop artist's sizable entourage, a drag queen who'd dolled himself up to look like Esther Williams (bathing suit and all), two Latina starlets kibbitzing (one in green plaid slacks, which made Lunt think of Jopp), and Benny Pompa, seated at the same chardonnay-colored couch where Mandrake had been earlier.

Accompanying the pop star tonight was only one of his two middle-aged female companions. Again she wore a leopard-print outfit, and again Pompa wore a jersey (this time the jersey read, "CAN I GET ME A WET NURSE?"). Lunt's first thought was to call Jopp, tell her to rush over right now, but he quickly decided not to. She'd focus on Pompa instead of Lunt, of course. Besides, he'd feel fresher when meeting Jopp at Gush for lunch tomorrow.

When the pop star popped a chartreuse-colored lozenge into his mouth, the Leopard Woman, as if on cue, ashed her Codex cigarette on the carpet. *Such are the bad manners of the privileged,* Lunt reflected. Was this Saffron or Trudi? Cigarette back in her mouth, she ran her hands through the pop star's ginger Afro. The tender way she did this made Lunt recall how his mother used to touch his hair during his childhood, smoothing it out, making it even straighter than it was. For a moment he was transfixed by the sight of the bigamous couple, how wrapped up in each other they looked, and how calm Pompa seemed after that crazy scene earlier in the day at Gush.

I need a girlfriend, Lunt decided, loneliness stirring once more inside him. *Jopp, ideally, but anyone will do. My new love doesn't even have to look like or act like Sharon Tate—that's how desperate I am!*

"Oh, I've been fine," said Mrs. Kruikshank at last, mildly startling Lunt.

"That's good," Lunt said, sliding his letter across the cool, smooth surface of the reception desk. As she accepted it, the inside of Lunt's right ear tickled him, so he jammed a finger in there, probing around, hoping he'd feel no hairs. To his relief, he didn't. "Please see that Mr. Trueax gets that letter."

After six seconds, Mrs. Kruikshank said she would. She still reminded Lunt of his mother, and he still couldn't put his finger on the reason why. Despite how pitiable, mellow-natured, and possibly wise the night clerk was, Lunt felt too out of it from the Mucaquell to want another prolonged chat with her. On the other hand, he didn't want to seem rude. And so, summoning up some cheer before bidding her goodnight, he said, "No ghosts prowling the halls tonight?"

The night clerk's face relaxed into a smile, and after a surprisingly brief pause, she said, "No cat burglars tonight, either." As ever, her breath bore the odor of mustard. "To tell you the God's honest truth, that cat burglar was the first thief I've ever heard of at the hotel, and I've been working here since 1967."

The year hit Lunt like a thunderbolt. "Sixty-Seven?"

Three seconds, then: "That's right."

"You mean you were working at the Ofotert *in the sixties?*"

After four seconds: "Yes. In March of 1967, I began in housekeeping, but I moved to this reception desk during my second year." Her eyes glowed with pride. "I know I look younger than my age. But no other employee even comes *close* to my longevity here!"

"And during your time," said Lunt, swallowing with excitement, "did you have any contact with a certain long-term guest, a young blonde movie actress named Sharon Tate?"

Mrs. Kruikshank appeared unsure, a questioning look on her face, and she looked up to the ceiling as if an answer waited there.

Lunt said, "If you could try to remember, I'd be so grateful! Blonde hair, hazel eyes... Have you heard about the Tate-World Conference at the Ofotert next weekend? It's a tribute to *her*, this actress I'm talking about!"

What ensued was a lengthy silence, during which Lunt rubbed the front desk's surface with a fingertip and studied the small, green-edged brass bell on the desktop. *Come on, lady—think!* Lunt silently commanded her. Had the night clerk's neurological problem affected her memory? How could anyone fail to recall Sharon Tate?

Then he thought of the image on his T-shirt, so he pointed to it with an index finger, saying, "Here, *she's* who I mean!"

This proved to be the charm. "Oh," said Mrs. Kruikshank at last, "you mean *Mrs. Polanski!*"

Lunt clapped his hands together like a mad-with-joy nursery-school kid. It hadn't occurred to him, not once, that any current Ofotert employees would have been here since Sharon's stay. What a gift the Hand of Fate had bestowed on him! *"Exactly."*

"Why, *yes,*" she said following another surprisingly short pause, "Mrs. Polanski was *such* a dear. It was awful, what those evil hippies did to her. What a gruesome business! Her husband must have been *so* shattered."

Feeling triumphant, Lunt said, "You know, ma'am, the reason I'm at the hotel—well, one reason, anyway, apart from that Sharon conference I mentioned—this reason I'm here is to work on a *book* about her. About Mrs. Polanski, I mean. I'm writing a biographical text about her, and I'll be glad to gift you an autographed copy once it's published. In the meantime, is it okay if I interview you?"

Five seconds of silence. Mrs. Kruikshank picked at her lower lip with a manicured fingernail. Meanwhile, Lunt mentally crossed his fingers. If she said no, how could he convince her?

"Oh, *certainly!*" said the night clerk at last. "Everyone here at the hotel adored the Polanskis. I have only good things to say about Mrs. P. That's what she asked me to call her, you know—'Mrs. P.'"

Lunt, still feeling dazzled by his good fortune, said, "If I come back tomorrow night with a tape recorder, or at least a notepad, you'll speak with me?"

Three seconds until, "Oh, of *course*, of *course*! Mind you, I knew Mr. Polanski a wee bit better than I knew his wife. He often stopped by to chat, just how we're chatting now." She leaned forward to speak confidingly, though this did nothing to cut the odor of mustard wafting into Lunt's face. "You know, I can't imagine how I'd *begin* to describe Mrs. Polanski's miniskirts. They were all the rage here, so very chic. There was one that even caused a furor, a suede skirt with an American Indian profile on her, well…"

"Her rump." Lunt chuckled. "I've seen it—the skirt, I mean—at an auction once. Too expensive for my blood, but…"

"Surely you didn't plan to *wear* it, Mr. Moreland!"

"No, I only wanted it for my, er, collection." (In fact, he would have tried it on, but only once—just to feel what *she* felt.)

Lunt asked if Ms. Kruikshank spoke with Sharon often. This led the woman to struggle to answer for four seconds before she came up with, "Sometimes I did. I remember she kept doting on that adorable Yorkshire Terrier they had."

"Dr. Sapirstein," said Lunt. "They named that dog after a character in Polanski's movie *Rosemary's Baby*. Sapirstein was a gift from Sharon's parents, but Polanski's friend Frykowski, who died alongside Sharon—Frykowski ran over the dog with his car when he was probably high on drugs." Lunt coughed, but only twice. "Polanski replaced the dog, and he never told Sharon the truth. He just said that Dr. Sapirstein ran away."

"That sounds like Mr. Polanski," said the night clerk after four seconds of silent struggling. "Always putting others first. But you mention their friend being 'high on drugs.' You know, there were many illegal drugs around Southern California back then. 'Stupefiants' is what my brother calls illegal drugs, you know. Here in the hotel, the smell of marijuana smoke got into the *carpets*, for goodness' sake! The former carpets, is what I mean. We used to have an OD, meaning 'overdose,' in the bungalows every week. Some were even fatal. Very sad." She leaned still closer to Lunt, voice dropping to a whisper. "Our previous owner made sure those got hushed up."

"I've heard that Dorothy Parker tried to kill herself in my bathtub."

"In Junior Suite Forty-Seven?" said Mrs. Kruikshank after two seconds. "Maybe fame is the problem. There is a Hebrew proverb which says, 'Eminence shortens lives.' So just imagine how bad the problem has gotten since those drugs arrived! Not that the Polanskis were ever the type to take drugs."

Lunt smiled in agreement, thinking, *This lady's pretty clueless.*

"The Polanskis were anything but drug types," the night clerk continued. "Good, wholesome parties they used to give here. I couldn't go to any, of course—the hotel staff is not permitted to cavort with guests. Even in those carefree days, it was forbidden." She lowered her voice again. "Do you know, I saw Warren Beatty walk into the Polanski suite once—with Steve McQueen!"

Before Lunt could redirect the night clerk's memory to Sharon, a new spasm of coughing took him by surprise. Mrs. Kruikshank looked concerned, and four seconds later, she said, "Have you looked into that Mucaquell yet?"

Lunt was coughing too hard to answer. But as soon as he returned to his suite, he grabbed the bottle and took a healthy swig of the stuff.

1985: Comatose for months following the auto accident that crippled Mr. Moreland, Lunt's mother surfaced into consciousness for eighteen hours before sinking back into the coma and perishing two months later. While conscious, Shirley Moreland mumbled a lot. Gibberish, as far as Lunt could tell. At one extraordinary interval, though, her mental fog seemed to clear. Her eyes sought out her son, who was sitting in a chair beside her bed. She hummed a few bars of "Goodnight, Irene." Then she whispered, "I've— I've been a *fool*."

"What, Ma?"

"A *sinner*, too! I should've let you love that girl, that poor dead girl, that blonde actress Sharon Fate. What was the harm? We don't live forever…" Her voice sounded feeble yet urgent. "I thought we go on, but we don't…so what's the difference whom we love?"

Bars of sunlight from the nearby window put golden stripes across the woman's wan face. Reaching out to take hold of her hands, Lunt moved his chair closer to the bed. Had he heard his mother correctly? Was her new perspective due to the heavy painkillers she was taking? By the coma's distorting aftereffects? Or was it the real thing, what Lunt had never dreamed he'd hear, something you usually just came across in movies (though none of Sharon's): a dramatic sickbed conversion?

"I've been so sinful," Mrs. Moreland went on. "Not just to you, Lunt, keeping you away from that dead actress. No, I treated your father bad, too, nagging, nag, nag, nag…but then our marriage, our whole *relationship*, was cursed…made under a bad sign…"

"*Cursed*? Why, Mom?"

"Because I *stole* him, stole him from someone else. It was this foreigner, this little minx he had. She was his girlfriend when I met him at Camden."

"Camden?" said Lunt.

His mother's voice rose, carrying a hint of her familiar irascibility. "College, Camden College. That's where we met, remember? And this girl—she was some foreign student, and she loved him, she adored him. But me, I set my sights on Jack Moreland, God knows why, and I just stole him out from under his little foreign girl's nose. I—I *put out*, you see, and she didn't, that was it, that did the trick..."

"Er, Mom..." Lunt looked around the room, embarrassed, although they were alone.

"I knew Curtis's mother would never let him marry *her*. No foreigners for Old Lady Moreland's precious boy, you see? Too bad the old witch didn't see that her husband, her *own husband*, was a faggot..."

"Wait," said Lunt. "Grandpa Moreland was *gay*?"

No response. Not to this question, anyway. The breathing of the critically injured woman grew more labored. Lunt let her sip some water from a cup by way of a plastic straw. Once she'd finished, he took her hands in his again and she found her way back to the previous subject.

"We felt so guilty afterward, your father and me, because his foreign girl, she tried to *kill herself*... She hung herself, we heard."

"Jesus," muttered Lunt. "I never knew any of this!"

"Why—why would we tell you? We never even spoke of it ourselves...not later on."

"Did she—did she *die*?"

"No, the girl's family found her in time...and saved her... They got her to the hospital, saved her life..." Mrs. Moreland nodded her head slowly, twice. "But it was *our* fault, Curtis's and mine, even though he blamed me, me alone. Your father never stopped the blaming, so I nagged him in return. Tit for tat, that's what our marriage was built on, tit for tat..."

"Oh, Mom."

"You know what, though? Curtis was right. Your father was right for *one* time in his life. I knew it wasn't good, it wasn't *kind*, what we did to that girl. I should have figured we'd be cursed, live under a bad sign...a bad *star*."

"You weren't cursed, Mom. You *aren't* cursed. It was an auto wreck that hurt you, not a curse. These things happen. It's like what happened to Sharon with Manson—just bad luck for her. The wrong place at the wrong time."

Now Mrs. Moreland's blue eyes met Lunt's own eyes, and for a moment, the son saw anger there, a fury that he believed was meant exclusively for him. But soon the anger drained away, the blue eyes softened, and his mother looked emptied out, a hollow shell of skin and bone.

"I'm sorry, honey..." She clutched his hands tightly. "I should've let you have your pictures, all your books, your little blondie Sharon Fate... She was dead, what did it *matter*?" The injured woman's eyelids fluttered. "What a shame."

"What's a shame, Mom?"

"Everything I did, every last thing..." She sighed, her eyelids too heavy now to stay open. "Such a shame, it was...and such a *waste*."

"**WHOSOEVER** treats people with no honor or humanity, he and his issue will get commensurate...er, *with* commensurate... Hey, how does your thing go again? Help me out!"

At the other end of the line came no response except for the now-familiar sound of faint breathing. Lunt had been editing a passage in his Sharon memoir when the room phone erupted into ringing, and as he answered it, he decided to give his nightly caller a surprise by reciting the man's own words to him.

"What's wrong there, Amarillo? Did I stymie you by stealing your routine? Come on, speak up! Cat got your tongue?"

"Amarillo" responded to this by launching into his nightly speech, each word pronounced precisely.

"That's more like it," said Lunt as soon as the speech was over. Then he fumbled with a pillow, one of his soft, smooth, white Ofotert pillows, and pushed the receiver underneath it, so that the only sound Lunt could hear now as he glugged down another draught of Mucaquell was the weak buzz of air-conditioning and the low drone of the TV. Let Amarillo speechify the whole night— Lunt had other business now. He would ride the Good Ship Muke, going Floaty P'Toaty, with his mattress morphed again to Sharon breasts and Jopp ass cheeks.

"Carry me back to Dreamland," he muttered, his body going slack, slipping into sleep.

And Dreamland became Bel Air.

This was a sequel to the Mojave Desert dream, but far less copacetic. The woman with the Sharon Tate mask made of Bubble Wrap, she'd returned, but now she huddled next to Lunt on a park bench, its green paint peeling, outside Sharon's Cielo Drive home. No lights shone from the death house tonight; everything was dark, a lattice-work of overlapping shadows. Cemetery fog drifted around, obscuring things further. Still, thanks to the occasional bolt of lightning lashing silently through the sky, Lunt could discern a metal chain across the driveway. Also, a "NO TRESPASSERS" sign. More than three decades earlier, a band of foul creatures, Manson's thugs, had swarmed all over this property. It was the last place Lunt ever wanted to be. Yet Sharon's Sharonness lingered here, even here, where she had gasped out her last word. Her "famous last word," which was *"Mother."*

A cool breeze. The fragrance of patchouli. More lightning streaks across the sky. What were these jittery streaks of energy telling Lunt? They did seem to herald something, signs and wonders. Was a dark force, a Great Beast of some sort, approaching? Near the "NO TRESPASSING" sign, a *kaffeeklatsch* of junkies had gathered, some pressing dolls to their chests. These were the Jolly Dolls favored by young girls.

Lunt turned his face to the sky. In time the breeze strengthened to wind, and a dune buggy roared by, its stereo blasting "Star," the Stealers Wheel song that most reminded Lunt of Sharon. The dune buggy almost struck a coyote trotting through the area. Before vanishing from view, the coyote padded up to Lunt and sniffed his left sneaker, which dripped with Bronson's moisturizer Beige Milk. Silence prevailed until the Sharon-masked woman broke it by saying, "Hey, do you know a way out of here?"

"Huh?"

From behind her mask, she sounded as frightened as he felt. "If you can get me out of here, I'll bring you to the desert and show you things that'll *blow* your mind."

"Sorry," said Lunt, "but I've heard that line before. What you just said comes from *Helter Skelter*. It's the book's most inadvertently comical moment. Manson whispered those exact words to some reporter during his trial."

The masked woman clucked her tongue the way Lunt sometimes did. "Why is it so funny?"

"Because that's gotta be the world's least appetizing offer. Even if someone *did* wanna go with Charlie Manson to the desert, even if they *trusted* him—which would be madness!—they'd still have to bust him out of prison, and how easy would *that* be?"

"Whatever," said the masked woman said, disdainful now. "I'm just here to pass along a message, birthday boy. With you turning forty years old soon, my boss wants you to let go of Sharon."

"Let her go?"

"Uh-huh. Let her stay dead. Stop turning a golden chalice into a slop bucket. That's what my boss says. You debase Sharon with your worship. That's why my boss is sending you those Santa Shots. He makes the Amarillo phone calls, too. They're a warning, birthday boy. If you don't let go of Sharon, give her up, leave her in peace, something evil will befall you."

Lunt was scornful of the advice. He said, "Sharon's not like some...some *light switch* that I can just flick on and off! She's my *muse*, my whole *life*. You might as well say, 'Stop breathing!' What could I ever replace her with?"

The wind rose, making the woman's head sway back and forth, and the lips of her mask parted slightly, giving Lunt a glimpse of the woman's teeth, her *real* teeth, which looked as smooth and as white as the Ofotert pillows.

"Take it off," Lunt told her. "Drop your mask, and *then* we'll talk."

"Impossible," the woman said. "That day is done."

"Why?"

"Because this mask has already eaten into my face."

5

WHO IS THE NEW GOD OF FUCK?

(Wednesday)

ON waking in midmorning, Lunt remembered Bronson's regular sign-off during their phones talks: "Sweet dreams, hon—and if not, enjoy your nightmares." Even though Lunt didn't find last night's Mucaquell-fostered nightmare fun, at least the Muke had vanquished his coughing. What's more, the new day was bestowing other blessings:

1. Lunt felt physically refreshed.

2. There was no new manila envelope under his door.

3. A line from the Dorothy Parker book, which he peeked into at a whim, made him laugh: *"Drink and dance and laugh and lie, / love, the reeling midnight through. / For tomorrow we shall die! / (But, alas, we never do.)"*

4. He was able to convey to Bronson in a single, less-than-four-minute voicemail all that he had experienced since they'd last spoken.

5. He was able to sound confident when he swore to Vishwa—in another voicemail—that he would "stop Mandrake's hate campaign," would increase Vishwa's cut of Lunt's profits "to forty percent" (*that ought to hook her good*, he figured), and would recruit more celebrities into joining Benny Pompa as contributors to Lunt's book. Lunt also vowed to "never, ever cause stress" for Vishwa again. With these concessions, how could she not take his Sharon project back onboard?

6. The coffee he brewed tasted better than ever and the shower he luxuriated in, steam coiling around his body, was equally fantastic.

7. The tiny swallow of Mucaquell that Lunt allowed himself on leaving the Ofotert—*Protection in advance*, he told himself—tasted rather good! How had he grown accustomed to the flavor so quickly?

8. As he'd hoped, the swallow gave him a slight high yet managed to still leave him in control. *A sort of functional Floaty P'Toaty*, he told himself.

Outside was a further blessing: glorious weather, with the air smog-less and smelling almost clean. Would the bad heat from Lunt's first day here return? Or was it "gone, baby, gone" like his coughing seemed to be?

In the hotel driveway, Lunt said a bright *"Hola"* to the squat, mustachioed parking attendant who was tapping his right foot rhythmically on the ground. No Baby Son in view; maybe he was getting his clipboard refurbished. A new graffito on the facade of Corpus Co-op—"GET THAT GIRDLE OFF, GIRL!"—amused Lunt. (Another new graffito, the Latin words "VULNERANT OMNES, ULTIMA NECAT" inscribed inside a clock image, made no sense to him.) And as Lunt hurried along the Strip toward Gush, humming a happy song—the inevitable Sharon theme "Star"—he tried to tune up his intuition: Would Jopp be there when he arrived?

No, his intuition answered.

But his intuition had never been much good, so as he stepped into the restaurant, where a bossa nova version of "Georgy Girl" blared, emanations of a certain color worked like a magnet on Lunt's eyes.

His breath caught when he saw her. Today her miniskirt was forest green instead of emerald; her throat was free of chokers, lime-green or otherwise; and her seafoam-green-colored hair was tied into pigtails instead of hanging free. But Jopp's pallor remained quite minty, her hands and cheeks were still dusted with green glitter, she wore the same forest-green Doc Marten knockoffs and Kelly green top, and her mouth looked even more Sharonesque than Lunt remembered.

"Fancy meeting *you* here," he said as he took the seat opposite her, exposing his back to the rest of the dining room.

Smiling in the curious way she had—without parting her Sharon-lips—Jopp pointed her chin at the image of La Tate on Lunt's T-shirt ("WHOLE LOTTA SHARON GOIN' ON!" were the words above Sharon's face). "I see you're crushing on Polanski's wife again," she told Lunt cheerily. "I'm getting jealous!"

Lunt's cheeks went fire-engine red.

"Not *too* jealous, though," she added, twirling a pigtail with her fingers. "I feel pretty connected to Polanski's girl myself."

"You do? Great! So that's something we've got in common."

Playfully, Jopp flicked Lunt's shoulder with a fingernail, leaving behind a sprinkle of green glitter. "Dude," she said with a thoughtful expression, "we've probably got *so much* in common."

Lunt's eyebrows shot up. They were off to the proverbial races!

As he told her all about his Sharonophilia, starting with *The Wrecking Crew* and continuing straight through to the upcoming Tate-World Conference, Lunt kept his posture straight, his paunch sucked in, and his eyes locked on Jopp's lips, her green Sharon-lips. How adorable they looked as she sipped the glass of iced tea she'd already ordered! Those lips were so bewitching that Lunt didn't mind not being at liberty today to scope out the as-many-as-usual beauties all around him. He also paid scant attention to the unopened menu at his table place and barely noticed the frequency with which Jopp's own attention kept drifting away from Lunt, roaming to the entrance of the dining room. The green woman only interrupted his Tate-talk when he went into details about the Sharonfest.

"Amazing, Jeepster. We'll have to go."

"We'll…you mean us?" said Lunt.

"No, duh, some *other* couple." Jopp chuckled, although she still managed to keep her mouth closed, hiding its interior from view. "Of *course*, us!"

Wow. Jubilation! Off to the races, indeed!

Relishing his good fortune, Lunt began to feel aroused, and imagined Jopp's silken lips pressed to his throat, then traveling south. She was delightful, this green woman, delightful! All his recent erotic fantasies of her, they were going to come true! But what if it was more than mere sex? What if he fell in love with her? Was she the one whom he'd wind up with, his lifelong partner? Quite a feat *that* would be, to bag somebody half his age—and with Sharon's mouth, no less. Eat your hearts out, Mandrake and Pandora!

But if we do get together, Lunt began to wonder, *will I be able to persuade her to dye her hair back to a normal color? She could wear a green wedding dress, no problem—I don't want her to change for me—but the hair, at least? Just the hair!* Lunt knew that his father would be happy with any choice Lunt made—any choice who wasn't a man—yet the green hair might nevertheless get Mr. Moreland's goat.

"Hey, what's wrong with my mouth?"

"Huh?"

"You're in a trance, dude, and you're staring at my mouth." Her smile was gone, and her green-mascaraed eyes blazed with anger. "You didn't see my teeth, did you?"

Lunt's own smile faltered. "Your teeth?"

"Forget it."

So she was ashamed of her dental status. While he pondered this matter (should he pursue it with some diplomatic questions, or simply drop it?), a voice from behind his left shoulder said, "Ready to order?"

Lunt swiveled in his chair to find the shag-haired female Jim Morrison he'd bumped into two days ago standing beside him. Her expression was as grim as her voice sounded.

"Cool your jets," Jopp snapped at the woman. "He hasn't even cracked his menu."

The waitress gave the green woman a Mandrake-like scowl, then addressed Lunt, asking what he wanted to drink.

"Scram," Jopp answered for him. "We're not ready yet.

"Well," the waitress told them both, "make hay while the sun shines—you only have this table for another forty minutes."

Which brought out the beast in Jopp. Glaring at the waitress as though she were a three-week-old unrefrigerated salmon filet, the green woman said, "Thanks. Now please haul your Tarot flesh outta here—you're crimping our appetites."

Sticking her tongue out at Jopp in that petutlant kid-fashion of hers, the waitress spun around and stalked off, her tattooed fists balled.

"Okay," said Lunt, laughing, "I've gotta ask. What the hell is 'tarry flesh?'"

"*Tarot* flesh, dude. Her whole body's covered with tattoos of Tarot cards."

"And you know that *how?*"

"She's a stripper at the Corpus Co-op down Sunset." Jopp tilted her chair back and balanced herself by placing her knees against the table's edge. "Her boyfriend's the lame-o drummer in this group that plays The Whisky every week, 'Muscle Memory'— so her stripper name, in honor of him, is 'Muscle *Mammaries.*' Witty, huh?"

"Even better would be '*Misty* Mammaries.'"

Jopp treated Lunt to another closed-mouth smile. "The boyfriend used to be in a band called 'Standard Nipple Works.'

Even worse than his current one. The critic at *Popfart* said their demo tape sounded like ten thousand toilets in Caracas flushing at the same time."

Lunt chuckled. "I can almost hear the din."

"The boyfriend's pretty inked up, too, but instead of Tarot shit, he's covered head to toe with I Ching hexagrams. *So* lame, right? Someone told me the one on his forehead means 'Youthful Folly.'"

"Well," said Lunt, "the couple that gets theme-design tattoos together stays together," but right away he regretted this, because instead of acknowledging the quip, with amusement or otherwise, Jopp once again directed her gaze to the front of Gush, looking past Lunt, apparently searching for someone. Observing her inattention, Lunt turned in his chair to follow her gaze. When he saw no one of importance there, he came back to the green woman and said, "Waiting for someone?"

Her lips formed her cutest closed-mouth smile so far today. It truly was remarkable, how alike her lips were to Sharon's! "Just watching out for the big P," she said.

"P? Oh. Benny." Lunt's eyes sank to his menu. The pop star competition. What a drag. Before Lunt could mention something, anything, else, Jopp asked when he'd first gotten into Benny's music.

"Oh, *way* back," Lunt lied. "College, I guess. You?"

"Me? Are you serious?" She shot him a look that asked if he'd gone daft. "I've been into Memento Morey Amsterdam since, like, *the womb*. My parents were big fans. And when Benny took the lead vocalist slot from Vascular Ted—*usurped* it, he likes to say—then I fucking flipped! You know their song 'Lichtenberg's Flowers'?"

"Lichtenberg?" said Lunt. "The German philosopher? The hunchback?"

"Nah, I don't think so. Different Lichtenberg. Maybe they're cousins? This one was a scientist, or doctor. Worked with lightning."

Too many Lichtenbergs, Lunt thought.

"Dude, how can you not know 'Lichtenberg's Flowers'? It was Benny's first great tune! It's epic—epic!"

"Well," said Lunt, "I love Memento Morey Amsterdam's stuff, and I'm sure I've heard that number"—*Not*, he thought, *if I could've helped it!*—"but I can't place it at the moment. How's it go?"

"Jeepster, fuck, I'm not gonna sing it here. Trust me, you know it. The lyrics are about Benny's lightning wound—his Lichtenberg's Flower."

"What's that?"

"It's this, like, scientific term for the bruise under your skin that happens where you got whacked by a lightning bolt. It's not made up, I Googled it!"

"And Benny really got struck by lightning?"

"Yeah, seven years ago. He talks about it in his interviews. It happened at his ranch in Australia. He calls it his 'Big Reveal.' He's got the flower on his chest. It's never faded, not at all. Sometimes he shows it in photos, or onstage during encores. You haven't seen it? Looks like a fractal, or a tree branch. A detailed red tree branch. Surviving the 'Big Reveal' gave Ben the strength to find himself, to find *his voice*, and then he rose up and took the mic away from Vascular Teddy. Who was the group's *first* singer."

Dog eat dog, mused Lunt. Even in the plastic pop world. *Especially* there!

Blaring on Gush's stereo system now was a bossa nova version of "It's A Small World After All," which made Lunt reflect, not for the first time, that this song, the theme song for the celebrated exhibit in Disneyland, ought to be the national anthem for pedophiles.

"Believe it or not," said Jopp, "getting hit by lightning is something I know something about. It wasn't me it happened to, it was my great-grandfather. My grandma New Leaf witnessed the whole deal. She was just, like, a girl. Thirteen, fourteen, something like that. Her name was still Marsha then, and her dad was playing golf at his country club near Boston. She was a good girl, helping out as his caddie. After a while, though, it starts to rain—thunder, lightning, everything—so Marsha says, 'Come on, Pop, time to go, let's head to the clubhouse.' She didn't like getting wet, my grandma, and she could feel her hair stand out from her head, which put the fear in her. She knew about summer storms." Jopp tilted her chair back again and did her balancing routine. "But her dad said, 'One more swing, Marsha, one more,' and when he raised his golf club to the sky—"

"Oh, no," said Lunt. "Zap?"

"Yeah, one gargantuan zap."

"Did his hair turn white?"

"Hair?" Jopp grinned, her Sharon-mouth remaining diligently shut as always, and she went on twirling one of her green pigtails. "More like his hair *caught fire*, dude. And the lightning bolt, it cut the guy in half. Two smoking pieces, my grandma told me."

"You're joking. In *half*?"

"I don't joke, Jeepster. Nobody in my family does. We're serious people."

"Jesus" was all Lunt could think of to say. Since Jopp didn't take up the conversational slack, he added, "What an awful story..."

"Yup. And what my grandma saw traumatized her so much that she dropped out of school, came out here to California, changed her name to New Leaf, and joined the hippies on their sixties trip."

Lunt was about to ask a follow-up question when a voice above his right shoulder—a female voice, but deeper than the waitress' voice, and snottier—derailed him. The voice said, "That menu *opens*, you know."

Lunt turned his head to find Latreena, the fur-vested hostess, glaring down at him. "I know," he said apologetically, "we're just—"

But Jopp wasn't having it. "Listen here, pepperpot," she cut in, countering Latreena's fierce look with one of her own, "he'll order when he's *ready*."

"You know the deal," the hostess said. "Thirty minutes till your table gets turned over. If you don't order in three minutes—"

Jopp gave Latreena a disgusted three-week-old-salmon look and the hostess spun around and left.

"I'm impressed," Lunt said.

"Listen," said Jopp with sudden conviction, flexing her green-glitter-dusted fingers, "I've got a question for you, okay? An easy one. And it's not whether you've been eating any eggs, even though I still advise those to help you cure your cough."

"Fine. I already know I want a seafood omelette for lunch. Shoot."

Jopp brought her chair down, ending her balancing act, and leaned forward to say, "When can I touch your dick?"

Not the kind of query Lunt expected. Once again, without conscious thought, he straightened his posture and sucked in his paunch. "Uh…"

"I bet I'll like it. I can tell by how a guy talks. So, when?"

Lunt felt his face get hot, and his whole body was instantly coated in sweat. "Touch it?"

"Any problem with that, dude?"

"No!"

"Didn't think so." She shifted in her seat. "With me working you, you'll be the new god of fuck! *My* new god of fuck, anyway."

"Oh." Lunt looked past Jopp, at the aqua wall behind her, and he swallowed, trying to moisten his dry mouth, feeling so aroused that he thought he might suffer a stroke.

"And all's I want in return," the green woman continued, "is for you to invite me to your hotel. To the Ofotert, I mean. Just get me, like, *inside* the place where Benny is. You don't have to introduce us, just get me near him, and I'll suck and fuck you so good that I'll actually increase your dick size. Permanently. *That's* how good I'll be."

Speechless, Lunt managed to nod his head, at first timidly, then less so.

"So invite me over. I can't come there without your say-so, because when I went to the Ofotert last night, some Mexican security goon, the house detective or some shit, got all *stormtrooper* on me."

"That would be Baby Son."

"Whatever. With *your* invite, though, I'm golden."

Bursting into laughter, triumphant laughter, Lunt felt his head swim. It was if he'd just quaffed Mucaquell. He needed a good retort for Jopp now, needed to say something suave, something charming, but all he could come up with was, "I always wanted to be someone's god of fuck!"

"Right on."

"So when—when can we start?"

Sitting back and twirling her pigtail some more, the green woman grinned her lip-compressed grin. "Soon as you like, Jeep."

"Maybe…tonight?"

Jopp blinked twice and said, "Why wait till then? I've got a cozy place in mind, somewhere close to here."

HOW can I talk about Philippe Fouquet? He was French, tall, only a few years older than I was, and—except for Roman, Marty Ransohoff, and, of course, my father—the most self-assured man I'd ever met. Philippe was also devastatingly handsome, like a Greek god, as though he'd been carved from the smoothest, coldest marble. I hate to say this, but Philippe made Richard Beymer and Jack Palance look, well, mortal.

My agent Mr. Gefsky had brought me to lunch at Dan Tana's one day in 1963 when an executive from Twentieth Century Fox strolled up to say hello. Accompanying him was Philippe, who was playing the role of male lead opposite Sandra Dee in a Fox romance entitled Take Her, She's Mine. *Even before we were introduced, I couldn't tug my eyes away from Philippe. I thought, Oh, my stars! I don't know if it was love at first sight, but without a doubt it was lust at first sight, plus fascination. Wowee zowee! His eyes were extraordinary, and his accent was so charming when we made small talk.*

"You are love-a-lee, mademoiselle," he said in parting, with a kiss for my hand, and Mr. Gefsky said, "Sharon, I can hear your heart fluttering from across the table."

He knew I didn't get excited easily. Men were always coming on to me, giving me their business cards, swearing that they were producers. Philippe was different. He called me soon after the lunch at Fox, and we got involved quickly. I felt guilty about Richard, but my relationship with him had started cooling down by then and we'd agreed we could see other people.

My days were still full of acting classes, auditions, and meetings. Philippe was equally busy, finishing and then promoting Take Her, She's Mine. *No matter how exhausted we were, though, we painted the town at* night, going to all the "in" spots on the Sunset Strip. Whenever we could, too, we'd drive out to Palm Springs.

Once the time came for Philippe to meet my parents, I was beside myself with nerves. Thank God our first dinner together turned out okay, although I don't think Philippe liked my parents very much. "Colonel Tate" was slowly coming around to the notion of his daughter being an actress, but his behavior toward me was as distant as ever. Philippe noticed. And Mom posed a bigger problem. Philippe viewed her as a typical "stage mother," overly ambitious for me, and overprotective, to boot. And she was that, it's true—she would even admit it! But what Philippe failed to see was that her ambitions stemmed from love, and her protectiveness was necessary in order to appease my father.

After my death, by the way, Mom spent a decade quietly mourning me, then roused herself to action—and what action! The humble housewife Doris Tate became a lioness, forming a "crime victims' rights" lobbying group, pushing hard for legislation on behalf of those victims, and helping to thwart all the Manson Family killers' attempts at getting parole. My sisters helped Mom a lot. From here in heaven, I've watched them work, proud of how effective they have been.

THE diaper-changing facility at Gush was small and plainly appointed, with a single bare lightbulb overhead, the odor of raspberry air freshener, and an aqua-colored table built at waist-height into the rear wall. As Jopp led Lunt into the room by his sweaty hand and locked the door, his heart was galumphing, his mind and member both aflame. Was this really happening? It was like a dream, a raspberry-fragranced dream!

Without a word, the green woman leaned her back against the table's edge and started fiddling with Lunt's belt buckle. No kissing. For some reason, she didn't initiate any, and Lunt was too nervous to do it himself.

"Wait," he said. "What about the hostess?"

"Who?"

"The woman with the fur vest."

"Latreena? "

Lunt tried to keep his voice down. Like his hands and knees, the voice was quavery. "Yeah. What if she catches us here? We still haven't ordered lunch!" He considered adding, "And isn't this room reserved for people with babies?" but realized before saying it how stupid this would sound.

Jopp, on hearing Lunt's concern, cackled with delight, still working on the belt. "Fuck Latreena, dude."

"Okay."

Okay, indeed. Lunt decided to surrender, to simply give himself over to the pleasure Jopp offered. Besides, it wasn't a felony to misuse a diaper-changing facility, was it? A misdemeanor, maybe, but not a felony! He wanted to make a funny quip along those lines, but had grown too anxious to speak at all.

"You ready?" Jopp said at last, shaking back her pigtails. Lunt's belt was open, his zipper down, and his khaki pants tangled around his thighs. She started playing with the top of his boxer briefs, teasingly tugging on and then releasing the elastic band. "You ready for Joppy?"

Unbelievably, yes, this was happening: right here and now, in semi-public, his body was about to be explored—and by a Sharon-mouth, no less! Before any fingers touched his penis, however, Lunt got a brain wave. A good idea, a bold initiative: he would beat her to the punch! Show her what great lover material he was, give her head before she got to give it to him. And so—surprising both of them—he reached down, stopped her hands from fondling him, placed his hands under her armpits, lifted her bony body into the air—she seemed practically weightless—and set her with a soft *thump* on the changing table, leaving her butt half-on and half-off it. Then he grabbed the cotton miniskirt at Jopp's hips, yanked it up, and looked down.

No underwear whatsoever.

He sucked air in past his teeth.

Her genitalia were obscured almost totally by a cloud of untrimmed pubic hair. *Pubic hair dyed seafoam green.*

"Wow," Jopp said, more breathless than ever as Lunt pushed her knees apart, "you like taking control! You really *are* a god of fuck!"

"Enjoy the show," Lunt said, having found his voice, and his charm power, once more. Gripping the girl's thighs, Lunt sank to his knees and buried his face in her cloud, his tongue already out and doing vigorous licking movements before it reached what the cloud concealed.

How long did it go on for? Four minutes? Five? Maybe longer? He got too lost in the heat of it to track time. Even so, whenever he would cast his mind back to this scene during the coming days and nights, he could summon up some aspects of it.

He remembered, for example, how drenched she was, and just how soft her pudendum-puff felt on his nose and cheeks and chin.

He remembered the taste of her, a taste mixed with the raspberry scent of the room.

He remembered wondering—fancifully at first but then out of true curiosity—whether his tongue would wind up stained green when he was done with her.

He remembered fearing that his actions would bring on a new coughing fit. (Why hadn't he thought to take along his Muca-quell today?)

He remembered looking up to see her ribs shift under the fabric of her miniskirt.

And he remembered the placid look on Jopp's face, how her eyes watched him with what seemed like only mild interest. Sphinx-like, kind of. Ordinarily, this would have worried Lunt—was he failing to please her?—but he could tell by other means that she was turned on. There was her heavy breathing; the occasional gasps and groans; her brusque command at one point to "Go, motherfucker, go"; the forest-green saddle shoes pressing down on his shoulders; her hips grinding her sex into his mouth; the way her tongue kept wetting her lips, those glorious Sharon-lips, but never revealing her teeth; and the way she plunged her hands into his hair, pulling on it and messing up his Sebring style (not that he minded).

While Lunt's tongue lapped away at Jopp, his throat humming with pleasure, he felt like he could devour her whole, swallow her down in one gulp. He wasn't sure but certainly hoped that he had one of his Instigator condoms in his wallet. After several minutes, he reached into his boxer briefs so he could stroke himself. "Self-interference" at its most frenzied! He did this in spite of the pain in his knees from the hard faux-marble floor, and in spite of some lower-back pain from the cramped position in which he kneeled. If he were younger, his back would not be such a problem. Damn this turning forty! But Lunt's tongue and jaw ached, too, which would have been the case, he knew, at *any* age.

On went the proverbial show.

Then, abruptly, it stopped. It stopped when, from the corner of his eye, Lunt glimpsed a used diaper near his left shin. The diaper, obviously fallen from the metallic trash bin beside it, overflowed with baby shit. A small heap of refulgent dark-brown shit. Even though the diaper didn't smell bad, or smell at all (the room-wide raspberry scent took care of that), the sight of it disgusted Lunt. So much so that it made him gag, twice, and threatened to wilt his hard-on.

"What's wrong?" Jopp asked, her hips still thrusting. "Is it *my* fault?"

"Huh?" Lunt's eyes leapt to hers from the diaper. "Oh, no, no, it's nothing."

"Then back to work you go."

After stretching his jaw a bit and running his hand through his hair to get it right, Lunt obeyed, resuming the process of oral sex while striving to block the soiled diaper from his thoughts. He would have physically nudged the vile thing farther from him but he didn't want to touch it in any way. *Forget it's there*, he counseled himself—just as the green woman spoke again, saying, "Know who you are now? In my fantasy, I mean. Know who I'm imagining is eating me?"

"Ugh?" Again Lunt suspended his oral labors. "*Me*, I assumed…"

"No, it's someone else. Doesn't everyone pretend the person they're with is someone else?"

Lunt sighed, not hiding his annoyance. He knew who Jopp was thinking of: Benny Pompa. Still, he wouldn't give her the satisfaction of saying it, and offered "George W. Bush?" instead.

"Ha!" She arched her torso. "No, I'm thinking about your girl."

"My *girl?*" Making sure no part of himself came in contact with the diaper, Lunt changed his position so that his back and knees would bother him less. Then he peered up into Jopp's face. The sheen of sweat there gave it a lambent glow, and the pubic puff he needed to look past made it seem as though she wore a seafoam-green beard. "*What* girl?" he said.

"*Duh.*" Jopp wagged a mock-admonitory, glitter-dusted finger at him. "Sharon Tate! I'm picturing *her* face mashing around there on my pootchka!"

Lunt settled back, crossing his legs and resting his rump on the floor. Though still sexually revved up, he was happy to take a break, to rub his jaw and to relax his knees and back and tongue. "So you're pretending that I'm *Sharon?*"

"Yeah, I think she's hot. Except I'm coming at her from a different angle than you are."

"Different?" He savored Jopp's aftertaste in his mouth. "What's that supposed to mean?"

"I'm into 'Charles Is Man's Son.'"

"Charles *what?*"

"Dude, I know you've heard of Charlie."

"Charlie…"

"Yeah!"

"Charlie *Manson?*"

"Bingo! I'm part of The Family, dude." She frowned. "Why doesn't anybody realize we're still around? I've been a member since, like, *the womb.* I thought you might've guessed by now."

Lunt's entire body stiffened.

"Third generation, Jeepster. My grandma, New Leaf, was one of Charlie's first wives up in Oakland, and now *I'm* one—a 'BOC,' which means 'Bride of Charles.' I write him a letter every day, straight to his jail cell in Corcoran. You know, Corcoran State Prison."

Lunt gaped at her, incapable of speech, until he finally began to laugh. "You're kidding me. You're—"

"Dude, we're serious people, we never kid! My Family is *for real.* Besides, why would I make jokes about Charlie? He's the only one of us who's allowed to joke. Trust me, though, he's hilarious! Matter of fact, Charlie's possessed by Anansi, the African trickster god. That's what he always says: '*I am the spider god Anansi!*' You ever read that guy Joseph Campbell? He was on our reading list last year. Charlie sends us a book list every month, and he's never made a bad choice. Oprah's Book Club ain't got *nothin'* on my man!"

"Manson?" Lunt said weakly. He stared at her in disbelief, not even noticing her exposed genitals anymore. "You—you like Manson?"

"Dude, you *deaf*? I'm fucking *married* to him! Spiritually, at least. But that's the best way to be married. And I would never be a bigamist like Benny is. Even though screwing Ben wouldn't be cheating on my husband, because Charlie says it's only cheating if it's anal."

Time juddered and jumped track. Lunt's mouth sagged open, fully open, and remained that way even after some saliva dribbled down his chin.

"Hey," said Jopp, "head's up, Jeepster, you're *drooling*."

The Sharonophile felt as though a fissure had opened in the floor beneath him and he was tumbling down. Meanwhile, high above him, the green woman smiled. And *this* time, for some reason, she actually parted her Sharon-lips, opening those lips wide enough for Lunt to view her teeth. Specifically the upper row of teeth, which were crooked and, worse, horribly discolored. Stained. Rotted. *Rotten.* And they weren't yellow, these teeth, or green like the rest of her, but brown. A rich dark chocolate hue. The same hue, or nearly, as the shit inside that diaper.

"Do I turn you on *this* much," Jopp said, cracking wise at Lunt's expense, "or are you just a chronic drooler? Eating eggs might help *that*, too!"

6

THIS PLACE WORSHIPS DEATH

(Wednesday, later)

DEAR Mr. Trueax,

This is very important. It now seems likely that an unwanted individual or individuals will attempt to harm me here during the balance of my stay at the Hotel Ofotert. I am referring specifically to a young woman with green hair and green clothing whose name (though she might not identify herself as such) is Jopp.

Drops of sweat fell from Lunt's forehead onto the letter. Lifting his elbows from their place on the mahogany reception desk, he stopped writing and turned to see if *she* was sneaking up the crimson-colored central stairway. Had she followed him here from Gush? Evidently not, praise Sharon. Not *yet*, anyway. No Mandrake in the lobby, either.

The past fifteen minutes had been a blur: Lunt barrelling out of the diaper-changing room, out of the restaurant, and down the sidewalk of the Strip. Shaking with terror, he ran as fast as his poorly exercised nearly-middle-aged legs would carry him, his blood gone cold but pumping, jumping, pounding through his throat.

At intervals he'd worked up some real speed, tearing along as though Satan was at his heels, and in spite of the mild weather, Lunt sweated through his T-shirt in no time. He got winded quickly, too, his chest imploding, yet he didn't dare stop, not even for the "DO NOT WALK" lights, and his head kept swivelling around to cast frightened looks behind him, making sure that Jopp was not in pursuit, running him to ground.

The green woman wasn't just *pretending* to be a Manson fan, she meant business—Lunt didn't doubt that. He recognized it in her face. He recognized it in her voice. That Sharon-mouth of hers, it was actually a cave of death. How unlucky could he get? Millions of citizens in the county of Los Angeles, literally millions, and he'd met one of *Manson's* people. A rabid disciple! Moreover, he'd not just met her but developed a crush on her. And put his mouth on her sex organs.

Her, a Manson *bride*!

On one hand (so Lunt reasoned as he ran past the shuttered-by-day Corpus Co-op), he'd been wise to flee from Jopp, because Manson and his ilk probably despised Sharon-lovers. They despised Sharonophiles because the Mansonophiles assumed, and rightly so, that the Sharonophiles hated *them*. On the other hand (and here was a thought that gave Lunt pause) did his Sharonophilia really offend Jopp? It wasn't as if he was in love with, say, Vincent Bugliosi, the prosecutor who'd put Manson behind bars and then wrote *Helter Skelter* about it. And since the Family had never targeted Bugliosi, they probably wouldn't care about Lunt. To them he was just a small fry. So maybe he hadn't needed to run from Jopp, after all. Maybe, in fact, she'd found his running away from her rude, and now she would lash out at him not for his Sharon-love but for his rudeness!

Somewhere up ahead of Lunt, a car backfired, loud as a bomb, and it stopped him in his tracks. *Was* it a bomb? Was this the start of a full-scale West Coast terrorist attack? Or, worse, the start of Helter Skelter?

After a moment, Lunt resumed his crazed dash to the Ofotert.

And now, recovering his wits in the apparent refuge of the lobby, he wiped the sweat from his forehead and forced a smile for the clerk who faced him from across the desk. She was the young woman with cropped hair and penciled-in eyebrows, the one whose name tag read, "SU WING SCHMIDT." Ms. Schmidt, her face as hard as wood, did not return Lunt's smile. Rather, she yawned without covering her mouth. Irked by this, Lunt looked down again at the cream-colored sheet of stationary on the desk and continued writing.

Mr. Trueax, please know that this is no laughing matter—Jopp and her confederates are affiliated with the murderer Charles Manson. The current situation is probably not related to those phone calls and strange packages I've written about earlier, yet it's far more perilous. Perhaps life-threatening! *Accordingly, please alert me to any attempt by Jopp, or anyone else, to make contact with me in the hotel even if it is merely by telephone. And please ensure that all of your employees—garage attendants, housekeepers, switchboard operators, and security guards, especially Baby Son—are aware of my request.*

Just as Lunt was signing the letter, his BlackBerry trilled. He checked the grimy plastic screen.

"JOPP."

Jopp, calling him!

"Oh, my God," Lunt said, fresh fear rippling up and down his spine, making him shudder. He let the call go to voicemail, asking himself, *Should I erase her number from my phone? No, because then I won't know that it's Jopp the next time she calls. What's more, the police won't be able to trace her if I turn up slaughtered, the latest Manson Family victim. So should I change my own number? If she keeps calling me, I'll have to!*

Pressing his BlackBerry firmly to his ear, Lunt listened to his new voicemail.

"Hey, Jeepster, I'm still here at Gush if you want to come back. You owe me an orgasm, okay? I guess we owe each other. And sorry if I gave you the heebie-jeebies. I should've mentioned my marriage sooner. Us Manson-ites and you Sharon Tate-ites don't exactly mix well, right? We're not most people's idea of a good fit. But that doesn't *have* to be the case! Don't believe what you read, dude—the Family never laid a *finger* on your girl. It was someone else who killed her, not us. I'll explain the whole deal when I see you. Anyway, it's high time we mended fences and got Charlie's energy and Sharon Tate's energy together. Won't that be cool?"

"Preposterous," Lunt couldn't help but say aloud. How stupid this green woman was! Of course the Manson Family killed Sharon! Claiming Manson didn't kill her was like denying the Holocaust, or saying that al-Qaeda were secular peaceniks! Bringing Manson and Sharon "together" was the *last* thing any Sharon-lover would want. Manson probably craved the moral absolution that such togetherness would grant him. But why should Manson get anything he craved? He'd slaughtered Lunt's darling!

"Anyway, I gotta admit," Jopp's message went on, "I'm kinda digging on you, dude. I like your haircut—it's, like, *so* sixties-sexy. Plus, I dig that you're a Pompa person. Let's hang out at the Ofotert tonight—maybe we can groove with Benny, Saff, and Trudi. Invite me over! I'll take you up on your offer to host me in NYC, too—we'll really make it *Fun* City. Call me back, 'kay? We're just getting started, Jeepster!"

Lunt clucked his tongue at his BlackBerry. The one good element of the message was that Jopp wasn't furious at him for running out on her. Meaning she wouldn't pose a threat, after all. Or was she just playing nice in order to ensnare him?

His first impulse was to erase the message, to remove the corrupting stain of Jopp's voice from his gadget. Yet he knew he might need to preserve it, with its citation of "Charlie" Manson, if she and her Family began tormenting Lunt. Besides, as much as he hated to admit it, he felt pleased by Jopp's finding favor with his haircut—"sixties-sexy" being exactly what he'd been shooting for with his tonsorial tribute to Jay Sebring. In addition, he couldn't help but feel flattered that Jopp was "digging on him." So she'd been

SET THE CONTROLS FOR THE HEART OF SHARON TATE

free for his taking all along, low-hanging fruit! And what delicious fruit she was, notwithstanding her evilness. A pity he couldn't have her. Or could he? If they had sex, nothing more, would it matter that she was a Mansonophile?

Yes, Lunt answered himself, *it* would *matter—big-time*! How could he think otherwise? Touching, much less fornicating with, a Manson-ite, would get him hounded out of the Sharonophile community. Perfidy, plain and simple!

"Please give this to Mr. Trueax as soon as he gets back," Lunt told Ms. Schmidt, pushing the letter across the front desk to her, unaware that Trueax was presently napping in his office. Lunt likewise gave Schmidt the thin black pen she'd loaned him. Her sole response, while accepting both pen and letter, was to belch without covering her mouth or excusing herself. Lunt stared at her, first with surprise and then with indignation. What was next, her unapologetically *farting* at him? Lifting a leg and shooting one his way? What kind of hotel *was* this? Then again, what kind of *galaxy* was it where one moment you're being intimate with a tasty young woman and the next you're running for your life?

"Very *delicate* of you," Lunt told Schmidt in a tone he made sure to saturate with sarcasm. Without waiting for an answer, he turned and mounted the staircase to the fourth floor. No elevator— he couldn't risk being trapped there if it went down instead of up, opened on street level, and allowed Jopp to step inside.

During his ascent on foot, Lunt paused at the third floor, his hand resting on the banister in order to listen for anyone pursuing him up the stairs. Nothing but the murmur of invisible Mexicana housekeepers and the squeak of their carts. Even so, he ran the last part of the way, fancifully imagining Manson himself right on his heels. Only after Lunt had inserted his key in the lock of 47 and started to open the door did he relax. Safety at last! He would

GARY LIPPMAN

change his T-shirt, which smelled of body odor, then call Bronson, who would probably scold him for chasing quasi-jailbait, saying, "Serves you right!" He would agree with her, then draw a hot bath, read some Dorothy Parker, and guzzle enough Mucaquell to bring down an elephant. After what he'd been through during the past hour, a long, restorative sleep was necessary.

As it turned out, Lunt would have to wait for all of that. This was because, on entering his suite, he found another package deposited on the butterscotch-hued carpet inside the doorway. The fifth and most harrowing package yet. The message on the envelope read, "A LONG TIME AGO, BEING CRAZY MEANT SOMETHING, BUT NOWADAYS, EVERYBODY'S CRAZY." What most shook up Lunt was the photograph inside the envelope. His intuition had warned him that the photo would be different than the Santa Shots, and this time his intuition was correct.

Lunt recognized the image, a color promo shot from when Sharon had portrayed the surfer-goddess "Malibu" in the Tony Curtis movie *Don't Make Waves*. The photo showed Sharon's figure to great advantage. Lunt's collection of Sharonabilia included three copies of it. But on seeing *this* copy—what had been done to it—Lunt gave a little cry and dropped his silver letter opener, the scimitar-shaped birthday gift from his mother. It struck his left sneaker with a relatively painless *bonk*.

Over each part of Sharon's body where Manson's monsters had stabbed her—stomach, breasts, heart, back, lungs, cheek, arms—some fiend had Magic Markered bright red "X's."

AFTER his mother's death, Lunt felt too guilty to leave behind his paralyzed father, despite the round-the-clock home nursing care, and so the Sharonophile said goodbye to Los Angeles (temporarily, he vowed), settled into his old home in Sulphurdale, and took a job as a local realtor. Before long, his Sharon books and videocassettes and photographs and mementos spread like kudzu from his bedroom shrine to fill the whole house. This did not displease Mr. Moreland—"You've finally blossomed," he told Lunt with tears in his eyes—but it sometimes taxed the patience of Jah Victor and the rest of the nursing staff, who had to work around the mess.

While living at home, Lunt began to write about Sharon, publishing articles in Sharon-oriented journals, especially that slick bible of Tate-World, *Sharing Sharon*. He mingled gladly with other Sharonophiles, too, but because these S-philes were distributed across the globe, Lunt's contact with them was usually at Tate-World Conferences or via phone calls, postcards, letters, and emails. Also, he used the vacation time from his work at the realty agency to visit Sharon-oriented sites around the world.

Lunt's first international voyage was to Argentina. An elderly film scholar who specialized in 1960s Hollywood had lured Lunt to Buenos Aires with the promise to, as the old man put it, "give you the big surprises about *la linda* Sharon." Sadly, Lunt's journey was star-crossed from the get-go. On arrival, he learned that a case of cholera had claimed the old scholar's life. And after spending a few days sightseeing in Buenos Aires, which was sweating through a heat wave, Lunt wasn't feeling so healthy himself.

The onset of some intense stomach ailment left Lunt writhing in his small room in the noisy Hotel Nebraska with all the symptons of, well, cholera. Not that it could actually be cholera, or so Lunt reassured himself: he'd never even gotten to meet with the film scholar. During the next four days in BA, however, Lunt lay naked and self-soiled on his damp, narrow bed, gazing dully at the brown-papered walls, reading the ink off the one book he'd brought along (*In Sharon Tate There Is No East or West* by Ingrid XZ) and listening to the one cassette tape he'd brought with him (The Doors' *The Soft Parade*).

After his tape player broke down, Lunt switched on the radio in the room, just in time to hear about a city-wide cholera alert. Now he really got writhing. To think that he'd flown all the way down here at great expense only to contract a case of cholera! His ailment turned out to be nothing more than a mundane gastric virus, but Lunt didn't discover this fact until days later, so while he suffered, hugging himself, ravaged by a breakbone-style fever, he prayed to Sharon's spirit to save him, and what he got was not salvation—not immediate salvation, anyway—but a roommate.

"*Konichiwa*," said the portly Japanese man with a prodigiously pimpled forehead who stepped into Lunt's room, a dented gray suitcase in each hand.

Rooms at the Hotel Nebraska were in short supply, it so happened, hence the management had sent a new guest to occupy the second single bed in Lunt's room. (Needless to say, had he not been so ill, Lunt would have complained about such managerial presumptiveness.)

At first the newcomer seemed confused by the sweaty, groaning, naked stranger in his new habitation, but he nodded politely to Lunt and repeated his native-tongue greeting. Intending to respond, Lunt lifted his head, focused his eyes on the new arrival—and promptly vomited all over himself.

In spite of his illness, Lunt grew to accept having a roommate. He'd felt lonely in his plight, and the only other human beings that he'd seen were the gum-snapping hotel maids and some giggling Norwegian schoolgirls who gawked at him from their window across the courtyard. *Perhaps*, he said to himself, *a sweaty, naked, American man is a sight they aren't familiar with from their previous school trips.*

Quickly Lunt and his roommate fell into a schedule of sorts. Each morning when the roommate got up and went forth to sightsee in Buenos Aires, he said a polite *"Sayonara"* to Lunt, and each evening when he returned he said *"Konichiwa,"* and when the roommate finally checked out of Hotel Nebraska, those dented gray suitcases in tow, he bade Lunt a polite farewell. Since he spoke no English and Lunt spoke no Japanese, Lunt felt sorry that he couldn't provide his pimple-foreheaded roommate with an explanation as to why he'd spent the last four days naked, sweaty, groaning, and, on occasion, dramatically puking.

What did he think of me? Lunt wondered after his roommate was gone. *Does he now believe that all Americans behave this way? Will he tell tales about me to future colleagues at business dinners to get a laugh? Or did he realize how ill I've been and even fear it was contagious, yet stoically—quite Japanesely—endure the fear?*

DOWN in the driveway, Lunt had no trouble finding whom he sought. As always, the tall Latino house detective had dressed well, held a clipboard, and smelled of Brut. Keeping a cautious eye trained on the driveway's entrance lest Jopp suddenly appear, Lunt showed Baby Son the latest package he'd received and summed up his situation, describing the green woman and emphasizing her nexus to Manson. As Lunt spoke, waving around the foul new envelope for emphasis, Baby Son listened patiently. He asked no questions, but sometimes his precisely shaved goatee shifted on his mocha-shaded, sparsely freckled face. When Lunt was done, Baby Son said he'd get to work on those packages and calls, his chin rising sharply on the last word of each sentence.

"Great," said Lunt. He took a twenty-dollar bill from his wallet and let the breeze give it a flutter. "For you."

The moment Baby Son registered the denomination, he reached for it. But Lunt moved his hand away, which left the security guard clutching at empty sunshine.

"Not yet, man. Before I give you this, and maybe many more to come, I want your sworn oath you'll help me. Help investigate my problems and protect me from intruders."

Baby Son's goatee shifted again, forming a polite smile. "You have my oath, sir."

"Good." To reinforce Baby Son's sincerity, Lunt gave him a second twenty along with the first. "And while I'm at it," he said, "I still want to change my room. From Forty-Seven to Fifty-Six."

The sorrowfulness that Lunt had previously glimpsed in Baby Son's face returned. "That's not going to happen, sir," Baby Son said. "No matter how generous you are."

Riding the clanging, metal grille elevator upstairs, Lunt re-minded himself that he was due to conduct an interview tonight, to speak about Sharon with Mrs. Kruikshank. Enlivened by the prospect, thinking how helpful it might be to his book—maybe he could get her to write something, too!—he heard the BlackBerry trilling in his front pocket. He fished it out and gave it a look. Not a call but a text message—and the name on the screen terrified him.

"Why no callback, Jeepster? Starting to think I scared you off. My teeth might not be white, but I'm no vampire! (I suck, but don't bite.) Invite me over, pretty please?"

This is not *good,* Lunt told himself as he stepped onto the fourth floor. *She won't rest till I'm caught in her web!*

Should he write her back, say, "Sorry, not interested," something congenial but firmly final? Eventually she'd get the message. But what a pity he couldn't sleep with her, couldn't taste that Sharon-mouth just once…! Despite her Mansonophilia, wasn't there a way of working it out?

No, positively not!

How could I live with myself if I crossed over to the dark side? Lunt thought. *Even if I could abide it, I might never get free of her. When I try to break up, she could turn spiteful and go after me with the weight of her Family behind her!*

Back in his suite, after throwing the dead bolt on his door, Lunt quaffed down a strong shot of Mucaquell. It tasted superb, a licorice delight. How had he ever found the taste of it unpleasant? He smeared some of Bronson's Beige Milk moisturizer on his face, then left an excited voicemail for his friend ("So much shit to tell you!") as well as a miffed voicemail for Mr. Trueax ("I've gotten *another* package, and it's ten times worse than the rest!").

While he left these messages, Lunt stood at his window. Pressing down one of the wooden Venetian blind slats gave him a view of

Seething Lane, where the daylight haze was softening, beginning the slide to dusk. Did anyone really live in the homes climbing those hills? Were the houses even real, or just optical illusions? Was Jopp crouched behind a bush out there, spying on Lunt? What trap was she baiting for him? What if she and her confederates, dressed in catsuits, planned to scale the walls of the hotel come nightfall, break into his suite, and do a Manson-style "creepy-crawly?"

Madness. Lunt forced himself to reject all those thoughts. No, he wouldn't be like Vishwa, would not let his fear carry him off, would not let it swallow him like the whale did Jonah, would not suffer a breakdown. The chances were, he had nothing to worry about. And in the bowl of sky above, Lunt caught sight of a hawk, perhaps the one from the other evening. Certainly the brownish stripes, rounded head, and narrow red tail looked familiar. Again the hawk traced lazy circles through the sky, lifted sometimes by gusts of wind, cruising about as if such an excursion was just for kicks, not hunting. Would Lunt be lucky enough to see the predator spot prey and bear down on it? Or was dinner, a live snake or something, already clutched in its talons?

Most of my life, he thought, *I've been like a hawk myself, scrounging through the world for any trace of Sharon.*

When the hawk plunged suddenly into a silver cloud, Lunt remembered the cat burglar who'd died at the Ofotert. Had this hapless woman been one of Manson's people? Had she been searching for Lunt and entered the wrong suite by mistake? Lunt tried to picture the female burglar in free fall, dropping alongside the hotel's facade. A broken drainpipe had sealed her doom, but no one had been present to witness how the burglar, unlike a hawk, failed to fly. Or how the ground had soared up to crush her before she'd received the gift of flight.

Soon the hawk was gone. Lunt gave the sky a final look. Above the highest hilltop homes was the faint outline of a moon. A pale-yellow moon, not full but getting there. Did this moon feed on our souls, as Sharon's favorite guru Gurdjieff claimed? Nonsense, of course—more madness. Lunt yawned. He felt unsteady on his feet. The Mucaquell was kicking in faster than ever. Wonderful! Bring on the slumber. He deserved it. But when would he do that interview with Mrs. Kruikshank? Not tonight, no way—he felt too whipped, too encased already in Muke-Jell-O, to speak with anyone. The interview could wait until tomorrow.

Lunt flipped on the television set, then washed his hands, making sure no trace of Beige Milk was on them. And just before he tumbled into bed, he guzzled some more cough syrup, finishing the chocolate-colored, blue-labeled bottle. Oblivion is what he wanted, temporary oblivion, and very swiftly he got it, floating off, going Floaty P'Toaty once again here in his lovely *sanctum sanctorum*, where the latest Dreamland sojourn was to the Daisy, one of Sharon's nightlife haunts in Hollywood.

The scene was sixties-era Babylonian splendor. Cigarettes burned, lightning flashed, and fog, not vampire movie-fog but psychedelic fog, drifted between the nightclub's tables. Every surface in the place was powdered with green sparkle. On the dance floor, which dominated the whole space, purple-velvet-waistcoated boys jerked their bodies in sync with the movements of long-haired girls in paisley-patterned microskirts. Here were the denizens of the "swinging world" La Tate once spoke of, that world whose cultural ruling class she belonged to.

"This is *my* scene, and it freaks me *out!*" someone bellowed.

Lunt, seated cross-legged at the center of the dance floor, understood the sentiment. "What a gas," he whispered to the people swirling around him. "So fucking far-out…"

Unfortunately, no one paid attention to him. Also irking him was the massive red hot-air balloon hovering overhead. Why, once it touched down, didn't everybody scatter? And why did the woman who emerged from the green rattan basket wear a Bubble Wrap Sharon Tate mask?

She waddled over to Lunt, the hem of her butterscotch-colored robe swishing along the glistening black marble dance floor. He recognized the waddle—it was how his mother used to walk. When she put her lips to Lunt's ear, her breath tickled the bushy hairs inside it and felt hot on his skin, like a furnace with its scorched iron door left open.

"Stop," said Lunt.

"Then *you* stop," the masked woman replied. Her voice sounded ancient, a crone's croak. "Let Sharon Fate go. When you were younger, decades still from turning forty, I warned you, didn't I? You debase her with your love. If you don't stop, you'll die a hard death."

Lunt struggled to his feet. "Who the fuck are you to talk like this?"

The masked crone hooted at the question, which wafted more hot breath into his face. "I'm your mother," she said. "Your gone-too-soon, long-gone mom. Call me Mother Fist. But I'm your sister's mother, too."

"I don't have a sister, I'm an only child!"

"So you say. But you forget your sister Sharon." She raised a gnarled finger to her mask and popped a single bubble with it. "I gave birth to Sharon Fate before I bore you. *Twenty years* before I bore you. Forty-three and sixty-three—do the math. You're siblings, Lunt."

"My God, we *are*?"

"So all your panting after Sharon, it's incestuous. And in this discotheque, that crime is punishable by death!"

Mother Fist's mask glowed like a lightbulb. Light poured out of it, and gradually a ringing sound, a bell, broke into Lunt's dream. Rising from the depths, he saw where he was, in Suite 47, and focused his eyes on the shiny black phone on his nightstand. The hotel landline, calling insistently to him. He shook his head to clear it and then glanced, frightened, at the carpet by his door. No new package. Praise Sharon! Narrow bars of sunshine streamed through the closed Venetian blinds. The bedside clock read 7:09. Lunt yawned, stretched, wished he could sleep more. He needed to sleep so much. But at the sound of another ring, which sang above the sound of the droning TV, he shoulder-rolled and grabbed the phone.

"Mr. Moreland? Randy Trueax here." The voice sounded a bit thick from (unbeknownst to Lunt) his illegal-drug-of-choice Plonk. "I received your messages, sir, and I apologize for those letters you've been—"

"They're not *letters*," Lunt hissed, trying to control his indignation. "Letters would make more sense. What I've been getting are photos, *upsetting* photos, with vile quotations. And don't forget those annoying phony phone calls!"

After Lunt ran down his recent woes, including the Jopp matter, he asked Trueax, "Aren't there cameras in the hallways here? You know, surveillance videos. They could catch whoever's leaving the envelopes. Or whoever might try to break into my suite."

"I'm sorry, no cameras," Trueax said. "It's part of our privacy policy. But we'll keep you safe, I assure you."

"I don't know how you *can* without cameras. And if you ask *me*, watching the guy in Suite Twenty-Three will really pay off. The guy there, Melek Randang, is—"

"We will investigate everything thoroughly, Mr. Moreland."

"Of course, if you want to make this trouble up to me, you can just shift the people in Sharon Tate's old suite somewhere else and move *me* there."

"Suite Fifty-Six?" At the aluminum desk in his office, the hotel manager's left eye twitched. "That's still not possible. Is there anything else we can do for you, Mr. Moreland?"

"No, that's—oh, wait. Yes, yes, there *is*. Cough syrup."

"Sorry?"

"I need more cough syrup. I've got this bad cough, and I've run out of my medicine. With the Tate-World Conference coming up, I can't risk the cough co—" He meant to say, "coming back" but went with "getting worse" instead. "Getting worse" sounded better. Much better. "I don't want to infect my fellow Sharonophiles. *Or* the other guests here. And with that girl Jopp on my trail, I don't dare step outside and buy the stuff myself. Why take the risk?"

"I—I understand. So how can we—?"

"Simple. Deliver me the medicine. With all the trouble I've suffered here, it's the least you can do. What I need is called Mucaquell. Don't worry, it's over-the-counter, no prescription needed. You can get it from Limsky's Pharmacy and put it on my bill."

"We can certainly do that," said Trueax, fiddling with a button on his coat sleeve. "Any brand of cold medicine will do if this one's not available?"

"No, it has to be Mucaquell. The cough syrup. '*Muke, do yer stuff*'—that's how the ads go. Your night clerk Mrs. Kruikshank, she's the one who sold me on it."

"Oh. Yes. We—we'll have a bottle sent up right away, Mr. Moreland."

Lunt drew a big breath and burrowed deeper into his wonderful white bed. He was too weary to pull his clothes off. Had he taken too much Muke? Could someone overdose on it? No, the only foreseeable danger would be if you mixed such things with alcohol, such as the complimentary still-unopened bottle of Dom Perignon on his writing table.

"You know what?" Lunt spoke up again. "Make it two."

"Two what?"

"Two more bottles. Just in case, in case this cough doesn't budge."

Trueax sniffed. "I see. Well, we wish you a speedy recovery."

No sooner had Lunt put down the room phone than his BlackBerry began to trill. He scrutinized its grimy screen, then answered with, "Bronnie, you won't *believe* the shit going on here."

"Yeah, well, hang onto your hat, pal, 'cause I've got a surprise for you, too."

Lunt's friend sounded anxious. Problems at her job? Some other distress? Lunt decided that he would listen to five minutes worth of her woes, spend another minute proffering his sympathy, then end the call and go to sleep. And later on, reinvigorated, he would rise and write his Sharon memoir like a demon.

"I've been trying to reach you, like, forever," Bronson said. Her concern, as it happened, was not about herself but Lunt. She wanted to know if he'd gotten any more mysterious packages.

"A couple, I think, since we talked last. It's unbelievable here, like a whirlwind! The most recent one came today, while I was at lunch. And what a lunch—that green-colored girl I mentioned, she's a fucking Mans—"

Bronson cut him off, asking, "Were there stickers on the new things? Stickers with messages? Because those stickers, the quotes written on them—I had a *feeling* about the last one you mentioned. An intuition. It sounded, like, *familiar*, so I did some research, and—"

"And what?" Lunt yawned, not concealing the sound at all, and cradled the phone between his chin and neck. "What'd you find?"

"Honey, they're statements made by *Manson*! On those stickers, it's all stuff that *he* said in the past!"

WHILE *Philippe and I fell deeper in love, my hard work began to pay off. I'd lost some self-confidence thanks to that* Whistle Stop *debacle, but I got it back with, of all things, a talking horse. In the autumn of '63, I filmed two episodes of the TV comedy* Mr. Ed. *In the first, I played a medieval maiden in a fantasy sequence, and in the second, I was a telephone operator whom the lonely horse rings up to chat with. In both parts, I worked in a black wig and got no billing. Both of these conditions were dictated by Ransohoff.*

"I don't mind the wig," I told him, "but can't I at least see my name on the screen?"

He shook his head, saying, "I'm sorry, Sharon, but I don't want you known out there, or even recognized, until you've paid your dues and gained the chops to make a splash."

As I said to friends at the time, I couldn't even fart unless Ransohoff said it was okay. A joke, sure, but I was truly feeling frustrated. "Miss Anonymous" is what I called myself whenever I heard about a big audition and Ransohoff refused to send me out on it. There was no arguing with him, either. Philippe, Mom, Dad—none of us could get anywhere with Ransohoff.

It started to feel stifling, being under Ransohoff's thumb to this extent, but by now I'd come to recognize something crucial: even though my looks had gotten me this far, they wouldn't get me all the way to the top. Only talent would make me a successful actress in Hollywood—and only talent would make me a good one. I wanted to be an American Catherine Deneuve because she played beautiful, sensitive, deep parts with lots of intelligence behind them. So I welcomed it when Ransohoff toughened up my daily schedule, increasing my time with all the coaches (voice, speech, dance, and film performance), not to mention the gym trainers and horseback-riding instructors.

(Contrary to what some later press releases said, I took no fighting lessons at this time. Those came later, when I trained for a kung fu scene in The Wrecking Crew with a wonderful young Chinese man who became my friend. Like me, he died young. His name was Bruce Lee.)

My nights got busier as well, with scripts to read, lines to memorize, and lessons to practice. Philippe began accusing me of ignoring him.

"Philippe," I'd say, "I love you just as much as ever, but I can't slow down now. Besides, I'm under contract!"

He'd shrug and finally grumble, "I give up," but his complaints were always worse the next time.

I made another unbilled and dark-wigged TV appearane, this time on The Beverly Hillbillies, and it didn't go over well. My damned nerves again! Once the director shouted "Action," all the lines I'd memorized just dribbled out of my head. Still, with every setback I felt more determined, and if you ask people who knew me in those days, most would say that I was well-liked and respected as a serious young professional, quick with a smile and a joke and a good word for everyone. Unlike most girls in Hollywood, I never bad-mouthed anyone. Perhaps I trusted people too much!

Life really began to look up when I got called back to The Beverly Hillbillies. I still had to wear a black wig, but in the credits beside the name of "Janet Trejo," a bank secretary in thirteen episodes—not one or two but thirteen!—was the first national appearance of "Sharon Tate."

AS Lunt brewed a pot of coffee in his kitchenette, sleepy but too freaked-out by Bronson's news to hit the hay just yet—*All those stickers on the envelopes bore Manson quotes!*—he filled in his friend on his recent travails: Mandrake's plot to undo Lunt's Sharon book, Jopp's unexpectedly sinister affiliation, and the new packages Lunt had received.

"The funny thing is," he concluded, "Mandrake didn't seem to know what I meant when I mentioned the Santa Shots."

"At this point," said Bronson, "who *else* could the bad guy be? Mandrake knows you're hitting a home run, writing a *meisterwerk*, and he can't bear it, so he's mucking you up by every means he can think of. Even with Manson-themed stickers and gruesome mailings."

"Wait a minute! What if it's *not* Mandrake but that green woman?"

"Behind the Santa Shots?"

"*Yes*! Why didn't I think of this before?" He poured coffee into a blue mug, brought it to his writing table, set it down well away from his laptop, and slumped into the desk chair. "It's far-fetched, maybe, but what if *everybody* at the Sharon conference next week is a target, and I'm just the Manson Family's first victim? I'm out here early, so I'm the front line. It makes *sense*, Bron! They want to shut us down, stop our conference from happening!"

"Who does?"

"I just told you. The Family! With Jopp as their agent! It adds up!"

Bronson went quiet for a moment, then gave her standard chortle. "You don't even know if your green woman was telling the truth. She hears you're into Sharon, so she claims she's into Manson just to fuck with you…"

"Trust me, Bron, she's for real. You didn't hear her. You didn't *see* her." He sipped at his coffee, which burned his throat a little. At least it would sterilize any of Jopp's remaining vaginal juices. "And maybe, just maybe, she's hoping she can scare me, so I'll spread the word about a Sharon-hating force around the Ofotert, and then our Sharonfest events will all get canceled."

"Paranoia, hon. Time to go nappy!"

"Or maybe Jopp wants to convert me to their cause? Just follow me on this, okay? Imagine the cred she'll get in her fucking Family if she converts me—if she can, like, flip a Sharonophile! I mean, it's one thing to turn a mixed-up runaway to their cause, but converting *a Sharon scholar*? Or else, like, uh, Jopp knows that she *can't* turn me, I'll never turn, never go for Manson, so what she's banking on, instead, is to torment me."

"Listen to yourself." Another chortle, though Lunt could tell from the sound of it that Bronson was growing impatient. She said, "I didn't realize you're so gullible. Are you on *drugs* or something?"

"Of course not!" Lunt shot back right away. He would keep the Muke his secret.

"Anyway," Bronson said, "didn't you receive the first Santa Shot *before* you met this green chick? And you only crossed paths with her because you chose to have lunch where she was eating, right?"

"True, that's a wrinkle in my theory. But what if they counted on me going there, to Gush, and falling in love with Jopp?"

"How could they count on that?"

"Because they knew how similar her mouth is to Sharon's. Meaning, she was, well, *bait*!"

"Bait? Luntie, you're not making sense. You really—"

Slumping in his chair, Lunt unsuccessfully fought back a new yawn, then took another sip of coffee.

"Am I boring you?" said Bronson tetchily.

"No, I've just…forget it. It's been a rough day. A rough *week*."

At which point Lunt heard three knocks on his front door. Knuckle knocks forceful enough to be heard above the ongoing TV drone. The knocking made him seize up in fear. He bolted up straight and quieted his voice to a fervent whisper. "Hey—someone's outside!"

"Outside your room?"

"*Yes!*"

"Who?"

"I don't know! The Manson people?"

"God, you're *losing* it!"

"Stay on the line till I check it out?"

"Lunt…"

"Please?"

Bronson sighed and said okay, she would.

Seriously flipped-out now, Lunt left his seat, making as little noise as physics would allow, and tiptoed to the door. There, pressing his palms against the thick varnished wood, he put his right eye to the peephole.

Out in the hallway, studying the clipboard in his right hand, stood Baby Son. In his left hand, the house detective held a white paper bag.

Eye still at the peephole, Lunt hollered to Baby Son through the door, asking if he'd intercepted the green woman outside. (Or had Jopp bribed him into working on her behalf?)

"No news about any green people, sir." Baby Son's goatee shifted on his lightly freckled face, forming an expression Lunt couldn't read accurately, and he raised up the bag to the peephole. "But I believe you ordered this?"

"I did?" Lunt narrowed his peephole-eye in suspicion. "Ordered *what*?"

The sorrowfulness Lunt had glimpsed before on Baby's face came back as he turned the bag in his hand so Lunt could read the words on its other side: "LIMSKY'S PHARMACY."

Stepping back from the door, Lunt clapped his hands together. His medicine was here!

ONE of Lunt's strangest vacations took him to Chicago. He journeyed there to buy a brassiere that Sharon had once owned, though whether she'd actually worn it could not be fully certified. At his hotel in the Loop, a convention of Jolly Doll collectors—a "Jolly-fest"—was in progress. Everywhere Lunt looked, grown men and women carried their Jolly Dolls around with them as though the objects were living infants. Lunt heard one woman boast that she loved her dolls more than she did her human grandchildren. And the match-up of doll to owner could be surprising, at least to Lunt: there were blond men with "Ethiopian Huntress" Jolly Dolls, for example, and black women with "Cold-As-Ice Norwegian" Jollies.

At lunch one day, Lunt noticed an especially strange sight. An underfed-looking older guy with a Buffalo Bill–style mustache was shuttling between friends at different tables while wearing a pink fez with a ring of Jolly Doll faces embossed around it. When Lunt inquired about where he'd obtained this item (thinking it might be a nifty kitsch item to buy for Bronson's birthday), the fez-wearer sniffed haughtily and said, "It was a door prize. It's *not* for sale."

Such buffoons, Lunt thought as he went on observing the Jolly Doll collectors. He considered them his inferiors because, as he told Bronson that night by phone, Sharonophilia was a far nobler passion—a passion for someone *real*. Or for someone, at least, who *used* to be real—not a fictional piece of painted plastic and fake hair that came packaged in a box.

Another Sharon-oriented trip that Lunt took was a week-long excursion to Paris. This was his first time in the celebrated City of Lights, and during the flight there he remembered Dr. Gluck, the

Francophile psychotherapist from his childhood whose office was decorated with French flags and images of the Eiffel Tower.

Lunt Sharonified his time in Paris by staying at the not-so-creatively-named "L'Hotel," which was where Oscar Wilde had died—and where Sharon had honeymooned with Polanski in 1968 (the year that Mucaquell came on the market). While at L'Hotel, Lunt found himself wondering, as he would continue to do later at the Ofotert, whether Sharon had stood in *this* part of the lobby, had passed through *that* entryway, had relaxed in one of *these* cushiony chairs...

Lunt also wondered, during his stay in Paris, if he would bump into Roman Polanski, who'd lived in the Gallic capital since 1977, when he'd fled punishment in Los Angeles for his statutory rape conviction. Everywhere Lunt went, he kept an eye peeled for Polanski, and asked himself how he'd react if their paths did cross. Would Lunt spit in the Polish dwarf's face? Or would he just verbally upbraid him, call Polanski a cad for having run around behind Sharon's back?

It was a dread-tinged time to be in Paris due to an ongoing series of terrorist attacks, attacks by suicide bombers who posed as street performers. Some were clowns, some jugglers, and some musicians; there was a rather limber acrobat, and even one celebrity impersonator. The impersonator pretended to be none other than Jim Morrison.

During Lunt's sixth day in town, the terrorist who looked like the Doors singer (and with his leather trousers and hippie shirt, he was *dressed* like Jim Morrison, too) appeared at the singer's grave in the Pere Lachaise Cemetery (Oscar Wilde's grave wasn't far away). To the delight of the Doors fans who milled around Jim's grave, which always drew a crowd, the "Jimitator," as newspapers world-wide would call him, sang certain Doors' songs without accompaniment: "Shaman Blues," "Wintertime Love," and Sharon's own preferred number, "Summer's Almost Gone."

Lunt wasn't present at this impromptu concert, but when he read about it later, he knew he *could have* been there, since he'd been planning to visit Pere Lachaise at some point before returning to the States. The Jimitator, by all accounts, sounded very much like Jim Morrison. He brought down the house with a stirring rendition of "The Crystal Ship." Then he took a bow, calling out *"Merci,"* and exploded by detonating an explosives-packed vest he wore. Eight people, including the Jimitator, were killed, and fourteen others were injured.

By Lunt's final night in Paris, he had wearied of all the sight-seeing and frightened avoidance of all street performers. So he decided to indulge a guilty pleasure: stopping in at a Champs Elysee multiplex cinema to see a mindless Hollywood romance. Starring Garth Chthonic, the actor whom Lunt would later glimpse at Gush, the movie was even worse than Lunt had expected. Once the credits rolled and the houselights came up, he found his way to the theater's restroom and took his place at a line of urinals. Beside him stood a diminutive old man with longish silver hair. Scrawled on the filthy gray tiles at eye level was a graffito. It was a poem, set down in blue ink, about a man who turned his lover's face into a mirror but polished the face so much that he made it a skull. Perhaps this would have held meaning for Lunt had it not been written in French, which he didn't understand.

While peeing, Lunt glanced from the graffito to the small man urinating beside him. As this man zipped up his fly, he leaned his head back slightly and everything clicked for Lunt. That wizened face in the dim-blue toilet light—the Sharon-lover knew it instantly. Shocked by this recognition, Lunt felt the blood drain from his own face, and he turned back to the tiled wall and kept staring at it until he was left standing all alone, his penis still out. The little man was gone. Gone for good. And what galled Lunt, truly galled him, was not the fact that he'd failed to harangue the dwarf. No, what galled Lunt was the fact that his first instinct, wisely repressed, had been to *bow* to him.

To beg Polanski for an interview.

To beg and to flatter him, and to touch those wrinkled hands that once touched Sharon.

"**WHOSOEVER** treats his fellows without honor or humanity, he, and his issue—"

"Got it," snapped Lunt. "Thanks. Buh-bye!"

Down he slammed the room phone, and back to his writing table he went.

Buzzing from a belly full of fresh coffee, Lunt had pledged to the poster-Sharon above his bed that he wouldn't sleep, or drink the Mucaquell that would bring on sleep, until he'd made progress on his Great Work. It had been too long since he'd written anything. When Lunt seated himself at his computer, however, he found it too hard to concentrate. Switching off the TV didn't help. His nerves were shot. And so, with the TV back on and his feet resting on the corner of his writing table, Lunt wound up doing research instead of writing. Research that was meant to bolster his knowledge about his possible new enemies.

Lunt typed "Manson Family 21st Century" into Google and looked first at the website allinthecharliefamily.com. Alas, the information on it concerned former Family members, people who were dead or still in prison or "born again" or "reformed and struggling to get on with their lives under new names." Nothing on Jopp or her grandmother New Leaf, and nothing about them on a site called mansonmegamaniax, either. But Lunt did find a plethora of facts about Manson, facts that Lunt, who'd always preferred to contemplate the mass murderer as little as he could, had been exposed to in the past but gladly forgotten.

During Manson's few years with the Family, he got obsessed with coyotes, whose yipping sounds he would imitate. Charlie also cultivated a mean stare and used it to unnerve foes, enhancing it sometimes by running his finger across his throat, suggesting decapitation.

While at Spahn Ranch, Manson took to wearing a gray corduroy vest, woven for him by his followers, who added locks of their hair to its brightly sequined images of goblins. At the ranch Charlie also took to brandishing a cutlass, a "magic sword" complete with knuckle guard. When he wasn't swinging it around, the cutlass could be found in a metal scabbard that was bolted to his dune buggy.

In spite of his self-described "knack with the opposite sex," Manson wasn't exactly a typical ladies' man. He kissed his women's feet a lot, but was often rough with their bodies. He'd threaten to cut their breasts off, for instance, would force them to fellate dogs, and demanded that they drink dog blood as a fertility aid. Speaking of dogs, the Family canines always got to eat at mealtimes before the women did. And whenever the women had sex with Manson, he insisted that they pretend they were sleeping with their own fathers.

Lunt looked up from the laptop and caught sight of himself in the mirror above his writing desk. For a moment he didn't recognize his slightly weak-chinned, rather flabby face; only the Sebringesque hair looked familiar. *Odd*, he thought. Then he surfed the net some more, finding more information about his sworn enemy.

Since his murder convictions and the suspension of his death sentence, Manson had been transferred from prison to prison in California: San Quentin, Folsom, the Medical Facility at Vacaville, and finally Corcoran State in the San Joaquin Valley, not far from Fresno. A "supermax" security institution, Corcoran had a reputation for sadistic guards. Moreover, it had been built on a filled-in lake that was once home to the brutally displaced Tachi Indians.

Well aware that he would never be set free, Manson spent his free time working the media whenever possible, promoting his crude brand of environmentalism, playing his guitar, reading the Bible, skimming through *National Geographic* magazines, and, as a committed vegetarian, chowing down potato chips and Ramen noodles.

Despite his incarceration, Charlie was very much in the world, if not quite, to quote the man himself, "at my will walking your streets, right out there among you." "FREE CHARLES MANSON" T-shirts were on sale everywhere. "Cease To Exist" and "Look At Your Game, Girl" and other songs that he'd composed in the sixties were still played by contemporary rock groups, while tribute songs such as "Charlie's '69 Was a Good Year" abounded. So did Manson fan clubs. One professional typographer had even created three typefaces in the madman's honor: "Manson Regular," "Manson Alternate," and "Manson Bold."

"People worry about Charlie the way they worry about cancer and earthquakes," a journalist wrote. Another journalist called Manson "the nation's leading anti-citizen." And the decades had not mellowed this anti-citizen at all: "I'm going to chop up some more of you motherfuckers," Charlie told a third journalist. "I'm going to kill as many of you as I can. I'm going to pile you up to the sky." Needless to say, his parole had been continually denied. "By the time I get out of here," Manson predicted, clearly recognizing how futile his yen for freedom was, "I'll parole to outer space."

With a few more strokes at his keyboard, Lunt learned that during a search of Manson's living space in Corcoran, prison officials not only found four bags of marijuana but one hundred feet of nylon rope and a mail-order catalogue for hot-air balloons.

Hot-air balloons: Why did those sound familiar?

After calling it quits on his research, Lunt checked his BlackBerry for texts. No more from Jopp—maybe she'd finally given up on him. Back on the net, he found his email box mostly full of quotidian stuff: a letter from his boss at the realty office re: a minor business matter; another invitation to that upcoming benefit for a victims rights organization; and some greetings from S-philes he knew, with lots of expressed zeal about the upcoming Tate-World Conference. Still, one email stood out from the others—way out. In fact, the instant Lunt finished reading it, he howled with rage, plucked his now-empty coffee mug from the writing table, and hurled it across the room. The cup, narrowly missing the TV perched nearby, shattered against a wall. Jagged pieces of blue porcelain rained down onto the carpet.

Dear Lunt (the infuriating email read):

Owing to the rancorous tone you took during our recent phone talk, I hereby request you to curtail any future communication between us. I'm sure you understand my need to buffer myself from loud hectoring and rancor, yes? I do not fully understand why your Sharon Tate project is so controversial among your fellow fans, but plainly it is controversial, and so, after renewed reflection, I must again affirm my unwillingness to represent the project. I hope this makes sense.

Good luck in finding new representation.

V. Mukherjee.

WHAT was the trouble with Philippe? Other people. Not other women, because if he slept with other women while we were together, I didn't know about it, and we were together so often that there couldn't have been many. Philippe certainly wasn't like Roman, whose philandering was so open and frequent that no one in our circle could understand how I put up with it.

(For instance, I was walking down the Strip one day and a guy in a car behind me honked his horn and yelled, "Lady, you've got a ba-yoo-tee-full *ass!*" My husband hadn't recognized me.)

To be fair, Roman wasn't always fully at fault. Women tended to throw themselves at his feet—grasping actresses, mostly, who hoped he'd cast them in his films. Even when they didn't fall for him, Roman wore down their resistance. Which really bothered me, as you'd imagine. There were nights when I cried myself to sleep and thought I'd die from grief. In my dreams sometimes, a different man appeared to me, a new suitor who tried to whisk me away from Roman. He was a humble real estate agent from New Jersey, and I knew he'd never cheat on me. Plus, more than my other lovers, this "Jersey guy" loved me for who I was, my essence, the Sharon who longed to (like the song "Nature Boy" goes) "love and be loved in return."

Over time, I learned to take Roman's cheating in stride. At least I got better at handling it. Why? Well, I didn't want to scare Roman off by seeming too confining, too smothering. According to the spirit of the times, jealousy was wrong, a "hang-up"—my own biggest hang-up, Roman would say. One of our best friends—Mia Farrow, I think it was, or else her beau in the late 1960s, Peter Sellers—said it best: "You're taking a partner, not a prisoner."

Roman wanted *to be faithful, or so I believed.* He's just frightened of monogamy, *I told myself,* and I have to help him move past this fear and show him how powerful and important this thing called love is.

I've never been a giver-upper, so I took my mission seriously, and I convinced myself that Roman's affairs were just about meaningless sex, whereas I was his wife, the only one he loved. At least I believed this at the time. So Roman pretended to be faithful, I pretended to believe him, and that was that.

Philippe, as I've said, was a very different animal. With my sexy Frenchman, the trouble that ultimately fractured and then finished off our relationship didn't have to do with other women but with the other important people in my life—my parents and my movie mentor, Martin Ransohoff. Philippe used to say, over and over, that the people around me were exploitative in one way or another—ripping me off financially, in the case of Ransohoff, or else, in the case of Mom, living out her dreams of a glamorous life through her actress daughter. God, the fights Philippe and I had over this!

"You're the goose with the golden œufs!" he would shout, and I'd shout back, "No, you don't get it—they only want what's best for me!"

LESS than one minute after smashing his coffee mug to smithereens, Lunt stood outside the entrance to an Ofotert room other than his own. The process of careening full-force down two flights of stairs had rendered him out of breath, but he still snarled emphatically, bristling with rage, white lines of anger showing at the corners of his mouth, as he pounded with his fists on the door marked "29."

As always, Lunt expected Glen Mandrake to be a formidable foe. Once the door swung open, however, and the men stood nose to nose, Lunt was surprised to find Mandrake in bad shape. For a start, the so-called Bad Boy with Blue Blood looked lost in an over-sized, monogrammed, Renaissance-red bathrobe; it was the first time Lunt had ever seen him, either in person or published photos, without his white suit. Under his red-rimmed eyes were sagging pouches. And how downcast Mandrake's face looked, speckled as it was with dots of moisture that might be—were they *tears*?

Lunt spoke first. Yelled, rather. "Fucking *dick*."

"Dear boy, your timing is always delicious." Mandrake's voice was cold and distant, nearly uninflected. He wiped away the wetness from his face with a sleeve. "If you would *please*—"

"Timing, schmiming. I'm not here to pussyfoot. You're emailing Vishwa right now and renouncing your threats."

"We can discuss this in the morning. You pick where and when. Now will you just *go*?"

In the suite behind Mandrake, near-total darkness reigned. Had he been asleep? Lunt hoped so—having interrupted the man's rest would be a true delight. Mandrake's whiskers, Lunt felt gratified to see, had flecks of gray in them, while Lunt's own hair, on the cusp of age forty, was as dark as ever. Not a single fleck of gray—none, at least, that he'd turned up yet. And had Mandrake actually been crying? Or had he just washed his face? Perhaps Mandrake sprinkled water on his mug to fool Lunt, make Lunt think he had a heart…

"Crybaby," Lunt said savagely, clenching and unclenching his fists. "Boo-hoo for you. Pandora must dig you in weepy mode."

A shadow entered Mandrake's bulging eyes now and his contemptuous look faded. "Since you mention Pandora again," Mandrake said, "I suppose that I—I owe you…"

"Owe me what?"

"No, drop it. Scratch that."

"What *is* it you owe me, you whack job?"

"Well…an apology. You've been furious with me, I know. And you do have cause."

Lunt looked idly at the cords in Mandrake's throat, not sure what he was hearing.

"What I mean…" Mandrake glanced nervously at his wristwatch, then picked at some lint on his bathrobe's collar. "What I'm saying is that I'm sorry for how it turned out with Pandora. All right? I apologize."

"*Now* you say this? What a put-on!"

"Not at all. When I met Pan, I knew I had to have her—I just had to have those Sharon-eyes. I couldn't help it."

"You think I'm *buying* this charade?"

"Buy it or not." There was resignation in Mandake's voice, unmistakable resignation, and he leaned his shoulder against the doorframe. "It doesn't matter."

Still not sure if he should trust the change, Lunt said, "Is this part of some twelve-step program you're doing?" he said. "Sadists Anonymous? Or did some shrink tell you to—"

"It's what Lichtenberg would want for me." He halted for a moment, indulged in some sniffles, and wiped at his cheeks again. "At any rate, we couldn't *both* have Pan, could we? Only one of us could, and I play to win, that's how I am. It's not as if I owed you anything, you weren't my friend. And remember, she *chose* me." He stopped again, his face once more forlorn. "She *chose* me, my little Sharon-eyes..."

Lunt clucked his tongue, disgusted by Mandrake's behavior even as it puzzled him. "We weren't friends, no," he conceded, his heart rate and blood pressure stabilizing, "but we were fellow Sharonophiles."

Mandrake's mouth tightened. He put his fist on the hip not leaning against the door. "You're right, of course. Live by the sword, die by it, right?"

"And scaring Vishwa away from my book? Will you say 'Sorry' for *that*, too?"

"No, definitely not. No apologies there, dear boy. I'll fight your book until the end. It's too dangerous for Sharon, for her reputation in the world. If you're here for a blanket 'I'm sorry,' *fuhgeddabout* it, as you say in your native state. But with Pandora—I..."

"What?"

A tear formed on the lower lid of Mandrake's left eye, and once gravity claimed it, making the tear roll down his cheek, Mandrake fell apart and began to weep. There in the doorway, right in front of Lunt and anyone who sauntered past, the bathrobed man slumped farther against his doorframe and sobbed, his shoulders rocking hard and his palms pressed to his eyes.

"Jesus," said Lunt. This wasn't theater, he could tell. Like Jopp's Manson affiliation, it was bona fide.

"She *left* me, Moreland! She fucking left me!"

"Who?"

"Pandora, you imbecile, who else? She threw me over for a chef! Can you *believe* it?"

"She *dumped* you?"

"Yes, yes, for some 'molecular gastronomist' from Westport. Westport, *Connecticut*!" He rolled his wounded eyes, his voice less controlled than Lunt had ever heard it. "Some two-bit cook with a TV show! Not even a real one, but *cable access*!" A new flood of tears issued from Mandrake, then he tried to speak in between more sobs that shook his body: "All the time she lived with me in Soho, Pan was sneaking out, stealing away under my nose to screw him, a fucking '*dish-jockey*.' He's not even a real chef, you know, not a *cordon bleu* man, but some asshole who makes *foams*. Foams and 'snail smoothies'—'Escargot Energy Drinks,' he calls them. And even *worse dreck*, I'm sure! But '*No*,' says Pan, 'he's an *artist*.' A foam artist! Snakes alive! He's probably never cleaned a grease trap, paid *one* due. Like my stepmother, that cow, he's just an arriviste… Well, I'll see to *him*. He'll get *his*! I'll render him down to mucilage! First Benny Pompa, then the chef!"

A giddiness filled Lunt, inside and out. He could not have concealed his triumph even if he'd meant to. This was true *schadenfreude*, an even richer taste of it than when Benny Pompa had hurled his drink in Mandrake's face. Far, *far* richer: live by the sword, die by the sword, indeed!

"How low the mighty have fallen," he taunted. "Wasn't it Lichtenberg who said that?"

Too dazed by his grief to notice the snideness, Mandrake said, "What would Lichtenberg *do*, that's the question. He described sixty ways people rest their heads on their hands, but nothing about heartbreak. I—I think he'd be stoic about this, Moreland. Nerves of cable. Lichtenberg would be…be…" But now another fit of weeping overtook Mandrake.

Lunt shook his head, once again stunned by the display. Stunned, amused, triumphant—and repelled, too, by how unglued his foe had become, how broken he was. "Shit, man, get a grip. Pop a Valium or something."

"I'm out of Xanax! I'm out of Onalull, too. Of all the times! Do you have any?"

Lunt considered offering him cough syrup, but only briefly, because he wasn't going to waste his stash on Mandrake, of all people! He also considered saying something vicious—sticking in the proverbial knife, while his enemy was vulnerable. But in the end Lunt chose not to. There would be time enough for that. So all he said was, "I'm outta here, but it's not done with us and Vishwa. Not by a long shot."

On his way upstairs, taking his time ascending the stairwell, Lunt left a phone message for Bronson, his voice bubbling with glee: "Hon, you're *not* gonna believe this latest news!"

His room phone was ringing as he reentered 47.

That scum from Amarillo, was Lunt's guess. *He didn't get to run through his whole routine tonight before I hung up on him, so he's calling back. Or maybe it's Mrs. Kruikshank, wondering when I'll show up for our interview. Or even Mandrake, phoning to beg me not to squeal to our fellow S-philes about how he embarrassed himself with me...*

Lunt picked up the receiver, said "Yes?" then listened to a young female say, "Hey, Jeepster, how's tricks?"

Freezing, too jarred by her real-time voice to speak, much less to disconnect the call, Lunt felt his body lower itself to the edge of his bed.

"Did I surprise you?" the green woman asked. "I *did*, didn't I?"

Fear, already gone creeping up and down Lunt's spine, had lunged as well into his throat, and his pulse soon drummed loudly in his ears. His eyes shot to the bulge of the BlackBerry in his pocket. She wasn't calling on that, she was calling on the hotel line! To *his suite*!

"Um...how did you get this number?" he asked.

"What do you mean, dude? It's the Ofotert's main digits! I just asked for you by name and they sailed me on through. If you wanna be incognito, use an alias next time. It's what Benny the Pomp always does."

"But..."

"You don't return my calls or texts, so what's a girl to do? Telephonic sneak attack, that's what! Anyway, when can I see you in the flesh?"

"You—you *can't*, I don't think..."

"Come on, I wanna see you! Invite me over! I wanna suck on you. We've got unfinished business, right?"

"Yeah," he gasped, "we do..."

"Did you admire my poozle?"

"Um..." His mind slowed.

"Do you remember what color my pubes are?"

How could he forget? It was tormenting him, turning Jopp down, Jopp and her Sharon-mouth, because the talk coming from that mouth had cast a spell on him, a sublime erotic hex, and he wanted her more now than he'd ever wanted Pandora, more than anyone he'd known except for Sharon. With labored breathing, labored as much from excitement as from anxiety, Lunt undid his belt, unzipped his khakis, reached inside his boxer briefs, and began to interfere with himself, the memories from Gush resurfacing. His mind, a spinning top, carried him back to the diaper-changing room, where he was going down on her, all those delirious sights and scents and sounds making him swoon. Before long, however, he thought about her teeth, those horrible rotten teeth, and his reverie screeched to a halt.

"No," he said.

"No? No *what?*"

"I—we—we *can't*, Jopp."

"What the fuck, 'can't'?"

He pulled his hands out of his boxer briefs. No, he couldn't sleep with a brown-teethed Manson girl. Those teeth suggested a deeper decay, a darkness nested inside her. She was evil, Manson-level evil, and sex with her would put his life at risk.

"Pretty please?"

Wavering, Lunt added, "God, I *wish*…but—"

"Dude, you scared? It's my marriage, right? My Bride of Charlie status? Don't worry, he's not a jealous guy. It ain't cheating unless it's anal, remember? And I told you, the Family did *not* ice Polanski's girl. We're blameless. The real killers were from this death-cult called 'The Thanatologists.' *They* did it—really! The Thanatologists hated Charlie. Competition, you know? *So*, with the help of the LAPD, the Thanatologists snuffed Tate and then pinned the crime on us. All the other victims, too. It was a frame job, I swear."

"But that's…no, that's wrong!"

Jopp tittered. "Don't believe the media, Jeepster. Charlie's First Commandment. Ratings over truth, always. We got a raw deal, just like Jesus. I've got a lot to teach you. Charlie *loves* life, he doesn't harm it. *Never.* Love's his thing, not death."

What horseshit. Total lunacy! Lunt stopped himself before he said this, however. If he spoke out against Manson, it might piss Jopp off, pit the Family against him. Was she laying a trap, tricking Lunt into dissing her "husband"? Caution, caution!

"No, I'm not, uh, worried about Charlie," he finally told her. "It's just that I—I've got a girlfriend. Not Sharon Tate, a *living* girl. And she's, uh, prone to getting jealous."

Jopp tittered again. "The old 'girlfriend back home.' I've done *that* trip before. What's her name?"

"It's...it's Pandora."

"Oh, cool name. Norse mythology. Don't open her box! She suck you good?"

Lunt cleared his throat, staring blankly at the still-unopened bottle of Dom Perignon on his writing table. He made a sound to signal yes.

"Well, not like *I'll* suck it," Jopp came back at him. "I see how you look at me, Jeepster. Girlfriend or not, you want my green lips on your girth-stick. So when can I visit you?"

Lunt's left hand returned to work inside his boxer briefs. He would finish off himself just after hanging up the phone, then he would drink deep from the Muke, his new supply, and everything would go Floaty P'Toaty, this broken world tilting into sleep, and Lunt's whole body, from top to bottom, would be covered with her lip marks. Green Sharon-lip marks!

"Tomorrow..." he said.

"Promise? Fine. But, like, *pick up* when you see my number on your phone. Oh, and Jeepster?"

"Yeah?"

"Sweet dreams."

Or else, he thought, his scalp prickling, *enjoy my nightmares.*

7

THE LIGHT POURS OUT OF LUNT

(Thursday, Friday, Saturday)

RED was the color of his true love's Ferrari. But tonight, in Dreamland, Lunt was driving a roofless green Mustang with his mother riding shotgun. Wearing Keystone Kop costumes, they were chasing down a hunchbacked old Nazi, who was on foot. This chase took place in a movie studio, the outdoor expanse of Spahn Ranch, Manson's favored hangout. As sunlight-dappled scenery scrolled past the open-air Mustang, rear-projection style, its engine made a scraping, rasping sound. So did the movie cameras set up along the road. Lunt mashed the gas pedal harder.

At one point a patter of rain got started and quickly strengthened, each drop sparkling on the car hood before it bounced off. Coarse-faced and bristly-haired, the hunchback stumbled as he ran, prompting Lunt to muse aloud that most hunchbacks usually weren't fast runners. Why couldn't they seem to catch him?

"Step on it!" his mother yelled, undaunted by how waterlogged they were getting. To be heard she had to yell over the howling— no, scraping—wind.

"Don't worry," Lunt hollered back, yanking the steering wheel from left to right. "It's only Lichtenberg, and he's dead, so he can't get far…"

But wait, thought Lunt. *How can Lichtenberg be dead if he's right out here in front of us?*

The Mustang thumped over a sudden rise. Soon they were on a highway ramp, then a six-lane blacktop heading south. The roadside was choked with weeds and candy wrappers. The Mustang slowed down. So did the wind and rain.

"I'm sorry, Ma, but I just figured out something."

"What's that?"

"Like Lichtenberg, you're dead."

"So what?" She shrugged her shoulders. "Who *isn't*?"

Lunt pondered this. Or tried to. But soon enough, he realized that this woman was not his mother. Not Mrs. Moreland, after all, but an imposter—someone wearing a Bubble Wrap Mrs. Moreland mask. He didn't know that you could buy one of those. When had they been made available?

Lunt woke up wearing yesterday's clothes, the bedsheets pulled to his chin. He huddled beneath them until he came back to some semblance of consciousness. What time was it? Groggily, he rolled around to peer at the clock on his nightstand. Four-something.

Four?

Four in the morning?

No—hazy daylight was streaming in from his window, where the wooden Venetian blinds were all open. Four in *the fucking afternoon*! This meant he'd slept for, what, twenty hours?

"Fucking cough syrup," Lunt mumbled, his voice slurry with sleep, like a person with brain damage. If he didn't cut back on Muke, he'd wind up like Mrs. Kruikshank, pausing for eons before he spoke. No more self-medicating for Lunt! *No more* excessive *self-medicating*, he corrected himself. *Not, at least, unless the coughing comes back.*

Sitting up in bed, Lunt shook his head to clear it, then remembered to check if any new packages had been pushed under his door. None. No sounds from the hallway, either. He exhaled with satisfaction. Would there be more "gifts"? Had his Manson-quoting benefactor, *whoever* it was, run out of material? *In all likelihood*, Lunt decided, *Mandrake's been the culprit, and he's too undone by Pandora's treachery to make any further mischief for me. It still seems peculiar that he'd desecrate those Santa Shots so badly, but obviously he's more unbalanced than usual.*

Lunt yawned, eyes shutting automatically. He wanted to glug down more cough syrup, to sleep longer, but "No," he answered himself out loud. "Make hay while the sun shines!"

Making hay meant interviewing the old night clerk tonight. It also meant that, in the hours before the interview, he should get cranking on his book. All the time he'd just lost, *twenty hours*, when he could've been at work! He loved writing about Sharon; it had become his truest form of worshipping her. *How did I let myself fall so far behind*? he asked himself. *And how, at this rate, will I ever finish the memoir before leaving LA? Once the Sharonfest starts here, I can't assume I'll get anything done!*

Of course, he no longer had a literary agent for the book that would contain that memoir, but soon enough he would put the screws to Mandrake, exploiting that imbecile's new psychological weak point, and then Lunt felt confident he could win Vishwa back and put his career on track again.

From Vishwa, Lunt's thoughts turned to another problematic woman. An erection swiftly followed. So did a brain wave: What if he could convince Jopp to reject Manson? A difficult task, admittedly, damn-near impossible—she'd been raised in the Family, after all. Yet if he succeeded, what a victory it would be. Not a victory for himself alone, but one the whole universe would benefit from, since as someone (Lichtenberg?) had phrased it, "To save one soul is like saving the whole world."

The question was, *how* could he sway her from Manson's influence?

I could butter her up, he reasoned, *win her loyalty by bribing her. Finance a set of new teeth, for instance. Expensive, sure, but I could do it by buying less Sharonabilia for myself and by giving up a few vacations. If this doesn't work, maybe I could hire a cult deprogrammer? How much do cult deprogrammers cost? An arm and a leg, most likely. Could*

I deprogram her on my own? Buy a copy of Cult Deprogramming for Dummies, *some book like that, or pay a deprogrammer half price to advise me in his methods? It might work! But what'll we replace Manson with in Jopp's mind? With Sharon-love, of course! This'll be part of her reprogramming, bringing Jopp to the light of Sharon. Then we'll be Sharonophiles together. And, oh, the credit in Tate-world I'll get, exposing a Manson lover to the glory of Sharon-consciousness!*

Lunt stretched his arms and drew the sheets up to his chin, leaving his arms out. Then he lifted his BlackBerry from the pillow near his waist and checked his messages. Two Bronson texts, both saying, *"Call me!"* and no texts from Jopp. There were, however, two breathless messages from her in his voicemail. In the first, the green woman spoke into her phone as people chattered in the background: *"Dude, where are you? Guess what? I'm at Gush, and you won't fucking believe who just graced us with his presence! Jesus, I can't breathe—get over here, dude!"*

In Jopp's second message, made two hours after the first, she was whispering no longer. *"Dude, it's unbelievable! I just had lunch with them! Benny, Saffron, Trudi—Saff remembered making out with me that time—and they're amazing! So real, so down-to-earth, so normal. Where were you, Jeepster? I told Benny all about you! I said you're into Sharon Tate and Benny said, 'That woman was a fox.' The wives think so, too! He calls them his wifeys. Cool, right? They told me they're starting their own religious commune, a place in Australia where they're gonna worship lightning, and Benny wants me to be a priestess! Amazing, right? Wanna join up? I'm fucking stoked. Oh, and my best friend wants to meet you! Maybe we can have a threeway? Call me, now! I'll give you all the details!"*

Lunt had profoundly mixed feelings about the voicemail. On one hand, he felt relieved that with Benny in her life now, Jopp would focus less on Lunt, and thus be less likely to pose a threat to him. On the other hand, Lunt felt jealous. With Jopp more Pompa-gaga than ever, would she still want to sleep with him? Talk of a "threeway" was exciting, yes, but talk was cheap, especially here in Hollywood. And even if she *did* still dig him, how long would that last?

Looking out his window, Lunt beheld a gorgeous, gem-edged, sun-kissed day. *Not just sun-kissed*, he reflected, *but sun-*French-*kissed*! While he scanned Seething Lane, empty as usual, for any sign of Jopp, Lunt felt his stomach growl and realized he was hungry. Should he raid his minibar? No, the low nutritional value and high prices to be found there scared him off. More than anything, he wanted Mucaquell, wanted that potion to bless his lips, to coat his throat, to warm his chest, his stomach, his core. Yet he knew better than to give in to his desire. So he telephoned room service instead and asked for the chicken parmigiana entree.

As he hung up the room phone, his BlackBerry trilled.

Jopp?

No, Bronson.

"Bronnie, wow, do *I* have to talk to you!"

And he did, pouring out everything that had gone down since they spoke last, with special attention paid to Mandrake's romantic downfall. Bronson's chortle at this news sounded not annoying to Lunt but welcome. She was glad to hear that no new packages had shown up. But when she mentioned his "green Manson girlfriend," the air went out of Lunt's balloon.

"No, I haven't heard from her," he lied. "And if she did call, I wouldn't notice, 'cause I've been writing like a beast of a scribe these past few days."

"Great," said Bronson. "You getting outside enough?"

"What does *that* mean?"

"Fresh air, swimming, taking strolls. You know, California-style health shit."

Lunt thought of the Ofotert's kidney-shaped pool. He'd never made it there. "Not yet. But I'm healthy, Bron. My cough is gone. Went away on its own."

"Remember that all work and no play makes Lunt a dull Sharonophile."

"Work is what I'm here for."

"Yeah, but *moderation*, hon. The Golden Mean. When you told me you were Ofotert-bound, I never figured that you'd stay locked inside there, shuttered away. Think of all that bounty surrounding you! All those gals you could be meeting while you're on your writing breaks. Some might even be *non-Manson-affiliated*!"

"Please stop with this Manson girlfriend shit. Just because I go down on someone doesn't mean I'm—"

"In Estonia it means you're already betrothed," Bronson goofed.

Lunt faked a laugh, but his friend's joking around was pissing him off, and he decided to say so. This made Bronson chortle again. Which only served to stoke Lunt's anger.

"I mean it," he said.

"So do I. Fresh air, strolls, social life. And here's a bonus suggestion: a new hotel."

"What, I should leave the Ofotert? Those Santa Shots have stopped coming. It was Mandrake, I think, and he's in no condition now to yank anybody's chain."

"Have those late-night calls stopped?"

"Probably."

"But you're not sure. Just quit the scene there, Luntie, light out for the territories. Find a fresh hotel with no bad vibes."

"So I just *run*? Flee like a coward?"

"No, you flee like a survivor. Like a smartie who doesn't need the headaches. You're obviously frazzled, so—"

"Wouldn't you be frazzled if you got freaky photos with Manson quotes? And started feeling sweet about some girl who turns out to be a Mansonophile?"

"I understand," Bronson said, reining in her strong tone, trying to mollify her friend, although he'd begun to irritate her, too. "That's why I'm suggesting you move. There's no shame in picking up stakes, Lunt."

"What about the Sharonfest next week?"

"You still go to it, naturally. You just drive there from the Mondrian, or wherever else you're staying. You've got a rent-a-car, right?"

"Yeah, a Mustang."

"Red, like Sharon's Ferrari, of course. Been in it lately?"

"Earlier today," Lunt said, realizing that he hadn't used the Mustang since the day he'd arrived in town.

"So rev that faux-Ferrari up, pack your bags, check out of there, and drive. You'll feel better, trust me."

Lunt gave a particularly exasperated sigh. "Whenever someone asks me to trust them, I know that that's exactly what I *shouldn't* do."

"Suit yourself. All the same, a change of scenery is what Doc Bronson's prescribing. Any digs will serve. Shit, Motel 6, even— they'll leave the light on for you."

Jesus, thought Lunt, *she's such a buzzkill.* She'd never gotten on his nerves this much before. What he needed was Mucaquell. Just a sip to smooth his edges, ease him down.

"Sharon never stayed at Motel 6, all right? The whole point is for me to live in this sacred space. Not just visit it, but *inhabit* it."

"And you *have* lived in it up till now, and you probably will again. Next year, say, in Sharon's suite after that tycoon, whoever he is, moves out."

"Ziggy Rosenwach."

"Right. You've got the freedom to vamoose and ought to use it."

"Thanks for the advice. But since you didn't bother coming out here yourself, you're not exactly well-positioned to be a sage."

"I *told* you," Bronson retorted, just as snottily, "I've got too much work at the office. And frankly, as I *also* told you, I'm not so keen on—"

"On what?"

"I'm not so keen on Sharon anymore. I just don't feel, like, so *comfortable* with her."

Lunt laughed sarcastically. "You want to hear my response to that?"

"No."

"Too bad. My response is, 'Traitor.'"

"*Me?*"

"You." He knew how wrong it was, assailing his best friend this way, but it felt too good to stop. Perversely good. Or *not* so perversely, because how *dare* she sit pretty hundreds of miles from the danger zone and give him advice about his well-being? Lunt was the one with his safety and his sanity on the line, not Bronson! "Sharon needs us," he said, "all of us—you, me, my book—to get the public wise to her. She shouldn't just be an answer in some dumb sixties trivia game. People need to know how fabulous she was."

"You think I don't agree?"

"So *now's* the time when you want to abandon her? Abandon me?"

"Lunt, I'm not abandoning anyone, okay? Besides, Sharon's dead. She's gone. She's past all abandoning."

"But that's the point! *Because* she's dead, she needs her fans to resurrect her! To keep the flame alive, keep her torch burning! She's only dead when we let the world forget her. Forget her glory, forget her pain..."

"Her pain, exactly. That's another reason I don't feel good about loving Sharon, all right? Because she suffered. And it's started feeling wrong to—"

"Wrong for who?"

"For *me!*"

"Justify it however you want," Lunt said. "You're still a traitor."

"Stop that!"

"You might as well be Mandrake. You're no better than he is."

"That's bullshit!" Bronson exploded. "Baloney! You're fucking *clueless!* Who are *you* to call me names?"

"And who are *you* to tell me how to live my life when you're not here?" Lunt boomed back at her. "Telling me to run scared from the Ofotert?"

"Where's this *coming from?*"

"So Sharon's too intense for you—fine, play it safe with Raquel Welch."

"I haven't settled on Raquel yet! It might be Claudia Cardinale!"

"Good luck with that. But remember—loving someone who's still alive is easy. Loving someone dead is what really counts. *That* shows big-time devotion. Nothing else."

"Bullshit! What does that—what does that *mean?* Listen to yourself!"

"And acting holier-than-thou when you can't even show *your face* here, that takes the cake." He couldn't believe what he was saying—even as he kept saying it. "You could've flown out to help me, to, like, support me. Just to *meet* me, meet me for once in our lives! Face-to-face, say hi to your 'Luntie.' But no, you're too fucking scared for that. Scared of your friend, scared of the world, scared of your fucking *self*."

"Oh—my—God."

"You're urging me to run out like a scaredy-cat, but you're the frightened one, you fucking *coward!*"

Ouch. No sooner had the words passed through Lunt's lips than he knew how wrong they were. How harsh they sounded. How much damage they would do. And they did. Bronson's silence, ominous and stark, seemed to create an echo chamber on the phone line, to bounce his cruelty back at him.

"Listen," Lunt said, coming to his senses, trying to rein himself in, to sound reasonable again, "I'm sorry, hon, I can't believe I did that."

No reply.

"I'm *so* sorry. Jesus—I'm fucked up here, so fucked up I freaked out on you. I really don't know what I'm saying…"

Still nothing. She'd clammed up.

"Bron?" he pleaded. "Bronnie?"

"Well, well," she said at last, and in her voice, usually so effervescent, Lunt heard pain, nothing but. "It's not the first time my kindness got repaid with insults."

"Listen—"

"*But*," she continued, pushing the trident of guilt deep into Lunt's psyche, "I never thought it would be you. You, the one person who *wouldn't* do that to me."

"Bronson, please—"

Too late. She put the phone down on him, killed the call.

Lunt's upper body sagged. And for a moment, he sat staring blankly at the phone, feeling acute self-loathing. How could he have been so heinous? How could he have scorned his loyal, loving Bronson? Her unwillingness to meet with him, it wasn't from hostility but from shyness. Her embarrassment, her shame. She felt so awful in her skin, so awful about herself—about her illness, her disabled state—that she wouldn't, *couldn't*, present herself to people. Not, at least, to anyone she cared for. Lunt knew he had to ring her back right now, to apologize profusely, to sort this out pronto. But she didn't pick up his call. He left a heartfelt message, then phoned again and left a second, longer voicemail. He had planned to keep on phoning until she answered. Yet before he placed the next call, he heard a soft knock on his door.

His back went straight with fear. He got up, tiptoed over to where the knock had come from, and peeked through the spyhole, bracing himself to see green hell outside, green death.

Instead—ah, yes, *room service*!

It was the waiter Lunt had once seen in the courtyard, the one with the crew-cut and tortoiseshell eyeglasses who'd been listening so attentively to Benny Pompa's stories.

"Chicken parmigiana, sir."

Lunt tipped him well. The problem was, he'd lost his appetite. The only meal he truly craved was his cough syrup. He would not allow himself the Muke, though. He had to eat, force down the food, phone Bronson once more, write his Sharon memoir (write a lot!), then go to interview the night clerk. Mrs. Kruikshank expected him. Hence no more cough syrup till bedtime!

As he was finishing the meal, Lunt heard a new knock on his door. Assuming it was the waiter come to collect the empty plates, Lunt bounded up, trotted to his door, and flung it open without consulting the spyhole first.

Mistake.

Time juddered, then jumped track.

Now.

Here.

Green.

And she'd brought somebody with her.

WHEN *Ransohoff reserved me a place in acting classes at the Actor's Studio in New York City, I pounced at the chance. This was the school where Marilyn Monroe had studied, not to mention Marlon Brando and James Dean! Also, I'd never lived in New York, so I was dying to go. I was even happier when Philippe said that he'd accompany me and take an acting course of his own at Carnegie Hall. Despite our fights, I still loved him. We found a nice apartment on the Upper East Side. Then, one night during dinner at a fancy, sky-high restaurant, Philippe put a cherry on top of everything by asking me to marry him.*

When I said yes, I felt like I was floating among the clouds that ringed the building where we were dining. (We could see those clouds clearly through the window near our table.) My elation wasn't so much about Philippe as it was about the general notion of being married.

Pleasing my man, this is what I wanted, just as I'd watched my mother please my father. A few years on, when I finally did get married to Roman, I found marriage suited me, too (apart from all of Roman's flaws). I loved cooking big meals for my husband and our friends, with Virginia Ham and upside-down cake my specialties, though I learned to make Polish dishes, too. And I loved cutting Roman's hair—I learned to do it from my ex Jay Sebring—and packing Roman's luggage for him before he went traveling.

Also groovy was all our globe-trotting together. Especially through Europe. London was my favorite destination, but I loved Paris, of course, and then there was Italy, my second home. In the 1960s, Europe was often ahead of America with its new ideas and fashions. In Europe, everything was so much more liberal and open. So much more realistic. The whole freedom outlook over there was just fantastic. People weren't worried about what society was going to think—as long as the feelings were present, and as long as the feelings were honest. Men in Europe cried openly, and in airports they kissed their sons right on the lips. Emotion made them real men.

As I summed it up for one journalist, "Americans are too inhibited, but they are slowly coming around to realizing what a swinging world we live in."

A "swinging world," yes—but a few years before then, my excitement about getting engaged to Philippe didn't last long. Life with him in New York turned disastrous, worse than ever. For one thing, I felt so intimidated by my courses at the Actors' Studio, as well as by the other students. Some of them were friendly, but every one of them seemed better at acting than I was. Unable to bear it, I dropped out after only a few weeks. (The best advice I ever got about the craft came later, by the way. On the set of The Fearless Vampire Killers, the one picture we did together, Roman said, "With acting, Sharon, all you need to do is to be able to relax and focus at the same time.")

A big hassle with Philippe stemmed from how my parents and my manager Marty Ransohoff reacted to the news of my engagement. Ransohoff even threatened me point-blank, in front of Philippe, that if I got married, he would terminate my contract. Sure, he'd invested a lot of money and time in my career, but this "Svengali" (which is what friends now called him) was so controlling that he even wanted to select my miniskirts for me!

Once Philippe and I moved back to LA, it was only a matter of time before the strain got to us. Our arguments grew so intense that we started lashing out at each other physically. Shoes, Coke bottles, wine glasses, silverware, toenail clippers—these all got tossed around. And when Philippe punched and kicked me so violently that I wound up in the emergency room at the UCLA Medical Center, I knew it was over.

"LOOKIE, Jeepster—I brought company!"

Standing beside the green woman in the doorway of Lunt's suite was a clean-cut young man. He looked about Jopp's age, but there was nothing green about him. Slightly glazed brown eyes, auburn hair combed straight back, a black-and-white varsity jacket, gray corduroy trousers, and a bland expression on his pale, mulish face—the only detail that didn't fit the wholesome "Joe College" appearance were the wire-rimmed glasses resting low on his narrow nose.

As Lunt took an involuntary half-step back from the visitors, questions swarmed through his suddenly disordered mind, questions such as:

"Which Ofotert staff members allowed Jopp in the building?"

"If she's not here to kill me, is she here to sleep with me?"

"Who's this asshole with her?"

"How can I have sex with her if *he's* here?"

Jopp spoke again: "Lunt, meet Seth Amaranthus."

"Not *Seth*," the boy scolded Jopp in a whiny, adenoidal voice. He gave her a scolding look to match. Then, more politely, he said to Lunt: "Call me Strangely Strange."

"Oh, right," Jopp said, "sorry, dude." And to Lunt, she explained, "His name *used to be* Seth, but he ditched that."

"Next year I'm signing up with the Foreign Legion," Strangely Strange announced, as if this illuminated the naming matter. He took a moment to tongue the cherry-flavored Life Saver in his mouth before clarifying, "The *French* Foreign Legion."

"Yeah," said Jopp, "as if the cause of French imperialism, like, *urgently* needs your help."

"Shut up, witch."

"Um…" said Lunt, his mind too derailed now to make much sense of the young people's dialogue, much less to furnish a response. An extra distraction was the iridescent T-shirt Jopp wore. Green, of course, it cast her bud-like breasts in sharp relief. Lunt could make out the contours of nipple perfectly. His groin commenced humming.

"Strangely here," she said, speaking in her customary closed-mouth, lips-hardly-moving fashion, "he's my best friend, like a brother. In the Family, I mean. We were on our way to Benny Pompa's and I wanted you guys to meet."

"I hear you're a fan of Sharon Tate," said the boy, his long, rather feminine hands beginning to fidget with each other. "That's cool."

"Come *on*," Jopp said, "invite us in! We've gotta talk, dude. Plus, we come bearing gifts."

"First, I need to use your toilet," Strangely said.

"No," said Lunt, "no, I…" This was going too fast for him. He stood motionless, trying to process everything, a bead of sweat dripping from his forehead to his bloated belly. (He hadn't digested his room service meal yet.) "I…I…I—" was all he could say.

"Whoa, the stutters! Guess that goes with your drooling from the other day, Jeep. You feel all right? Still got that cough?"

Strangely turned to his companion, a troubled expression now crossing his face. "He's got a cough? It's not the *flu*, is it?" The whine in his voice turned insistent. "Jopps, you *know* I can't afford to get the flu again!"

"Cool your jets, Seth."

"*Heyyy*," he reminded her.

"Yeah, sorry, *Strangely Strange*. Don't worry, it's not the flu, it's just hay fever. The Jeepster gets it every summer, right, Jeep?"

Lunt wiped his brow. He didn't answer. He was staring at her mouth, entranced as ever by its Sharonness, and also by how well

GARY LIPPMAN

she managed to speak without revealing her wrecked teeth. She looked fantastic today, with her seafoam-green hair tied once more into pigtails.

"Have you tried eating eggs?" Strangely asked Lunt. "Eggs have been medically shown to reduce coughing."

Smiling seductively, Jopp reached out with a fingertip to draw a circle on Lunt's left cheek. This action left behind some glitter he wouldn't notice until his next time in front of a mirror. "You gonna keep us standing out here all night?"

"Please *don't*," said Strangely, "I've gotta make yellow. And this hallway has a draftiness issue. I really *can't* afford to get—"

Trying to sound as civil as he could, Lunt said, "I'm sorry, guys, but, uh—not now?"

"Why not?" Strangely challenged him.

"Because my place, it's a mess...a major, like, *pigsty*."

"You want messy," said Jopp, "you oughta see our Family HQ!"

Then, without further ado, she took the hand of her "best friend" and tugged him along behind her as she pushed past Lunt into the suite.

Once he realized what she was doing, Lunt resisted—but only feebly, raising both hands in the universal "stay back" gesture. By then Jopp had already moved around him, bumping his tricep with her bony shoulder.

"Nice digs!" Strangely said, surveying the place as soon as he got inside, his glazed eyes taking in everything. Including the TV, which at the moment was broadcasting a game show.

What just happened? Lunt thought, his insides going tingly and his mouth cottony with panic. *They're inside my room! They're* inside!

"Very nice," the green woman agreed with Strangely, nodding her head yet keeping her eyes on the man she called Jeepster.

"This'll definitely do," Strangely said, still tonguing his Life Saver.

Now Jopp touched Lunt's flushed right cheek with her fingertips. This action left behind more glitter. She said, "We need to crash with you a few days. Just a few. Benny says we can't stay with him in his own pad upstairs, but everything'll be easier if we're set up near him."

"In the same building," Strangely elaborated. "Hey, can you drop the A/C three or four degrees? It's chilly in here."

"Remember I mentioned Benny's new commune in Australia?" Jopp said to Lunt. "And how Ben wants me to be a lightning priest-ess? That's why I have to be close to him till my training's all done."

"Wait," said Lunt, not sure he'd understood what she meant. "You want to live *here*? With *me*?"

"Me and Strangely, yeah. But just us, no one else. Unless you want more roommates."

Lunt shook his head. Were they mocking him? They must be! "This is a gag, right?"

"A week is all we need," said Strangely. "Or a couple of weeks, I guess." He pointed to the bed. "You can't say that's not roomy enough for all three of us! Is it a queen?"

"Looks it," Jopp answered.

"But we'll have to kill the air-conditioning altogether. This draftiness issue is—"

"But that's—you're—*no!*" said Lunt, his voice shooting up.

"No what?" said the green woman, her smile undiminished.

"No you *can't* stay here!"

"We can't? Why not?"

"You just—just can't. Sorry."

Now Jopp's smile *did* diminish, and her face darkened. "Come on," she said, "don't be greedy. Being greedy's so *lame-o*."

"You're not a greedhead, are you?" This query came from Strangely, who'd stopped glancing around the suite to focus on

Lunt, his fingers busily fidgeting. "You know what Charlie calls greedheads? 'Bredda Gravalicious people.'"

"That's Jamaican," Jopp put in, assuming a helpful tone of voice, as if such courtesy would persuade Lunt to accept them as lodgers. "Charlie speaks twelve languages, plus Jamaican patois." She placed her bony hands on Lunt's chest and pushed him gently backward, guiding him against the nearest wall. Lunt bumped his head on it, but not hard. He wondered at this moment if his life might no longer be under his control.

"He's not a Bredda Gravalicious, is he?" Strangely asked Jopp.

"No, he's not. I know this dude too well. Besides, like I said, we brought him gifts, right? Stuff to trade for squatting rights."

With his head awhirl and his armpits now soaked with sweat, Lunt glanced from Jopp to her companion.

"For instance," the green woman said, exchanging a nod with Strangely while massaging Lunt's shoulders with a strength that surprised him, "Seth, or, er, Strangely works for our Family Research Council, the FRC, and he's been hitting up the web for intel. *Vital* intel."

The boy shifted from one foot to another. "Can't we do this *after* I make yellow?"

"Nope," said Jopp, "we can't," her tone growing stern. "Give him a taste."

So Strangely made an exasperated face, and in his adenoidal voice he said, "Sharon Tate gave birth out of wedlock to a child, a male, in 1963."

Lunt narrowed his eyes. "That's not true."

"Sure it is."

"No, it *isn't*." Clearly, they were mocking him. "That's absurd! It's just—"

"The dad was a Hell's Angel, and the kid's whereabouts? Unknown. But the FRC can find that child for you."

Lunt rounded on Strangely, fuming. "Who told you that? It's *lies*! Just gossip, stinking gossip!"

Strangely, thrown by this response, soon regained his poise. "Not according to the FRC," he said. "We dug up more, too. Did you know that Sharon Tate was the sex slave of the movie actor Steve McQueen? Supposedly McQueen was dynamite in bed, a real macho king."

"Wrong. *Wrong*! They were just friends."

But the boy held his ground. "The FRC has proof, hard proof. And did you know that Sharon Tate, Steve McQueen, and some hairdresser named Jay used to play ménage à trois games together?"

Lunt clenched his jaw, his fright and confusion superseded now by rage. It was one thing for them to invade his home, to threaten him that they'd move in. But slandering Sharon was beyond the pale! Before he got to say so, Jopp's thin hands flew like birds to his belt buckle and started to undo it. Meanwhile, Strangely spun on his heels in a goofily executed pirouette and marched through the open door of the bathroom.

"I've waited long enough," he called out. "Time to do something no one else can do *for* me!"

At the first sound of his urine hitting the water in Lunt's toilet bowl, the green woman stopped fuhtzing with Lunt's belt and shrugged (adorably, Lunt had to admit to himself) and said, "Seth always says stuff like that when he pisses." Her hands resumed their work. "Dopey, huh?"

"My goal," Strangely called to them, still in full flow, "is to teach myself to do this in rainbow colors. *That'll* blow the Legion's minds!"

By now, Lunt's belt was unbuckled, his zipper was down, and his indignation had subsided, had turned to wonder. "What're you doing?" he managed to say to Jopp, his voice dying off on the last syllable.

"A little treat. Where's your girth-stick, Jeepster?" She reached with nimbleness into his boxer briefs. "Ah, yeah—*got it*." While watching her barely moving Sharon-lips, he'd grown erect again with notable speed. She said, "If you let us crash here for a few weeks, we'll give you this treatment *every hour*. Like Abe Lincoln said, it'll be good *and* good for you."

Lunt didn't hear the "we" in her message. That is, he heard it but failed to hear it, to process it, just as he heard but failed to understand other aural data inside his suite: the toilet flushing, the Manson ditty "Look At Your Game, Girl" that Strangely hummed, and the *pock* sound caused by Strangely removing the lid of Bronson's Beige Milk moisturizer from its jar. Lunt couldn't apprehend any of this because his attention, all of it, had been reduced to feeling Jopp's warm, thin, strong hands. With one of these clutching his penis at its base and the other tenderly cupping his testicles, Jopp dropped to her knees, bringing the Sharonophile's underwear and khaki pants down with her. And now Lunt's focus shifted to her mouth, which engulfed that "girth-stick" of his entirely.

Oh, my stars, Lunt thought, simultaneously pulling in his paunch, straightening his spine, and inhaling sharply, *her lips, her lips—they're on me finally!*

Pleasure cascaded through him, lighting up his damp face and drawing moans from him as he stared down at the green woman, etching the image into the wax tablet of his mind. But along with such rapture came worry. Where had he left his Instigator condoms? What if she found him too fat? What if his hair looked bad? What if his groined smelled, *tasted*, as sweaty as the rest of him must have been? And what if she suddenly, viciously chomped down on his penis, vagina dentata-style, biting the whole thing in two?

Such concerns were short-lived, because what she did simply felt *too* good.

"You like?" Jopp wanted to know, once she'd paused to take some shallow breaths.

"Oh, *yeah*," Lunt gasped, pressing his back harder against the wall so he wouldn't slide down it. His legs had turned wobbly; he didn't trust them to keep him upright. "Don't stop, please!"

Fixing him with her unblinking green-shadowed eyes, regarding him the same placid way that she had when he'd been the one going down on her, Jopp took him into her mouth again, no glimpse of the teeth he knew were there, terrible teeth he didn't want to think of. *Stay with her lips*, he commanded himself, *concentrate on the Sharon-lips, nothing else, don't think about what's just behind them in that awful mouth, that cave of death.*

To help with this he tried to listen to Jopp's gulps, her "Mmms" and her moist wheezes.

It's all right, he thought, grinning stupidly, *it's just a blow job, a normal act, and no one ever has to know, not even Bronson, there'll be no evidence I got involved with Manson's girl, I'll just deny it, deny it all…*

When Jopp tightened her grip on his testicles, Lunt idly brushed a strand of green hair from her forehead, then wiped his hands, as sweat-slick as hers were dry, against his bare hips. Soon, with his eyelids fluttering, he was completely under her spell, able to see nothing until he happened to glimpse movement, rhythmic movement, across the room.

What was it?

Lunt's eyes cleared. Using them to squint, he found Strangely standing against the suite's writing table. The boy had left the bathroom, yet his gray slacks were still gathered around his ankles; his milk-white midsection was bare; and his penis was in his right hand. He was shaking his organ in sync with Jopp's head-bobs while the fingers of his left hand had found something else to fidget with.

"What the *fuck!*" Lunt bellowed, furious all over again when he noticed what Strangely was doing, and the Sharonophile swung around so sharply that his penis got wrenched from Jopp's mouth and she toppled over sideways. Then Lunt pawed at his pants and underpants until he'd pulled them to his waist. "You're crazy! *Both* of you!"

"What's wrong?" said Jopp. "Is it my fault? Seth'll take over if you want. He's a suck-artist, I swear."

"Yeah, they're gonna *love* me in the Legion, all those ex-cons and fugitives in kepis." Strangely dipped two fingers into the jar again, then resumed "interfering with himself," as Mrs. Moreland would have characterized his behavior.

Jopp sank to her rump on the floor, tucking her legs up beneath her, as Lunt recognized the object into which Strangely had been sticking his fingers.

"And it's Strangely Strange, not Seth," the young man corrected Jopp again.

"No!" Lunt boomed once he recognized the jar and realized the use Strangely had found for it. "No, no, *no!*" And he stamped his foot for emphasis—stamped it as a spoiled toddler would.

"Maybe you *are* a greedhead," Jopp teased Lunt with a "baby's-been-naughty" finger-wag. "You can't *always* be the first to come, rich boy."

Once more, Lunt hadn't really heard her, or heard anything. His full attention was on Strangely, half-naked Strangely, who'd picked up the Beige Milk once more, sniffed at it, and said, "Nice scent."

"Put that down, you freak! That's *my moisturizer!* Stop it!"

The green woman frowned, newly confused. Why was Jeepster getting so worked up? Was the suck-work she gave him bad, or had he gotten a peek at her teeth? She'd tried so hard to keep them hidden…

Strangely, himself untroubled, gave a whiny little chuckle. "Don't get your crap hot," he told Lunt, swallowing what was left of his Life Saver. "Next time I'll bring my own lube, 'kay?"

"Get out, you monsters! *Out!* I'll call the manager! I will!"

"Whoa, Jeepster, whoa—keep your voice down!" Jopp got up from the floor and began to stretch her slightly aching legs, first the left and then the right. "Listen—"

"No, *you* listen, bitch! I'll—I'll call the cops!"

"You'll *what?*" she said, vexed by Lunt at last. "You want us bounced out of the Ofotert a *second* time?"

"Yes! Exactly! I'll chuck you out *myself!*"

"What's gotten into him?" asked Strangely, too disturbed to go on masturbating. "Jopps, this friend of yours is rude. Besides, he's not cute like you said."

"You're *murderers!*" Lunt cried, both hands swatting with fury at the air in front of him.

"Jeepster, *pipe down.* Jeez! What's *eating* you tonight?"

"You killed Sharon, that's what, you scum! You and your people slaughtered her! And you expect me to smile, to be *a host*, to say, 'Cool, move right in, can I fix you guys a drink?'" He clenched his jaw, grinding his teeth. "As if your murders never *happened?*"

The green woman's eyes welled up with tears. "Something's cooked his brain," she told her best friend. "Maybe he *does*, like, have the flu."

"He does? Oh, *shit!*" Strangely dropped the Beige Milk, which hit the carpet with a *thunk*, and pulled up his corduroys, then dashed to the front door, which he promptly flung open. "I knew it—flu! I can't afford this!"

"*Lower your voice!*" Jopp hissed at him.

But Lunt's voice was even louder now than Strangely's. Once again, he threatened to "call the cops," adding, "You're trespassing, you scum! You'll go to jail and never see your Benny Pompa again!"

Biting her lip, the tears still swelling in her green eyes, Jopp knew that she—they—had no choice. Not anymore. This lame-o Moreland meant business. He would shop them to the police, bring the heat down on their asses. Their Ofotert base was blown. How wrong could one girl be? Blinking away her tears, she hurried over to Strangely, who held the door for her, turned to Lunt and snapped, "Go and rot in this pesthouse here. I hope your flu gets *worse*." Then, before he followed the green woman into the hallway, Strangely hawked and spat onto the carpet inside the door. It was the precise spot where the Santa Shots always showed up.

The instant Lunt slammed the door shut, he double-locked it and took a fast peek in the spyhole. Were they gone? Yes: empty hallway, no trace of green. Cowards, like Bronson, they'd fled without a fight. Well, good riddance! To think he'd let Jopp go down on him. Had even thought of *marrying* her!

Grumbling curses, his whole body quivering, Lunt went over to grab the Beige Milk, brought it with him to the bathroom, and hurled the jar into the trash pail. He didn't care if the jar shattered, Strangely had spoiled Lunt's moisturizer forever. How could he use it again without recalling that defilement? Next, Lunt carried a bath towel to the doorway and spread it out over the butterscotch-colored carpet, covering the saliva stain, and finally he seized hold of the room phone and rang the switchboard operator.

As soon as friendly Nancy began to greet him, Lunt cut her off, shouting, "The green bitch, she *got in*! I said '*No green bitch*,' but she showed up! You—you—you *fucking let her in here*!"

"I'm sorry, sir. 'Green bit,' you say?"

"Green *bitch*! Green *bitch*! I told that twitching asshole Trueax, and Baby Son, *too*. Hotel detective, my *ass*!"

"If you'd slow down, please…"

"She came straight up to my *room!*"

"But, Mr. Moreland, we don't have a guest named 'Greenbit' staying with us. And have you tried placing our 'Do Not Disturb' sign on the doorknob?"

With a screech of frustration, Lunt slammed the phone down, then took his BlackBerry from a twisted hill of bedsheets. *Bronson,* he thought, *I need Bronson. Need to speak with her, beg her forgiveness, and tell her about the ambush, how Jopp invaded here!*

Yes, Bron would know what he should do.

But as Lunt delved into his contacts list, scrolling for Bronson's name, the phone vibrated in his hand with a new text.

Seeing who the text was from dissipated Lunt's rage, changed it to fear all over again. Spine-tickling fear.

"You insult ME, insult SETH, insult our FAMILY—that's bad enough. But one thing I will NOT tolerate is when someone THREATENS TO CALL THE COPS ON ME. It's WAR, you asshole. You're LUNCH MEAT."

"I'm lunch meat…" Lunt said in a flat voice. "I'm lunch meat…"

And less than a minute later, he was "back on the Muke," glugging the stuff down until the bottle was drained dry.

A few months after I broke up with Philippe, he'd moved back to his native land, and I was living with a white poodle I named "Love" in the small apartment of another actress, a girl named Sheilah Wells. ("Don't forget to pronounce the h," she used to joke.) I never mentioned to Sheilah, or anyone else, how violent Philippe had been with me. It was too upsetting, and embarrassing, for me to even think about, just as I kept trying to forget a horrifying "date-rape" experience I had back during my high school years in Italy. (Even now, up here in heaven, I can hardly bear to mention it. All I'll say is that the rape involved a serviceman my father introduced me to, but I didn't mention it to either Dad or Mom.)

When I had the free time after leaving Philippe, I went skiing with friends or else visited my family. Unfortunately, there wasn't enough free time. I spent all of my weekdays working from early morning until late night on The Beverly Hillbillies, and afterward I cooked for myself and watched TV or else read magazines or books before going to sleep.

Reading became more important to me because I'd grown self-conscious about my intellect. Later on, during my few years with Roman, I would read more than ever, because I was striving to keep up with him. Will Durant's History of Philosophy and Thomas Hardy's Tess of the d'Urbervilles were two of my favorites. Even the original title of Tess before Hardy changed it—Too Late, Beloved—haunted me. I left the book in our London bedroom just before I left Roman temporarily to sail on the Queen Elizabeth II back to New York and then on to Bel Air. I wrote a note to Roman and placed it with Tess. The note said, "This would make a marvelous script. It's filled with popular debated material—sexuality and society, religion, good vs. evil, forgiveness and fear. Tess will enchant you."

Roman didn't seem to take my suggestion about Tess *too seriously. Even so, ten years after I was gone, he did make that picture. He cast his then-girlfriend, a very young German named Nastassja Kinski, in the lead role. I was tickled that we shared a birthday, Nastassja and I—January 24. And I was touched that Roman had dedicated* Tess *to me and to Paul, our never-born child.*

1964 was busy for "Sexy Little Me," as I used to call myself with friends. Ironically, of course. I read sometimes that I was supposed to be Hollywood's new sex symbol, even groomed to be Marilyn Monroe's replacement, but I thought I was the most unsexy thing that ever was. I was open for new ideas, sure, but I certainly was not aware of being sexy. Anyway, looks had nothing to do with what I felt like inside. When I wasn't dressed up for a public event, I kept my hair in a ponytail and didn't wear makeup. Who cared if people saw me like that?

Back to '64. That year, two bummer experiences happened and then, at Thanksgiving time, something great.

The first bummer was that I muffed an important screen test. Actually, I think I did pretty well on it, but the director of the film, a loud, rude man named Sam Peckinpah, argued with Ransohoff against using me. The picture was The Cincinatti Kid, *and my role would've been as the girlfriend of a professional gambler, played by Steve McQueen. Steve seemed to dig me, and our test together got a little steamy. If he weren't married, who knows what else might have happened? But marriage was an institution I always respected, and both Steve and his wife, Neile, became good friends of mine. Ransohoff pushed hard for me at the casting—I know for a fact that he did. But in the end, Peckinpah won the battle and he cast Tuesday Weld instead.*

As for the second bummer, it came about because Ransohoff could see my disappointment about The Cincinnati Kid *and wanted to make it up to me. So he scheduled a photo shoot on the beach at Big Sur, a place I fell in love with and later went back to for visits. The shoot went fine, but* during my drive back to Hollywood on the Pacific Coast Highway, a pea-soup fog developed out of nowhere and shrouded my new Triumph sports car. It got so difficult to see that I missed a turn and my car went flying off the road and rolled three or four times before it stopped. I don't remember much about the crash—it seemed to go not so much in slow motion (which is how Steve McQueen later told me his own racecar crashes went) but as if it was a bad dream.

I went on to have some other near-death experiences. When we were filming the beach-blanket picture Don't Make Waves, I jumped from a plane into a swimming pool, but my parachute opened prematurely and spread over the top of the pool, not allowing me to come up to breathe. But it was only on August 8 in '69, that night when Manson's people marched me and Jay out of my bedroom and shouted threats at us and shot Jay and choked me with a rope and began to stab me that I realized, "I'm really dying!"

My only injury from the auto wreck up the coast turned into a tiny scar near my left eye. But it didn't feel much like a miracle, seeing how badly the Triumph was wrecked. This wasn't the first car I'd smashed up, either; I was always a horrible driver. "Clumsy" is a word people often associated with me. I even dislocated my arm once by falling out of bed! Gaping at the ruin of the Triumph, I knew that Ransohoff would be enraged with me, and he was enraged, even more than I'd feared. After that day, he dragged his feet with my career still more. The auditions he sent me to getting fewer and fewer.

"I hope he hasn't given up on you," my mother said.

"Don't worry, Mom," I answered, "we have a contract, and he doesn't want to lose the value of his investment."

We both chuckled at this, but I was starting to worry that it was true, that Ransohoff saw me as a business deal that wasn't working out.

CONVICTED of Sharon's Tate's murder—he'd trained dolphins to maul her in her swimming pool—Lunt Moreland languished in prison, in a cramped, windowless cell. Although his hands were manacled to the wall, he was able to feel inside his ears for growing hair, the fingers probing deep. His only consolation while locked up was a bottle resting by his side. Because of the bottle's chocolate color, he assumed it contained Mucaquell, but when he'd finished drinking it down, emptying the sucker, he felt a rumbling in his stomach and noticed the word "Lustrate" on the label.

Lustrate, he recalled, was that libido-suppressing drug mentioned decades ago by Dr. Gluck, the Francophile therapist his parents had made him consult.

"No one here gets out alive," he mumbled to himself. "Or if I do, it will be so long from now that they'll parole me to outer space."

Through the bars of his cell window he saw lightning, spiderweb-shapes of it against velvet darkness, unaware that pure light had started pouring from his mouth. He went back to probing inside his ears, and when his fingers felt a long hair in the left one, he tugged on it until someone outside the cell, the prison warden, struck a gong, and Lunt awakened to raw sunshine.

Only gradually did he realize where he was.

The TV was blattering on, an inane talk show, and the clock on the nightstand read 6:19 while morning light streamed through his closed blinds. Friday already! Once again he'd lost so much time sleeping! Asleep, and not writing! But sleep was so delicious—especially in this suite, this well-appointed womb. There was nothing "junior" about it! And with Jopp and her cohorts having marked Lunt for destruction, it was also his only safe place.

Jopp.

Sitting up with fear-stoked speed, Lunt looked around the suite, checking for intruders, and then his eyes leaped to the space just inside his front door. Nothing there, just carpet with a bath towel covering Strangely's spittle. Praise Sharon! Mandrake's Santa Shot campaign did seem to have ended. Lunt's eyes now traveled to the room phone beside him. A memory came doggy-paddling into consciousness: halfway through his slumber, the black and shiny phone had started ringing outrageously, forcing Lunt awake, and after fumbling around for the receiver, finding it, and then holding it in the vicinity of his head, he'd heard that "Whosoever" bullshit once more.

What happened next?

Lunt could not recall. But the receiver rested on its cradle now, while his BlackBerry lay in the tangle of bedsheets near his waist.

Lunt took hold of the thing, stared at its grimy screen, poked at some buttons. Zero texts or calls from Jopp. Well, no news was good news—unless she didn't plan to make further threats but meant to just attack. Lunt shivered at this possibility, something catching in his chest. No word from Bronson, either. *Shit.* He had to call her again, to apologize as best as he could.

Anyway, was Bronson right, should he flee the Ofotert?

When the room phone rang, startling Lunt nearly out of his skin, his intuition told him, *Don't pick it up.*

Still, he answered back to it, *what if it's Jopp? I have to know where I stand with her. Or what if it's Bronson? Yeah, Bronson calling to say, "We went too far, that argument was stupid, you're my best friend, we're not like Mandrake, we stick together." Ah, loyal Bronson!*

Stretching his arm toward the nightstand, Lunt's hand reluctantly bypassed a Mucaquell bottle there, the still-full one, and took the receiver from its cradle.

"I hope I'm not, er, *waking* you," said Randy Trueax. The hotel manager had just blazed through a self-rolled, Plonk-laced cigarette, his first of the day, and this accounted for the lopsided grin on his face despite the present task of appeasing the kook in Suite 47. "I got your message about yesterday's snafu, the visitor in your junior suite."

Which outraged Lunt all over again. "She wasn't *a visitor*, man, she broke in here! She could've killed me! She's a threat to the whole place—*Charles Manson's wife*. The exact woman I warned you about, the green one."

"Well...I apologize, Mr. Moreland, and I assure you it won't happen again."

Lunt didn't want to alienate the manager of Sharon's former home, but his anger prevailed. "It better *not!*"

As Trueax launched into a defense of the hotel's policy on guest privacy, Lunt switched the phone to his left hand and the right reached for his Mucaquell. *Just one sip*, he cautioned himself, unscrewing the bottle top, tossing it across the room, then raising the bottle to his lips. He slurped in that self-promised sip and loved the warmth that coursed right away through his chest. After wiping his mouth with the back of his free hand, he decided to interrupt the still-blabbering Trueax by mentioning the mysterious phone calls and packages: "They stopped, I think—those packages, at least—but I still want proof of who was behind them."

Seated at the desk in his unadorned office, Trueax felt his head go into its latest Plonk-powered whirl.

He thinks I'm barking mad, Lunt figured, taking another sip of Muke. *That, or else he suspects I'm running a number on him.*

Maybe I planted the Santa Shots myself in order to file a lawsuit against the hotel, or to blackmail its owners, or to con them some other way. I hope he won't think all the Sharonophiles are bad seeds! What if the Sharonfest gets canceled, or won't be permitted here next year? Everyone will blame me! Then again, I'm blameless, right? I'm not a con man but a victim, a paying customer who's suffered major breaches of my security!

"Of course," he told Trueax, "there *is* one way you make this up to me."

The hotel manager sniffed at the notion. "Let me guess: Suite Fifty-Six. You want to change rooms, move to the former suite of your favorite actress." His right eye began to twitch. "As I've been informing you consistently since you arrived here, Mr. Moreland, transferring you there is simply not possible."

"Fuck *that*," said Lunt. "I've given up on that. No, what I want is more Mucaquell."

"Muca...Ex*cuse* me?"

"You know, the cough syrup I've been using."

Absently Trueax fiddled with a button on his coat sleeve. "Didn't you receive the bottle? *Two*, if memory serves?"

"Yeah, but, er—I dropped one. It shattered on my floor." With a yawn, Lunt remembered his suite's carpeting. "The *bathroom* floor, on the tiles. And the other bottle's running low." To support the veracity of his request, he pretended to cough now, and instructed himself to fake more coughs as the conversation went on.

"Why don't we just get you a doctor?" Trueax said. "We can have one visit your room."

"No, I've already spoken to my internist in New Jersey. He recommends I continue with the Mucaquell. So please get me more. Send someone out to pick it up. You can put it on my bill, just like you did yesterday. Or, wait, was it the day *before*?"

"I understand," said Trueax, breaking into a new lopsided grin. And he did understand, finicky as he was about his own drug of choice. "And I presume you're too ill to get the medicine yourself?"

Lunt faked another cough. "It's not that I'm too ill, it's that I'll be *in danger* if I leave here. Manson's wife, remember? The odds are, she's laying a trap for me right now. I don't *dare* leave the hotel, Mr. Trueax. My going out for even *seconds* might mean murder! Better safe than sorry, right?"

"We will send out for another bottle," Trueax said. He couldn't wait to tell his boyfriend about this madman. "And it will be brought to your junior suite once—"

"Thanks," Lunt jumped in, "but I'll need two bottles. Like before. Or, no—three. *Three* bottles."

Right away he wondered if even three would be enough. Probably not. Three would hardly last him through the week! Here it was, Saturday, and the Sharonfest would be starting next Friday evening. Wow, *so soon!* But was it Saturday now, or Sunday? Did it matter?

"Make it a case," he said.

"A *case?*" Both of Trueax's eyes were twitching now. "Isn't that excessi—"

"One dozen bottles." Lunt faked yet another cough. "Don't worry, I'll pay you something extra, as a tip. I'll write you a check, I promise. Two hundred dollars? No, let's say three. Or five! Yeah, five hundred dollars if you do this for me, Mr. Trueax."

"That's generous," Trueax said, not believing for a second that he'd be paid the quoted figures. Still, he knew from experience that he could add a hefty service charge to this cretin Moreland's hotel bill. That charge was entirely at the manager's discretion.

Lunt's own reasoning, once he'd hung up the phone, went: *Once I've flown home from here after the Sharonfest, I'll stop payment on*

*that five hundred bucks to Trueax. Let him complain all he wants—we
don't have a written contract! He probably won't still be working here the
next time I come to stay. Besides, by using Mucaquell I'm saving the money
I would've spent on food! Why didn't I hear about this medicine till now?
It's terrific!*

Stretching out on his bed, the talk with Trueax ended, Lunt
looked wistfully at his remaining cough syrup. What he wanted
was to drain the bottle in one go. He wanted the taste, that licorice
delight; he wanted the feeling, that stupendous Floaty P'Toaty; and
he wanted to dream, to savor the shelter that dreams conferred.
True, Dreamland hadn't been any picnic lately—it was more like
Nightmareland—but he wanted to go there, anyway, because he
sensed that he was due for a sweet one. As he was reaching for the
bottle, resistance gone, the BlackBerry in his hand began to trill.

His father phoning.

The bedridden Mr. Moreland was probably worried by the lack
of recent contact with his son. Lunt wished he could ignore the
call, deal with it later, but having alienated Bronson, he felt too
guilty not to pick up.

"Hey, Surfer Boy, how's tricks?" said the old man, as jaunty-
sounding as ever. Being a paralyzed widower was a constant trial
for him, of course, but he was able to watch TV around the clock
without being nagged by his wife. Could this be the reason for his
sunny mood every day? "Still driving those California girls wild?"

Yawning throughout the conversation, Lunt told Mr. Moreland
extensive falsehoods about getting his writing done, keeping in
good shape, and dating a variety of "surfer girls." Mentioning his
cough syrup was out of the question, and Lunt realized that he
would have to get clean, to "get off the Muke," when it was time
for him to fly home to New Jersey. "Dope," he could hear his father
saying, "is the gateway to homosexuality!"

For his own part of the phone conversation, Mr. Moreland spoke about the banal comings and goings of his nursing staff. He said he missed his son and asked about the upcoming Sharon Tate conference. Then—"Oh, I almost forgot!" said Lunt's father. "You've got mail here. Lots. A mound of oversized letters."

"Oversized…" murmured Lunt, his eyelids slowly sinking shut. The familiar Muke-sleep was coming on, fast. Once the "o" word got through to him, however, his eyes popped open. "*Oversized?* Did you just say *oversized?*"

"Right," said Mr. Moreland, "postmarked from Texas. They look kind of important, too. Love letters from one of your sweethearts, maybe?"

"Are they *manila?*"

"What, *from* Manila?" The old man chuckled. "In the Philippines?"

"No, the *color!* Are they manila colored? The envelopes!"

"Oh! Hmm. Yeah, I guess so. Should we open them, see what's inside?"

"Yes! God, yes! Dad, listen—this is crucial."

"Then hold the line. I'll ask Jah Victor to bring them over." Raising his voice as much as his strength allowed, Lunt's father hollered, "Yoo hoo!"

"Not at *my house,*" Lunt muttered to himself, shifting nervously around in bed. "Not *there*, too! It *can't* be…"

But it could be, and was.

As soon as the Jamaican male nurse got on the phone and greeted Lunt and described the seven packages sent to the Moreland home in Sulphurdale, New Jersey, Lunt had no doubt about their provenance, especially after Jah Victor confirmed that there was a sticker on each envelope. Lunt asked what each sticker read.

"Hmmf," said Jah Victor. "We see, yah." Over the line came the sound of paper rustling. "On *this* one, it says: 'In my mind's eye, my thoughts light fires in your city.' Hmmf, that's funny."

Manson—Lunt recognized the quote. Something that appeared in *Helter Skelter.*

Lunt swallowed hard, dread washing over him, thinking, *What if it isn't Mandrake behind all this? And Texas, where the phone calls come from—so those are connected to the Santa Shots! But why are the packages being mailed to my home? Is the sender trying to say he can find me anywhere—by land, by sea, anywhere he* pleases?

"Shall I open the envelopes?" asked Jah Victor.

"Yes, yes," said Lunt in a tumble of words, "yes, yes, open all of them, right now!"

Maybe inside one of them would be an explanation for the weirdness. But what if there wasn't an explanation, only new disturbing photos? Worse ones?

"No!" Lunt cried out abruptly, changing course, "hang on, Victor, *don't* open them."

"Make up your mind, mon!"

"Wait till I get home."

Whatever was inside there might alarm Lunt's father. "But read me the rest of the stickers on the outside of the envelopes."

So Jah Victor did.

According to one of them: "I MAY HAVE IMPLIED ON SEVERAL OCCASIONS TO SEVERAL DIFFERENT PEOPLE THAT I'M JESUS CHRIST, BUT I HAVEN'T ACTUALLY DECIDED YET WHAT OR WHO I AM."

Another sticker read: "WHEN IT COMES DOWN AROUND YOUR EARS, YOU'D BETTER BELIEVE I'LL BE ON TOP OF MY THOUGHT. I WILL KNOW EXACTLY WHAT I'M DOING."

And another: "NOW IT'S THE PIGS' TURN TO GO UP ON THE CROSS."

And: "IN THE NAME OF CHRISTIAN JUSTICE, SOMEONE SHOULD CUT YOUR HEAD OFF!"

There was one more, according to Jah Victor, but Lunt had heard too much already.

MY love life in 1964 was not exactly thrilling. I missed Philippe and couldn't seem to get in the groove with other guys I met. None of them were as appealing as Philippe had been. My roommate Sheilah tried to cheer me up, and so did Mom and Dad, but nothing worked. Then came Thanksgiving—which means it's time for me to tell you about a guy named Thomas John Kummer.

Like Roman, Thomas John was born in 1933, ten years before me. The fourth child of an accountant and his wife, he learned to cut hair while in the Navy during the Korean War. After four years in the service, he came to Hollywood, where he found work in an upscale hair salon. (He might as well have invented that word "upscale" because he used it so much with me!) While in "Tinseltown"—another term he might as well have invented—Thomas changed his name to Jay Sebring, after the Sebring Auto Race in Florida. He thought "Sebring" sounded glamorous, and glamour was important to Jay, because he figured it would compensate for his uncool Michigan background as well as his short stature: Jay was only five feet and six inches tall, just a little more than Roman. You can't say I only went for tall guys!

Chic hairstyles were big during the early 1960s—Vidal Sassoon started the trend, and Jay recognized his chance and grabbed it with both hands (and brush and comb and scissors). Actors and actresses, Jay knew, were only as good as they looked, and great hair was as accessible as a good suntan. Kirk Douglas was Jay's first celebrity client: Kirk needed to give the slaves in his picture Spartacus a distinctive appearance, and so he turned to Jay.

Within a few years, Jay had his own chrome-decorated salon, Sebring International, on Fairfax Avenue, with Paul Newman, Warren Beatty, and Steve McQueen among the rich and powerful clients. After separating from his wife, a fashion model named Cami, Jay ran wild as a bachelor. Despite his height, Jay was sexy, nearly as handsome as Philippe, and he started squiring gorgeous women around in his Cobra sports car. Aside from his wanton ways, Jay had a real sweetness to him—he was "the kindest playboy in town," as our friend Elmer Valentine called him. Elmer owned the Whisky A Go-Go, a Sunset Strip hotspot where the Doors would soon get their big start.

Through a mutual friend, Jay naughtily arranged an "accidental" meeting with me, and we got together right away. I liked how self-confident yet sensitive he was, dominant but not too dominant. After only two or three dinners together, with some late-night visits to jazz clubs, we were "the new thing in town." I loved to sit in the private room at the back of his salon, chatting with Jay and his top clients while he cut their hair! None of them ever complained about my being there.

Jay and I fell hard for each other, no question about it. My parents also adored him. But Jay fell harder than I did. I was always trying to convince myself that he was my soulmate, and I never quite managed it. Maybe, it seems to me now, I should have tried harder.

INCARCERATED in a Nazi death camp, Auschwitz or Dachau—whichever one had the smoke-colored *"ARBEIT MACHT FREI"* sign above its gate—Lunt and a few other ragged-looking prisoners were being marched by armed storm troopers past tall snowdrifts cloaked in mist: that same old cemetery fog. Lightning bolts zigzagged in the distance. After an anxious wait, the warden, a brutal catsuited female commandant named Mother Fist, ordered her prisoners to a squat, gray cinder-block edifice, where showers awaited them. The showers inside were filled with poisonous gas instead of water. All the prisoners dutifully headed that way except for Lunt. The commandant stopped him, thumping his chest with a black-gloved hand. Her Bubble Wrap Sharon Tate mask curled into a wolfish grin.

"For you," she said, "we have a special ordeal planned."

"Why me?" Lunt protested. "I'm not a Jew. I'm not a Gypsy, either!"

"Maybe not," snarled Mother Fist, "but what's that symbol you're wearing?"

Sure enough, when Lunt followed the commandant's eyes to his chest, he found a pink triangle sewed into his black-and-white striped uniform.

"No!" Lunt burst out.

"Oh, yes," said Mother Fist with a cackle. "You're exactly what your father fears—as queer as a mislabeled *Deutsche Mark* bill."

"That's wrong!"

"You don't love Sharon, you love *Roman*, and that French actor Philippe, and Jay Sebring, and all the rest. Oh, how you wish you could've forced your way into their steamy sessions, those faggy bacchanals with Steve McQueen!"

"Those are just *rumors* about McQueen."

The sky's coloration slowly turned to pewter around them.

"Being queer," said Mother Fist, "that's the source of your Sharonophilia. You're a fag—and Sexy Sharon is your mother. Who do you think that child born in sixty-three was? Sharon's child! You're the bastard child of Sharon and that biker! She popped you out of her fizzy womb, then she dumped you, she didn't *want* you, and the Morelands took you in, they filed the papers and legally adopted you. They were infertile because their union was cursed. Under a bad sign from the start. Don't you remember what your mother, your fake mom, told you on her deathbed? They got rid of your father's foreign sweetheart and that sweetheart tried to kill herself. Opened her wrists, like Dorothy Parker in your Hotel Ofotert bathtub."

"No! That's *lies*! All lies!"

"So the least you can do, *faggot*, is let her go. Let Sharon stay dead."

Something woke the sleeper. Something, a sound very different from the constantly droning TV. It was a distant rasp, a scraping of some sort. Emerging from his nightmare, Lunt blinked his eyes and rubbed both his temples, his breathing fast and shallow. Except for the modest sunshine winking through the open Venetian blinds, the suite looked washed-out, as if it was ailing, had grown moribund, from lack of light. Maybe it *was* a junior suite, after all— not senior enough to resist decay. His mind clearing, Lunt flopped over in bed, tangling himself up in the sheets, and looked around in puzzlement. What time was it? Before he could learn the answer, he thought he heard the scraping sound again, so he rolled to his left and tried to listen. Nothing more, just the TV. What had made that sound? An object of some sort. A bottle, maybe? His new supply of Mucaquell! Had they pushed a case of medicine under the door? How'd they manage *that*?

Lunt felt too weak to sit up, so he rolled off the bed, and once he got his sea legs, he stumbled over to his front door, where a manila-colored package waited on the carpet, waited right beside the spittle-absorbing towel. Lunt's horror on seeing the package cut through his grogginess like his scimitar letter opener.

He glanced at his door, making sure it was bolted, then put the lights on in his suite, picked up the envelope, and carried it to his writing desk. From the outside, it resembled all the other unmarked packages he'd received, but the sticker on the back was blunter than ever. "READY TO DIE?" it said. As Lunt knew, Manson used to ask this question of his disciples, and when they answered "Yes," he'd instructed them, "So live forever."

While he held the silver blade that opened letters, the Sharonophile's intuition warned him not to view the contents. He ignored his intuition, and once he'd seen what was inside, seen his tormentor's *chef d'oeuvre*, a sob rose in his chest and his knees buckled, betraying him. Down he went, clobbered to the ground by his new "gift."

Inside the package were Xerox prints, copies of Polaroids dated August '69.

Autopsy photos.

Hers.

8

MOON-FEED

(Sunday, Monday)

NAKED Sharon lay on a gurney, a cold metallic slab, her belly reduced to normal size since the baby inside her was gone. Someone had pinned her hair back and aimed a hot white light at her, at her startled-looking open eyes.

What monster is behind this? Lunt kept asking himself. *Who hates me so much that they want me to see this madness? And how did he or she obtain it? It can't be Mandrake or any other Sharonophile. Some monster, probably in Texas, is trying to destroy me!*

Splayed across his carpet, Lunt felt too poleaxed to try to stand. Taking a second look at the autopsy images had proved foolish since it made him vomit, emptying his guts. He hadn't eaten much lately, so there wasn't much mess, but the physical act of puking, those grueling convulsions, wearied him. He buried his face in his hands. His stomach felt inside out now, like a child's winter mitten. He considered setting fire to the autopsy prints, destroying them as they deserved to be destroyed, but he knew that, as with the Santa Shots, he needed to preserve them. For evidence.

After some minutes, Lunt leaned over and took hold of the bath towel that covered Strangely's spittle. He placed it on top of both the vomit and the Xeroxes. The besmirched towel, and what was under it, would remain there on the carpet at the entrance to the suite until the following Thursday morning, when officers of the West Hollywood Police Department would break through the front door and discover it.

Lunt hoisted himself up and staggered to his bed, where his Mucaquell awaited. He took a long pull from the chocolate-colored bottle, swishing it around in his mouth, appreciating the taste. When there was no more, he dropped the bottle to the floor. It made a *gunk* sound. He closed his eyes, trying to push away the images of Sharon on that gurney. Still, those images only vanished once he'd climbed under his blanket and the Floaty P'Toaty took him.

This time Roman Polanski wore the catsuit; it was Polanski who took the role of Mother Fist. Her voice was *his* now, Polish accent and everything—Lunt recognized it from the dwarf's filmed acting performances and taped interviews. And with her, *his*, gloved finger tapping Lunt's forehead, Polanski said, "Even *I*, her true love, let Sharon go. I found a new wife, made new children, moved on. Nothing stops me—not the Nazis, not Manson, *nothing*. But you, you're too chicken to fight the past, dear boy. Or fight yourself. So sweet dreams, dear boy. Or as your false friend Bronson says—she's the *real* enemy, you know—*your nightmares will eat you.*"

When he came awake, Lunt felt short of breath, queasy, hot, with perspiration dotting his forehead. There was no Mucaquell to give him solace. How had he polished off two bottles so speedily? He lay in bed for a long time, wondering when his case of Muke would arrive, his body bathed in light that streamed through his picture window. That sunshine made his optic nerve ache. Just in case a new Santa Shot package showed up, Lunt turned every few minutes to gaze at his door. Nothing appeared there, praise Sharon. After those autopsy photos, the images of her body cut to pieces on that slab, what could possibly be the encore?

The clock on the nightstand read 2:46. Sunday afternoon. If the "Whosoever" prankster had phoned him again last night, Lunt could not remember it. How wonderful it would be to flee the hotel, to breathe fresh air, to sashay along the Strip, to drive his red Mustang around. But he knew that going outside would be too risky.

While leaving a voicemail for Trueax—"Where's my cough syrup? A case of it, you *promised!*"—Lunt experienced a tiny twinge of hunger. Yes, he needed food, needed non-Mucaquell nourishment. So he rang room service and ordered a full meal. Chicken Marsala this time. The concept of a hunk of white-meat poultry under a drizzle of Marsala sauce seemed enticing—right up to the moment when the silver tray arrived. Then, once Lunt beheld the real article, his appetite vanished, simply left him, and after forcing himself to eat, he felt queasy. Something had been rearranged inside him, or his organs had somehow been reprogrammed, because the only nourishment he knew he could handle at this stage was Mucaquell.

At his window, Lunt looked down upon tranquil Seething Lane, searching for any green hair, green clothes, or otherwise suspicious sights. The curving street was as humdrum as ever, with no hawks swooping around. Soon the wooden Venetian blinds began to concern him. Why were they open? He didn't think he'd left them open. Had someone been in his room while he was sleeping? Had the housekeeper crept in here quietly to clean up, working around the slumbering man in bed? Or was it Jopp, she and her people? Had they done a creepy-crawly on him, moving the furniture, changing things around to bug him out?

Lunt eyeballed his suite, studying various nooks and crannies. Nothing looked unusual. Lunt pulled on the cord to shut the blinds, then hurried to his door, stepping over the bath towel on the carpet, trying not to think of what lay underneath it. Hoping to find someone to ask about his blinds, he poked his head out into the hallway, but the hallway, like Seething Lane, was empty, from the crimson-carpeted main stairwell on the left to the glass "Emergency Exit" door on the right. No one to be seen, not even a housekeeper. Except for a vacuum cleaner's buzzing in the distance, silence ruled.

Taking a seat at the writing table, he sought to distract himself by writing his Sharon memoir. Alas, he was too jittery to focus. Besides, what was the point? Mandrake had torpedoed his book, his Great Work, the one achievement in Lunt's life that mattered, and this discouraged him too much to get anything done. Nothing he wrote, anyway, could properly express how much he loved Sharon, just as nothing he wrote would be sufficient to convey his true love's essence, what a miracle she'd been, how all those amazing attributes got vacuum-packed into a single being. A goddess, in fact! Why not just live and die in silent worship?

Lunt looked forlornly at the "WHY?" poster, La Tate's eyes as ever refusing to meet his.

"I betrayed you, yes," he told the poster, "just like Bronson's betrayed me with her refusal to phone back, to forgive me, and her refusal to ever *meet* me, and her switching over from you, Sharon, to Raquel Welch. Maybe I'm a *worse* traitor—I betrayed you with a Mansonophile. But I was just so *lonely*, so lost without you…"

Not sure what to do with himself now, Lunt shut down his laptop and turned to the Dorothy Parker book, but he just kept reading the same poem over and over, hardly comprehending the text, which started with, *"Death's the lover that I'd be taking."* After that, he half-watched the dreck on his TV while glancing over at his front door (*Where the* fuck *is my Muke?*), and glancing sometimes at the champagne resting on his writing table. Could the bottle's alcohol content serve as a panacea, some kind of substitute, for the Muke, those Muke-ingredients his body craved?

Finally, toward evening, the room phone rang, which scared Lunt silly. The good news: it was Trueax, calling about the Muke. But the bad news was extremely bad.

"No more Mucaquell *where*?" said Lunt. "At Limsky's Pharmacy?"

"No more Mucaquell *anywhere*, Mr. Moreland. Your medication is no longer available. It's been recalled."

"*Recalled*? What, like, *remembered*?"

"Not remembered," said the hotel manager with a snicker he didn't bother to conceal, though Lunt was too preoccupied to notice. "Mucaquell has been *called back* by its manufacturer. Production is discontinued."

"Discontinued? But that's outrageous!" *Is Trueax deceiving me,* Lunt wondered, *holding out on me, bogarting the Muke for himself?* Trying to keep his anger in check, he said, "I don't understand. Discontinued *why*?"

"There's something wrong with it, I'd say. Wouldn't that be the case if something gets called back by the manufacturer?"

"There's *nothing* wrong with it! It's terrific!"

"Plainly," said Trueax, his tone turning snarky, "not everyone agrees with you. We haven't learned any details yet, there's nothing solid on the Internet. But a recall is definitely in effect."

"That's *wrong*," Lunt said. "Mucaquell works fine. I can *prove* it!"

The manager exhaled, grinning lopsidedly, and glanced at his hands, worried that they were trembling. No, steady as stone. So should he roll another cigarette? Yes, he would need the extra one today, with more Plonk than usual sprinkled in it.

"Enough talk," snapped Lunt. So much for keeping his cool. "You're all hot air. Just get me my Mucaquell."

Trueax snorted, growing equally miffed. "Mr. Moreland, I'll repeat myself *again*, since you can't seem to take on board the basic concept. Your cough syrup is not available. Take it up with the people who produce it. Or go hunt for it yourself. Or find yourself another brand."

"No, it's got to be Muke! My doctor said so. If it's not available in LA, then try Fresno. Santa Barbara, Vegas, *anywhere*!"

Another snort from Trueax. Had he not been forced to enroll in an anger management course last year, he would have had some

GARY LIPPMAN

choice words for this buffoon. "The recall is national," he said, leaving it at that, pleased that he'd maintained what his anti-anger instructor had referred to as "chi parity."

"Well," Lunt forged on, though he was on the verge of weeping, "I won't give up so easily. Not like *you*. There must be some bottles out there..."

"You may be right." This was the stock response Trueax used for ideas put forth to him by crazy people, whether they were elite hotel guests or schizophrenic beggars on the street. "At any rate, we've tried our best on your behalf, and now I need to end this matter."

"So you're a quitter—is that what you're saying?"

Shaking his head, his eyes beginning to twitch in sync, Trueax told himself, *Chi parity, chi parity, chi parity.* Once he regained control of himself, he said, "Sir, there are any number of independent concierge services you can—"

"Services, *schmervices*, you clown!"

"*Clown?*" Fuck chi parity! Oh, how Trueax would have loved to strangle the breath from this imbecile! To run upstairs and choke him dead with bare hands! But after taking three deep breaths through his nose, the hotel manager was able to master his rage once more. Keeping his voice even, he said, "Mr. Moreland—"

"Keep searching, clown!"

"*Again* you call me that?"

"Do your job, Trueax! Search!"

"*You're* the clown!" Trueax boomed, losing every ounce of that chi parity. "*You're* the clown, you—you—"

A host of hostile phrases followed, some of them quite creative. Yet these epithets got muffled by a pillow—the pillow under which Lunt pushed the phone receiver.

JAY Sebring turned out to be as nice a man as Richard Beymer, though Jay did possess a dark side. There was his house, for example, which he bought a few months before I met him. A mock-Tudor mansion on a cul-de-sac just off Benedict Canyon Drive, Jay's home had been owned by Jean Harlow and her producer husband, Paul Bern. On Labor Day in 1932, Bern committed suicide. Some years later, someone drowned in the swimming pool, and this was followed by two more suicides, including a housekeeper who hanged herself.

The first night I visited Jay at his mansion, which was also the first night we made love, he told me these stories. He also said that the house was haunted. "That's a major reason why I bought it," he said. "Don't you feel the vibes? They're fascinating!"

I didn't feel anything except for his well-built naked body next to me in bed. Yet I lied to Jay and told him that I did indeed feel those vibes. Why not? I wanted to feel them! Ghosts were cool, as long as they were benevolent.

Nothing weird manifested itself in the house until one night in early '65 when I was staying there alone. Jay was working late on a film set in the Valley, and I woke up to find a creepy little man, even smaller than Jay or Roman, standing beside my bed. He was peering down at me, his eyebrows arched, as if he was curious who I was. With one lollapalooza of a scream, I bounded up, ran past him, and barreled down the home's main stairway, where I saw another terrifying sight: a female corpse who looked exactly like Yours Truly. She was naked, with a rope looped around her neck and her throat slashed open and her eyes horribly bulging.

"It must have been Paul Bern, that figure beside your bed." This is what Jay theorized once he got home. It took a long time, plus some joints and glasses of milk, for me to calm down.

"And who was that woman on the stairs?" I wanted to know, still shaking.

Jay smiled. "Probably the housekeeper who hanged herself."

"But why did she look like me?"

Jay couldn't answer this. He gave me a massage, tried to relax me, and in time, thanks to the grass and milk and TLC from my boyfriend, I fell asleep. Never again did I see any ghosts at Jay's place, or anywhere else. Still, I couldn't forget that woman's popped-out eyes and peeled-open red throat.

While I was with Jay, the flower children were on the rise, and I considered myself one of them, burning incense and getting off on Bob Dylan and Janis Joplin and the Doors. I also loved wearing the Mod Look. How fantastic all the fashions were in the 1960s! One of my favorite outfits was the cream-colored taffeta wedding dress I designed for myself. As I described it to reporters at the ceremony, "It's Renaissance until you get below the knees."

Designing clothes was a passion for me, and I couldn't wait to get started making my own children's wardrobes from scratch. Then there was shopping. I loved to browse through Melrose Avenue boutiques, especially Betsey Bunky Nini, and Jack Hanson's Jax Department Store. (Jack also owned the Daisy, one of my favorite Hollywood nightclubs, which had a $500 annual membership fee!)

What was my single most cherished outfit? Probably the blue-and-yellow Pucci print minidress that I was buried in, with the body of Paul, my unborn baby, in a white shroud right beside me.

Back in the 1960s, the drugs seemed as innocent as the fashions. At least they did at first. Jay, I will admit, was an enthusiast. You name it and he liked it: pot, speed, cocaine, mescaline, and LSD. He was hardly alone in this—everyone in our circle of show business friends used stuff to turn on. Because of his popularity with people, though, Jay became known as a vital connection between the dealers and the customers. Here was another aspect of his dark side. Now, I wasn't exactly a stranger to getting high: I'd taken my first sip of beer back in junior high school, and in Italy I discovered wine. But only in Hollywood did I discover the pleasures of smoking hashish and marijuana. I wouldn't say it was "love at first toke," but it did feel as mind-expanding as advertised, and later on, with Roman, I became famous in our Hollywood and London circles for the deliciousness and potency of the hash brownies I baked.

Generally speaking, drugs were good for me. Before I started using them, I felt so knotted up inside, too shy sometimes to even dance at parties. Drugs opened me up to the world like a flower in bloom. One of my favorite things was to drop LSD and go with friends out to the desert—the Joshua Tree National Monument, usually—and watch sunsets from the top of a boulder. Nothing sordid, in other words; nothing like the scandalous stories that came out after my murder, gossip that our parties were drug-fueled orgies. What rubbish!

Nevertheless, I quit smoking grass when I got pregnant, and LSD became problematic even before then. Acid could take me a little too far "out there," and I had my share of bummers. The first time we tripped together, for example, Roman teased me by putting on a Frankenstein mask, and I screamed like a madwoman, even more than I did when I saw those ghosts in Jay's house.

Roman said he'd had some bad drug experiences as well. Once, while he was high on some especially strong acid, he saw swastikas in the eyes of a friend, and this reminded him of his childhood in Nazi-occupied Poland, where his parents were sent to concentration camps (his father survived, but not his mother). That same time, according to Roman, he discovered "the secret of life," which he took the trouble to write down: "First love, then sex, then work."

"Sounds accurate to me," I told him as soon as I stopped giggling. But even though I didn't say it then—I didn't want to alienate him—having children was, for me, more important than my acting or even love or sex. I knew that, once I got married, I would find being a mom so fantastic. Parenthood was right up there with romance! Which was why I begged Manson's people to let me live long enough to have my child.

Begged them in vain.

"ALL right, you win," Lunt told Randy Trueax's answering machine at noon on Monday, another mild-temperatured, sun-French-kissed day in West Hollywood. "It's just this cough," he lied, "it drives me bonkers. You can send something else—it doesn't have to be Muke! I'll pay anything, just send it now! And whatever you do, *don't let Jopp or other people in to get me!*"

This message, once he heard it, made Trueax cackle with delight. In the heat of his fury last night, the hotel manager had considered removing Lunt from the Ofotert by force. Such a strategy would not just be vindictive but prudent as well, since who could predict in what filthy and wrecked condition the cough syrup addict would leave his junior suite? It probably required fumigation already! Besides, they couldn't afford another guest being carried out of the hotel on a stretcher, having already reached their monthly scandal quota with that dead cat burglar.

After mulling over the matter, Trueax decided to leave Lunt Moreland where he was, at least for now. To cover himself, the manager made sure to charge Lunt's credit card in advance for his entire projected stay, with three thousand additional dollars held as collateral for damages. That, in addition to a special charge Trueax would levy.

As for the hotel guest in question, he hated to keep ringing up Trueax, especially after their nasty recent talk. Yet what other options did Lunt have? The staff at every drugstore he phoned had told him that they no longer stocked Mucaquell. The nation-wide recall Trueax had mentioned was, yes, the new reality, though Lunt still suspected the hotel manager of hoarding some syrup for himself. No pharmacies seemed willing to deliver other cough syrups, either. Was it Lunt's desperate, hectoring tone that caused these refusals? Or had he been black-listed? Was it Jopp behind his troubles—was this possible?

Monday proved quite unkind to Lunt. Before then, still in possession of Mucaquell, he'd spent the majority of his time doped into dream-rich slumber, but now that he'd run out of his elixir, sleep had become a problem. Despite bone-deep fatigue and dozing off for ten-minute intervals, Lunt couldn't get any rest. And with his whole system newly under siege, insomnia was the least of the troubles.

He felt dirty, sticky, listless, and had a thirst no amount of drinking water could slake, although sweat came pouring out of him and turned icy in the AC-ed air. His libido had departed without ceremony and his testicles hung low while the skin on his arms and legs felt strange, almost like paper, and when this "paper" got to itching, he couldn't stop scratching it. In time he'd scraped open little wounds. His stomach felt unwell, too, pulses of nausea gathered into a steady state. His body ached from toes to scalp, dull pain alternating with needle-sharp stabs. Moving his eyes hurt in particular. Hell, even his hair hurt—and everything, *everything*, burned with fever, that bad old breakbone fever, as though some gargoyle fed a furnace inside Lunt.

The only affliction he *didn't* suffer from now was a cough.

Is this cholera? Lunt wondered, wiping a line of froth from his lips. He'd dodged that disease down in Buenos Aires. But perhaps he hadn't, after all. Perhaps the cholera microbes had lain dormant in his body until this horrid moment. Or what if it wasn't cholera but poisoning? Had Jopp or Mandrake or even Trueax spiked his Muke with something toxic? He'd read once that Manson planned to crash Tinseltown soirees and dose the punchbowl with belladonna, a potent psychedelic, then rob the partygoers blind. Was Lunt in the throes of a belladonna trip?

In truth, Lunt was undergoing acute drug withdrawal—what bohemians like Manson called "cold turkey." Yet this fact did not dawn on the Sharonophile. Nor did he speculate how he'd gotten hooked on Muke so quickly. He was past such curiosity. All he knew—or *thought* he knew, given how disordered his thoughts were—was that Sharon's ghost would intervene. She would not let Lunt sink too far. Not *all the way* down. Wasn't this Hollywood, where all the endings must be happy? She would soar to his aid; she knew how much he worshipped her, how long he'd been her devotee, and she knew he'd resurrect her with his book, the Great Work that Mandrake was so hell-bent on pulverizing. Mandrake, and Manson, and maybe even that dwarf Polanski—all the "man" men: <u>Man</u>drake, <u>Man</u>son, and Ro<u>man</u>! Sworn members of an anti-Lunt conspiracy, they labored day and night to punish him, just as the gods punished Prometheus for stealing fire and then presenting it to humanity...

They won't win, though, Lunt vowed silently. *In the end, thanks to Sharon—here's the outcome she'll engineer!—me and my book will survive. Survive, and* triumph. *Yes, sir, I'll reach forty without senility (clear memory intact, no hair in my ears) and never speak again to Bronson, that female Judas. I'll strike it rich and be famous and find a wife with the five S's, and write more books about La Tate, and when I die, a very old man, everyone will say, "He gave us Sharon, restored her to us, made her a fire for humankind."*

Come nightfall, Lunt's suite seemed to be in constant motion, dipping and swooping around him. While tossing around atop his sweat-soaked mattress, he felt his fever spike, and it whipsawed him between extremes of cold and hot. Meanwhile, his throat was as dry as chalk, his tongue had swelled, and his nose began to run, its viscous output flecked with blood. He thought of it as a faucet someone had carelessly left open. There was a buzzing in his ears, his teethed chattered, he farted frequently, and he reeked as badly as he felt. He didn't dare bathe himself, however, because he worried how his skin would feel, the terrible scalding, when water touched it.

By midnight, Lunt's BlackBerry had gone dead, as drained as his Muke bottles were, and his mind was too far gone now to think about recharging it. *Am I like Vishwa, cracking up?* he asked himself. *Loony bin bound? "We cannot truly know whether, at this moment, we are sitting in a madhouse." Where did I hear those words? This isn't just a madhouse, it's a pesthouse. That's something else I heard recently. But where?*

With his bowels constantly astir, he wondered if he would soil himself in bed. Was his life no longer under his control? And what was this new itching, this awful internal itching, as if some creature (he pictured not ants but a rat, a single overgrown rat with fangs and claws) was scratching at the inside of Lunt's flesh, its inner layers, tickling him into madness?

Wistfully Lunt remembered the balcony one flight up, that peaceful aerie from which he'd watched the hawk fly, soft sunset light evaporating around the creature. That had been his first full day at the Hotel Ofotert, his first full day away from home. So long ago, it seemed. How he wished he could return there! But he was trapped in this sound-proofed prison cell, this junior suite as silent as the grave, this air-conditioned lowest circle of Ofotert hell.

Near dawn he fell into a quasi-sleep, but it was short-lived because he woke to find his legs thrashing about, twitching and jerking as if galvanized by their own mad agenda. This terrified Lunt more than his other symptoms. He'd never lost control of body parts before. What's more, the rat inside him had scampered southward, tickling him through his middle. What did *that* mean?

The room phone had to ring for fifteen minutes, stopping and starting many times, before it could break through Lunt's mental sludge, the buzzing in his ears, the drone of the TV, and the cavalcade of other noises in his head. It took him another full minute to get the receiver near his face and mumble "Hello?" into it.

"Apology *not* accepted," a female voice announced.

And while he was still working out who this voice belonged to, it hurtled into a loud, rude, expletive-laced monologue.

"Listen," Lunt finally broke in, surprised for an instant by how ravaged his speaking voice sounded. "I *swear*, I'm sick, Jopp…"

"Yeah, and you took down *Seth*. Remember my Seth? He's sick, too. You gave him that lame-o *flu* you've got! He hasn't been outta bed since he met you."

"No, honestly—this is worse…worse than flu…I'm *dying*!"

"You've got bigger problems, trust me. You finked on us yet?"

"Ffff-inked?"

"Yeah, shopped us. Ratted us out. Squealed on us to the heat."

Lunt felt his right leg start to thrash and couldn't will the thing to stop. He licked his cracked, snot-crusted lips, or tried to lick them—not enough moisture in his mouth. God, he was thirsty! "Uh…*what*?"

"If you wanna make it right, Mr. Bredda Gravalicious, you know what I need."

Not understanding her, Lunt shook his throbbing head to bolster his brain function, but gently, so it wouldn't throb worse.

"I want to occupy your Ofotert room," the green woman said, and her voice had an edge to it, an iciness he'd never heard before. "I get to live there, no charge, till I'm done with Benny's priestess training. You had your shot at living with me and, like, you blew it. So out you go. Take your bad germs somewhere else. When I'm done at the Ofotert, you can move back in."

She had more to say, but when Lunt shifted his position on his sick-bed, trying to get comfortable, he lost hold of the receiver and dropped it, and by the time he was able to retrieve the thing from the carpet and put it back to his ear—actions which caused him great strain as well as more groan-inducing head-throbs—Jopp had hung up. Hoping she hadn't believed that *he'd* hung up on *her*, he put the receiver back in its cradle and waited for her to call back. It was a short wait, one minute only, but during it he licked his lips again, or tried to lick them. He was so *thirsty*. But how, with his tongue so swelled, softball-size, could he get water, champagne, *anything*, down his throat? Moreover, his left leg had joined the right one in thrashing about now, thashing with a will of its own.

As soon as the phone rang again, these problems were temporarily forgotten. Lunt seized the receiver, an action that caused another groan, and went right on pleading with her to show him mercy.

The only problem: it wasn't Jopp on the line now.

Once Lunt paused to draw a breath, that solemn male voice said, "Whosoever treats his fellows without honor or humanity, he, and his issue, shall be treated with commensurate inhumanity and dishonor."

It took Lunt a few accelerated heartbeats to recover from his surprise. Then he asked, "Are you the one...the one who sent those...those *awful pictures*?"

Silence, punctuated by faint breathing. Then the breathing changed back to voice, a voice from Amarillo, Texas, and this by-now familiar voice, instead of answering Lunt's question, posed one of its own: "Ready to die?"

Lunt gasped.

"They dressed her sexy for her funeral. You gonna dress that way for *yours*?"

ANOTHER aspect of my boyfriend Jay's dark side was his sexuality. There's no easy way to say this: Jay was into sadomasochism. He was never really violent with me; all he did was tie me up with silk cords, then gently whip me, and I always gave him my full permission. Jay would get so excited by this—he even took pictures of me bound and gagged, which he confessed he liked to look at while he masturbated. It was all so silly—I had to struggle not to laugh out loud, which might have offended him. But I found it sad, too, and I wondered what was in his psyche, in his past experiences, that made this behavior such a turn-on.

Apart from the S&M stuff, making love with Jay was normal, and usually really good. My previous lovers appreciated my figure, of course, but not the way Jay did. I felt like he wanted to know, and took the trouble to know, every inch of me. Even the not-so-sexy parts. This was fantastic— it boosted my self-confidence, especially on those days when I felt a little chubby. Then again, as a rule, I came to feel open about showing off my body and did so gladly in nude scenes for films as well as in a Playboy "pictorial" that Roman would shoot himself. "The Tate Gallery," the editors titled it.

Comfort with one's own nudity was a virtue, as Roman saw it; my "letting it all hang out," he said, was another way of being authentic, being Sharon without shame. Of course I would never have done outright pornography, although Roman did privately film us making love. But as long as the nudity had an artistic purpose, why not?

(Which reminds me of a joke Roman once told me, a joke that cracked me up: "What's the difference between eroticism and kinkiness? Answer: with eroticism you just use a feather, whereas with kinkiness you use the entire ostrich!")

Looking sexy, acting sexy, and dressing sexy sometimes had its costs. Along with sexiness came wolf-whistles and catcalls from men, not to mention vicious looks from other women. One time in Paris with Roman, I was on crutches owing to a minor skiing accident, and a band of drunk Spanish boys yelled some vulgar things at me. One of them even dared to pinch my rump! So Roman thumped him one, but the others ganged up on Roman and beat him up.

Another time, five months before my murder, I was at home on Cielo Drive when this creepy-looking hippie came strolling across our front lawn. Even smaller than Roman, he had long hair, a messy beard, and piercing eyes. Not exactly the sort of stranger you want waltzing around your property! A friend who was with me, the Iranian photographer Shahrokh Hatami, confronted the stranger. While this hippie explained that he was looking for the previous tenant, a record producer named Terry Melcher, I stepped out onto the porch to see what was going on. Our eyes met, the hippie's and mine, and it shook me up. A lot. The way those eyes looked at me, into me, cut deeper than any catcall or unfriendly look or butt pinch. It was as if he wanted to rape not only my body but my soul. And rape me not out of lust but rather from pure hatred.

Hatami spoke brusquely to the hippie, maybe too brusquely, explaining that Melcher no longer lived in the house, and the hippie shrugged and shambled off. Even so, I couldn't forget him. The eyes of that freak stayed with me until my last moments alive, when I guessed, correctly, that my murderers had taken their orders from him, the little man who was their god.

Back to Jay. In March of '65, his divorce from his ex was finalized, and we spoke about getting married. I was in love with Jay, of course, but I wasn't sure if I loved him enough to want to spend the rest of my life as Mrs. Sebring. Anyway, I believed I was too flighty for Jay, not organized enough. I could be unpredictable—very, very impulsive. Sometimes I didn't know what I wanted from one day to the next. I couldn't enjoy anything premeditated; I just did stuff as I felt it. "Spontaneous" is the word. But whatever I did was motivated by honesty. So I decided to be honest with Jay, and put off making a decision about marriage with him. I said I'd been down this block once already with Philippe, and heck, I was only twenty-two!

"I need time," I told Jay—time being, of course, what none of us, even people who'll get to live out their full life spans, have enough of.

Disappointed as he felt, Mr. Sebring told me he'd accept the delay, especially when I gave him my high school class ring as a sort of pre-engagement offering. Then, to help sway me, he took me with him to Hawaii for a vacation with our friends Steve and Neile McQueen.

My career at this time was still in the dumps. Ransohoff kept dragging his feet, not sending me out on enough auditions. While we were in Hawaii, both Steve and Jay brought up this bad situation. They were concerned, and tried to persuade me that, while my problems with Ransohoff could not be addressed—a contract was a contract, after all— my agent Gefsky was fair game. It was true that Mr. Gefsky wasn't doing much for me anymore, and Steve said that his own agent, the top-drawer Stan Kamen at William Morris, was willing to take me on.

I saw the point. Then again, Mr. Gefsky had always been so good to me that in the end I agreed to switch agents on one condition: that Mr. Gefsky continue to get his usual ten percent commission from all my work. Basically, this meant that I was paying two separate commissions to two separate people, one of whom wasn't even working with me any longer, but if we're not loyal to those who deserve our loyalty, what good is anything else in our lives?

THANKS to the "DO NOT DISTURB" sign placed by Lunt days earlier on his doorknob, no hotel housekeeper disturbed him in his agonies. This did not mean that the Ofotert cleaning staff was unaware of those agonies. Throughout Monday and Tuesday, the chambermaids parked their squeaky carts near Suite 47 and took turns putting their ears against Lunt's door. They couldn't comprehend what words he babbled—he had the TV and the A/C going nonstop, to blot out the silence he'd come to find oppressive. The housekeepers listened anyway, chuckling or shaking their heads in sympathy, each of them thinking, *Loco—another wealthy loco gringo*. They had heard worse at the hotel, and knew they'd most likely hear worse in the future. But he sure was in bad shape, this *loco gringo*.

Astounded at how heavy his head felt, Lunt theorized that it might be filled with concrete. He considered the possibility that his gastric gurgles were speaking prophecy. And he believed— for a while, at least—that his suite was shrinking, its walls slowly yet steadily, *stealthily*, closing in on him until it would turn into a sepulcher and seal him up inside itself forever.

Tuesday was when Lunt's spiritual crisis began, when his faith in Sharon's grace finally wavered. Whether the sick man was curled in fetal position on his sofa, was crawling to the bathroom, or was shivering in the empty tub where Dorothy Parker had failed to kill herself, his headache, thirst, sweats, runny nose, buzzing ears, chattering teeth, fever, and stench, not to mention all the itching and those involuntary frantic leg shakes, kept battering his body. How could his faith in La Tate *not* waver? Perhaps she even meant well, wished to save him, but she was, alas, powerless, with her new home in the sky just too far away for her to be of earthly help.

"I'm over and I know it," he told his Sharon poster. "Snakebitten. Done for. Lunch meat. Kaput. It's the end of me, Lunt Moreland. Was this how you felt when death came?"

Meanwhile, he felt the rat set loose inside himself go scampering up to his head, where its claws and fangs tickled brain meat and skull walls alike. He wet himself, the urine soaking into his bed. He didn't care. Hygiene was irrelevant. The odor was gross, true, but everything in the universe smelled bad now, and nothing mattered. Nothing but Mucaquell, the nectar that ran out on him when he needed it most. He cursed everyone who'd made it, from the executives and the chemists to the factory foremen and the truck drivers who'd placed that fickle substance in his hands.

At one point, Lunt felt rational enough to want to phone 911, to beg whoever answered to send an ambulance for him, but to his muddled mind, this claustrophobic Ofotert prison was his best bet, a cocoon that sheltered him from greater horrors. Leaving it would prove more dangerous than staying, so 911 remained undialed. More than once, however, he rang the switchboard operator, pleading with her, *Bring me my medicine.* Like Mrs. Kruikshank and the rest of the staff, Nancy had been instructed by Randy Trueax to ignore the guest in Suite 47. And in the end, he yanked the phone cord from its socket. What use were telephones anymore? He couldn't bear to hear another word from Trueax. Nor could he stomach any new "Whosoever" scary talk or further guff from Jopp or Bronson. No hex they might call down on him, no psych-out whammy, was worse than what he currently suffered.

Outside, tar-black clouds gathered, the moon wheeled through the sky, and a tidal wave reared up from the Pacific, prepared to engulf the land. So Lunt imagined. Chaos couldn't be denied; the

Hand of Fate, that karmic hammer, would ball itself into a fist, punch through the ceiling, and smash Lunt into powder, a powder the hotel maids would eventually blithely vacuum up. To distract himself from such thoughts, Lunt started watching—or sort of watching while sliding in and out of consciousness—a movie rerun. It looked familiar. The plot was like Polanski's *Tenant* but set in London instead of Paris, and filmed in black-and-white, not color.

Gradually Lunt realized, with his bloodshot eyes fixed on the glass screen, that this was *Repulsion*, Polanski's opus from 1965. And as he watched now from his sickbed, wheezing through mossy clenched teeth and farting more prolifically than ever, a blonde with Sharon-hair—Catherine Deneuve—listened as a couple in the room next to hers had sex.

Later, Deneuve wiped her mouth compulsively after letting her boyfriend kiss her.

Then she lingered on her phone, repeating "Hallo?" to an unseen obscene caller.

Then she dreamed of being raped, raped in silence except for a loudly ticking clock.

And finally, with a straight razor, she slashed a man.

Hang on, Lunt thought, jarred into a moment's mental clarity. *She murdered a guy*? This was unsettling. Totally! Weren't Sharon blondes, even French ones like Deneuve, destined to be the victims? It ruined everything, the entire moral setup, if women were killers instead of killees! What kind of planet would this be if Sharon Tate murdered someone? Even if that someone was Charles Manson?

IN 1965, I did a "villainess-in-black-leathers" role for the TV show The Man From UNCLE, but nothing else turned up until the autumn, when Ransohoff gave in to my pleas and agreed to cast me in an English horror film that he was producing in France. Its title was Eye of the Devil (Thirteen, in its foreign release), and the lead role was played by David Niven, the movie star crush of my girlhood. How wild that, of all the world's male actors, Niven was the star of my first real movie production! Wowee zowee!

"Don't you fall in love with that mustachioed English twit," Jay cautioned me, laughing, before I left for France. He was laughing, I think, to show me that he wasn't really frightened of losing me to Mr. Niven. But Jay was worried about losing me to someone else, anyone who was younger and more handsome and glamorous than himself.

The script for Eye of the Devil was majorly eerie. David Niven played an olden-days marquis, Philippe de Montfaucon, who brings his wife and two children with him from their home in Paris back to Montfaucon's family chateau. He's returned so he can try to manage a disappointing grape harvest. What the marquis knows, but won't admit to his loved ones, is that the entire village surrounding the chateau belongs to a pagan fertility cult, and in order to improve the harvest, the cult leaders plan to kill the marquis as a sacrifice to their gods.

The part of France where we shot Eye of the Devil, the Perigord, had a foggy, mystical atmosphere. It was perfect for the story. So was the castle, the Chateau d'Hautefort, which was our principal setting. The character I played was a sinister young witch named Odile de Caray, who lived in the area with her warlock brother, Christian. Playing Christian was the sexy English actor David Hemmings, who was so good the *following year in Antonioni's picture* Blow-Up. *The characters of Odile and Christian are key members of the harvest cult, and in the end, it is Christian who kills the marquis with an arrow to the heart during an elaborate death ritual.*

David Niven was so generous to me, and he really got a kick out of it when I told him that as a schoolgirl I'd planned on marrying him. He said some really nice things about me in the press, stuff like, "She's up on Cloud Nine, Sharon is, a marvelous girl, and she's got all this fun and spark and go—a great discovery!"

Originally, the actress playing the marquis' wife Catherine was Kim Novak, who was so fantastic in Hitchcock's Vertigo. *(I told Roman when he was making his thriller* Rosemary's Baby *that* Baby *seemed to me like "Hitchcock on grass.") When Kim injured her back while shooting a scene, Deborah Kerr was brought in as Kim's replacement. Contrary to what the gossip papers said, trying to play up trouble between me and Kim, she was thoughtful, kind, and helpful. (Unlike Elizabeth Taylor, who one year earlier got me blackballed from a small role in her film* The Sandpipers. *No matter how friendly you are with them, certain stars just can't stand having a starlet around. Sometimes I think that my being friendly with that type of person made it worse—they saw my friendliness as weakness. And when you get to the point where you have the power to run your own career, they call you a bitch.)*

Not only was Deborah Kerr terrific in the role, a total professional, but she was as supportive to me on set as David Niven was. She kept passing on helpful tips and telling me that, as long as my luck stayed good, I'd be a huge success.

When I heard this, I wondered why she emphasized "good luck" so much. Now I know.

FINALLY she came. Peeled herself off the "WHY?" poster on the wall so she could join him on his fever-dampened mattress.

In other words, delirium set in.

Delirium, or at least a twilight state with full-production values.

"Hi," she cooed, coiling around the perspiring naked man, her pregnant belly pushing out from under her velvet dress, her wig askew. Through the closed Venetian blinds (at least they'd stayed shut!), slivers of moonlight asserted themselves. The vise grip of drug withdrawal, as if wearying of Lunt, would begin to loosen in several hours' time, but he was still getting squeezed by it, hard. When the poster-Sharon smiled at him, beaming pure compassion, he noticed that her teeth, unlike Jopp's, were white. As white as whipped-cream clouds. And in the sultry voice Lunt recognized from films and taped interviews, she said, "What a *swinging* world we live in!"

Lunt tried to kick free of his damp bedsheets, to embrace her more directly—this time he'd wanted his legs to thrash!—but he was too tangled up to manage it (and was afraid of hurting her). His bid to speak also failed—his mouth and throat might as well have been Death Valley, his tongue still as swollen as a softball. In spite of her presence, everything hurt him as keenly as ever. Nevertheless, with great effort, Lunt could finally croak two words: "Help me."

"Sorry," said Sharon with a sigh, "no can do. It's the 'insane game.' You chose Manson over me. You made his Family *your* Family, therefore *my* Family. Now I can't get rid of them. They've wrecked my fun and spark and go."

"Forty," he managed to whisper. "Please, Sharon, forty...I'm almost there, there at my birthday..."

Charmingly, she shook some wig hair from her eyes, then consoled him the best she could, blowing air into his nostrils, cooling his forehead with her kind touch. She said, "Do you remember my famous last words? Actually, it was just one word, the word I said before they finished me…"

He nodded.

"It wasn't 'Daddy' or 'Dad,'" said Sharon. "It was 'Mother.' Do you remember what Dutch Schultz said on his deathbed? 'Mother is the best bet.' Nutty, right?"

Lunt tried to smile, but saw that she'd begun to look past him, looking at the foot of the bed. Struggling to lift his boiling head, he finally raised it several inches off of his pillow, and once he succeeded—Yikes!

She'd brought company.

Lunt gasped with recognition. Ranged around him, encircling his bed, was a rogue's gallery consisting of Jopp and Strangely, that Japanese tourist from Buenos Aires, plus Benny Pompa, Polanski, Bronson, and Mandrake. What about Manson? Lunt couldn't see him, but he knew that wicked Charlie must be outside, racing a dune buggy through the Ofotert hallways while crooning "Star," Lunt's theme song for Sharon.

"Light a candle," Bronson advised the ailing man. "Someone's getting hurt here very badly."

"We warned you," said the Japanese man, in flawless English.

"You can't say you weren't told," added Polish-accented Polanski.

Everyone seemed so witchy. They were sorcerers, all of them joined together to preside over his extinction. Eyes watering, Lunt whimpered, "Mother, oh, mother, mother," quoting Sharon's last word. So he wouldn't live to forty, after all. No, he would join his mother and his Sharon, and once he died, somebody else, a perfect stranger, would replace him in this suite and go on living, loving the women Lunt loved, while Lunt went totally forgotten.

"Gird your loins," Bronson said, and then she chortled. Her trademark chortle. It seemed like years since Lunt had heard it. He narrowed his eyes and glared vehemently at his ex-friend, whose lips were parted, her teeth exposed. These teeth were thoroughly Jopp-ish, crooked and rotted brown by her devotion to all things Manson.

"You're just a cripple," Lunt spat at her, "a lousy dyke, too pathetic, too ashamed to ever meet me face-to-face. I know *why*, too. It's 'cause Sharon loves me more than *you!*"

"Wrong," said Lunt's ex-friend. "A Jolly Doll can't love its owner. Not that we ever owned La Tate. Or even, like, *understood* her."

At which point the whole sick crew in Lunt's suite, including Sharon, began to chortle, mocking Lunt's plight. He couldn't bear this, he really couldn't. Rolling away from his bed's wet spot, away from Sharon, he gazed up at his window, wishing he could rise and fly through it and flee this place, not fall the way cat burglars did but soar away, just fucking *fly*, a proud, free hawk, and the wind would purify his lungs, restore his health, and lift him higher, higher, higher, to that source of light, the moon.

Except the moon was not his friend.

And never had been.

It was a round, gold vacuum cleaner, stealing all the life from Lunt, all his vitality. Whatever Hoovers the housekeepers used here, those things had *nothing* on this sucker, this hungry moon. It fed on us without remorse, just as Gurdjieff had believed. He'd known his stuff, that wizened sage; Sharon's taste in wise men was laudable. And now the moon had chosen Lunt and it was feeding on *his* soul, and his enemies were feeding, too, devouring him, and he knew that when they stopped, he'd be no more than a mere husk, his essence hollow, all scooped out, with the moon just a reflection on the curved bones of his skeleton.

I was pretty nervous when Eye of the Devil *started production, biting my nails like a demon. I didn't have a super big part, they listed me seventh in the credits, but I was featured in nearly a dozen scenes, and one of the promo posters for the film showed a close-up of my eyes with this tagline: "LOOK AT HER LONG ENOUGH AND SHE JUST MIGHT BE THE LAST THING YOU EVER SEE."*

The director helped a lot, reminding me, "Don't worry, Sharon, the camera is your friend." One big challenge I overcame was learning the British accent I had to use for my part. In the first big scene I shot, the marquis' children happen upon me, the witch Odile, sitting beside a pond near the chateau, and just before I use the magic charm on my necklace to turn a toad into a dove, I say to the boy, "Do you believe in magic?" I had to repeat this line hundreds of times in my trailer to get the ring of it, the Britishness, just right. By the end of our shoot, people told me that my accent was pretty accurate!

Another fun scene to play was when the marquis is whipping me for being a witch, and instead of looking pained, my face is transported with bliss, and I flip him out by saying, "You're mad—quite, quite mad." As you'd imagine, I kept thinking about Jay doing his own gentle whipping routine with me, and I made a promise to myself to say those same words to him the next time he tied me up and used his whip on me.

My best scene in Eye, *I think, was one that we filmed on the roof of the chateau. When Deborah Kerr finds me hanging out again with her children—I'm tempting them to play on the castle's high ledge—we have a showdown. Deborah warns me to stay away from her family, then asks, "Didn't my husband already tell you to keep your distance from us?" In the scariest vacant tone of voice I could manage, I reply, "Did he say he* would do that, did he lie to you? Oh, but you must be used to that by now. Men always lie. Personally, I have no use for them—except for my brother, Christian!" And while I'm saying this, my fingers are fingering the magic charm on my necklace, turning it so it catches the sunlight and reflects it into Deborah's eyes. Basically, I hypnotize her—so much so that I finally command her to leap from the roof to her death! And she's about to make that leap, too, when my brother, who's in the distance, blows a hunting horn, which accidentally breaks the spell and saves her.

One downer from the Eye shoot was this freaky guy Alex Saunders. He referred to himself as a "professional warlock" and wanted everyone on the set to address him as "Verbius, King of The Witches." Alex claimed that the master magician Aleister Crowley—the self-styled "Great Beast 666"—had tattooed his little body as a tenth birthday present. (Not most people's idea of what to give a child for his birthday, right?) One of our executive producers had hired Alex to advise all of us on "occult authenticity," and he and his wife offered to teach me how to fly on a broomstick. All I had to do, they said, was undress and apply "an ancient balm" to my private parts.

"No, thanks," I told Alex, "I'll stick to flying with Pan Am."

After my murder, "Verbius" claimed that he'd initiated me as a witch. Like hell he did (no pun intended)! The truth is, Satanism scared me, and I only paid attention to it because my friend Mia Farrow, fresh from shooting Roman's film Rosemary's Baby, kept blabbering on about it. For me, spirituality was all about positive vibes, although even my favorite mystic, Gurdjieff, wrote some creepy stuff. How the moon, for example, nourishes itself on human souls.

9

A SLOW NIGHT AT THE CORPUS

(Tuesday)

WITH his withdrawal symptoms at last receding, Lunt felt—well, not *better*, exactly, but a little less unwell. He had an appetite, for one thing, and so, with sore joints and stiff legs, crying "Ouch" along the way, he hobbled to his kitchen, where he opened the minibar, gingerly sat himself on the warm linoleum floor, and then got busy drinking soda pop and "feeding," as Pompa would call it. Feeding in a big way. When he was finished, more than half the candy, peanuts, popcorn, potato chips, and soda bottles in the minibar were gone. Lunt was disgusted by all the money he would be charged, by the poor quality of nutrition, and by the wasteland of torn-open plastic wrappers he'd just created. Still, the sustenance proved good for him right off: he could fall asleep, for one thing; his sleep was free of nightmares; and just before he woke, he heard a voice say, *"You know how to score it."*

He understood what "it" meant, too.

Mucaquell. And he *did* know how to score it. Where he could obtain it. Oh, splendid brain wave! He understood at last. That voice had spoken truth.

So, time to leave Suite 47.

First, though, he would need a shower. Before climbing into it, Lunt caught a glimpse of himself in the bathroom mirror, and what he saw there disconcerted him. Sunken cheeks, puffy red eyes, a snot-caked mustache, and a bluish tint to his face, while his stomach had never appeared more bloated. As for his hair? Jay Sebring would've *plotzed* (a favorite word of Bronson's) to behold such greasy hair. Worse, some of the whiskers on Lunt's cheeks were white. White! He looked hunted, haunted, years past his real age. Forty? Fuck, no, over *fifty*. Sixty, even. A haggard drifter...

Despite how cool Lunt kept the water, the shower still scalded him, just as he'd feared. Still, he forced himself to endure it until he'd soaped up everything. Getting dressed seemed to take a century, so he didn't bother shaving, but he did brush his teeth, and the clothes he put on were fresh: boxer-briefs, khaki slacks, his usual sneakers, and a T-shirt reading, "A MIGHTY FORTRESS IS OUR SHARON." Remembering to bring along his red-tasseled key, he headed to his front door, legs still stiff and aching. Then...

Elevator, going down.

10:08 P.M.: From her station behind the Ofotert's reception desk, Mrs. Kruikshank failed to recognize the man stumbling toward her. Judging by how he looked and moved, this person, whoever he was, was plainly in a bad way. And such a grumbly look on his face!

Halting before he reached the front desk, Lunt turned to squint at the revelers in the lobby, who were in raucous high gear. He was searching for a flash of two colors, orange being good (Benny Pompa's Afro) and green being the opposite. What would he do if Jopp was here? All would be lost! Likewise, he hoped Mandrake wasn't lurking nearby since he couldn't bear for his foe to see him in this state. Then again, did anyone really matter anymore?

Stay focused, Lunt ordered himself. *Keep your eyes on the prize!*

Recognizing him at last, Mrs. Kruikshank pursed her lips, opened her eyes as much as they would go, and brought both hands up to her face. "Mr. Moreland," she said after two seconds, "it's *you*! I didn't... Oh, you poor thing! You're green around the gills... What the heck has happened to you?"

Lunt, startled by the woman's tone, how suffused it was with kindness, moved forward, lurching the final distance to its source. So she was here—great! Wise like Yoda, she would recognize his plight, sympathize, give him assistance.

"Sir, are you *ill*, or—" Mrs. Kruikshank paused to shake her head. "Can I call you a doctor?"

"No doctors," said Lunt, his voice cracking. His nose, jammed up as it was, still picked up the scent of mustard coming off her. "I *need* you, lady..."

The night clerk blushed. After four seconds, she said, "Yes, I know you're keen to interview me, it will be my pleasure, but surely we can do that later, when you feel up to it?"

"*Please,*" Lunt insisted. His hands dropped to the smooth cool mahogany of the desk and gripped its curved outer edge, holding on to it for support. "Please—I need to find that pop star Benny Pompa. He's staying here, in the Ofotert. He might have something I need. What's his room number?"

Closing the magazine she'd been perusing (it featured an article about Roman Polanski's current wife, the French actress Emmanuelle Seigner), Mrs. Kruikshank said, after five seconds, "Does this involve our interview? Because I'm certain Mr. Pompa won't make *half* as good an information resource as I will!"

"Forget the interview…I need Pompa. *Right now!*"

More than usual, a full nine seconds, were required for the neurologically-impaired Filipina woman to understand this and to then reply. "Mr. Moreland," she said, as if speaking to a child who should've known better, "the staff is *not* allowed to share this information."

Lunt's voice rose, growing desperate. "But I'm a guest here."

"Yes, I know, and we're pleased to have you—but *it's forbidden*! Mr. Pompa deserves his privacy."

"I know, I know, but—"

"And Mr. Trueax said that with *you,* for some godforsaken reason…" She was going to refer, discreetly, to the hotel manager's new grudge toward Lunt. But instead she paused to ask herself a silent question: *What harm would come if she* did *give this poor man Lunt Moreland what he wanted?*

10:14 P.M.: Tonight, Saffron Jane Rubinowitz and Gertrude "Trudi" Albertson—routinely referred to by *Popfart Magazine* as "the Brides of Pompa"—had chosen to stay in. So when they heard someone's knuckles knocking on their suite's front door, they were lounging on the living room's indigo couch, sharing a bong. The bong was loaded with Bolivian Bronze hashish, which had been smuggled from Taipei inside a prep book that Trudi used for her notary public exam. Instead of the up-market attire that these sharp-featured brunettes usually wore—garments made from the processed outer flesh of rattlesnakes and leopards—the two were dressed down tonight. All they had on were underpants (Trudi's a white thong with the words "DADDY'S GIRL" in red script on the front, Saffron's an oversized pair of ice-blue panties) and midriff-exposing T-shirts (Trudi's bearing the logo of the Hotel Kempinski-Corvinus in Budapest and Saffron's showing the side-by-side faces of Minnie Pearl and Pearl Bailey beneath the words, "OUR TWO MOST PRECIOUS PEARLS"). Both women wore lipstick—matching candy-apple red.

Saffron wasn't sure she'd actually heard the first knock; Bolivian hash was notorious for inducing auditory hallucinations. And she'd begun to forget the matter when, wait, hark, there it was again! A knocking sound that was slightly louder this time, loud enough for Trudi to glance over at Saffron in a fashion suggesting that she had heard it, too. Both women thought, *Benny must've forgotten his key.* Neither woman said it. But Saffron did say, after blowing two jets of smoke from her nostrils, "Let's hope he kicked that green bitch to the curb." Then she handed Trudi the bong before lifting herself off the couch.

A mere twenty feet separated Saffron from the front door, but this distance was not easy to navigate, especially not while barefoot. First, she had to swerve around the altar in the center of the room, a wooden structure devoted to our globe's many deities of lightning. Arranged on the altar were statues formed from iron, plastic, wood, and stone, statues that represented Thor, Zeus, the Roman god Summanus, the Teutonic Donar, the Haitian Sobo, the Indian Indra, the Japanese Futsu-Nushi (male) and Kaminari (female), the Bantu Umpunduto, the Magyar's sky goddess Verka, plus two Aboriginal deities: Mamaragan (whose voice was thunder) and Namarrkun (who liked to strike clouds with axes attached to his celestial knees and elbows).

In threading her way to the door, Saffron went past picture windows entirely covered with felt sheets, a hooded grill dragged in from the balcony, candles burning everywhere, and electric lights covered with colored scarves and snoods. Saffron also had to pass over a vast field of debris. This debris had collected spontaneously on the charcoal-colored carpet of the suite during the two months the women had been living there with their male mate, and now it formed a galaxy of garbage—an ever-shifting, clumpy-textured, cigarette-ash-dusted "skin," as Saffron referred to it. ("Floor-paper" was Trudi's own term for the mess.) Needless to say, housekeepers were never permitted into this place by the occupants.

Among the objects on the carpet were:

An empty porcelain piggy bank; three brunette wigs (still in their packaging, with one labeled "The Rebecca Schaeffer Look"); an unopened box of Tampex sanitary napkins; a "Happy Goth Girl" Jolly Doll; a paperback copy of Gore Vidal's novel *Myra Breckinridge;* a football jersey reading "GET THAT GIRDLE OFF" across the front; an antique yet recently sharpened cutlass; nineteen stolen street signs reading: "DANGER: LIGHTNING!" in seven different languages; a gigantic American flag; various video cameras with tripods; a dog-eared biography of Bruce Lee; a length of barbed wire; plastic devil horns; a book entitled *Coconuts, Constipation, and You;* a golden tube of a patchouli oil–flavored "personal lubricant" called Arabian Silk; a rubber coyote mask; a hernia belt; scuffed-up white go-go boots; a sack filled with ostrich feathers; a "Gap-Toothed Giddy-Up" Jolly Doll; shaggy blue cheerleader pom-poms; a pair of purple-tinted shooting glasses; Lone Star firecrackers; a book entitled *How To Live Like A Lord Without Really Trying;* three blonde wigs (still in their packaging, with one labeled "The Nicole Brown Simpson Look"); a photograph of Oscar Wilde with the caption "He's Hot, He's Sexy, And He's Dead!"; a jewel-encrusted goblet; a clear, plastic packet containing dyed-green pubic hair; a black Bic ballpoint pen with its end chewed off; two electric bass guitars; a crash helmet used by a stunt man on the set of the film *Le Mans;* paper flyers for something called "THE PERPA MIND LAXATIVE SYSTEM"; a book of Victorian ghost stories; a salt-encrusted surfboard; assorted, unlicensed handguns (one loaded with live ammunition, the rest with blanks); a thick brown leather weightlifter's belt; a black, very different kind of belt; a book entitled *Petting As An Erotic Enterprise;* three garments from last year's *haute couture* collection of the prestigious "House of Szombathelyi"; a dark-brown witch's hat; a torn poster of the carpenter Jesus Christ accidentally striking his finger while hammering a nail and shouting out in pain, *"ELVIS H. PRESLEY!";* a batch of brand-new adult diapers; a Santa Claus hat; cartons of Codex and Santa Fe cigarettes; two uneaten beef stroganoff TV dinners; a variety of dildos and vibrators, all colored yellow; the Doors CD album *LA Woman;* a large coil of thin yet strong rope; many unpopped sheets of Bubble Wrap; and a glazed gray meat-hook with a fat long chain attached.

Two paces from the front door, Saffron stubbed her big toe on the meat-hook, harshly enough so that she hollered, "Mother*fuck!*" It was not the first time that this toe and this object had collided.

Another knuckle knock on the door, this one slightly bolder than its predecessors. Saffron, her toe still smarting, yanked open the front door. Instead of her husband on the threshold, she found a square-looking loser. He was slumped against the doorframe, not suavely but Skid Row–style. She gave him the once-over, twice. Not that two times were necessary. Autograph seeker, was Saffron's guess. Except that he looked more disheveled than the run-of-the-mill Benny Pompa fan.

In a shattered-sounding voice, the loser said, "Sorry to bother you, miss… I'm a neighbor…I live downstairs, on the fourth floor…"

"So what," Saffron snapped, "you want a medal?" She jerked a thumb over her shoulder at the junk-strewn floor behind her. "We probably got one here."

While riding the clanging, metal grille elevator upstairs, Lunt had sensed new energy coursing through him. Much of this energy derived from hope, a nervous jangling hope that he might soon score Mucaquell. Since Benny Pompa was renowned for his illicit-drug use, it made sense that he'd possess Lunt's favorite potion, or else would know where Lunt could snag it. And with Pompa being so charitable to orphans, how could he refuse a fellow doper, one in need, and one who was half an orphan himself?

Another reason Lunt felt energized was the suite where he was heading, the sacred site where Sharon had lived in the late 1960s. How unfair that the current resident wasn't Lunt but Benny Pompa—or "Ziggy Rosenwach," the falsely-identified "European bigwig." What a stupid alias Pompa had used for himself! Even so, Lunt did not hold it against him. Lunt didn't dare to, since he required Pompa to get him Muke. "Beggars can't be choosers," as

Lichtenberg or Dutch Schultz or someone else once said, and Lunt would *beg* Pompa if necessary—beg for Muke, and beg to hang out in Sharon's once-and-forever suite.

On arriving at the fifth floor, Lunt left the elevator, forgetting to glance at the balcony from which he'd watched the sunset of his first full day here. As he knocked on Sharon's old door, focusing on the numeral "56" (which was shaped from the same kind of brass as his own door's "47") and thus failing to notice the "DO NOT DISTURB" sign on the doorknob, he felt an extra power surge. Sharon's spirit had come through for him, after all! Why had he doubted her posthumous ability to give him succor?

Once the door to 56 swung open, something unrelated to Sharon or Mucaquell threw Lunt for a loop. It was how little clothing the woman who now faced him wore. *So much for snake- or leopard-skin*, Lunt thought. He'd foreseen that he might encounter one of Pompa's fetching wives, but—wow. Straightening his posture, sucking in his belly, he felt his groin hum for the first time in days. Just her bare, smooth-muscled thighs were enough to rile him up.

"Well?" Saffron prompted him, arms folded, regarding Lunt with obvious distaste.

Stay focused, he commanded himself. *Keep your eyes on the prize.*

Averting his eyes from any body parts but her eyes, Lunt spoke again. "It's an emergency," he said. "A big one...I need to see your husband—as soon as possible!"

10:36 P.M.: The air was warm and smelled clean to anyone who cared to take a whiff, though the stars had to fight their way through light pollution to glimmer down onto Sunset Boulevard. Ignoring the sky, Glen Mandrake motored west. Hertz had run out of red Ferraris, and he'd always had a yen to drive a Jeep, so a Jeep it was—an open-air blue one. Cleaned up efficiently, out of the bathrobe and back in his white suit with a brand-new pumpkin-colored ascot, Mandrake was cruising around, wondering what local singles bar would suit him. Tonight was his first time outside the Hotel Ofotert since Pandora had ditched him, and he needed to replace her. Someone temporary, either for one night or the week. Two or three replacements at one time would be ideal, of course— the thought of multiples made his ears twinge with excitement. In his still fragile state, though, self-confidence might be difficult to summon.

A green light at Fairfax. Another green at Crescent Heights. Outside the mall where Schwab's Drugstore once stood, an off-the-leash bulldog barked at Mandrake. He showed it his middle finger. The Ofotert was still visible in his rearview mirror, its turrets like iron nails against the dark sky, when a messed-up-looking middle-aged man stepped in front of the Jeep, right out here in moving traffic. This sudden appearance gave Mandrake a scare—"Snakes alive!" he shouted, and he had to swerve fast to avoid striking the fool, whom he failed to recognize.

Lunt hadn't recognized Mandrake either, but the Jeep had spooked him as much as he'd frightened Mandrake because Lunt briefly mistook it for a dune buggy, Manson's vehicle of choice.

"Fucking *goon*," Mandrake yelled back at the jackass he'd nearly run over. After long enough on the street, these homeless guys forgot how to walk, didn't they? Scowling, he drove on.

Outside Corpus Co-op, a curious scene failed to catch Mandrake's eye. In a cone of streetlight, a rheumy-eyed, snaggle-toothed, blotchy-faced drunkard wearing bib overalls lay sprawled on the sidewalk singing the old tune "Violent Love." Egging him on tonight was the strip club's bouncer, a thick-shouldered, pin-eyed man. Siberia-born and bred, the bouncer wore a bear-claw necklace he'd purchased last year at a shop on Melrose, and his nickname, which even his new wife called him, was "Bullet Head." Although he'd taken several lives with his bare hands while growing up (including a childhood friend during a vodka-fueled bar fight), Bullet Head had an amiable disposition. In fact, he considered the inebriated crooner his friend.

Why did Mandrake fail to notice the two men? Because he was lost in his own thoughts again, brooding about Pandora. And as his Jeep blasted past the gaudy Strip billboards, accelerating through a yellow at Doheny and nearly knocking down two Mexican girls who were holding hands, Mandrake heard the Fuikksho smartphone resting on his lap go off. Its ringtone was Sharon Tate's voice, but computer-modified by a techie friend of his to say, "I cherish you, Glen." Mandrake, the Glen of that fake love-declaration, squinted down at the phone's plastic screen, which he polished daily. (He hated the thought of his earwax existing outside his ears.)

"BRONSON," the spotless screen informed him.

10:43 P.M.: *Fuck this shit*, thought the shag-haired, barely clothed, but comprehensively tattooed female Jim Morrison look-alike who was lap-dancing in Corpus Co-op's VIP section. Her name was Nadine Gilroy but her stage name was "Moral Uplift," recently changed from "Muscle Mammaries." (Her boss had groused that the latter monicker had too many syllables.) Nadine wished she could stick out her tongue at her whole workplace tonight—colleagues as well as customers, her mood being sour for three reasons:

1. She'd come here straight from her waitressing job at Gush, so her feet were killing her.

2. She aesthetically disapproved of the crude fiberboard-and-exposed-brick décor of the club—especially the rubber plants everywhere.

3. The song currently playing, a techno take on George Jones' country weeper "He Stopped Loving Her Today," stank.

Admiring Nadine's lap dance from their seated positions on a magenta leather banquette were half-a-dozen people. Five of them were members of the female motorcycle club "The Rolling Eggs," and the sixth was the exhausted-looking famous actor Garth Chthonic. As always, Chthonic's personal enema bag rested beside him. Buzzing on a bourbon jag since early this morning, the actor had commissioned Nadine's dance because he liked how much she looked like the late Doors singer. (His soft spot for Jim Morrison dated from the spring of 1970, when Chthonic had watched his big sister Vicky [nickname: "Vulturine"] have sex with the soon-to-be-dead vocalist in a Long Beach nightclub restroom.) Moreover, Nadine's Tarot card tattoos enthralled the sozzled man.

"What's *that* one?" he insisted on knowing, pointing a finger through the red gloom of the club at the dancer's chest. What he meant to indicate was the image emblazoned between the breasts there: a person dangling upside-down.

"Oh, that's my Hanged Man" was Nadine's response. (Talking about her tattoos always perked her up. The Tarot and her body's ink tributes to the cards were, along with her drummer boyfriend, her blind cousin Jules, and Vicodin, the only things that made Nadine feel happy.) "And here's the Tower," she added, touching a lightning-struck stone cylinder rising from her shaved groin, "and the Sun" (proudly touching her right breast, where yellow rays shone from her nipple), "and the Moon" (the other breast, which radiated moonbeams), "the Emperor and Empress" (one on each forearm), "the Hierophant and the High Priestess" (one on each thigh), "the Wheel of Fortune" (an elaborate ring around her navel), "the Magician" (turning and stretching an arm backward to point at her shoulder blades), "the Devil" (on her lower back), "and here's the Lovers" (a young woman and man facing each other from each buttock, with the crack of her rump dividing them).

Once she'd finished explaining, Chthonic nodded with satisfaction, but Nadine soon sank back into tetchiness. The biker women were sort of cute (cuter than their local enemies, The Menstrual Cycles, whom Chthonic sometimes brought to Gush), but Nadine had long ago grown weary of actors in this town, successful like Chthonic or not, no matter how appealingly worn-out they might look. So *Fuck this shit*, Nadine thought, dancing on and not noticing a man who slowly shambled through the club. If Nadine had glimpsed the man as he went past Chthonic's banquette, she might have remembered him from Gush.

Someone two banquettes away from Chthonic had *not* missed Lunt, however. This someone—Pondicherry Jocelyn Brit

Experience Jordan, known to her friends and fellow latter-day Manson Family members as "Jopp"—spotted and recognized Lunt as soon as he'd edged into the VIP section, which tonight, a slow night at the Corpus, was unguarded by any staff.

"Hey!" Jopp yelled above the throbbing music. "C'mere and lemme spit on you, Jeepster!"

On hearing the voice, Lunt swung around, looked, and did a double take.

Oh, no, not her.

And not with him.

Lunt froze in place, fear twiddling up and down his spine. How could he buy drugs from Pompa if *she* was here?

Tonight her miniskirt, perhaps the same one she'd been wearing when they first met, was emerald-colored. Her throat was free of chokers, lime-green or otherwise. Her seafoam-green hair hung free, not bound in pigtails. And her mouth, that Sharon-lipped treasure, looked as glorious as ever.

Sharing the magenta banquette with Jopp was a man whose legs were extended in front of him and whose fingers were laced behind his ginger-Afroed head. The name on his passport was Donald Benjamin Hanover, but "Benny Pompa" was how people knew him. His music group's latest album, *I Wanna Die in My Sleep Like My Dad Did (Not Screaming in Terror Like All His Passengers Were)*, had just achieved platinum-record status, so Pompa and his young green companion were celebrating at his favorite Ofotert-vicinity watering hole. Unlocking his hands, drawing in his legs, and sitting forward, the pop star was curious to know to whom Jopp was shouting abuse. His eyes took in Lunt, who stood frozen in place near their banquette. Both Jopp and Pompa's faces, lit by two small lamps on their table, looked grotesque to the Sharonophile. Demonic, even! Most likely the green woman was trying to "Mansonize" the pop star, corrupt him, sup on his essence the way Lunt believed the moon had Gurdjieff-wise supped on his. Was she *brainwashing* Pompa? Would his charity from now on go not to orphans but to Manson's acolytes?

Lunt swallowed hard, tasting a new despair, and he felt like weeping. He couldn't stay here, couldn't do this—he had to flee, run from this place out to the Strip, where he'd dodge more dune buggies en route to the Ofotert, his sanctuary...

But before he fled, something happened. Something as subtle as a smile.

In fact, it *was* a smile.

Before Lunt could hurry off, he saw a change in the pop star's face. Pompa's expression seemed to mellow, to glow resplendently just like it did that day at Gush when he'd grinned at Lunt. Or had showed to Lunt a grinning mask. Tonight, again, Benny was doing his friendliest, most beatific, teeth-so-white-they-shone-in-the-red-gloom grin. And there wasn't anything mask-like about him.

This grin, Lunt's intuition told him, delaying him from running away, *is unfakeable. It, he, this pop star, is sincere. So stick around, Lunt—this enemy of your enemy Mandrake, he wants to make friends. He hurled his drink in Mandrake's face because he glimpsed the wickedness there, but with you, he sees the goodness. Hell, he might even recognize a brother!*

Lunt rubbed his bloodshot eyes. Standing upright now was growing difficult; thanks to his still-weakened condition, he needed to lie down, not to sleep, just to *rest*, until...

Until what? his intuition challenged him, its tenor turned confrontational. *Until some stripper squirts Muke in your mouth from her fake breasts? There's no free lunch, you jive turkey! Gird your loins, man, hold your mud! Sharon up and get that cough syrup!*

Lunt stared at his black, pebble-grained sneakers, making up his mind. And soon, as if plunging into a vortex, he started toward the pop star, murmuring, "Eyes on prize, eyes on prize, eyes on prize" under his breath.

AFTER the Eye production wrapped, I flew back to London to do looping, a few PR photos, and other postproduction stuff. The producers shot a fantastic promotional film about me, a little something called All Eyes on Sharon Tate, and they rented me a flat in Eaton Place, which was a happening spot in town. I lived there with my voice coach and my latest pooch, an adorable Yorkshire puppy named Guinness. I named Guinness after the drink I came to like, even though it was so fattening.

During the days when I wasn't working, I exercised at a gym near my apartment, lay under a sunlamp, strolled around Hyde Park, shopped on the King's Road and Carnaby Street, and stopped in at museums. Jay came over to visit, and we had fun, and when he flew back to LA, my beau left me "in the care" of one of his friends, Victor Lownes, who was the head of the British edition of Playboy magazine as well as of the Playboy Club on Park Lane. Victor was a terrific friend to have, very charming and hospitable. He "really got me," to quote the title of a song I loved to dance to at Alvaro's and the Antelope Bar and other favorite discotheques. Victor brought me to all the grooviest parties, and through him I got friendly with the French actress Leslie Caron. Something about Leslie struck me as so trustworthy that I felt safe to confide in her about my problems and my doubts about staying with Jay.

Once all the postproduction work was done, I invited my Hollywood friend Wende Wagner to come and stay with me in London. I knew Wende and Leslie would dig each other, which they did, and Wende and I really wowed the squares in town with our matching go-go boots and miniskirts. Oh, and our leather motorcycle jackets! These outfits, it so happens, were what we wore to a particular luncheon that Victor set up for us and some other friends of his. One of these friends turned out to be a not very tall Polish film director.

We had a rocky start, Roman and I, but eventually we fell in love, and so I broke it off with Jay, though we remained dear friends. Jay stayed close with my parents, too, and he made sure he became friendly with Roman. Many people we knew thought Jay was just biding his time until Roman and I broke up. "He's never stopped loving you, Sharon," they explained. They didn't have to say this—it was obvious to me. Women understand more than men realize! In the friendship sense, I never stopped loving Jay, either. He became like a brother, my older brother. And when Jay got murdered right beside me, he was still wearing my high school ring on a gold chain around his neck.

(NOTE: The text of *Excerpts from the Memoirs She Didn't Live Long Enough to Write: The Life of Sharon Tate as Told from Beyond the Grave to One of Her Biggest Admirers, Lunt Moreland* stops here. It was never completed by its author.)

THE banquette's slate-gray Formica tabletop was cluttered with debris, though this debris was less diverse than the stuff on the carpet in Pompa's hotel suite. The objects here consisted of an overflowing ashtray; some Codex cigarette packs; a tall, tapered, unmarked, navy-tinted bottle; a bowl of melon balls soaked in kirsch; and two balloon glasses filled with a sky-blue liquid. The same liquid, perhaps, that Pompa had hurled in Mandrake's face at Gush.

"Greetings," the pop star said to Lunt, drumming his fingers on the table, not offering a hand to shake. His voice was raspy yet convivial. "What does your mother call you?"

"She's dead, but, uh, Lunt. Lunt Moreland." He focused all his attention on the pop star, ignoring Jopp, and tried to conceal from them how nervous he felt in their presence. Could they sense his nervousness anyway? "I'm staying at the Ofotert, too. In Suite Forty-Seven."

"Hi, Lunt from Suite Forty-Seven. You sure your name's not Fritz?"

"Fritz? No."

"Or Mr. Stuyvesant Fish, maybe?"

"*No!*"

"Well, I'm Benny Pompa."

Still no handshake. Up close, Lunt noticed, the pop star's forehead was crisscrossed with creases, deep ones that probably got airbrushed out in photos. Pompa was dressed in his usual uniform, blue jeans and a jersey. Whatever message was printed on the front of the jersey was hidden from view by a new addition: an old gray corduroy vest with faded sequined goblins. *Where did I read about a vest like that?* Lunt wondered. Then, still ignoring Jopp—in spite of how he yearned to optically savor her Sharon-mouth (yes, his libido was coming back!)—Lunt shifted on his feet and cleared his ravaged throat and began delivering the speech he'd mentally rehearsed: "Mr. Pompa, sir, I'm a big fan of your music, and I would've said hi earlier, introduced myself, but I've been sick, and, er…"

He stopped so that he could swallow and wipe sweat from his brow. *I'm still sick,* he told himself, *still fucked-up from having no Muke, not really lucid.*

Seizing on Lunt's pause, Jopp said, "Dude, your new boho look ain't working for you. Shave that beard, huh?" She scrunched around on the banquette so she could turn to face Pompa. "This is that Sharon Tate freak who gave my friend the flu, *plus* threatened to phone the heat on us!"

Lunt clenched his jaw, jamming his hands into his trouser pockets and thinking, *How dare she spew insults at me, and publicly! Lies, to boot! After everything I've suffered because of her, now this Manson trash turns Pompa against me? Unbelievable!*

Mutual hatred radiated from each of them in nearly visible waves. Lunt felt the urge to kick her rotten crooked teeth in, but Pompa spoke up, elbowing Jopp rather savagely and informing her that Lunt was "turkey-ing," whatever *that* meant. "Frosty-cold," the pop star added. "F-R-O-S-T-Y. All the classic signs. Isn't it obvious?" Now Pompa addressed Lunt. "Nothing worse than that ole dope-hunger, huh? Except maybe kidney stones." He turned back to Jopp. "Now *those'll* put you through changes!"

"Straight up!" The green woman took a fast sip of the blue liquid in her balloon glass, then said, "You know, Ben, I can quote your lyric from 'We Met Cute': '*We met cute, me and Marsha—she was doing her taxes and I just passed a kidney stone.*' Brilliant!"

Pompa shook his head dismissively. "I didn't write that song, slave—our first singer did. And keep a civil tongue."

Slave? thought Lunt.

The pop star brightened again. "Join us, comrade," he told Lunt in that hoarse voice of his. "Lots of space here, as you can see. How'd you find us?"

Choosing his words with care, Lunt said, "Your wives. They, uh, told me you were here."

"They did? Uh-huh. Hoping to ruin my tête-à-tête with our green slave, no doubt. Mischievous wifeys! Well, all's fair."

Red-tinted stripper flesh flashed at the edges of Lunt's vision. He mopped more sweat from his forehead with a wrist. This place was like a boiler room!

Meanwhile, Pompa was studying Lunt, patting his stomach as he peered at the newcomer long enough to see what he apparently wished to see. Then: "Codex?"

As soon as Lunt figured out what this meant, he said, "Oh, no thanks, I don't smoke."

"Me, neither, comrade, I just quit two minutes ago. Of all our most popular intoxicants, tobacco's got the most costs with the least benefits." He pointed his chin at the blue-tinted, unmarked bottle. "Care for some laudanum? It's amaretto mixed with liquefied opium. Special blend, made by Gabriela, my band's private chemist."

"No, no," said Lunt, "none for me tonight, thanks." All he needed, on top of his Muke-trouble, was swishing opium into the mix! A recipe for disaster. But slowly, carefully, he eased his creaking body onto the firm magenta banquette seat. How hospitable Pompa was! To think that Lunt was hanging out with someone as famous as La Tate—and with the same birthday as her! He wished he'd brought along with him that never-opened complimentary bottle of champagne. It would've made for a great "getting to know you" gift. Or was Dom Perignon not classy enough for this high-life afficionado?

He also wished he could ring up Bronson and say, "Guess where I am!" *But she's my ex-friend now*, he reminded himself. *Another thing to blame myself for. But maybe Benny will replace her, be my new friend? And let me live in Sharon's suite, crash in a spare room, be his roommate? He might even share one of those wives of his with me!*

"Let's hear it again for Mercy!" the nightclub deejay's voice erupted from the hinterland beyond the banquette as the last song, which was a techno version of Morris Albert's "Feelings," faded out. "Give it up for Mercy!"

Lunt assumed, on hearing this, that the deejay referred not to the dancer currently descending from Corpus Co-op's raised mirrored stage but to the concept of mercy. This error gave Lunt a flutter of magical hope: yes, Benny would show him mercy!

By the time he'd figured out what was what, the new song, a sitar-laden techno version of "The Mary Tyler Moore Theme," had gotten underway and a new dancer had strutted onto that elevated mirror-forest. Instantly she drew all of Pompa's attention, therefore Jopp's and Lunt's as well.

"Let's give it up for *Gretchen*, people," the deejay bellowed. "Direct from the Swiss Alps—*Gretchen!*"

Because of the dancer's name and origin, Lunt expected someone Nordic-looking, perhaps along the lines of a Swiss Miss–type, or a Valkyrie. Why, then, was the young woman now prancing in the limelight Middle Eastern in look—an Israeli or an Arab (with nothing Sharonesque about her)? Interestingly, too, she wore nothing but platform boots, a halter top, and a diaper, and above the din of music she kept crying out to everyone, as if cautioning them, *"Tan, don't burn! Tan, don't burn!"* This made no sense until a mangy Schnauzer came trotting out from stage left, bounced up at Gretchen, and started to tug her diaper down with his miniature teeth. Finally Lunt got it. It was a spoof of the old Coppertone ad! One of the many print ads Sharon had done as a starlet was for Coppertone. Lunt considered the coincidence another good sign—a reminder from Sharon's spirit that she was with him.

Halfway through Gretchen's act, Pompa looked abruptly upward, pressed a forearm to his mouth, and began to bark, sounding not unlike the dog onstage might sound. Lunt frowned, mystified. Were these barks how the pop star showed respect for the dancer? Garth Chthonic, three of his female biker associates, and even Gretchen herself glanced at Pompa, plainly curious about this barking act he was doing. Jopp, for her own part, seemed nonplussed about it, as if Pompa's canine-like behavior was charming.

"Benny, I *told* you," she said with a chuckle, "eating eggs will get rid of that."

Pompa ignored her. Yet what she'd said illuminated it all to Lunt: the pop star wasn't barking, he was *coughing*! So this was something else he and Lunt had in common.

Maybe, Lunt mused, *I even caught my cough from him. Which would be kind of cool—* "I got this bug from a famous pop star!" *We shared germs. Or does everyone who stays at the Ofotert long enough come down with something like this?*

After three particularly severe "barks," Pompa's coughing spasm finally subsided. Then he took a long pull of laudanum from his balloon glass and said to Lunt, "So that's Sharon Tate on your T-shirt, huh? I hear you've got a 'black belt' in Sharon Tate studies. Expert in the field. Or does my green slave here exaggerate?"

Swiftly inflating with pride in the smudged light of the club, Lunt said, "It's true."

"As you might know," Pompa said, his grin returning, "Sharon Tate and I have the same birthday. Last week some big-eared bald mutant tried to remind me of that fact while my wives and I were feeding at some seafood restaurant on the Strip. Not cool. If there's one thing I hate, it's when my feeding gets interrupted."

"I'm the same way!" offered Lunt.

"And if there's one thing *I* hate," Jopp jumped in, "it's someone snitching on me to the cops. That happened way too much when I went fundraising door-to-door once for the Family…"

Ignoring her, Pompa told Lunt, "Sharing Sharon Tate's birthday is something I'm really proud of."

Lunt said he understood. He mentioned that the "mutant" Mandrake was his enemy as well. He briefly explained why, elaborating on how heinous Mandrake was. And he was about to bring up Mucaquell when Pompa, as if by some Bronson-quality intuitive power, beat Lunt to it. He said, "How long've you been turkeying?" Seeing Lunt's blank face, he added, "Deprived of your drug of choice, I mean. In withdrawal."

"Oh. Er—days, I guess. Three?"

Pompa winced. "Been there. How's your noodle?"

"I still feel bad in general. Really washed-out. To tell you the truth, I'll need to lie down when I leave here." His stomach remained turbulent as well, but more from tension now than illness, so he didn't cite it.

"Serves you right to suffer," hissed the green woman, all malice.

Pompa would not abide this. "I told you, *slave*, keep a civil tongue."

"But, Ben," she protested, "he's a snitch!"

"And you're *surprised*?" Pompa came back at her. "Your boy Manson chopped this guy's girlfriend to bits. You're his natural foe."

"No," said Jopp, "that's wrong, Charlie's innocent! It was a *frame-up*, I *told* you. The Thanatogists killed Tate and all the others, not Charlie, and with the cops' help the Thanies pinned it on us. Charlie's *peaceful*, dude! He's Charles Is *Man's Son*!"

Pompa went quiet. He poured more laudanum into his balloon glass, took a sip, and swished it around in his mouth before he swallowed. Then, smacking his lips, he said he had a question for Lunt: "She ever get struck?"

"Struck?" Staring dully at a prancing silver goblin stitched into Pompa's vest, Lunt mopped more sweat from his forehead. It was the club's fault, not his: the temperature inside here was positively unconscionable. "I'm not sure I—"

"*Struck,*" the pop star said, as if the emphasis would clarify the question. "My guess is that she *did*, yeah."

"'Starstruck,' you mean?"

"*Lightning-struck.*"

"Oh! Oh, so—wait, you mean was Sharon struck by lightning?"

"In her *youth*, is my guess," Pompa said. "Am I right, Fritz?"

"It's Lunt, actually."

"Lunt, yeah. Am I right?"

"Sharon, hit by lightning? Not that I know of..."

"Not that you *know of*?" Jopp said, scoffing. "I thought you're a pro. An *expert.* "

Before Lunt could think of a suitably snide comeback, Pompa shut the green woman down with a single fierce stare.

"I *am* a pro in these matters," Lunt finally asserted, "a Sharon Tate scholar, and if there was a lightning incident, I'd have heard about it. Trust me."

"Gimme a '*whoop-whoop*' if you like girls!" the deejay shouted.

At the neighboring banquette, all the female bikers obliged him, roaring with glee.

"Not even in her *youth*?" Pompa pressed the issue. "I could've sworn... All the signs of a lightning strike were *there*! Her voice, her tit size..."

"Sorry," said Lunt, thinking, *Tit size? This is getting bizarre.*

Just then, an especially loud techno version of Ravel's "Pavane for a Dead Princess" blasted from the sound system, drowning out Lunt's thoughts. The music heralded the three strippers who now took the stage. This was "Harmony," a tri-racial act, which featured a Haitian-American called "Bustma Hymen," a Korean-American who went by "Bibim-Bap," and a Quebecoise whose name was "Je T'Aime." ("'Jet' for short," she later told Garth Chthonic while treating him to a private dance).

"Lemme guess," Pompa said after a new belt of laudanum. "My guess is, it's H."

"H?"

"The thing that's got you turkeying. Skag. Junk. Smack. Sugar. Horse."

"*Brown* sugar," Jopp explained condescendingly for Lunt. "What Benny means is *heroin*, you lame-o."

Lunt stared fiercely at her, racking his sluggish mind in vain for a suitably vicious retort.

"Nah," said Pompa, "it's not smack, uh-uh. But it's an opiate, for sure. That's why I'm urging you to try the laudanum. Similar silkiness. Wait—is it Oxy? No," he changed his mind quickly, "not Oxy, either. Or codeine." Looking frustrated, the pop star took a Codex pack from the tabletop and knocked out a cigarette. Instead of lighting it, he used it to meditatively stroke his jaw. Finally, just as the three dancers of Harmony simultaneously flung off their bikini tops, Pompa said, "Hang on, I've got it! Mucaquell?"

Lunt gaped at Pompa, his glassy, bloodshot eyes opening wide. "You...but that's *amazing!*"

"He got it right?" said Jopp.

"Yes. *Yes!*" Lunt laughed, shaking his head. Pompa's intuition—it was wicked good!

"Bully for you," the pop star said, grinning again. "You're a man of subtle taste. Only *sophisticates* appreciate a good cough suppresant. Though Muke is controversial, as you know."

Uh-oh, controversial? "Why is that?"

Pompa swung his legs onto the banquette and crossed them in an impressive semi-lotus position. "Gone from the shelves, *ka-poof*. Till last year, it was just another syrup. But then they added this new enzyme, this ingredient *SzV*, and it's a totally different ballgame. Freaky shit—way, way addictive. Insidious! Not like anything I've tried, on- or off-market. Psychopathic dreams, right?"

"Uh, yeah," agreed Lunt, too excited by their talk for it to occur to him that Pompa might lack the Mucaquell to sell him.

"We all need a good hallucination sometimes," the pop star breezed on. "Like my uncle Billycoo always says, 'It's easier to bury your reality than it is to get rid of your dreams.' Nice, huh?"

"That could be your next song title!" chirped Jopp.

Once more refusing to look at her, Pompa stayed with Lunt, regaling him with Mucaquell data. "No one's saying what SzV is made from, or even what those initials *stand for*. Really hush-hush. Lots of rumors on the web, though—talk about stuff like gold salts, noxated zinc, stuff like that, plus some fermentation process called 'The Brewster Method.' It's the main reason thieves are hitting drugstores now instead of banks or 7-Elevens. So—RIP, Muke. Matter of fact, I'm shocked it stayed legal for so long."

"Wow," mumbled Lunt, still stuck on the armed robbery mention, which called back to him the sign in the window of Limsky's Pharmacy, that sign forbidding guns from being brought in. As if Muke-hungry gunmen would heed such a ban! He wanted to mention this to Pompa, to share this observation, but his face was soaked in sweat, which distracted him. What's more, the pop star had already moved on, digressing now on the vanished cough syrup's name.

"Did you know '*muca*' means 'pussy' in Hungarian? So does 'punci.' I picked that up last time I played Buda. Or was it Pest? Anyway, there was this promoter's daughter there who loves Muke. We called her 'Punci-Shmunci.' Anyway, Mr. Tate, Mucaquell was huge all over Europe."

"Hang on," said Lunt, straightening his posture. "Who's 'Mr. Tate'?"

"*You* are. It's what I think I'm gonna call you. Because 'Mr. Sharon Tate' *becomes* you, comrade."

"But you can call me by my real name. I'm—"

Pompa reached forward to place his hairless hand over Lunt's wrist. "Please," he said, "let me honor you by calling you by *her* name."

Holy shit, thought Lunt, gaping down at the pop star's hand on his, *this is the nicest man I've met in my whole life*!

"Do I have to call him Mr. Tate, too?" asked an irritated Jopp.

While Pompa polished off the laudanum in his balloon glass, Lunt turned to the green woman, smirked at her, and cocked his head triumphantly, as if to say, "You *think* he likes you, you Manson-slut, but all he wants to do is to fuck you—if *that*. Me, on the other hand, I'm Benny's *new friend*."

Fading slowly, "Pavane for a Dead Princess" eventually gave way to a techno version of the Tiger Ichisan number "Never Bring Ants to Our Picnic." The members of Harmony sashayed off the mirrored stage. Mounting it in their place was the next dancer, Moral Uplift. Lunt was too busy exulting in one-upping Jopp to glance at the woman onstage, much less to recognize her as Nadine Gilroy, the Jim Morrison look-alike waitress he'd encountered a week ago at Gush.

"I'm bored," Pompa announced. "Let's go home and get you fixed up."

"Who?" said Lunt.

"*You*, Mr. Tate, who else? You're kvetching for Mucaquell, right? Well, I just happen to be sitting on a case of it in my suite. Or half a case—I don't recall if I busted it open yet."

"You have it? *Really?*"

"Comrade, I've got everything except for A-bombs. And I hear you can even buy *those* on Amazon.com these days."

Lunt felt as though his heart just burst from his chest like a bazooka shell and *kazoomed* across the club. *Oh, my stars!* he thought. "And you'll sell me some?"

"*Sell* you? Nah, try *give* you, free and clear."

"Wow," said Lunt, clapping his hands delightedly together before he realized how childish this must have looked. "*Thank you, Benny!*" Tears sprang to his eyes. *I'm saved*, he thought, *fucking saved! I don't deserve this goodness...I mucked up my life so badly, run the whole thing off the rails, but everything will be different now that Benny's here to help!*

"Ants at our picnic," went the pounding techno music. "*Ants, ants, ants, ants at our picnic...*"

"Do I owe you something in return?" Lunt asked. "Because anything, *anything* I can give you, just say so! I—I've got some Dom Perignon, for instance..."

Instead of answering, Pompa looked to the ceiling, pressed forearm to mouth, and went back into a barking-dog coughing fit. Lunt leaned away from him as politely as possible. He didn't want to offend the pop star, but he didn't want to catch his germs, either, and acquire a new cough. Jopp, who'd been watching the pop star closely, put her thin hand on his shoulder, and as she did, she parted her lips, once again revealing her teeth. They looked as chocolate brown as ever. Even in the red gloom of the Corpus, Lunt saw, they were repugnant.

"Let's have a party," she said to Pompa. "An indoor picnic! Like the song that's playing now. You hear it, dude? And what good is a picnic without lightning?"

10

THE HELTER STARTS TO SKELTER

(Wednesday)

IN the new dream, she was with him. Not some imposter with a bubble mask or the woman from his "WHY?" poster but *her*, the real her, and she was naked. Wowee zowee! He was naked also, yet unlike Sharon, who could roam about at will, he was held fast in a web, a spider web, wrapped up in netting not sticky but strong— lines of web binding his whole body. No, not "whole," because his face and hands and feet and buttocks were free; he could feel blowing air, cool air-conditioning, on them. Still, with his arms pressed to his torso and his legs pressed together, Lunt was floating in this dream-web, bent forward at the waist and swaying slowly, his toes two inches above a carpet. A junk-strewn carpet.

Sharon looked different tonight. Her body was waifish, not voluptuous at all; her breasts were tiny, bud-like; and her newly trimmed thatch of pubic hair was seafoam-green, the same hue as her other hair. What's more, her navel and nipples had been pierced and fitted with emeralds, perhaps not real ones, and tattooed across her upper chest was the word *"EVERGREEN."* As for her hands, hands she used to stroke his face, these hands were made of water. Water-hands, imagine that! Like melted dolphin fins. Still, it was Sharon, truly Sharon—he'd know the contours of her lush mouth anywhere. Even after he shut his eyes, the eyelids too heavy to battle open, he saw that lush mouth in his mind, and the fragrance he discerned, a fragrance distinct from the scent of burning wax, a fragrance filling every corner of his dream—it was patchouli! La Tate's favorite. She, his goddess, was using patchouli oil to, like, *anoint* him, to rub his forehead with this balm, this hippie nectar, making him holy!

GARY LIPPMAN

In fact, he wanted, *needed*, to close his eyes, in order to shield them from the white light. Specifically, the hot white spotlight aimed now at Lunt. Nevertheless, he wished he could watch her, and watch the pair of other women, likewise nude, who'd been pointing their cameras at him since the spotlight had been switched on. Their bodies looked older than Sharon's; they'd lived past twenty-six, been granted more life, and the extra years showed slightly on them. Both women had large rounded breasts and well-defined ribcages. And both had shaved their pubic hair into shapes, each shape a letter of the alphabet—one was an "S," the other a "T."

Hey, those were Sharon Tate's initials!

Who were these women, Sharon's sisters?

And were they working for the spider, the unseen spider whose web held Lunt?

But did that matter?

No, nothing mattered but for how Sharon was presently anointing Lunt. So he relaxed, offered his body to the webbing, letting his weight sag into it, and he just listened to the soft whir of the cameras as they filmed him, and to Jim Morrison singing "Strange Days," and later on to other voices. Non-singing voices. *Distracting* voices. He felt his face construct a frown; they had torn him from his dream. The loudest of the voices, gruff and male, issued from somewhere to Lunt's left. Was this the voice of the unseen spider?

"Physiological results," the male voice said, as if reading or reciting from memory, "include depression, fatigue, insomnia, memory loss, impotence, dizziness, cataracts, and broken eardrums. Fifty-four percent of victims get struck in open fields like golf courses and ballparks. And twenty-three percent?"

"Twenty-three percent," said Sharon, "get hit while under trees, right?"

"Good. Thirteen percent?"

"Uh..."

"Here's a hint, slave: two b's."

"Oh, *yeah*, thirteen percent on boats and beaches!"

"And seven?"

"Seven, on farm equipment! And the last four are miscellaneous? Riding bikes, standing by windows, stuff like that?"

The male voice grunted with satisfaction. "Good work. Now, what about our offering? Is he ready?"

What offering? Lunt wondered. *Who are these people? How did I wind up in this web?*

Had he been thinking clearly, he would have recalled leaving Corpus Co-op with Jopp and Pompa ninety minutes earlier. On their way to the exit, the dancer called Moral Uplift recognized Jopp and Lunt and stuck her tongue out at them. Once the trio got outside, they were forced to step around the drunkard in bib overalls who still lay splayed across the sidewalk singing "Violent Love" while the nightclub's Siberian-born bouncer egged him on.

"Catch you next time, Benny," Bullet Head called after Pompa, pronouncing each word precisely. The bouncer was proud of how good his English was, and deeply grateful to the Berlitz organization.

Pompa, Lunt noticed, had a loping kind of walk. During a break in traffic, the two men along with Jopp had to run for it, charging together across the Strip. To Lunt's relief, no dune buggies were on the road. Still, the sight of the Ofotert's turrets frightened him; they looked like iron fingers pointed accusingly at heaven; and then a gray Volvo zipping around the curve there almost clipped the group. They paused on the sidewalk, catching their breath, and when Lunt's knees turned temporarily to jelly, Pompa helped to prop him up. So did Baby Son, who was stationed as usual with clipboard at the entrance to the Ofotert. Lunt waved them off. He wouldn't allow himself to appear weak in front of Jopp. Or in front of Mandrake, for that matter, should Mandrake be lurking nearby.

Then, elevator, going up. On the five-story ride in close proximity to one another, Pompa sang one of his own songs while Lunt and Jopp avoided making eye contact.

"*You* again," Saffron snapped once she opened the door to Suite 56 and found Lunt standing beside her husband and the green woman. By now so many candles were lit in Sharon's old suite, candles of different shapes, sizes, colors, that everything glowed a lambent yellow.

"Glad I texted ahead," Pompa told Saffron as he ushered his guests inside. "You made it just right for the ritual. We'll need more candles, though."

Immediately the wives leapt to work, opening a closet door, pulling out more cylinders of wax, placing them around the suite, then touching Bic lighters to each wick.

What ritual? wondered Lunt as he gawked at his new surroundings. In the doorway earlier tonight, he hadn't had the opportunity to glimpse the junk that engulfed the living room's charcoal-colored carpet. Now, welcomed past the threshold, he couldn't help but think what slobs these people were. Utter pigs! It looked as though a pawnshop's entire inventory had been delivered here by truck and then unceremoniously dumped out. They'd desecrated Sharon's home. Had this rubbish been in any order before entropy asserted itself? Did it all belong to Pompa, the giftings from countless groupies? Or was it plunder, the pilferings of an indiscriminate kleptomaniac? Lunt ran his eyes over one sector of the floor, keen to spot any bottles of Mucaquell.

"It's a good night for a ritual!" Pompa announced to everyone.

"What ritual?" Lunt said.

"I *told* you, lame-o!" Jopp groused at him. "Benny's got a new cult, I'm his slave, and Saff and Trudi are priestesses."

"It's not a cult, it's a secret society," Saffron corrected her, "and we're *high* priestesses."

"Or call us sibyls," Trudi said. "We like that word, too."

"Weren't *you* supposed to be a priestess?" Lunt taunted Jopp. "Demoted to *slave*, I guess."

On hearing this, the green woman—in the spirit of her "sibling" Strangely Strange—hawked up phlegm and spat it with passion at Lunt. Bull's-eye, or close enough: it caught the lower part of his throat.

Once he recovered from the shock of this assault and used his wrist to blot at the spittle, he got ready to respond in kind. Before any saliva passed his lips, though, Pompa intervened, rushing forward to clamp a palm over Lunt's mouth.

"*Uh-uh*," he said. "Nix-nix. No spit-fights in the parlor. That's what we call this room. It's our parlor. Sounds *old-timey*, right, comrade? Gives it a Stephen Foster feel. So let's keep it quaint between Team Manson and Team Tate." He crooked a finger at the green woman. "Slave, you come this way." Taking her elbow, he looked Lunt squarely in the eye. "Guest, make yourself at home."

As they vanished behind a door, Lunt leaned against the indigo sofa, resting, and stole a few peeks at Saffron whenever she wasn't looking. He also checked out the suite, Sharon's old suite, some more: the felt sheets on the windows, the hooded grill, the colored scarves and snoods, and the candles everywhere, which gave the place a diabolical vibe, making it like a set from Sharon's movie *Eye of the Devil*. The odor of burning wax was too strong, almost sickening. As for the altar thing—what was *this* for? Was it where they'd do the so-called ritual?

Trudi, obviously the friendlier of the wives, appeared from the balcony, shut the door, drew a curtain across it, then greeted Lunt with a moist peck on his cheek. Like Saffron, she was clad in underwear and T-shirt. But their husband, once he emerged from a side room with a bottle in his hand (Lunt couldn't make out the label, but the glass was an encouraging chocolate shade)— the husband, once he emerged, was stark naked. Naked, that is, but for that gray corduroy vest with goblin images stitched into it. And visible despite the vest was a red streak, a curious marking, down Pompa's pale and hairless chest. The marking resembled a marijuana plant, yet it didn't seem like a tattoo. This was his Flower, the "Lichtenberg Flower" Jopp had mentioned—the trace left by the lightning strike Pompa dubbed his "Big Reveal."

Lunt would've liked to peer at it more, but Pompa's nudity unsettled him, causing him to look away. If his father ever learned how close Lunt now stood to a nude man, old Mr. Moreland would throw a fit.

"Hey, Jeep."

Lunt wheeled around in the direction of the new voice, then cringed and said "Ugh" and covered his eyes. Jopp had reappeared, and she was just as unclothed as Pompa.

"Green was the color of my true love's nether-hair," Pompa sang in a surprisingly rasp-free falsetto.

As if this lyric was a cue, music flooded the suite. It was an all-Doors playlist on some centralized PA system. Giggling between themselves, Pompa's wives also got naked, tossing their thongs and T-shirts on top on the lightning altar. This served to expose still more female anatomy for Lunt to surreptitiously leer at. Their bodies, so splendidly muscled, looked almost airbrushed.

"You cool with Doors?" Pompa asked. He was scratching his pale, shaved genitals with one hand while the other poured his blue laudanum into a jeweled goblet. "The music, I mean."

"Oh, sure," said Lunt, who hadn't realized the nude pop star was speaking to him. He took a quick glance at Pompa, then looked away again. "The Doors was one of Sharon Tate's favorite groups!"

Pompa didn't seem interested in this, although he raised his eyebrows slightly. He drained the laudanum in one slurp and dropped the goblet to the floor.

From the carpet everything comes, Lunt reflected, *and to the carpet everything returns.*

Leaning down, Pompa rummaged through the flotsam and jetsam there until he came upon purple-tinted shooting glasses, which he picked up and put on his creased face. "Jim Morrison got struck by lightning," he informed Lunt. "When he was 'sweet sixteen.' People don't talk about it, but it's true. So he was a lightning shaman like *I* am."

As Pompa spoke on about shamanism, Lunt hazarded some fast new peeks at Jopp's mouth, her groin, the emeralds stuck through her nipples, and her mouth. Always that mouth! When she caught him at it and gave him a Mandrake-style smirk, Lunt lowered his eyes guiltily to a Jolly Doll on the floor and thought, *Is Pompa one of those Jolly Doll collector nuts? What do the hotel housekeepers make of this pigsty? Does Pompa even allow the staff inside? How did the suite look when Sharon lived here? None of the furnishings are the same—or are they? This indigo sofa, for instance, looks pretty antique...*

Pompa interrupted his reverie by commanding Lunt to "strip off."

"Huh?"

The guttering candlelight reflected psychedelically on the pop star's purple glasses. "I always strip off as soon as I come home, and I ask that my guests do, too." He rubbed his belly unselfconsciously. "Strip off, Mr. Tate."

Shit!

"Actually," said Lunt, "er, I'd like to keep my clothes on. But thanks. And you really don't have to call me Mr. Tate…"

Lunt's host gave the bottle in his hand a kinetic shake. "House rules. *Parlor* rules. Go naked or nothing. N-E-K-I-D. The 'nothing' option means no Muke." He poked Lunt's breastbone with a finger, his face hardening. "And 'Mr. Tate' is *exactly* what I'll call you."

Three minutes later, a pair of khakis, boxer briefs, black pebble-grained sneakers, and a Sharon-themed T-shirt lay piled on the carpet beside an unopened box of Tampex, and the doleful owner of that clothing stood bare-assed in the parlor with both hands placed over his penis. He didn't want it being stared at by Pompa's wives or Jopp. *Especially* not by Jopp. As it happened, though, Jopp and the wives were too busy now to pay him any mind. For some reason, they were setting up a pulley system, with Trudi handling a meathook, Saffron hauling a cable around, and Jopp searching by hand through the hoarder's paradise on the floor. What the green woman finally came up with looked like a tube of toothpaste—except that no toothpaste tube Lunt knew of was labeled "Arabian Silk."

Politely, he asked Pompa for the cough syrup.

"One sec," was the answer. Pompa had just uncovered an old-looking cutlass from the carpet. "Hey, I've been *searching* for this thing!" He gave the weapon some swings, slashing the smoky golden air with it. "To think that *he* once held this same blade in his hands!"

Lunt's eyes followed the movements of the cutlass with new apprehension. Pompa didn't intend to *use it*, did he? To run Lunt through with it, perhaps? No, Pompa wouldn't, because Pompa was famous—and famous people didn't kill people, they *got* killed. They were the prey, not the predators; the rabbits, not the hawks; the flies, not the spiders. *Then again*, Lunt reminded himself, bumming out anew, *O. J. Simpson, Robert Blake, Phil Spector…*

His good cheer was restored when Pompa seemed to lose interest in his sword and ambled over to present the chocolate-colored bottle to his guest. Yes, it *was* Mucaquell! Lunt recognized the label as soon as he grabbed it.

"Go on," the pop star said, "knock some back. Have a good belt. It's still got the hair on it, as oldtimers say. Just don't overdo it, you'll get ill. Trust me, going back on *anything* post-cold turkey, you need to take it slow."

I'm saved, Lunt thought, exultant, *fucking saved*, and in a flash he twisted the bottle open, hurled the cap away from him (the carpet would serve as his trash can, too), and drank deep. He felt so thirsty for it that he forgot to keep his hands over his groin. Jesus *fuck*, this tasted glorious, a licorice dream! He felt it swish over his gums, flow down his throat, and deliver a sunburst finish to his heart and brain alike. He would've kept going, too, but a hand tapped hard at his drinking arm.

"I warned you, comrade—*slow*. You just chugged most of that down. Take it in stages or else you'll puke. No need to panic. I've got a case with your name on it. You help us with our ritual, be our offering, and I'm giving you the whole thing. 'Mr. Tate,' that case says. M-R-dot-T-A-T-E. In seven languages."

"*Colonel*," Lunt corrected him, his voice already slurry, though this was due most likely to the vaunted "placebo effect." "Don't call me Mister, call me Colonel. Like Sharon's father, Colonel Tate."

Pompa gave a husky laugh. To Lunt's ears, it didn't sound too different from Bronson's chortle. The pop star said, "Oh, really? You sure I can't call you 'leff-tenant?' That's how I pronounce the word 'lieutenant'—*leff*-tenant. Cool?"

Lunt shook his head, drying his Muke-moistened lips with two fingertips. "No, 'Colonel,' please."

"Colonel it is then. I'm gonna pronounce it 'Coll-a-nell,' though."

Lunt was no longer listening. He was too occupied quaffing more Mucaquell, pouring it down his gullet. Liquid manna, this drink was, manna from heaven! How would he ever stop drinking it? How could he ever live without it? Life would be like a desert, Death Valley—like an existence without Sharon. Impossible!

"Are you sure your girlfriend never crossed paths with lightning, Coll-a-nell Tate?"

"Yeah, I'm sure," said Lunt, already in a swoon, his legs falling out from under him and his mind cut loose and drifting, back in Floaty P'Toaty mode, with its warm familiar shedding of all concerns. The Muke had zapped him fast, faster than usual, or so it seemed, with everything made over into Jell-O, Muke-Jell-O, and Lunt now sank to the floor, gently, beautifully collapsing, so zonked out he hardly felt the Jolly Doll's head sticking into his right thigh.

What he *did* dimly make out was Pompa looming above him, Pompa with his flaccid penis (decidedly not "huge," as Jopp had claimed). What was Pompa doing now? Why was he holding out to Lunt a sheet of cream-colored Hotel Ofotert paper and a black Bic ballpoint pen with its end chewed off?

"The pen is mightier than the sword," Lunt mumbled. This struck him as hilarious. Why wasn't anyone laughing along?

"Sign here," Pompa instructed him in a newly business-like tone. "You can read it if you want, but it's so boring I'll grok it if you don't. It's a release form. It says you give permission for us to film you for a video we're making."

"A *rock song* video? For MTV?"

Pompa gave another Bronsonesque chortle, which made Lunt think, *Oh, if Bronson could see me now!*

"MTV, right, Coll-a-nell, and you're the star." The pop star slapped his belly for emphasis. "My wives and slave are at your service. And later on, they'll munch on your dick, all three of them, how's *that* sound?"

Carefully Pompa put the pen in Lunt's right hand. "Signature, please. Saffron and I will sign it, too, as witnesses, and then Trudi will notarize it. Trude doesn't look like a notary public, but she is."

Lunt tried to center his vision on the man who hovered in the sky above him. The grinning, orange-eyebrowed visage had gone back to looking like a mask—the mask of fame, eaten into his face. And Lunt wished that he could stand, be face-to-face with Pompa, man-to-man, but he knew that was impossible. *He's so famous*, Lunt told himself, *and I'm just a—a what?*

A loser, said a voice within. This inner voice was getting scabrous with him again. Cutting through the Floaty P'Toaty, it said, *Here you are, Lunt, on a star-trip sex-trip drug-trip, but mostly it's a bummer, and a loser is what you are, trumped by everyone. By your betters.*

With a prolonged Muke-redolent sigh, Lunt squinted at the document Pompa held out to him, striving to make sense of it. Words, dumb words. The only truth was in Sharon's soul. So with a hand that felt enfeebled, Lunt scrawled his name, then chuckled bitterly, remembering when he'd signed another contract, the one with Vishwa, the one she'd gone on to cravenly rescind. How puffed with pride and hope he'd felt that day! And how low he'd fallen to the here and now. He'd tried to capture Sharon's soul in words, and he'd failed. So whatever they planned to do to him (speaking of which, why were the wives coming toward Lunt with coils of thin rope?)—*whatever* they did, it couldn't be worse than living without his Sharon book, his Great Work, ever being published.

Or without a lifetime supply of Mucaquell.

Forty-five minutes later, the Muked man found himself enmeshed in a complex spiderweb, while Jopp had been transformed—by Muke-magic!—into Sharon, and her wet hands, hands of cool patchouli water, massaged his forehead.

In reality, Lunt was tied from shoulders to ankles in a strait-jacket made of rope, something he merely imagined was a spider-web. This was "The Catbird Seat," a simple yet effective bondage apparatus that Trudi had invented, though not yet patented. It was composed of a thick leather weightlifter's belt (buckled snugly over Lunt's waist), a meat-hook (attached to the belt), a powerful wire cable (fixed securely to the hook), an ovoid steel eye bolted to the ceiling (through which the cable was threaded), and another eye bolted to the nearest wall (which held the cable taut).

"*Summer's almost gone,*" sang Jim Morrison in his low voice, the voice that once pleased Sharon. *So it is,* thought Lunt, who'd been hoisted into midair. *My youth's almost gone, too, age forty's at hand*—while other voices, speaking voices, intersected Jim's. That gruff male voice, for instance—the spider's.

"How many strikes occur per year?" it asked.

A female voice replied, "Forty million?"

"Correct! But is that figure for the States, or international? Take it, Saff."

"Yoo-hoo!" Lunt struggled to say. Yet no sound could seem to cross the gulf from mind to mouth.

"Forty million *in the States*," put in a brand-new female voice.

"Florida has the most of them," said the man. "But Wyoming's got four times more when you adjust for population."

Meanwhile, Sharon had disappeared from view. Her liquid fingers, too. But then one finger, just the tip of it, appeared on Lunt's left buttock, then his anus, and the fingertip massaged that aperture, going around, around, around—circling it so deftly, so *delectably*, that he knew he'd implode from the grooviness.

"Whoa, you've got a hole here," Sharon remarked, and then she giggled. How like a playful child she sounded! "Funny, *I've* got one, too." And gradually Sharon's finger sped up, each rotation stealing breath from Lunt's throat, patchouli swirling into pleasure, building heaven in his heart, and finally a different finger, different but just as liquid, slid deep into him, penetrating Lunt the way that Roman, Jay, and Philippe had once penetrated her. *So I'm like Sharon now*, Lunt thought, *Sharon herself, and she's become them, all her lovers*, and she, Lunt's angel, dug deep inside him, drilling into him like a penis, each plunge inside him drawing moans from within his chest.

A world away, Jim Morrison kept crooning.

"Okay, I got him buttered up for you," Sharon said after a slice of time—minutes or hours?—and took her finger from his anus. A vacuum sucked all sound away. All but Jim's bass rumble of a voice.

Why has Sharon stopped? Lunt wondered. *I miss her hands!* He whispered "Yoo-hoo?" in the hope she would hear him, yet no one answered. There were footsteps near him, however, and a dog barked.

"Give me Myrna," said the spider as soon as the barking stopped.

Whispers, more footsteps, laughter.

Something electric got switched on. A humming sound.

The spider said, "I'll do a test, just a few volts."

And then it happened.

"*Oh, FUCK!*" Lunt screamed, eyes popping open from the pain.

Searing pain.

Outrageous pain.

Pain that he hadn't known was possible.

It attacked his heart, detonated there, and shot pain through his spinal column straight to his skull.

"*Oh, FUCK!*" again.

Then Lunt blacked out.

Time for the ritual.

"HE'S not, like, *dead*, is he?"

Wiping the patchouli-flavored lubricant from her hands onto her bare narrow hips, the naked Jopp looked from the dangling unconscious victim to Benny Pompa. Specifically, she looked at the cutlass that Pompa brandished in his left hand and then at the gadget he clutched in his right hand. This gadget, which had electrocuted Lunt, was a long black wand with yellow lightning bolts painted on it. At one end of the wand were a handle and on-off switch; from the other end protruded metal electrodes.

"Nope," Trudi replied to Jopp, shutting off her video camera without a glance in Lunt's direction. "That was the very weakest setting."

"Our slave did good work anointing him," the pop star said. "Coll-a-nell Tate must've dug it."

The green woman still felt buzzed from laudanum, but Lunt's stark agony had somewhat undone her. Her gaze stayed fixed on the bound man, who continued to sway a little from the force of his convulsion. "But what if—what if he *does* die? Accidentally, I mean?"

"He won't," said Trudi as she mounted her camera on a tripod before the Catbird Seat.

Saffron, doing the same thing with a tripod that stood to Lunt's left, told Jopp, "We haven't lost one offering yet."

"Let's stay with low voltage," Pompa told Trudi while handing her the black wand. "We'll make this last."

"What *is* that thing?" Jopp asked.

"This *thing*," Pompa explained, grinning more beatifically than she'd ever seen him grin, either in photographs or in person, "is what you'll be learning how to use. It—she—has a name: 'Megawatt

Myrna.'" And now, as if conversing with the object, Pompa held it before his face and said, "Myrna, meet slave. No, Myrn, I'm *not* sure why she's green. I don't even think *she's* sure, though I'll bet she *thinks* she knows why."

Both Saffron and Trudi guffawed at this, Saffron for a longer time. Having finished setting up their movie cameras, they each moved on to other tasks. Trudi loaded AA batteries into what looked like a new weightlifter belt while Saffron massaged Trudi's shoulders and cooed in her ear, softly singing along with "Love Street," the Doors song currently playing.

Pompa, Jopp noticed, had grown erect. This ritual always aroused him. He said, "We named Megawatt Myrna after Trudi's mother. She doesn't really approve of her son-in-law, does she, Trude?"

In the Catbird Seat, Lunt moaned and stirred. It seemed that he was coming back to consciousness. The green woman watched his movements, thinking, *Thank God*. He might be a snitcher and a greedhead, a Bredda Gravalicious, but he didn't deserve to die. Then, glancing nervously again at "Myrna," she asked if it was a Taser.

"Tasers," Saffron said coldly, "are not permitted here."

"Tasers," added Trudi with a bit more warmth, "are commercial things, and what we do is sacred, not commercial."

Using his cutlass, Pompa pointed to the weightlifter belt that Trudi now fastened around Lunt's chest. "As for that stun belt there," he told Jopp, "we haven't given him a name yet. I say 'him' because we think he's male. And he makes Myrna seem like, well, Eleanor Roosevelt."

Jopp didn't know who this Eleanor person was, but Trudi and Saffron guffawed at the remark despite being occupied with their respective business. With Lunt still suspended in the air, one wife took Lunt's chin, opened his jaws, and poured more Mucaquell down his throat while the other wife peeled ropes away from his midsection so she could attach a snowy-white adult diaper to him.

"What's *that* for?" Jopp asked. The creepy surprises kept on coming.

"Sometimes the drug addicts we use as our offerings lose sphincter control," Trudi explained.

"Too late for squeamishness," Pompa told Jopp tartly. He slashed the air again with his cutlass. "You pledged obedience to us. To *me*. We take that seriously, don't we, wifeys?"

The wives exchanged a glance, broke into laughter.

Pompa ran his right index finger along the blade of the cutlass. Like the corduroy vest Pompa wore, this seriously sharp weapon had been a loaner from Jopp, a temporary gift to her "master." The sword and vest had been Manson's "most prized possessions."

"Charlie was wearing this vest the night before he got busted," Jopp had explained, "and he loved to wave around the cutlass. So with you borrowing his garment and his weapon, Ben, you'll plug into Charlie's powers. The only catch," she made sure to add, "is that you have to give them *back* to me, okay? Someday, I mean. I hate to be an Indian giver, but these are sacred Family heirlooms. If I lose them, my grandma New Leaf will have my head."

Pompa agreed to return the items, not mentioning that he had zero intention of honoring his word. Why would he honor it? These relics were too wondrous to part with—even more valuable to him as the leader of a new secret society than Jopp's insights about her Family. The way Pompa viewed it, Manson was a madman—a vicious, probably-never-struck-by-lightning madman—but in his own way Manson had been a shaman nonetheless. A visionary. And possessing the man's vest and cutlass would transfer Charlie's vibes to Pompa. Already, in fact, the pop star could feel a certain

Mansonness burgeoning inside him, sparking the shaman-spirit into lightning. *Human* lightning.

He did a few of his barking coughs, then touched the sword's tip to his chest, the curious marking he bore there. "You see this Flower, slave?"

Beginning to feel frightened, Jopp whispered, "Yeah."

"Speak up! Share your voice!"

"Yeah, Benny, yeah."

"Well, come and *lick* it. And while you're licking, here's a flash quiz. True or false: the ancient Romans built lightning shrines?"

PAIN. Not just the discomfort of being bound and suspended in the air, but pain, something terrible set loose inside him, lashing at each meridian, every molecule, of his body, torching through bones, nerves, tissue, bloodstream, making his heart a cinder. This is what Lunt felt. And *"AAARRRRRGHHH!"* is what he screamed. He could sense the belt across his chest but didn't realize, *couldn't* realize, that all his torment branched from there. His eyeballs spun around, his thoughts got whipped to tapioca, and all the hair on his head stiffened before he plunged back into darkness.

"Sorry," said Trudi with a shrug. "I hit the button by mistake."

"Oh, *sure*," said Pompa, throwing her a sidelong glance. "We know *all* about your supposed 'accidents.'"

At this stage of the ritual, they'd eighty-sixed the Doors and put a sugary 1960s pop tune on repeat mode: Bakalaka's "Lightning Lucy." This was Pompa's self-proclaimed theme song. A version of it, dissonant and loud, appeared on his pop group's first live album.

"Trudi, hand that remote to our slave and let her use it."

But the slave in question was too distressed to speak now, much less accept the object Trudi proferred. What Jopp had just viewed—Lunt's wild convulsions from the shock, his body jerking like a misused puppet, his crying out in agony—these shattered the remnants of her laudanum high. The green woman's eyes, widening with fear, kept jumping around the parlor, jumping between Pompa, his wives, their cameras, and Lunt, whose limbs still quivered, though he'd blacked out once again. How many more jolts could he take? This wasn't pretend death, this was *for real*! This was what the Thanatologists did to Polanski's girl (and then blamed her husband, Charlie, for)—this was murder! And she wasn't just a bystander, a witness—she was sort of *helping* them! She'd share the blame! Why was Benny going this far? What had changed him? Was it some fit brought on by the lightning damage he'd sustained? Maybe getting lightning-struck wasn't good for him, after all...

Jopp asked herself what Seth or her other Family confederates would do if they were in her place.

How about grandma New Leaf?

Charlie himself?

"Slave, please take what Trudi's giving you."

Jopp couldn't bear being in the pop star's gaze now, especially not through those crazy purple glasses he wore. Looking away from him, her voice starting to falter, she said, "Uh...I'd rather not? Please?"

"I knew it," said Saffron sharply. "She's out of her depth. This chick's for shit."

"Hey," Trudi spoke up, "give her a chance!" Unlike her wife, she still believed that Jopp, with care and patience, could be groomed as a useful slave. "Remember *your* first time?"

Saffron went into a snit and didn't answer.

Eager to get on with the ritual, Pompa finger-drummed his Flower and said, "Let's use Myrna again. Saff, give him a few volts on his leg."

"Which one?"

"The left. Always the left in everything, remember?"

"That's our new 'theory of sinistrality,'" Trudi filled in Jopp. "Left is superior to right. Benny just came up with that last week."

After shuffling over to Lunt's flank, her bare feet kicking aside debris (but carefully—she didn't want to stub a toe yet again), Saffron put the stun gun to his leg. Jopp couldn't hear the crackling sound it made—Lunt's resulting shriek was chilling, and the web creaked loudly from how his body bounced in it.

Can someone outside the room hear this? Jopp wondered as Lunt's throat made gurgling sounds. *Hear* anything *above this music?* She hoped so, but the Ofotert suite seemed soundproof.

"Now do the right leg," Pompa ordered Saffron. "Lightning— *strike!*"

Lunt's reaction to electric shock this time was his most extreme so far. Followed by another swift blackout.

Tears rushed to Jopp's eyes. She'd never seen something so awful. "He'll *die*," she cried out, growing as sick to her stomach as she already was in her heart.

Humming along with "Lightning Lucy" in his husky voice, Pompa tossed his cutlass to the carpet, where it clattered on the floor-paper. "No, he won't," he answered Jopp. "Skin effect, the experts call it. It stops each shock from being lethal. Lightning's a charm, a noble gift, and we're *enobling* our offering by granting it to him. Putting him in a state of grace. Just like we pay homage to the storm gods by presenting *him* to *them*. It's a win-win!"

"*Lightnin'—is strikin'—*again!" Bakalaka sang.

"But, *Ben*," said the green woman, hoping to chill him out, restore him to his true self, "you're better than this. Like, *much!* What about your—your foundation? You know, Pompa Pride? That charity stuff you do for orphans?"

Husband and wives tittered at this together. And Pompa, more turned-on by the ritual than ever, the ordeal of their offering, began to fondle himself. "My manager set that shit up as a tax dodge. Who gives a shit about orphans? If you ever took a Perpa Mind Laxative, you'd know that being parentless is good for you. Now *focus*, slave, and prove Saff wrong."

"Huh?"

"Last chance to show us you fit in. Get hold of Myrna, find her switch, and give the Coll-a-nell some volts."

Jopp swallowed hard.

"Start with his arm."

Enough, she thought. She'd had enough of this.

"The left, I mean."

"*No*," she said. Her voice, coming from far down inside her, had meager power to it, but she'd worked past her fear sufficiently to make a stand.

"Louder," Pompa boomed at her. "I want to *hear* you!"

With her voice gaining its own force now, its own edge, its own authority, she said, "*Fuck* no. And fuck *you*, Ben. It's *wrong*, this lame-o shit you're doing."

Infuriated, Saffron lowered the stun gun she'd been trying to hand to Jopp and crossed her arms. Her face was as smooth as marble, but her voice betrayed her feelings. "What did I tell you, Ben? She's no good!"

Trudi, for her part, was less angry than puzzled, asking Jopp, "Didn't you tell us you *hate* this guy? Why should you care if he gets struck?"

"I *don't* care," Jopp explained. "Not when it comes to a *little* suffering. Hang Jeepster from the rafters, fine by me! Keep him swinging there all night...but giving him electric shocks? That's just *sinister*, dude."

Trudi shook her head. She still had faith in Jopp's slave potential, but that faith was ebbing fast. "How is it evil when we're *purifying* him? Benny just told you, it's a win-win. Anyway, we've got a signed release form."

"*Plus*," Pompa weighed in without curtailing his self-pleasure, "isn't it ironic?"

"What is?" said Jopp.

"Isn't it ironic that *you're* the one who's accusing us? You, of all people—it's the pot calling the kettle black, slave! Or *ex*-slave, I have to say, because you're hereby excommunicated."

Jopp wasn't sure what "excommunicated" meant. But she was even less sure about the pot-and-kettle business, so she asked about this first. "What pot?"

"Listen to Ms. Manson Bobbysoxer here question *our* values! As if Charlie M. was famous for his *tenderness*. Not exactly a man of peace, was he? When the Helter began to Skelter, Sharon Tate and her pals got chopped into kindling. Yeah, we're giving the Coll-a-nell some volts'n'jolts—how's that worse than *your* Family's behavior?"

"I *explained* it was a frame-job! Charlie never killed a—"

"Murderer or not," the pop star cut her off, "for him the turn-on was Helter Skelter. For you, it's Manson. For Coll-a-nell Tate, it's his girlfriend. And for other fools, it's superhero comics, or old Doors tunes, or *my own* music, or Jolly Dolls, or sitting around and popping Bubble Wrap. All of it's just dumb distraction."

"*Lightnin'—is strikin'*—again!" sang Bakalaka.

Lunt groaned and shuddered, his body swaying in the Catbird Seat.

"People need distraction from themselves," Pompa spieled on, holding Jopp's glare. "Those selves are too dark to face. And *that's* why lightning matters, because it fucking *illuminates*. It's better than all that other crap. It *shines a light*, cuts through the black, cracks it apart. You understand? It burns, it cleanses!"

Jopp felt confused; she didn't know how to respond. What the pop star, her *favorite* pop star, was saying *did* have a touch of wisdom to it. In a zany way, it did! But killing someone—even this lame-o Lunt!—was exactly what the Thanatologists had done to Sharon Tate. And no wisdom could change how wrong that was.

Fed up with his ex-slave, Pompa turned to face his wives, his priestesses, his sibyls, and, with his husky voice breaking he demanded that they strike, hurl new lightning bolts, at Lunt. "Go, wifeys, go! *Make him feel fire!*"

The two obliged, with Trudi setting off the stun belt while Saffron pressed Megawatt Myrna to Lunt's back, the region just above the diaper.

Shocked awake, he screamed, convulsed, and blacked out once more.

"Stop!" Jopp cried out, covering her ears with her glittery green wrist.

"Lightnin'—is strikin'—again!"

"More!" Pompa howled, the shooting glasses falling from his sweat-dampened face. He was leaping up and down, tugging harder at his penis, feeling as orgasmic as he felt while performing onstage. Electrocution, watching *others'* electrocution, had been getting Pompa's rocks off since his own experience of it, the Big Reveal that nearly killed him, gave him his Flower, and changed his life, transforming Pompa from a mere dope pig to a person with a new need. A *better* need. Yes, what were drugs, even good drugs, compared to lightning? Nothing satisfied like nature's harshest kiss! And sharing this with other druggies, helpless addicts like himself, was the highest high of all. True sex magic! Therefore, witnessing Lunt's ordeal took Pompa higher, ever higher—right to the brink of the night's first climax.

Yet before the pop star came—before he burst like a firecracker, yelping *"Yes"* and toppling over to the carpet, emptied out, with his wives' applause filling his ears—before this happened, he heard loud knocking on his door. The suite's front door. And this knocking was being made not by knuckles, a human fist, but something else: a wooden clipboard.

"The neighbors, probably," said one wife.

"Our music's too loud," said the other.

More knocking. Louder.

And so, with a growled "Fuck" and an adjustment of his glasses, the husband set out across the parlor, feet moving confidently through the detritus, the floor-paper, staying clear of the cameras' range. He would quiet the music, fine, but not by much, because no strangers would be permitted to ruin his ritual. Not in *his* parlor! And while he twisted a silver knob on the stereo, removing substantial bite from the singer Bakalaka's voice, he turned his back to Jopp. Which gave her the break she needed.

Hearing those knocks, those aural signals from the "real" world, had reignited the green woman's courage, put iron back in her spine, and so when Benny turned away, she gave an anxious little cry and sprang to life and into motion. That is, she darted to the door, unbolted it, and flung it open before the wives could scramble after her.

Framed in the doorway were two men.

Two tall men.

Their eyes needed a moment to adjust to the dim candlelight of the suite. Then...

"Jumping Jehosaphat!" one of the men exclaimed.

WHEN Lunt woke up, he saw a rectangle of blue marred by a single shredded-looking cloud. Surrounded by a darkness that smelled of soil—soil and patchouli—he moved his arm so that he could touch that darkness with a finger, and it *was* soil, worm-riddled soil packed densely around him. Next he looked down at his supine body and found himself wearing a dress. It was Sharon's favorite blue-and-yellow Pucci print minidress, the one she'd been buried in.

Although the sight of his hairy legs poking out of the dress was grotesque, he rather liked how he looked in it. This was his first experience wearing drag and it felt glorious. Still, the sound of a shovel hitting dirt pulled his attention back to the sky above him. A rain of that dirt came falling on him. Sharon, wearing a dress identical to his, was using the shovel to bury him alive. For some reason, however, this bothered Lunt less than his possibly having missed the Hotel Ofotert's Tate-World Conference.

"What day is it?" he shouted up to Sharon, once he'd brushed the dirt and dust away from his face.

"August eighth," she replied, panting heavily from the exertion.

"So it's my birthday!" A grayish clod hit Lunt squarely in the forehead. "And I *did* miss the Sharonfest…but at least I made it to forty!"

Light poured from Sharon's mouth as she spoke. "Not quite. It's August eighth in sixty-nine. Meaning, you just turned six, and it's my death-day, and I've decided to take you with me."

Lunt frowned, thinking, *My fault—mine alone. I didn't heed Mother Fist, didn't let La Tate stay dead, so it's come to this, with me back here in Holy Cross Cemetery not to pay respects to her but to join her, to honor Sharon the way I always hoped I wouldn't have to: with my life.*

Tears dribbled down Lunt's cheeks, rolled into his mouth. He could taste salt along with the dirt and dust. "You died too soon," he called up to her.

Now light came pouring from Sharon's ears and nose while her lips, so much like Jopp's, formed a smile. He could see this smile clearly. Yet she still looked sad to him when she said, "I think I always knew I'd die young. Young, and by violence. My intuition's as good as Bronson's. You didn't write that in your Sharon memoir, did you? When I cried, 'Please don't' to those killers, I knew they wouldn't listen. 'I want to live!' I pleaded, 'to live, and have my child!' I even begged them to take me with them, to keep me with them till I gave birth. *Then* they could kill me. But all for naught. They were too far gone for empathy. Just like *you* are."

And light came pouring now from her whole face, blinding Lunt, and when he woke up—for real this time—he was back in his suite. So he *hadn't* been buried alive, although he felt groggy, hurting badly, and was naked except for a diaper firmly attached to his middle. The clothes he'd worn last night were piled beside the bed on which he lay. The worst of the pain was concentrated in his lower back and left hip; it was as if all his body's woes of the past week had settled there. The diaper, on the other hand, felt comfortable—as smooth and as soft as the bedsheets. Did all diapers feel so fabulous? Wait, why was he wearing this thing, anyway? All he remembered with any clarity was stripping bare in Pompa's—*Sharon's*—suite. Maybe everyone got into diapers, as a goofy party game?

Scootching up to a sitting position made Lunt yell out, because his back and hip themselves cried out in pain. Gingerly he eased himself around to check the trouble areas, where he found bruises in each spot. Even to touch them with a fingertip brought on a keen hurt. The bruises puzzled him as much as the diaper did. Moreover, he was feeling hungry, terrifically hungry, and a licorice taste in his mouth made him think of Mucaquell. Where was the case of it Pompa had promised?

Lunt peered around his bedroom. As far as he could tell, it was in the same shape as he'd left it: the TV blaring, the unopened champagne bottle, the stack of defaced Santa Shots, the stickered manila envelopes they'd come in, the towel on the carpet that covered spit and puke and vile photos. An awful stench, too. And no sign of Mucaquell.

That scumbag Pompa! He'd broken their agreement! For a man who was kind to orphans, he sure seemed untrustworthy!

What time was it?

According to the clock on the nightstand it was 8:28. Morning or night? Night, according to the dark lines etched between the closed Venetian blinds. (At least they'd stayed shut, free of creepy-crawly tampering.) But what night was it? Had the Tate-World Conference begun yet? Begun *without him*? Lunt didn't know. He *did* know that moving around in bed even slightly made his hip and back lacerate him with more pain. Nevertheless, he needed his Mucaquell. Even more than food, he craved it. Which meant that he would have to use his room phone.

Unfortunately, once he'd picked up the receiver, which felt cold against his ear, it had no dial tone. Dead—like his uncharged BlackBerry. Had Jopp cut off his landline to toy with him? Jopp, or that twitching goofball Trueax?

After a moment, Lunt remembered that he'd unplugged the phone himself. His stretching down to plug it back in brought on new physical agony. Three rings, however, and he was connected to Pompa's suite, where a woman, Saffron or Trudi, chirped, "Oh, hi" when Lunt announced himself. Then her husband got on the line.

"Coll-a-nell!" The pop star's voice was hoarser than ever. "I'm glad you called."

"Really?" Lunt was proud to hear it. "Good to hear you, too, Ben. But, uh…"

"Speak, comrade."

"What night is this?"

"What *night*? Last I checked, Wednesday."

Wow, thought Lunt, *praise Sharon! So I haven't missed the conference, there's still time to get my Muke, hang out with Benny, bond more with him, ogle his wives, then sleep through Thursday, and rise refreshed for the start of the Sharonfest!*

"You feeling charged up?" Pompa asked. "You should be. We put the lightning lords inside you. Not enough, but *some*, at least."

Lunt didn't know what Pompa meant, but said, "Yeah, thanks."

"You're welcome, Fritz. Grok away at that feeling. Listen, we're going out to do our feed, then maybe back to Corpus Co-op, so I'll sign off, but—"

"Wait! Er, have fun…but what about that Muke you promised me?"

Following a brief pause, Pompa began to laugh, to chortle Bronsonesquely, but soon it changed to that barking sound, and again it took Lunt a moment to recognize that this was coughing. Then he waited anxiously until Pompa could speak again. What he said was, "I oughta save that syrup for *myself*, huh? Well, we can give you a taste, I guess—we're philanthropic types. But only that, a taste."

"But you owe me! A *lot* of it—you promised!"

"Owe?" The pop star chortled again, but more modestly, so that he wouldn't relapse into coughing. "What we agreed was, you'd deliver yourself for our ritual, be our offering, but we had to cut it short, so—"

Lunt wasn't sure he'd heard this correctly. "Ritual? I—I don't know what that is."

"Don't be coy, comrade, you'll piss me off. P-I-S-S-M-E-off. Thanks to your oafish pal, that clown in the white suit, everything got burned, so the blame I lay is on you."

"Wait, stop. Oafish pal? *Who?*"

Splayed across the indigo couch in Suite 56, Pompa squeezed a muscular naked left calf—not his own but Saffron's. She and Trudi were dozing beside him. "I don't like my rituals getting fucked with," he said to Lunt. "Your pal interrupted our deal, which means you're technically in breach. Breach is a contract law term—our notary public Trudi will explain that if you want. The point is, we don't owe you bupkus. Unless you wanna receive some *new* volts, which we can work out, trade for Muke. Stop by and we'll rig you up tonight. Fresh diapers, free of charge."

"But that's—that's *not fair!*" Raising his voice made his lower back sing with pain, so Lunt kept it in check when he added, "It's not!"

"Fair?" Pompa chortled some more. "If you want fair, you can find it in the dictionary between 'fab' and 'fuck.' Talk to White Suit."

"White Suit…" *Hold on.* "Mandrake? Mandrake was there last night?"

"Is that his name? Yeah, right during the ritual. *Significant* interruption. So point your finger at him, not me, for burning our arrangement. Oh, and another thing." The playful nastiness in Pompa's hoarse voice changed to just plain nastiness. "That green-colored chick said you're a tattletale. Prone to finkage. So while you're here, or even when you go back to where you're from—Sharon-Tateland, or *wherever*—you will *not* get second thoughts and drop a dime on us. Got it?"

"Drop a dime?"

"Grass, rat, tattle, squeal, fink, inform." The pop star's voice grew nastier still. "We didn't finish what we started, but you've been lightning-struck. That means I'm your master. Plus, I've got the Flower in my flesh, and it protects me. We're with the storm gods, my wives and me. So don't make waves."

Don't make waves, thought Lunt. The title of a Sharon film. How far away that carefree world seemed, the world of 1960s beach-blanket movies.

"Besides," Pompa said, "that contract you signed was a release form, it was notarized and witnessed. My attorneys are pretty heavy, they'll bleed you dry if you give so much as a chirp. And don't forget, we've got the ritual on video. I'm not in frame, but *you* are—you're the star, you with that green chick. Make one chirp and it gets uploaded to the internet. You'll go worldwide. Got it, Mr. Stuyvesant Fish?"

"Er...I..."

"Sounds to me like 'Roger that,'" Pompa said, and then hung up, enraging Lunt, who nearly hurled the phone at the nearest wall.

The bastard! Fame *was* a mask that had eaten into his face. A basilisk mask! Cursing loudly, which hurt his lower back again, Lunt wasted no time in ringing up a different hotel room. While it rang there, Lunt's eyes shot over to the champagne on his writing table. Lord, he could use a fucking drink! If not Muke, at least Dom Perignon! Ordinarily he didn't drink alcohol—his hangovers tended to be atrocious—but this was not the time to worry about tomorrow.

"Welcome back, dear boy!" Glen Mandrake said once Lunt had identified himself. "Just rising? Oh, what a titanic sleep you've had! The things I've done in the meantime. Hey, have you washed your diaper yet?"

"So you *were* in his suite!"

"You mean *Sharon's* suite? Indeed, I was. I should have guessed that 'Rosenwach' was an alias for Benny Pompa. It's a sin how badly that beast has trashed the place. They'll need a Hazmat squad when he checks out."

Asleep and snoring faintly in Mandrake's bed was a voluptuous young African-American woman with a fur vest hanging half-on and half-off her otherwise naked body. Not only was this woman, Latreena Bates, the regular hostess at Gush, she was also Mandrake's latest lover. Their first sexual congress had occurred this afternoon, following her lunch shift at the restaurant.

Smiling down at Latreena now, Mandrake in his oversized, monogrammed, Renaissance-red bathrobe thought of mentioning her presence to Lunt, but he didn't want the envy-prone New Jerseyan to sour his new affair. He would find time for boasting and gloating later. So all Mandrake said was, "Do you know what came to mind when I saw that lunatic tableau in Sharon's suite last night? Or I should say this morning... My first thought was, 'Ooh-la-la, an orgy!' You know, everybody naked, complete with sex toys. But then I saw how you were all trussed up, tied top to bottom, maybe dead, and *then* I thought of Lichtenberg, my hunchbacked homey, and his quip that 'We cannot truly know whether, at this moment, we are sitting—'"

"The madhouse, yeah, yeah." To Lunt's chagrin, Mandrake's romantic heartbreak about Pandora seemed to have receded; he sounded as vile as ever. "What were you doing at Pompa's?"

Mandrake sighed. "Again, it's not Pompa's suite, it's Sharon's. Keep that straight, Mr. Would-Be Sharon-Themed Author. You really don't remember? Well, I was *saving* you, dear boy. Baby Son and I were like the cavalry, thundering to your rescue."

"Baby Son?"

"Yes, our supposed house detective with the very mature first name. He's the one who carried you over his shoulder back to your dingy, disgusting room. That Hazmat squad should pay you a visit after Pompa. In the end, though, the only work that that Baby Son did was the heavy lifting. Your greater debt is to me."

"I still don't know what you saved me *from*!"

"Well, I can't say for certain—it looked *arcane*, that rig they had you in." Mandrake did one of his tut-tuts, which incensed Lunt. "But you were obviously being tortured in a most baroque fashion."

Lunt felt his rectum pulse. Twice. Had he really been tortured? That would explain the pain in his back and hip. Was it Pompa who'd tortured him? And what was the story with the diaper?

In Mandrake's bed, Latreena Bates shifted position, draping a downy forearm across her eyes. Reluctant to wake her until his refractory period was over, Mandrake spoke more softly when he told Lunt, "He was spitting mad, that Pompa. He said some savage things to me. Even called me 'an eater of broken meats,' whatever *that* means. The wives were just as bad. Balloon smugglers, the two of them, and splendid-looking without clothes, but hostile, *feral*, spitting abuse while Baby Son untangled you from those ropes. Snakes alive, have *they* got anger issues! Only when we mentioned the police did Pompa change his tune. Yes, *that* backed him up efficiently enough. All of a sudden, he was sweetness. Pure light. His wives, to boot. And finally we reached an understanding."

"Understanding? You and him? What kind?"

"Let's just say that Baby Son got a cozy sum of cash on the barrelhead, and I got something else."

"From Pompa? *What* something else?"

"Gentlemen don't discuss such things."

"So Pompa paid you off?"

"That's one way of characterizing it. In exchange for our not yelling 'Cop,' or summoning a doctor—because doctors tend to yell 'Cop' on their own—Baby Son and I each got renumerated. And then some."

Unbelievable, Lunt thought. *Is there any bribe Baby Son would refuse?* "Tell me what Benny's giving you!"

"I repeat, etiquette forbids." He tut-tutted again, glanced at his wristwatch, then again took in the sight of the dozing woman. She wasn't as comely as Pandora, or nearly as intelligent. What's more, there was little Sharonesque about her. Yet until he found someone more suitable, she would serve adequately enough as his date at the Sharonfest. "All you need to know, dear boy, is that I saved your diapered ass and you owe me for it."

"Why are you breaking bread with Pompa?" Lunt cut in. "Especially after what he did to you at Gush!"

"Oh, I'd been planning revenge for that, he was definitely in my sights. *Then*, when your handicapped friend phoned me to say you were in danger, I suspected Pompa might be behind it, and I was right. Even if he *wasn't* behind it, I would have framed him if possible."

"Handicapped? Who?"

"The lesbian. She does seem to care about you, despite your Jersey pedigree and that churlish book you're flogging."

"Bronson called you? *You*?" This was getting crazier and crazier, worse and worse. "She wouldn't!"

"But she did. And it was poignant, how worried for you she was. She found out you were imperiled, so she pulled my number from the Sharon listserv and rang me up. Next, Baby Son and I discussed the situation with that brain-damaged old night clerk, that annoying Filipina Kruikshank, and she suggested that we could find you in the abode of Ziggy Rosenwach. Meaning, Benny Pompa. Which suited me, in vengeance mode, just fine."

Lunt shook his head, astounded by everything he'd heard. Had all this truly happened while he was sleeping? And *tortured*! Did someone, Pompa, actually *torture* him?

"By the way," said Mandrake, "there was a girl with green hair in Sharon's suite. Fetching, and stark naked like the others, but she got dressed and ran away once we showed up. Lickety-split, she went."

Lunt nearly said "Jopp," but clapped a hand to his mouth to stop it.

"Pompa was yelling insults at her," Mandrake continued. "He seemed more furious with her than he was with us. Anyhow, do you happen to know who she is?" The mental image of the green woman made Mandrake's nostrils quiver with excitement. He lowered his voice in case Latreena was waking up, or only pretending to be asleep. "She's a little underfed for me, but did you notice that green-haired girl's *mouth*? Just like Sharon's! Remarkable, really. I presume you saw her too. Well, I want her contact info. Pompa wouldn't share it. So you have to find it for me, Monsieur New Jersey. Bear in mind your debt to me."

Lunt, grinding his teeth, was about to explode, to blow his proverbial top, but caught himself in time, and pondered the offer. Striking a bargain with Mandrake—trading Jopp's number for Mandrake's promise not to trifle with Lunt's Sharon book—might be worth it. And how delicious when Mandrake found out he was wooing a Mansonophile! But what if Jopp quit the Manson Family at some point in the future and then wound up in Mandrake's arms? Lunt knew he couldn't bear this—not with the memory of his losing Pandora still fresh. "Mandrake," he said at last, "thanks for helping me. *And* for helping Bronson. But I still consider you a turd, I owe you nothing, and I hope you get an aneurysm, *right now*."

Cackling with mirth as he put down the receiver, Lunt waited just a second before he lifted it again and dialed Bronson, whose number he knew by heart. The inside of Lunt's non-phone-covered ear tickled him, so he jammed a finger in there, and felt some hair. *Oh, shit, a lot!* Before he could fret too much about this, though, Bronson picked up, sounding sleepy.

"Did I wake you, Bronnie?"

"Lunt? Oh, shit, fuck—thank *God!*"

"Bronnie, I'm sorry, so, *so* sorry, for what I said."

"Forget that for now."

"Can you forgive me?"

"We'll deal with that some other time. Where are you?"

"Now? In my suite."

"At the *Ofotert?*"

"Yup."

"No, Lunt, no! You were supposed to split, to get out! Didn't Mandrake warn you? That scum, he *swore*, I made him *swear*, he'd move you out! Did you get my messages?"

"Which ones?"

"On your cellphone!"

"My BlackBerry's been dead for days."

"Fuck, I could *kill* you!"

The Sharonophile clucked his tongue. "Bronnie, stop. I've already been through hell." He wasn't certain that he'd been tortured, but the possibility of it so shamed him that he couldn't mention it to her. Not even to *her*, his dearest friend.

"Well, get out of there. Go!"

"Hey," he said, "you're scaring me."

"You *should* be scared," said Bronson, fully awake now.

"But why'd you phone Mandrake?" Lunt asked.

"Come on, what choice was there? You weren't answering my calls, I couldn't trust the hotel staff, and Mandrake seemed to be the only Sharonophile on the premises! I couldn't bring the cops in, either, because I didn't have hard proof…"

"What proof?" said Lunt. The worry in her voice had his pulse racing. "And what's the problem with the staff here?"

"My intuition kept *ping-ping-pinging*, I did a bit of research, and you know those packages with Manson quotes? *Someone who works there sent them to you.* Her name is Cory Baha. She's a member of that dumb Polanski fan club, Polanski People—remember them? They're the ones who own the Santa Shots, so she must've stolen some from their stash and marked them up."

"They sent me Sharon's autopsy photos, too!"

"Christ! You serious?"

"You have no idea how revolting they were, Bron. They made me puke…"

"I can guess. This Cory Baha seems unhinged. A lunatic!"

"Hold on," said Lunt, "so let me get this straight. The Santa Shots were given to me by this girl Cory, and she works at the Ofotert?"

"Cory *Baha*. Do you know her?"

Lunt bit his lower lip, his mind oscillating. Baha sounded Hispanic, and most of the hotel's chambermaids were Mexican, or Mexican-American, so was this Cory Baha a housekeeper here? Had he met her, or was she keeping to the shadows, avoiding him? Had she even been in his suite while he was sleeping, opening and shutting the Venetian blinds, creepy-crawling?

"And that's not all," said Bronson. "Guess where *her brother* lives? Amarillo! They work together, her and him!"

"I can't believe it…"

"It fucking adds up."

Lunt shuddered. "How'd you find this out? Find *her*, I mean?"

"I told you, basic research. I Googled Manson's people, Family members, their associates, and nothing clicked, so I looked at Polanski People and *bingo*! I found a member who works at the Hotel Ofotert. So I delved deeper, learned about her what I could, and—"

I can't handle this without my Muke, Lunt thought. *I'll have to cut a deal with Pompa, submit myself to his ritual. Whatever that is! Even if it's mild torture...*

"Hey!" said Bronson. "You there?"

"Uh? Oh, yeah, yeah..."

"So have you met this Cory Baha?"

"Not that I know of, no."

"Well, it's personal, all the same."

"Why, because I hate Polanski?"

"No, hon, your parents."

"My *parents?*"

"Yup. Apparently, this Cory Baha bitch grew up in Jersey, and she went to college there, Camden College, and she had herself a sweetheart, some nice young college boy named Moreland."

"Wait..." Lunt felt his jaw start to sag. Time juddered and jumped track.

"*Then,*" Bronson continued, knowing she had to spell it out, spill every last bean, so that Lunt would understand how serious this was and run for refuge, "some other chick, she came along, stole this Cory's guy, they jilted her, and Cory flipped out, slashed her wrists."

"But she survived," said Lunt. "I *know* this story—my mother told me before she died! She and my dad, they cheated on his college girlfriend, hooked up behind her back..."

"It's some coincidence, I know. A small world, right?"

Lunt closed his mouth, swallowing saliva before it spilled out, and stared at the phone on the nightstand. Was this really happening? Was he still dreaming?

"There are still some missing pieces," Bronson continued. "A shitload, actually. But I think I've got the main facts. After she botched her suicide, she and her brother came out west to LA, and she went gaga for Polanski and joined his fan club. Then her brother splits, he moves to Amarillo, but she's still working at the Ofotert, and she's still pissed at both your parents when you show up, two weeks back, and put new sting in her old wound. So she and her brother gaslight you, they use your Sharon-love to drive you nuts. And who knows how far they might go? That's why you *have to leave*, right now."

Lunt's thoughts returned to what the man in Amarillo said each night: "Whosoever treats his fellows without honor or humanity, he, and his issue, shall be treated with commensurate inhumanity and dishonor."

"So I'm the issue," said Lunt. For once, his intuition was as accurate as Bronson's. Or perhaps it was just logic. At any rate— oh, splendid brain wave!—he finally got it. Cory Baha, who'd been "treated without honor or humanity"—he realized who she was.

11

LAST WORDS: FAMOUS AND OTHERWISE

(Thursday)

IN Paris, the city where he'd honeymooned with one wife and currently lived with another, Roman Polanski, nearly seventy, took a sip from the day's first espresso.

Thousands of miles to the west, the sixty-eight-year-old Charles Manson slept in his California prison cell. He dreamed of the river Styx, where hawks wheeled through a granite sky and where, in bare trees, spiders formed webs between adjacent dripping, brown branches.

Farther west of Paris, the Hotel Ofotert towered over Sunset Boulevard. In a junior suite on the fourth floor, an empty Dom Perignon bottle lay on a butterscotch-colored carpet. A wasteland of torn plastic food wrappers surrounded the bottle. On a nearby writing table, letters had been placed over a book by Dorothy Parker, and scrawled across a sheet of paper beside the letters was this message: "FOR THE AUTHORITIES TO DISTRIBUTE TO THOSE NAMED HEREIN—MY SURVIVORS."

Lunt Moreland had been swigging Dom Perignon from the bottle as he composed the letters by hand. Given the solemn circumstances, emails did not seem formal enough, so he'd issued his farewells on cream-colored hotel stationary with a thin, black, Ofotert-monogrammed pen. The booze had boosted his courage for what he had to do, and also blunted the pain he still felt in his lower back and left hip.

In the first letter, embarked on when Lunt was halfway through the bottle, he implored his former literary agent to find a publisher for his unfinished Sharon Tate memoir.

"Perhaps, Vishwa," he wrote, *"you'll even pen a preface to my Sharon Tate book, explaining why I couldn't complete it. I doubt that,*

given my fate, Mandrake will strive to block you on this. But if he does, please persevere for the sake of my memory."

In a letter to Polanski, Lunt apologized for maligning the film director's name, concluding, *"Roman, I envied you your wife."*

Another letter was addressed to Jopp: *"Right now, Manson seems alluring to you, and as a third-generation Family member, you probably won't find it easy to break yourself free from the mindset. But if you ever think of me—fond thoughts, I hope!—consider looking into Sharon, what a great artist and person she was. Perhaps her spirit will guide you from the darkness to the light."*

He added, in a PS, that Jopp's friend Strangely had been wrong about Sharon sleeping with Steve McQueen. *"They were just friends, and she never got to bear anyone's child, biker or otherwise."*

By the time he wrote to Bronson, Lunt was nearly out of champagne, his stomach gassy. He thanked his best friend for her friendship and hoped her future would be radiant—*"whether La Tate plays any part in it or not. If you do move on from Sharon to Raquel Welch, I say 'Go for it.' You have my blessing. We're friends forever, no matter what. And please ensure that I get buried at Holy Cross, as close as possible to Sharon's grave. Most likely they only accept Catholics there, so please lie to them and convince them that I was one."*

With each successive letter he wrote, the still-diaper-clad Lunt got drunker, and his handwriting grew shakier. Some letters—addressed to his father's nurse Jah Victor (*"You've been a saint to my poor dad, and I pray that you'll continue"*), and to his father himself (*"I'm sorry, Dad, for how low I've fallen"*)—were sweet in nature. Other letters—to Randy Trueax, Benny Pompa, and Lunt's ex-girlfriend Pandora—expressed scabrous sentiments. And by the time he started writing to his mother, a woman two decades dead, he had grown so unhinged by Dom Perignon that he couldn't write legibly at all.

12:08 A.M.: In the Hotel Ofotert lobby four stories down, Mrs. Corazon Kruikshank (*nee* Baha) stood at her post behind the mahogany reception desk. She was speaking with a guest, a beautiful young Hungarian human rights lawyer who'd just arrived by taxicab from LAX. Within a day, dozens of denizens of Tate-World—Sharonophiles who'd signed up for the Ofotert's Sharonfest—were due to also arrive at this hotel and check in at this front desk, eager to move into their temporary new lodging. Thanks to one of their own, however, the conference would be canceled.

"Alas," Mrs. Kruikshank told the jetlagged Hungarian, whose nose wrinkled at the night clerk's mustardy breath, "no, I'm *not* sure whether meals at our restaurant can be prepared without garlic. Still, I know how serious people's allergies can be. If you inquire tomorrow, our manager Mr. Trueax will be glad to help you."

As the stout Filipina night clerk finished the word "you," she glimpsed a figure stumbling drunkenly toward her. Except for a puffy white swimsuit, he was naked. Barefoot, too. And stinking of champagne—she could smell it from here. The swimsuit, was it *a diaper*? It surely looked like one! But why would an adult wear a diaper in public?

The Hungarian, spinning around to face the panting, inebriated, nearly middle-aged man coming toward her, asked herself the same thing, her nose wrinkling at the champagne smell. Was this one of those Hollywood eccentrics she'd heard about?

"Can I help you, sir?" said Mrs. Kruikshank.

Then she recognized him. "And boy," to echo one of Sharon's killers about a not entirely dissimilar scenario, "was she surprised!"

Indeed, the look on Mrs. Kruikshank's face was the same look she wore whenever she strained to get her words out. By the time she would have been able to speak, though, Lunt was upon her. Snarling as he lunged past the Hungarian, he leaped up against the front desk (the exertion of it sending sudden pain to his injured back and hip—pain not even his present drunkenness could suppress), plunged his left hand into Mrs. Kruikshank's cloud of white hair, got a good grip, and yanked her head toward him.

The old desk clerk had been taken by surprise; she hadn't seen the letter opener, that scimitar-shaped eighteenth-birthday present from Lunt's mother, clenched in his right hand. The Hungarian had better luck. Having glimpsed the silver object, and believing it was meant for her, she dashed away, rushed to the lobby, which was filled with revelers, while Lunt reared back, swung his right arm, and brought the shiny weapon down.

Kruikshank has to die. So his drunken reasoning went. She'd been against him all along, this crone with her neurologically challenged manner. What an *act*, a crock of shit! So she had a gripe against his parents? Fair enough. (And now he understood why she'd reminded him of his mother: he'd sensed her link to Curtis Moreland, his old man.) But did her gripe against his parents justify *tormenting* him? Or *desecrating* Sharon's image?

No!

She had to pay for the damage she'd done.

Still, this wasn't just about vengeance. Lunt had to kill her because of the damage she had *yet* to do. With this evildoer, this madwoman, holding power at the hotel, she could wreak havoc on the entire Tate-World gathering, do as much harm to Lunt's fellow Sharonophiles as she'd done to him alone. He had to stop her.

Preemptive strike time!

(Drunk as Lunt was, drunk and deranged after what he'd suffered lately, his thoughts were obviously disordered.)

His plan had been to stab her where she stood, then clamber over the front desk and finish her off with more blade thrusts. However many would be needed. After which he would retreat to his sanctuary, Suite 47. There he would fill the bathtub with hot water, remove his diaper, play on the suite's stereo the Stealers Wheel song "Star," take the "WHY?" poster from the wall, bring it with him into the tub to bid *"Adieu"* to La Tate, his lovely Sharon, and finally slice his wrists with the letter opener. Suicide would be easier to handle than prison. And sleep, the Big One, he hoped, would bring Lunt no nightmares, only sweet dreams.

12:09 A.M.: The Sharonophile's arm, swinging downward, moved fast. But thanks to all of that champagne—and thanks, perhaps, to a deficient killer instinct—Lunt fucked it up. Instead of striking the woman's soft throat, he struck her bony shoulder. Mrs. Kruikshank gave a yelp—no delay now in her verbal response—and tears jumped instantly to her eyes. Stunned, she looked at the new wound, which began to sting as soon as the blade pierced the skin and muscle and then met bone. She couldn't fathom what she saw, the liquid seeping through the gray polyester of her uniform. But she could fathom what she *felt*, and oh, it hurt.

The last time she'd felt such pain, acute physical pain, was when, rejected by her love, the nice quiet Curtis Moreland, she'd opened her wrists with a razor. She hadn't believed she'd die then, not truly. She'd longed to die, but being young, she did not imagine it would happen. Not for real. This time was different. This time, she wanted life, more life, to *stay alive*, if only for a day, one more day, and she knew she might not make it. Curtis Moreland's grown son, this foolish boy, he'd overreacted to the tricks she and her brother had played on him. Overreacted to the extent that this fool now seemed bent on killing her. Cory's lips began to quiver; so did a thick vein in her throat; and "Mother," she cried, "Mother, *Mother*," calling to the dead parent who'd once been Cory's great protector, even more so than her brother.

"Mother," she cried, "*Mother!*"

And this word, as it turned out, protected her.

Big events awaited Lunt. At 12:24 a.m., he would be arrested in his junior suite by two members of the West Hollywood

Police Department, both of them with guns drawn. Lunt's rented Mustang, that affordable substitute for Sharon's Ferrari, would be impounded from the hotel's garage, and the garbage from his first day's take-out lunch discovered inside the car. His electrocution wounds and Mucaquell addiction would be treated in the medical wing of the county jail. As soon as Lunt was charged with attempted murder, the media would go wild for the "man who loved Sharon Tate not wisely but too well," and as soon as Benny Pompa got linked to the whole affair, news of it would circle the globe. Next would come Pompa's own arrest, his own indictment for attempted murder, and his eventual acquittal at trial. Next, too, Lunt would publicly renounce his Sharonophilia. He would enjoy his first face-to-face meeting with Bronson. At his trial, his lawyers would pioneer the first so-called "Muke defense." Alas, to no avail: At trial's end he would be convicted of his crime and sentenced to a year in prison. Ironically, or perhaps not, that prison would be Corcoran State, Charles Manson's own current "home." Thanks to various maneuvers by his attorney, Lunt would only have to serve ten months there. And to his great relief, he and Manson would never encounter each other.

Yes, a busy year lay in store for Lunt.

But nothing would shake him up, would change his life, as much as hearing Mrs. Kruikshank's cry of *"Mother."*

It's real, he saw now, sobering up fast. He'd just stabbed someone—*a living person*. And she was helpless, he saw this too, bitter yet helpless—a troubled person whom he had just troubled some more. He, a Sharonophile, had behaved like, like—*a Sharon-killer!* And in the mirror behind his victim, Lunt saw a face, destroyed and ghostly, that he hardly knew.

"Mother," said the night clerk, right hand pressed to her wound.

"Mother," left hand raised to stave off any new blows.

"*Mother*," afraid to lose the life that she believed Lunt's parents ruined.

"*Mother, mother, mother, mother.*"

Long ago, someone else, another victim, had spoken this word. She'd spoken it while in her death throes, with her sweet eyes pointed skyward. Alas, no mercy was to be had; the light poured out of her, all out. And so amazed was Lunt to hear it now, to hear this word "Mother," that he dropped his letter opener. He let it fall, and watched it bounce on the front desk's polished surface before it settled near the bell turned green with rust.

Several people in the lobby viewed the attack. Not keen to tangle with a madman in a diaper, each of them dialed 911 from their cell phones. Mrs. Kruikshank, too terrified to move, much less to try to scurry off, merely gaped at Lunt, wobbling a little on her feet. He didn't move a muscle, either. Nailed to the spot, he was staring at his hands and at the blood, Ferrari red, that spattered them. After a moment, he lay his palms flat on the desk, also bloodstained, and then his eyes rose to his victim's and he said, "Sorry! God, *I'm sorry!* I didn't *mean it*! I'm *sorry*, lady! *Please FORGIVE ME!*"

Speaking also, in a way, to someone else—the other victim.

That long-gone woman, gone too soon.

Neither Jolly doll nor goddess, but a person.

A human being.

He'd never grasped this most important truth about her until now.

("ALS ICH KAN")

AUTHOR'S NOTE

BEWARE of authors who make explicit any theme or (yikes!) moral in their work. Because of this novel's sensitive historical material, however, I wish to assure readers that, unlike my "Sharonophile" protagonist, I deeply respect Sharon Tate's humanity, admire her work, and do not intend at all for my story to minimize the tragedy of her terrible early death. I mourn her passing and sympathize with her survivors. As I've tried to show, the worshippers of dead famous people often end up doing harm both to themselves and to the memory of the worshipped one.

RESEARCH

IN researching this novel, I drew upon the multitude of articles, essays, and videos re: Sharon Tate to be found online. Also of assistance was the "Charles Manson's Hollywood" sequence of Karina Longworth's superb podcast *You Must Remember This.*

By far the most helpful of the books I consulted was the excellent, highly recommended *Sharon Tate and the Manson Murders* by Greg King (2000).

Among the other books I looked at, several stand out: *Helter Skelter* by Vincent Bugliosi and Curt Gentry (1974); Ed Sanders's *The Family: The Story of Charles Manson's Dune Buggy Attack Battalion* (1971, 1990), as well as his *Sharon Tate: A Life* (2015); *Kaddish* by Leon Wieseltier (2000); *Manson: The Life and Times of Charles Manson* by Jeff Guinn (2013), and Debra Tate's *Sharon Tate: Recollection* (2014).

ACKNOWLEDGMENTS

MY late friend Harry Crews said about each of the books he pounded out on his trusty typewriter, "Before me, this was not; because of me, this is." Of course, Harry had help and so have I, with my gratitude to my loved ones and friends being boundless. Alas, these folks are too numerous for me to thank them all by name in this limited space. Hence I mention here only the subset of hearties who aided in my composing or publishing this particular novel.

For professional support, I thank Tyson Cornell, Hailie Johnson, Julia Callahan, and Guy Intoci at Rare Bird Books—I've really enjoyed working with you. Thanks as well to Chris Calhoun (who, like me, once met Colonel Sanders), Walter Bode, Yfat Reiss Gendell at Foundry Media, and George Sheanshang.

For their early feedback, guidance, and encouragement, I am grateful to Michael Imperioli and Jillian Lauren. Not only are they my pals, but they're the fine authors of books that I dig a lot.

Speaking of great scribes who provided me with assistance, my thanks as well to Laura Albert, Jennifer Belle, Lydia Lunch, Ann Marlowe, Patricia Marx, Daniel Menaker, Nicolas Richard, Larry "Ratso" Sloman and Christy Smith, Jerry Stahl, and Michael Wherly (Carson).

For personal support, artistic inspiration, and/or good advices, I'm grateful to Laurie Anderson, Brigitte Bako, Stacey Bell, Carla Capretto, Chrisy Cardy, Juan Guzman, Sergio and Susana Medina, Steven List, Bob Neuwirth, Jimbo Ospenson, Lou Rittmaster, Eileen Salzig, Sara Sugarman, Ronen V., and Jonathan Young and Audrey Grumhaus.

Further thanks to Jerry Arellano, Scott Asen, Sarah Bloom, Lorraine Bracco, Tamara Braun, Nikki Cantello, Maryellen Cataneo, Alan Dreher, Barry Ellsworth, George Dawes Green, Yasmine Hamdan, Alosha Ipatovsiev, Heidi James, Simon Kirke and Maria Angelica Figueredo, Dorka Keehn, David Keil, Danny "Kootch" Kortchmar, Steve Krulwich, Ilene Landress, Larry Marshall, Myra Pasek, Gabrielle Penabaz and Pippin, Dan Seligman, Scott Shriner, Dalia Sofer, Jeff Stein and Angela Janklow, Sean Sullivan, Judith Weinstein...

Oh, and where would I be without Arnie Civins and Larry Kirstein?

Deeply missed are Mr. Crews, Gypsy Boots, David Bowman, Irving Cooperberg, Bea Dunmore, Yankel Gladstone, Madeleine Jensen, Gordon Kato, Nina Mattson, Marla Ruzicka, Rona Smith, and Scott Sommer.

"You can't choose your family," no. But I've been gifted with "blood" whom I'd gladly choose. So thank you to Ethel Lippman ("from here to the moon and back 100 million times"); Bernard Lippman (Charlie Samsam says hi); David and Lena (Lily) Fern; David and Lena (Lulu) Lippman; my lovely coparent and best friend Ingunn Egset; Prester John Bliss; Szombathelyi Marika and Istvan (the glorious parents I dreamed of and finally found); my dear Norma and Bobby Lippman; the fabulous fjord-dwelling Egsets, Bodil, Ola and Ols; plus Szilard (Dr. Meyer) and Ginger.

Speaking of choices, even if I had my pick to parent any child in the universe, I'd go with Gabriel Olai Beauregard Egset, whose wit, warmth, resilience, and brilliance "make me feel ten feet tall." Now get back to work on *Finnegans Wake*, son!

If I owe my sanity—indeed, my existence—to a single person, it's my uncle Dr. William H. Fern. Without him, no me. How patient Billy's been during five decades of listening to me vent, helping me to "tailor expectations," sharing family lessons, imbuing me with his courage, and serving as my foremost teacher/mentor/ surrogate father. What's more, I'm just one of hundreds of people whose lives he's enhanced.

Finally, this book would not exist if not for the flower of Veszprem, my wife Szombathelyi Vera Kata. Tender, wise, beautiful and fun, she's given me a loving home while helping me to "grow up." She has also, as my first and best reader, ensured that this novel got improved, finished, sent out into the publishing world, and recognized. Gratitude and blessings and a *"Szeretlek nagyon* big-time" to you, *Mutyi!*